I'M NOT
STILLER

I'M NOT STILLER

BY

Max Frisch

TRANSLATED FROM THE GERMAN BY MICHAEL BULLOCK

NEW YORK : VINTAGE BOOKS

A Division of Random House

VINTAGE BOOKS
are published by ALFRED A. KNOPF, INC.
and RANDOM HOUSE, INC.

Reprinted by arrangement with Abelard-Schuman Limited

Translated from the German. © 1954 by Suhrkamp Verlag

MANUFACTURED IN THE UNITED STATES OF AMERICA

A NOTE TO THE READER

THE strange history of Anatol Ludwig Stiller, sculptor, husband, lover . . . prisoner, is divided into two parts. Part One contains Stiller's seven notebooks written in prison. Part Two is a Postscript written by the Public Prosecutor.

PART · I

Stiller's Notes in Prison

"BEHOLD, for this reason it is so hard to choose oneself, because in this choice absolute isolation is identical with the most profound continuity, because through this choice every possibility of becoming something else—or rather of remolding oneself into something else—is ruled out."

"As the passion for freedom awakes in him (and it awakes in the choice, as it is already presupposed in the choice), he chooses himself and fights for this possession as for his happiness, and this is his happiness."

Kierkegaard, *Either-Or*

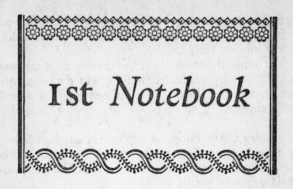

1st *Notebook*

I'M not Stiller!—Day after day, ever since I was put into this prison, which I shall describe in a minute, I have been saying it, swearing it, asking for whisky and refusing to make any other statement. For experience has taught me that without whisky I'm not myself, I'm open to all sorts of good influences and liable to play the part they want me to play, although it's not me at all. But since the only thing that matters in my crazy situation (they think I'm a missing resident of their little town) is to refuse to be wheedled and to guard against all their well-meaning attempts to shove me into somebody else's skin, to resist their blandishments even if it means being downright rude—in a word, to be no one else than the man I unfortunately really am —I shall go on shouting for whisky the moment anyone comes near my cell. I told them several days ago it needn't be the very best brand, but it must be drinkable, otherwise I shall remain sober; then they can question me as much as they like, they won't get anything out of me—or at any rate, nothing that's true. In vain. Today they brought me this notebook full of empty pages. I'm supposed to write down my life story—no doubt to prove I have one, a different one from the life of their missing Herr Stiller.

"Just write the truth," said the defense counsel provided for me by the State, "nothing but the plain, unvarnished truth. They'll fill your pen for you whenever you want."

It's a week today since the clip on the ear that led to my arrest. According to the evidence I was rather drunk; I therefore find it difficult to describe the (outward) course of events.

"Come with me," said the customs officer.

"Please don't make difficulties," I said. "My train will be leaving any minute."

"But without you," said the customs officer.

The way he pulled me off the footboard deprived me of any wish to answer his questions. He had my passport in his hand. The other official, who was stamping the travelers' passports, was still in the train.

"Is there something wrong with my passport?" I asked.

No answer.

"I'm only doing my duty," he said several times. "You know that very well."

Without answering my question as to what was wrong with the passport—an American passport, with which I had been halfway round the world!—he repeated in his Swiss intonation:

"Come with me."

"Now look officer," I said, "if you don't want a clip on the ear, please don't pull me by the sleeve; I can't stand it."

"Come along now."

I boxed the young customs officer's ear just as he was telling me, in spite of my polite but unambiguous warning and with the arrogant air of one protected by the Law, that they would soon let me know who I really was. His navy blue cap rolled along the platform in a spiral, and for an instant the young customs officer, now capless and consequently much more human, was so flabbergasted—too much taken aback even to be angry—that I could easily have got into the train. It was just beginning to move off, people were leaning out of the windows waving, and one carriage door was still open. I don't know why I didn't jump in. I believe I could have snatched my passport, for, as I have said, the young man was completely dumbfounded, as though his whole soul was in the rolling cap; and it was not until the stiff cap had stopped rolling that he was seized with understandable rage. I ducked down among the people, determined at least to brush some of the dust off his navy blue cap with its Swiss cross badge before handing it back to him. His ears were lobster red. It was strange: I followed him as though under some compulsion to behave myself. He didn't say a word and without taking hold of me, which was quite unnecessary, led me to the police station, where I was kept waiting for fifty minutes.

"Please sit down," said the Inspector.

The passport lay on the table. I was immediately struck by the changed tone in which I was addressed, a kind of solicitous and rather clumsy politeness, from which I gathered that after looking at my passport for an hour the police had no further doubt about my American citizenship. As though to make up for the young customs officer's churlishness, the Inspector even fetched me an armchair.

"You speak German, I hear," he remarked.

"Why not?" I asked.

"Do sit down," he smiled.

I remained standing.

"I'm of German origin," I explained. "An American of German origin—"

He pointed to the empty armchair.

"Please," he said, and hesitated for a while to sit

down himself. . . . If I had not condescended to speak German in the train I might never have found myself in this scrape. Another passenger, a Swiss, had spoken to me in German. The same traveler, who had been getting on my nerves ever since we left Paris, was also an eyewitness of the blow I gave the customs officer. I didn't know who he was. I'd never seen him before. He got into the compartment in Paris, woke me up by stumbling over my feet, forced his way to the open window with apologies in French and there said good-bye to a lady, speaking in Swiss dialect. No sooner had the train started than I had the disagreeable sensation that he was staring at me. I took refuge behind my *New Yorker*, whose jokes I already knew by heart, in the hope that my traveling companion's curiosity would eventually be exhausted. He was also reading a paper, a Zurich paper. After we had agreed in French to close the window, I avoided every unnecessary glance at the passing landscape; meanwhile my unknown companion, who may have been a charming fellow for all I know, was so obviously waiting on tenterhooks for an opportunity to start a conversation that finally there was nothing for it but the dining-car, where I sat for five hours and had a drink or two. I didn't return to the compartment until compelled to by the approach of the frontier between Mulhouse and Basle. Again the Swiss looked at me as though he knew me. I don't know what it was that suddenly encouraged him to speak to me; possibly the mere fact that we were now on his native soil. "Excuse me," he asked in a rather embarrassed manner, "aren't you Herr Stiller?"

As I have mentioned, I had drunk a certain amount of whisky. I couldn't make out what he was saying. I held my American passport in my hand, while the Swiss, relapsing into his dialect, turned the pages of an illustrated paper. A couple of officials were already standing behind us, a customs officer and another man holding a rubber stamp. I handed over my passport. I now realized that I had drunk a lot and was being looked at with suspicion. My luggage, of which I had little, was in order.

"Is that your passport?" asked the other man.

At first I laughed, of course. "Why shouldn't it be?" I asked, and added indignantly: "What's wrong with my passport?" It was the first time doubt had been cast on my passport, and all because this gentleman had confused me with a picture in his illustrated paper. . . .

"Herr Doktor," said the Inspector to this same gentleman, "I needn't detain you further. Many thanks for your information."

As the grateful Inspector held the door open for him, the gentleman nodded to me as though we knew each other. He was a Herr Doktor; there are thousands of them. I didn't feel the slightest desire to nod to him. Then the Inspector came back and pointed to the chair again.

"Do take a seat. As I can see, Herr Stiller, you're pretty drunk—"

"Stiller?" I said. "My name's not Stiller."

"I hope," he went on unperturbed, "you can nevertheless understand what I have to say to you, Herr Stiller."

I shook my head, whereupon he offered me a smoke, a Swiss cigar. I naturally refused it, since it was obviously offered not to me, but to a certain Herr Stiller. I also remained standing, although the Inspector had settled down in his chair as though for a long chat.

"Why did you get so excited when you were asked whether it was your proper passport?" he asked.

He turned the pages of my American passport.

"Look, Inspector," I said, "I can't stand being taken by the sleeve. I warned your young customs officer several times. I'm sorry I lost my temper and hit him, and of course, I'll pay the usual fine at once. That goes without saying. What's the damage?"

He smiled indulgently. It wasn't quite as simple as

that, he told me. Then he lit a cigar, carefully, rolling the brown stump between his lips, leisurely, thoroughly, as though time was no object.

"You seem to be an extremely well-known man—"

"I?" I asked. "What makes you think that?"

"I don't know anything about these things," he said, "but this Herr Doktor, who recognized you, seems to have a very high opinion of you."

There was nothing to be done. The confusion had arisen, and whatever I said was taken as affectation or genuine modesty.

"Why do you call yourself Sam White?" he asked.

I talked and talked.

"Where did you get this passport?" he asked.

He took it almost good-naturedly and sat back smoking his rather evil-smelling cigar, his thumbs hooked in his braces, for it was a hot afternoon, so that the Inspector, especially as he no longer considered me a foreigner, had undone some of the buttons of his not very suitable jacket, while he gazed at me without listening to a word I was saying.

"Inspector," I said. "I'm drunk, you're right, perfectly right, but I'm not going to have some wretched Herr Doktor—"

"He says he knows you."

"Where from?" I asked.

"From the illustrated paper," he said and took advantage of my contemptuous silence to add: "You have a wife living in Paris. Is that right?"

"I? A wife?"

"Julika by name."

"I don't come from Paris," I declared. "I come from Mexico, Inspector."

I gave him the name of the ship, the duration of the crossing, the time of my arrival at Le Havre, the time of my departure from Vera Cruz.

"That may be," he said, "but your wife lives in Paris.

A dancer, if I'm not mistaken. She's supposed to be an extremely beautiful woman."

I said nothing.

"Julika is her stage name," the Inspector informed me. "At one time she had T.B. and lived at Davos. But now she runs a ballet school in Paris. Right? For the last six years."

I only looked at him.

"Since your disappearance."

I had involuntarily sat down to hear what the readers of an illustrated paper knew about someone who obviously, at least in the eyes of Herr Doktor, resembled me; I took out a cigarette, whereupon the Inspector, already infected by the esteem spread by this same Herr Doktor, gave me a light.

"So you yourself are a sculptor."

I laughed.

"Is that right?" he asked without waiting for an answer, and immediately proceeded to the next question: "Why are you traveling under an assumed name?"

He did not believe my oath either.

"I'm sorry," he said hunting through a drawer, from which he pulled out a blue form. "I'm sorry, Herr Stiller, but if you continue to refuse to show your proper passport I shall have to hand you over to the C.I.D. Make no mistake about that."

Then he tapped the ash from his cigar.

"I'm not Stiller," I reiterated, as he began conscientiously to fill in the voluminous form, but it was as though he simply didn't hear me any more. I tried a different tone of voice. I spoke solemnly and soberly: "Inspector, I haven't got another passport." Or with a laugh: "That's a lot of nonsense." But in spite of my drunkenness I could clearly feel that the more I spoke, the less he listened. Finally I shouted: "I'm not Stiller, devil take it." I yelled and banged my fist on the table.

"Why get so excited?"

"Inspector," I said, "give me my passport."

He didn't even look up.

"You're under arrest," he said, turning the pages of my passport with his left hand, copying down the number, the date of issue, the name of the American consul in Mexico, everything the blue form demanded in such cases, and said in a not unfriendly voice: "Sit down."

My cell—I have just measured it with my shoe, which is a trifle less than twelve inches long—is small, like everything in this country, so clean one can hardly breathe for hygiene, and oppressive precisely because everything is just right. No more and no less. Everything in this country is oppressively adequate. The cell is 10 feet long, 7 feet 10 inches wide and 8 feet 3 inches high. A humane prison, there's no denying it, and that's what makes it so unbearable. Not a cobweb, not a trace of mildew on the walls, nothing to justify indignation. Some prisons get stormed when the people learn about them; here there's nothing to storm. Millions of people, I know, live worse than I do. The bed has springs. The barred window lets in the sun—at this time of the year until about eleven A.M. The table has two drawers and there is also a Bible and a standard lamp. And when I have to do my business I only have to press a white button and I am taken to the appropriate place, which is not supplied with old newspapers one can first read, but with soft crepe paper. And yet it's a prison, and there are moments when you feel like screaming. You don't do so, any more than in a big store; you dry your hands on a towel, walk on linoleum, and say thank you when you're locked into your cabin again. Apart from the already autumnal foliage of a chestnut tree I can see nothing, not even if I climb up on the sprung bed, which incidentally (with shoes) is forbidden. Sounds of unknown origin are the worst torment, of course. Since I discovered they still have trams in this town I have almost been able to ignore their rumbling. But the unintelligible announcer on a nearby radio, the daily clatter of the dustcart and the wild beating of carpets in echoing courtyards are bad. It seems that in this country people have an almost morbid fear of dirt. Yesterday they started entertaining me with the stutter of a pneumatic drill; somewhere they are tearing up the street so that later they can pave it again. I often feel as though I am the only unoccupied person in this town. To judge by the voices in the street, when the pneumatic drill stops for a minute, there is much cursing and little laughter here. Round midnight the drunks start bawling because at this hour all the pubs are shut. Sometimes students sing as though one were in the heart of Germany. Around one o'clock silence falls. But it's not much use putting out the light; a distant street lamp shines into my cell, the shadows of the bars stretch across the wall and bend over on to the ceiling, and when it is windy outside, so that the street lamp swings, the swaying shadows of the bars are enough to drive you crazy. In the morning, when the sun shines, these shadows do at least lie on the floor.

Without the warder, who brings me my food, I shouldn't know to this day what's really going on here. Every newspaper reader seems to know who Stiller was. This makes it almost impossible to get any information out of anyone; everybody acts as though you were bound to know all about it, and they themselves only have a rough idea.

"—for a time, I believe, they looked for him in the lake," said my warder, "but without success, then all of a sudden people said he was in the Foreign Legion."

While he was speaking, he ladled out the soup.

"Lots of Swiss do that," he told me, "when it gets on their nerves here."

"They join the Foreign Legion?" I asked.

"Because it gets on their nerves here."

"Yes, I know," I said. "But why the Foreign Legion? That's worse still."

"It makes no difference to me."

"So he just left his wife at Davos," I asked, "ill as she was?"

"Maybe it was a blessing for her."

"Do you think so?"

"It makes no difference to me," he said. "Since then she's lived in Paris."

"I know."

"She's a dancer."

"I know."

"As pretty as a picture."

"How's her T.B.?" I inquired sympathetically.

"Cured."

"Who says so?"

"She does."

"How do you know all this?"

"How do I know?" said my warder. "Why, from the papers."

I can't find out much else.

"Eat," says my warder. "Eat the soup while it's still hot, and don't lose your grip, Mr. White. That's what they're waiting for, these Herr Doktors, I know them."

The soup, a *minestra*, was good, in general I can't complain about the food here, and I think my warder has a soft spot for me; at any rate he doesn't address me (like everyone else) as Herr Stiller, but as Mr. White.

So they want me to tell them my life story. And nothing but the plain, unvarnished truth. A pad of white paper, a fountain pen with ink that I can have refilled whenever I like at the expense of the State, and a little good will—what's going to be left of truth, when I get at it with my fountain pen? And if I just stick to the facts, says my counsel, we'll get truth in the corner so to speak, where we can grab it. Where could truth escape to, if I write it down? And by facts, I think my counsel means especially place-names, dates that can be checked, details of jobs and other sources of income, for example, duration of residence in different towns, number of children, number of divorces, religion, and so on.

P.S. Where was I on January 18th, 1946?

Walking in the prison yard.

It's not nearly so bad, not nearly so humiliating as you expect, and as a matter of fact I'm glad to be able to walk again, even if it's only round and round in a circle. The yard is pretty big—paving stones with moss growing in between, a fine plane tree in the center, ivy on the walls, and of course the fact that we are not yet wearing convict's clothes, but the civilian clothes we had on when we were arrested, makes a lot of difference. If we widen the circle in which we have to walk we can see a flat roof with flapping washing; apart from this there is only sky around the roofs, which are covered with cooing pigeons. Unfortunately, we have to keep in single file, which makes proper conversation impossible. In front of me walks a fat man with a shiny bald patch (like myself) and folds of fat on the back of his neck, who paddles himself along with his arms when he's made to walk—probably a newcomer; when a friendly warder tells him it's time for his walk, he looks round (which costs him a physical effort) half stubbornly, half bewildered, dumbly seeking support. Support against what? Behind me goes the Italian who is so fond of singing in the shower bath, and the warders can't help laughing at his comic imitation of myself. Once I looked round to see my portrait. It was funny enough: hands behind the back, the attitude of a thinker, always slightly out of line through absent-mindedness, a look of nostalgia for distant places combined with yearning glances over the nearest brick wall, a man who shyly flatters himself he doesn't belong here, and on top of this the awkward cordiality of the intellectual. It's probably a good likeness, anyhow even the Jew has to laugh, the only intellectual among the prisoners, who unfortunately walks in the other half of the circle, so that we can only converse in grimaces and gestures. He seems to have very little faith in Swiss justice . . .

Suddenly someone began playing football with a raw potato; there were a few brisk passing movements before the head warder, a very correct man who always takes it as a personal insult when anything discreditable happens, finally spotted the potato. Squad halt! A serious inquiry as to where the potato came from. We stood in a circle grinning, not saying a word. The head warder walked from man to man, the peeled potato in his hand, and looked each of us in the eye. Everyone shrugged his shoulders. The head warder had missed the chance of simply throwing the potato away; against his wish, the matter had suddenly become important, a matter of principle. I had the feeling it was all a farce and the head warder himself was finding it hard not to laugh and dismiss the lot of us. At the same time I felt that perhaps they had a torture chamber after all, perhaps the stolen potato was enough to make them come with red-hot irons. Suddenly my Jew put up his hand, to the accompaniment of general laughter. Even the head warder realized that this admission could only be an act of derision (he had never seen a Jew who played football) which was worse than the theft of an uncooked potato. The Jew, white with agitation, had to step out of the ranks. The rest of us were told to go round at the double for five minutes. Of course the poor fat fellow in front of me, wobbling like a hot-water bottle, was left behind on the first time round and ran in a spiral to shorten the distance, until a warder told him to fall out. They were not inhuman. But order must be maintained and also a certain gravity. After all, we were in a remand prison . . .

There are times, alone in my cell, when I have the feeling that I have only dreamed all this; that at any moment I could stand up, take my hands away from my face and look round in freedom, as though the prison were only within me.

"I've done my best," said my defending counsel, "to make your stay in the remand prison, which I hope will be short, as comfortable as possible—whisky is not allowed. You have the best room in the building, believe me, not the biggest, but the only one with morning sunshine; you have this view into the old chestnut trees. As to the bells of the Cathedral, they're very loud, I admit; but what do you expect me to do? I can't put the Cathedral somewhere else!"

That was quite right, just as everything my counsel says is right in a way that never convinces me and yet always puts me in the wrong. The ringing of the cathedral bells, a metallic hum, which breaks out at least twice a day, and more often when there are weddings or funerals, makes it impossible to hear oneself think; it is like a trembling of the air, a soundless quaking, a noise like a man diving into the water from an excessively high diving board; it makes me deaf, dizzy and idiotic. But my counsel is right: he can't put the cathedral somewhere else. And as I then remain silent out of sheer hopelessness, he picks up his folder and says:

"Right, let's get down to business."

My counsel is a thoroughly decent, or at least inoffensive fellow, from a well-to-do family, virtuous through and through, rather inhibited, but even his inhibitions are turned into good manners; and above all, he is just, no doubt of that, just in even the most trivial matter, desperately just, just out of an almost inborn conviction that justice exists, at least in a constitutional State, at least in Switzerland.

At the same time, he's not stupid. He knows a great

deal, he's as reliable as an encyclopedia, especially where Switzerland is concerned, so that there is really no point in discussing Switzerland with my counsel; every idea that casts doubt on Switzerland is smothered under a mass of indisputable historical facts, and in the end, if you don't actually praise his Switzerland, you are always in the wrong, just as I was wrong over the bells of their cathedral. Perhaps it's only his lack of temperament, his virtuousness, his moderation, which so immoderately irritates me; he is superior to me in intelligence, yet he employs all his intelligence simply to avoid making mistakes. I find such people unbearable. I can reproach him with nothing; he considers me a thoroughly decent, or at least inoffensive, fundamentally sensible fellow, a man of good will, a Swiss. This is the basis on which he is conducting my defense, and every time I see him I nearly explode. Then I turn on my heels, leave him sitting on the bed and turn my back to him; I maintain an almost insulting silence and stare out of the window at the old chestnut trees with my hands in my pockets, simply because in the long run I can't stand people of his sort—people who can't imagine committing murder themselves, and therefore can't imagine that I could commit murder either.

"I understand you perfectly," he said, "I understand you perfectly. You're annoyed with Switzerland because it greets you with imprisonment, understandably —I mean, understandably annoyed, for it is painful to look at one's homeland through bars—"

"What do you mean, homeland?" I asked.

"Only"—he skipped my not unimportant question— "don't make it difficult for me to defend you. Unfortunately, some of the remarks you made when you were arrested have found their way into the Press. What's the use of making bad blood? I beg you, in your own interest, to refrain in future from criticizing our country, which is your country too, after all."

"What did I say?"

"People here are very sensitive," he replied with splendid frankness, but at the same time evidently unwilling to utter remarks uncomplimentary to Switzerland with his own mouth, and continued: "To keep to the matter in hand, I have now examined all the papers, and if you will be good enough to tell me, at least in general terms, where and how you have spent the last six years—"

He asks me that every time. And yet I swore not to make any statement without whisky. It's a positive dossier he takes out of his leather brief-case, so full that one can't even turn the pages without first undoing the clip. I laughed in his face. He is convinced that this dossier is mine, nothing will prevent him from reading it aloud for hours on end. As though the boredom he inflicts on me day after day were not also a kind of torture.

"Herr Doktor," I interrupted him today. "I've just come from Mexico—"

"That's what you say, I know."

"I've just come from Mexico," I repeated, "and you can take it from me, the famous human sacrifices of the Aztecs, who cut human hearts out of the living body as offerings to the gods, were child's play compared with the treatment you receive on the Swiss frontier if you come without papers—or with forged papers—child's play."

He only smiled.

"So you admit, Herr Stiller, that your American passport was a fake?"

"My name's not Stiller!"

"I have been informed," he said quietly, as though I had not shouted, "that you are presumed—I say presumed—to be none other than Anatol Ludwig Stiller, born in Zurich, sculptor, married to Frau Julika Stiller-Tschudy, disappeared six years ago, last address 11 Steingartengasse, Zurich. I have been appointed—"

"—to defend Herr Stiller."

"Yes."

"My name is White."

But I cannot make him understand, however often I repeat it. Our conversation runs like a gramophone record with the needle stuck in the same groove.

"Why aren't you Stiller?" he asked.

"Because I'm not."

"Why aren't you?" he said. "That's what they told me."

In the end I kept my mouth shut. His time is limited; that's my only salvation from this thoroughly decent fellow who considers himself my defense counsel and is therefore offended because I don't do as he asks, after he has read the whole dossier. Finally he puts it back in the brief-case, presses the catch without a word until at last it clicks, stands up, makes sure he has got everything, his fountain pen, his glasses, and shakes hands with me as though he had just lost a game of tennis, telling me what time he'll be back tomorrow.

P.S. He's "convinced of my innocence." What does he mean by that? Suddenly the idea enters my head that there is some suspicion hanging over Stiller; that is why the authorities here are so keen to lay hands on their vanished citizen—some affair has to be cleared up.

Knobel (that's my warder's name) is a real gem, the only person who believes what I say. While he is cleaning the cell, I lie on the bed, and he goes on cleaning until the water he wrings out of the floorcloth is clear enough to drink. It seems they take a lot of trouble over outward appearances. Even the window-bars get dusted in this country.

"Well, if you tell me yourself you murdered your wife—," said my warder.

Fourteen years ago he was a greengrocer with a cart and a horse called Rössli, of which he speaks very affectionately. At first I thought he was talking about his wife. He has worked as a warder ever since he became a widower, and he tells me I'm the first in all this time who didn't protest his innocence every time he cleaned his cell. He says he simply can't bear to listen to the twaddle talked by all those honest men. It must be nauseating. I hear the next cell is occupied by a banker, who weeps for hours at a time, and the next cell but one by a ponce, who likewise talks about honor. My warder is pleased with me, I think. While he was a greengrocer, and still under his wife's thumb, he obviously imagined a remand prison very differently. The things you'd hear there! he thought to himself. But not a bit of it. If he wants to hear criminals, he has to go to the cinema (he says) like everyone else . . .

He quite understood that I didn't want to talk about my first murder, since it was my wife.

"But your second?" he asked.

"My second," I said, skinning the sausage, "oh, that was nothing. I already knew I was a murderer, so I didn't have to get into a particular frame of mind first —it was in the jungle."

"You've been in the jungle, Mr. White?"

"Indeed I have."

"Well I'm blowed," he said, "well I'm blowed."

"Do you know what the jungle's like?"

"Only from the films, Mr. White."

"Well, that's just how it is," I said and made quite a pause before coming to the point. "I knew this Schmitz was knocking about in Jamaica and I went around for months with a dagger in my left boot."

"Who's Schmitz?"

"Director Schmitz," I said.

"Never heard of him."

"The hair-oil gangster," I said. "A millionaire, you know, the sort you can't get at in a civilized country."

"And you took a dagger and——"

"That's right."

"Well I'm blowed," he said.

"An Indian dagger."

Unfortunately, since he has eight cells to look after, his time is short. Nevertheless, he always stays longer with me than with the others, the honest men. He's a real gem; whenever they feed the prisoners their over-ripe Swiss cheese, he always brings me a saveloy bought with his own money. True, saveloy (beer-sausage) isn't exactly my favorite dish, especially if I've no beer to go with it—it's a rather garlicky sausage you can still smell hours afterwards, when you're thinking of something else; but I'm touched by the thought behind it.

Frau Julika Stiller-Tschudy, wife of the missing man, had asked for better photos, in order to avoid a fruit-less trip from Paris. For three-quarters of an hour they surrounded me with their lamps, so that I couldn't help sweating. And on top of that they kept saying:

"Relax. Be quite natural."

Fortunately my public prosecutor (or examining magistrate; I'm not well up in these things) is a pleasant character, a skeptic, who doesn't even believe every-thing he says himself; also he was the first one with the good manners to knock before coming into the cell.

"I suppose you know who I am?"

"The public prosecutor?"

His smile baffled me. He stared at me for a long time with both hands thrust into his jacket pockets, some-how embarrassed. My first idea was: This man has some confession to make to me. He seemed to lose himself in private thoughts of his own. For a while he behaved as though he were deaf, staring at me openly as adults rarely do, and in any case longer than was polite, so that when he realized what he was doing he blushed slightly.

"Do you smoke?" he asked, and when I refused, he

added, taking a cigarette himself and lighting it, "This is an entirely personal call. Please don't regard it as an interrogation. I felt the urge to make your acquaintance . . ."

A pause.

"You really don't smoke?" he asked.

"Only cigars."

"My wife sends her regards," he said, sitting down on the bed like a regular visitor and gazing round for an ash-tray, just to avoid looking at me, I believe, "— that is if you really are Herr Stiller."

"My name is White," I said.

"I don't want to anticipate the judicial inquiry," he said with an undertone of apology or relief, went on smoking and obviously didn't know what to say next under the circumstances. It wasn't for some minutes, after an exchange of small talk that was suddenly quite impersonal and rendered even more threadbare by the fact that his mind was elsewhere—chiefly about motor scooters and the fact that whisky, and alcohol generally, was "unfortunately" strictly forbidden to prisoners on remand—he declared abruptly: "Personally, I've never seen Stiller. At least not consciously. We once had a talk over the telephone, as you may know; it was a call from Paris, but I can't tell whether it was you."

Then his tone changed and he suddenly became good-humored:

"You murdered your wife, Mr. White?"

I had the feeling that he didn't believe me either. He was smiling, but his smile disappeared when we stared at one another in silence, and he asked me why I murdered my wife.

"Because I loved her," I said.

"Is that a reason?"

"Look," I explained, "it was a sacrifice for her to live at my side. All my friends thought so, to say nothing of her friends. She herself hardly said a word about the way I made her suffer. She was a very noble person, you know, and you can ask anyone you like about that, everybody thought so. They had never seen such a noble, such a fine person as my wife, they all said. And we moved almost exclusively in educated circles. Besides, I thought so myself, I admired her, you know. Her nobility attracted me. That was her undoing. I can't tell you how often that woman forgave me, how often!"

"What for?"

"For being as I am."

Every now and then he asked a question. For instance:

"Did you often quarrel?"

"Never."

"Not even before the murder?"

"Certainly not," I answered, "otherwise it would never have been committed. You obviously can't picture my victim. She would never have dreamt of raising her voice, so I didn't dare to either. I told you, she was such a noble person—can you imagine what it's like to be married to such a noble person? For nine years I was plagued by a bad conscience. And if, once a week, I couldn't stand my bad conscience and smashed a plate against the wall, for example, I felt like a murderer, my wife's murderer. Yes, that's how hard this frail woman's life was with me."

"Hm," he said.

"There's nothing to smile about," I said. "It took years of my life before I realized that I was her murderer, and finally drew the logical conclusion."

"Hm," he said.

"I deny nothing," I said. "But don't expect to see me with a bad conscience. I haven't got one any more. Somehow it has simply been used up. I had so much bad conscience while she was still alive: It was terrible for her, simply terrible, to have to live at my side."

"And that's why you—murdered her?"

I nodded.

"I see," he remarked.

"It's unbearable," I said, "you can't go on having a bad conscience for years, without knowing why you have a bad conscience."

And so on.

I don't know whether he understood me.

Once a week, every Friday, we're allowed to take a shower, ten minutes each, ten prisoners at a time. Otherwise I never see my neighbors; but then I see them stark naked and to the accompaniment of a steamy splashing, so that we can scarcely talk to one another. One of them, who considers himself innocent, refuses to soap himself out of spite. One little Italian always sings. There is not much to be learnt from the faces under the shower, distorted by strands of wet hair and soap. Added to this is the nakedness of the whole body: after being used to seeing the face as the only naked area, you are more or less compelled to look at the whole naked body, which is not very pleasant. All you can guess is that it belongs to a workman, an intellectual, an athlete, a clerk. On the whole, our naked bodies are thoroughly embarrassing, because they are inexpressive; at best they are natural, but generally they are rather ridiculous. I have made friends with a German Jew; we soap one another's backs, since he can't reach all over his either, and we agree that we ought to have a shower every day. After an almost childish outcry over the cold water with which the head warder drives us into the drying-room, we are all very quiet as we rub ourselves down, with the pink faces of babies and hair like boys'. Apart from myself, I fancy, there is no one guilty of a serious offense among us. Thanks to the fact that they put me near the end of the alphabet (as "Stiller"), I have a little more time to chat to the German Jew. We have both come to the conclusion that physical hygiene in Switzerland is in remarkable contrast to the rest of their obsession with cleanliness. He told me that where he lived in the town he was only allowed by contract to take a hot shower at weekends, as in the prison. Then we march off to our cells one by one with bath towels round our necks.

Today I received the following letter:

"Dear Brother,

"You can imagine that since getting the news from your local canton police I have scarcely slept a wink, Anny too is very excited. Anny is my dear wife, I'm sure you will like her. Don't be angry with me for not coming to Zurich at once, but it's simply impossible at the moment. I hope you are not ill, at least, dear brother. Your photograph gave me a shock—you looked so thin on it that I could hardly recognize you. Have you been to see Father in the old age home yet? Don't listen to what he says, he is an old man now and you know what he's like. You know that Mother is dead? She suffered less than we feared she might. We will visit her grave together. When the canton police told us you had returned, I thought most of Mother. She often used to think you were on the point of coming home; she didn't say so, but we knew very well why she stayed up later than usual, she imagined you were coming back that evening. I just want to tell you that Mother always took your part. Whenever your name cropped up she used to say she hoped you were happy.

"Of course, we are very anxious to hear your story, dear brother, for nothing much has happened to us. I'm a manager here, so you see nothing came of my farm in Argentina—it was simply impossible to leave Mother just then, but we're doing quite nicely.

"Have you heard yet that your friend Alex took his life? So I've been told, anyhow; he put his head in the gas oven, I believe. Or wasn't Alex a friend of yours?

But I don't want to give you a list of deaths. I'll just tell you again how pleased we are. I don't suppose I need tell you about Julika, according to the newspaper things are going much better with her now. She came to Mother's funeral. I can well understand that afterwards she didn't want to see any more of us, being your family. But I think she's still living in Paris. Perhaps you've already spoken to Julika.

"I hope you won't mind, but I must stop now: we're just having a fruit show that's to be attended by a member of the Federal Council, and I've hardly asked you a proper question yet about your life and your future. I hope you will very soon be free.

"Meanwhile, all good wishes from

Your affectionate brother
Wilfried.

"As soon as I can get away from work for a couple of days I shall certainly come to see you. Today I just wanted to write and tell you that of course you can come and stay with us at any time."

Nobody believes a word I say and in the end I shall probably have to take an oath that the fingers with which I am taking the oath are my own fingers. It's really laughable. Today I said to my counsel:

"Of course I'm Stiller."

He stared at me.

"What do you mean by that?"

For the first time the idea entered his honest head that I might not be their missing Herr Stiller after all. Then who could I be? I gave him a few suggestions: Perhaps I was a Soviet agent with American papers. No joking please, and anyhow, in his opinion, anything connected with the Soviets was not a fit subject for jokes; it was simply too evil, just as, on the other hand, anything to do with Switzerland was too good to be a fit subject for jokes. I made another suggestion: Perhaps I was an S.S. man who had been underground for a bit and now saw an opening, the Unknown War Criminal with experience of the East, now very much in demand. But how could I prove I was a war criminal? However candidly I swore to it, they wouldn't let me go without proof. My counsel doesn't even believe that Mexico is more beautiful than Switzerland. Whenever I tell him so he just gets irritable and asks:

"What's that got to do with it?"

My counsel isn't interested in the way the Indians tear the cobra's fangs out in order to use them for their celebrated snake dance. He is even less interested in the Indians' attitude to death. And not at all in who ordered the murder of the Mexican revolutionaries. And he doubts whether it is true that the Mexican sky belongs to the vultures and Mexican mineral resources to the Americans. It's really not easy to keep this man entertained for an hour a day. He interrupted me in the middle of a story which I, at least, was finding enthralling:

"Orizaba—where's that?"

He whipped out his Eversharp and wouldn't rest until he had made a note of my polite but brief reply. Then he immediately asked me:

"So you worked there?"

"I never said that," I replied. "I earned money and lived there."

"How?"

"Fine, thanks," I said.

"I mean, how did you earn money?"

"Oh just the way people do earn money—" I said. "Not by my own labor anyhow."

"How then?"

"With—ideas."

"Explain that a bit more fully."

"I was a kind of estate manager—," I said with a gesture indicating honest profits, "—on an hacienda."

He pretended not to notice the gesture.

"What's an hacienda?"

"A large estate," I replied and gave him a full description of my position, which was inconspicuous, but the meeting place of the indispensable bribes from both sides, and my ideas on this subject, and then the topographical situation of Orizaba, which is heavenly, close to the tropical zone yet just above this zone, which I can't bear with its humid luxuriance, gorgeous butterflies, slimy air and damp sun, its clammy silence full of murderous fertilization—Orizaba lies just above this zone on a plateau that gets the air from the mountains; behind you can see the white snow of Popocatepetl, in front the blue waters of the Gulf of Mexico, while all around is a blossoming garden about the size of a Swiss canton, blossoming with orchids, which grow there like weeds, but also blossoming with useful plants— date palms, figs, coconut palms, oranges and lemons, tobacco, olives, coffee, pineapples, cocoa, bananas and so on . . .

Today my counsel opened with the remark: "You don't seem to be very well informed about Mexico."

My counsel had been working.

"What you told me yesterday is a lot of rubbish. Look," he said and showed me a book from the municipal library. "Benito Juarez tried to do away with large-scale landed property. He was unsuccessful. Porfirio Diaz was overthrown because he ruled with the support of the big property owners, and as you may know there followed a series of bloody revolutions aimed at breaking up the big estates. Monasteries were burnt, land-owners shot, and it ended with the dictatorship of the revolutionaries. You can read all that in here. Go on, have a look. And then you talk to me about a flourishing hacienda that's supposed to be as big as a Swiss canton—"

"Yes," I said, "if not bigger."

"Why do you tell me such tall stories?" he said. "You must see that we shan't get anywhere like this.

It's just not true. I don't believe you've ever been to Mexico."

"All right," I said, "have it your own way."

"Who could have owned an hacienda like that in modern Mexico," he said, "under a government that expressly forbids all large-scale land ownership?"

"A member of the government itself—"

This was a point my counsel didn't want to go into. Anything not quite above board makes him feel uneasy, and above all as an honest Swiss he can't bear to see abuses laughed at instead of being denounced and definitely relegated to the other side of the Iron Curtain. To back up his viewpoint he quickly pointed out that Mexico was a Communist country, an explanation which, from my first-hand knowledge, I could not accept. Apart from the fact that Mexico's mineral resources are mostly in American hands and therefore mostly protected, I did not consider the taste for large-scale land ownership Communistic, but human, and why should we not, free as we were, discuss everything human? . . .

Said my counsel: "Let's come to the point."

Meanwhile I find the story of my hacienda minister so amusing that I cannot forbear to tell it: He was, I believe, a manufacturer of office chairs, such as every State needs in large quantities. He wasn't the only manufacturer of office chairs. Once he had been elected Minister of Trade—so that he personally occupied a State office chair—for the sake of something to do, he imposed a ban on imports, to the great distress of those who delighted in the manufacture of office chairs. Raw materials fell into short supply everywhere. The Minister of Trade did not sit easy in his chair, as may be imagined, and when the right moment came—that is to say, when he had bought up the materials in short supply in the United States and stored them tidily on the other side of the frontier—he could no longer resist the entreaties of his competitors, and lifted the import ban for a fortnight. All the rest, of course, were too late with their orders, went bankrupt and were only too glad to accept the merger that was offered them. But the Minister of Trade, although above reproach, felt no further urge to sacrifice himself for his fatherland; he retired to the dilapidated hacienda with which the State, so to speak, rewarded him, and tended it with heart and soul and some thousand laborers, whose picturesque straw hats I shall never forget. As we sat on the shady veranda, we used to see them like white mushrooms out in the flowering, burning hot fields; and soon it was indeed a model hacienda, a paradise on earth . . .

Received from the public prosecutor the following information:

Anatol Ludwig Stiller, sculptor, whose last address was his studio in Steingartengasse, Zurich, and who has been missing since January 1946, is suspected of some offense the nature of which cannot be revealed to me until my identity has been proved. It seems to be a matter of some gravity. Espionage? I don't know what sets my mind running on this particular track, and anyhow it makes no odds to me; I'm not Stiller. How they wish I were. They obviously need him badly, guilty or not, as one small pawn may be needed in a game of chess—to clear up a whole situation. Drug traffic? Somehow I catch a whiff of politics rather than ordinary crime, and something in the attitude of my public prosecutor suggests to me that the suspicions of the Federal Police rest on rather shaky foundations. The mere fact that a man has suddenly disappeared naturally gives rise to rumors.

P.S. Looking back (in the meantime I have been reading the Bible again) it strikes me that both my defense counsel as well as my public prosecutor have asked me from time to time whether I know Russian, a question to which I replied, "Unfortunately not." "For Russian is supposed to be a wonderful language," I added, "all the Slav languages in fact . . ." Isn't one allowed to say that here?

I'm being put through the mill. Now they want to confront me with the lady from Paris; a blonde or redhead, to judge by the photographs, and very attractive to look at, rather skinny, but graceful. She and the missing man's brother have been sent a photograph of me. She insists she is my wife and is arriving by plane.

A walk in the prison yard—alone! It is very pleasant, but it makes me wonder. The favored treatment proves that those in authority still (or more than ever) take me for their missing Herr Stiller. They even let me out without a warder, so I don't have to walk in a circle; I sit on a bench in the sun and draw in the sand with a twig. But I must never forget to rub out my scribbles with my shoe, otherwise they take them for art and see in them further proof that I am the missing man. Autumn is on its way. Here and there, as though from an empty sky, a yellow plane leaf flutters on to the sand. You can see it in the sky too; its blue is already paler and more transparent. The air is fresh, especially in the morning. A hazy spaciousness. Pigeons coo, and when the cathedral bells chime they swish up into the air like a silver-gray cloud and their fluttering shadows follow them silently across the walls. They flutter on to rooftops and gutters; later they sail down again into my silent courtyard, waddle round my bench and coo.

I shall tell her the little story of Isidore. A true story. Isidore was a dispensing chemist, that's to say a conscientious fellow who made a pretty good living, the father of several children and a man in the prime of life, and there is no need to emphasize that Isidore was a faithful husband. Nevertheless, he couldn't stand his wife's perpetual inquiries as to where he had been. They made him furious—inwardly furious, he didn't show a sign on the outside. It wasn't worth quarreling about, for at bottom, as I have said, theirs was a happy marriage. One fine summer, as was the fashion just then, they made a trip to Mallorca, and apart from her never-ending questions, which annoyed him on the quiet, everything went well. Isidore could be extremely affectionate when he was on holiday. They were both delighted with the beauty of Avignon, and walked along arm in arm. Isidore and his wife, whom we must imagine as a very amiable woman, had been married just nine years when they arrived in Marseilles. The Mediterranean sparkled as it does on posters. To the silent annoyance of his wife, who was already on board the steamer for Mallorca, Isidore had to go back at the last moment to buy a paper. It may be that he did it partly out of pure spite because she asked him where he was going. God knows, he didn't mean to; it was simply that, as their steamer wasn't going yet, he went for a bit of a stroll. Out of pure spite, as I have said, he plunged into his French newspaper, and while his wife was actually sailing to picturesque Mallorca, Isidore, when the wail of a siren at last made him look up with a start from his paper, found himself not at the side of his wife, but on a rather dirty tramp steamer filled to overflowing with men in yellow uniforms and also under steam. The great hawsers had just been cast off. Isidore watched the quay recede into the distance. Whether it was the devilish heat or the uppercut from a French sergeant that shortly afterwards rendered him unconscious, I cannot say; on the other hand, I venture to assert with complete confidence that Isidore the chemist had a harder life in the Foreign Legion than before. Flight was out of the question. The yellow fort, where they made a man of Isidore, stood alone in the desert, whose sunsets he learnt to appreciate. No doubt he sometimes thought of his wife, when he was not simply too tired, and he would probably have written to her; but writing was not allowed. France was still fighting against the loss of her colonies, so that Isidore had soon seen more of the world than he would ever have allowed himself to dream. He forgot his chemist's shop, of course, as others forgot their criminal past. In time Isidore even lost his homesickness for the country that claimed in writing to be his home, and it was pure decency on Isidore's part when—many years later—he came through the garden gate one fine morning, bearded, lean as he now was, his sola topi under his arm, so that the neighbors—who had long ago assumed the chemist to be dead—should not be distressed by his somewhat unusual attire; naturally he also wore a belt with a revolver. It was a Sunday morning, his wife's birthday, as I've said, he loved her, even though he had not written her a postcard in all those years. He paused for an instant, looking at his unaltered home, his hand on the garden gate, which had not been oiled and creaked as it always used to. Five children, all bearing a certain resemblance to himself, but all seven years older, so that their appearance took him by surprise, were already shouting "Daddy" from a distance. There was no turning back.

So Isidore rode on with the determination of a man who has seen hard fighting, and in the hope that his dear wife, if at home, would not ask for an explanation. He strolled across the lawn as though he were coming back as usual from his shop, and not from Africa and Indo-China. His wife sat speechless under a new sunshade. Isidore had never seen the expensive dressing gown she was wearing before either. A maid—another innovation—immediately fetched a second cup for the bearded gentleman, whom without doubt, but also without disapproval, she took for the new "friend of the family." "It's cool here," said Isidore, pulling down his rolled-up shirtsleeves. The children were delighted at being allowed to play with the sola topi, which naturally led to some quarreling, and when the fresh coffee arrived it was a perfect idyll, Sunday morning with bells ringing and birthday cake. What more could Isidore want? Without a thought for the new maid, who was just laying the cutlery, Isidore grabbed his wife. "Isidore," she cried and was unable to pour out the coffee, so that the bearded guest had to do it himself. "What is it?" he asked affectionately, filling her cup up at the same time. "Isidore," she cried, close to tears. He put his arms around her. "Isidore," she asked, "where have you been all this time?" The man, as though momentarily stunned, put down his cup; he was simply not used to being married, and stood in front of a rose tree with his hands in his pockets. "Why didn't you write me so much as a postcard?" she asked. Thereupon he took his topi away from the dumb-founded children without a word, set it with military precision on his own head, which is supposed to have left an indelible impression on the children for the rest of their lives—Daddy with a sola topi and revolver holster that were not only genuine, but showed visible signs of use—and when his wife said, "You know, Isidore, you really shouldn't have done it," it was all over with Isidore's cozy homecoming. He drew (once more, I expect, with military precision) his revolver from his belt and fired three shots into the still un-touched cake decorated with sugar icing, which, as may readily be imagined, caused a pretty frightful mess. "Isidore," screamed his wife, for her dressing gown was spattered all over with whipped cream—if the innocent children had not been there as witness she would have thought the whole visit, which cannot have lasted more than ten minutes, a hallucination. Surrounded by her five children like a Niobe, she watched Isidore the irresponsible walk coolly out through the garden gate, the impossible topi on his head.

After this shock the poor woman could never look at a birthday cake without thinking of Isidore, a pitiable state of affairs. Her friends advised her confidentially to get a divorce, but the brave woman still hoped. Her husband's guilt was obvious. But she still hoped he would relent, lived entirely for the five children she had by Isidore, and like a Penelope put off for another year the young lawyer who paid her a visit and urged her, not without reasons of his own, to divorce her husband. And sure enough a year later— again on her birthday—Isidore returned, sat down after the usual greeting, rolled down his sleeves and once more let the children play with his topi; but this time their delight at having a daddy lasted less than three minutes. "Isidore," said his wife, "where have you been this time?" He stood up, without shooting, thank goodness, and without taking his topi away from the innocent children, rolled up his sleeves again and went out through the garden gate never to return. His poor wife wept as she signed the divorce petition, but it had to be, especially as Isidore did not put in an appearance within the legally specified period; his chemist's shop was sold; the second marriage proceeded without ostentation and after the legally specified period had elapsed was also sanctioned by the registry office; in short, everything followed an orderly pattern, as was so important for the growing children. There was never any answer to the question of where Daddy had got to. Not even a picture postcard. Mummy didn't want the children to ask where he was; she ought never to have asked Daddy herself . . .

They have no money for whisky, but plenty for telegrams to Mexico to confirm from the Swiss Embassy that there is not only a Mexican dump called Orizaba, but in very truth a whole lot of flourishing haciendas, some of them really occupied by ex-ministers, some of them larger than the canton of Zurich and some of them smaller. On the other hand, however, (my able counsel informs me) the Embassy cannot confirm that a Swiss citizen was ever employed on a Mexican hacienda.

"Well," I said, "now you know."

"What?"

"That I'm not a Swiss citizen, Herr Doktor, and therefore can't be your missing Herr Stiller."

Whenever one of us thinks with razor-edged acuity, the other is in no way convinced; my counsel reached into his leather case and actually offered me a cigar he had specially bought for me—not the brand I wanted, unfortunately, but I nevertheless showed I was touched.

"Word of honor—have you really been in Mexico?" he asked. "Joking apart."

It's funny how a little thing like a one-franc cigar immediately puts you under an obligation, making it quite impossible for me to turn my back on the donor without a word, in answer to his question . . . Have I really been in Mexico! Anyone can say Yes, but not everyone, I thought to myself, can relate what a backache a lower shrub-leaf, like the one on this cigar, gives the poor picker on the plantation; for these lower leaves are tougher than the upper ones, gray with dust, sandy and brittle, so that they are all too liable to break. But the picker is only paid for absolutely faultless goods. These lower leaves are used to wrap the fine cigars. Only the perfect article can be employed . . .

"Yes, yes," said my counsel. "No doubt, but what has that to do with my question?"

I smoked. I described my work on the Uruapan tobacco plantation. A hard time. On my knees from morning to evening. You can't pick the lower leaves any other way; even on your knees you have to bend to find the best leaves. Once, I shall never forget it, I was crawling along from shrub to shrub, a Mexican straw hat on my head, without catching a glimpse of the other pickers. I waited in vain for the overseer's whistle. Despite my economic position I simply couldn't stand the heat any longer, wages or no wages. The stench of sulphur was getting stronger and stronger. I yelled out, suddenly seized with terror. From the gray earth just behind me a little cloud of yellow smoke billowed forth. In vain I shouted to the other laborers, mostly Indians; they had already fled. My feet, too, could bear the heat no longer, and I ran, but where to? The air was full of smoke like a stag party where everyone is smoking cigars, and I could see fissures opening up in the earth around me, soundless fissures from which came the stench of sulphur. I run on at random until I was panting so hard that I could run no further. Then I looked back at our plantation and saw it rise and arch itself and become a small hill. A thrilling spectacle, but heat and smoke drove me on. I cried out the news in the village. The women gathered together their children and sobbed; the men decided to send a telegram to the owner of the plantation that was turning into a volcano. After a few days and nights, during which the village lived in a continual state of alarm, it had developed into a not inconsiderable mountain enveloped in yellow and greenish smoke. The village could neither work nor sleep; the sun shone as always, but it stank of sulphur, poisonous and hot, so that one would have liked to stop breathing; and the moon shone out of a cloudless night-sky, but there was thunder. The little church was filled to overflowing, the bells rang without pause, occcasionally drowned by the thunderous eruptions of the mountain.

No answer came to the telegram, so we had to take steps to save ourselves. Fire glowed through the smoke that clouded the moon. And then came the lava, slowly, but irresistibly, cooling and setting in the air, a black broth giving off swirling white steam; only during the night could you see the glow inside the stone broth that came nearer and nearer, as high as a house, nearer and nearer—thirty yards a day. Birds flitted about in bewilderment because they could not find their nests, and forests disappeared under the red hot lava, mile by mile. The village was evacuated. I don't believe a single human life was lost. Carrying their weeping children in their arms or on their backs, laden with bundles containing little of value, they drove their distracted beasts in front of them, the donkeys braying and becoming more stubborn the more despairingly they were beaten. The lava flowed casually between the houses, filling them and swallowing them up. Being one of those who had no animal to save, I stood on a hill and watched the lava advancing: it hissed like a snake, turning every drop of water it came upon into steam, and it had a skin like certain snakes, a metallic gray skin, crusty over a soft, hot and mobile interior. Finally it reached the church; the first tower fell to its knees and was swallowed up with all its hurtling debris; the other stood fast and is still standing today, a tower with a little Spanish dome, the only thing left out of the whole village . . .

"The village was called Paricutin. Now that is the name of the new volcano," I finished my story, "and if ever you go to Mexico, my dear Doktor, drive out to this Paricutin. The roads are terrible, but it's worth while, especially at night; glowing stones fly fifteen hundred feet into the air, and there is a rumbling like the rumbling of an avalanche, and just before it begins smoke always billows up from the crater like a giant cauliflower, but black and red, red underneath where it catches the light from the flames below. Not so long ago the eruptions succeeded one another at pretty short intervals—six minutes, ten minutes, three minutes, each eruption throwing up a cascade of glowing stones, most of which were extinguished before they struck the ground. It's a first-class firework, believe me. Especially the lava. From the middle of a dark heap of dead slag, on which the moon shines without detracting from its blackness, the lava shoots out bright crimson, in spurts, like blood from a black bull. It must be very thin and runny, this lava, it sweeps down over the hillside almost as quick as lightning, gradually losing its brightness, until the next eruption comes glowing like a blast furnace, gleaming like the sun, lighting up the night with the deadly heat to which all life is due, with the molten heart of our planet. That's a sight you must see. I remember that our souls were filled with a jubilation that could only find an outlet in dancing, in the wildest of all dances, an outpouring of horror and delight, such as the incomprehensible people who cut the warm heart out of the living breast might have understood."

My counsel made notes.

"Paricutin?" he asked. "How do you spell that?"

"As it's pronounced."

We chatted about this, that and the other. The cigar was new to me, but very good of its kind. Once more we never got down to business (as he calls his heap of papers).

"Herr Doktor," I shouted after him down the corridor, "you needn't bother to inquire about my working on that plantation, Herr Doktor, you can save yourself the trouble. Even your Swiss Embassy won't be able to find anything."

"Why not?"

"Because of the lava."

He'll telegraph just the same.

I'm not their Stiller. What do they want with me? I'm an unfortunate, insignificant, unimportant person with no life behind him, none at all. Why am I lying to them? Just so that they should leave me my emptiness, my insignificance, my reality; it's no good running away, and what they are offering me is flight, not freedom, flight means acting a part. Why don't they stop it?

Herr Dr. Bohnenblust (that's my counsel's name) has fetched the lady from Paris, who thinks she is my wife, from the airport and seems to be very charmed with her.

"I just wanted to let you know," said my counsel, "that the lady has landed safely. Of course she sends her love—"

"Thank you."

"She's now at the hotel."

My counsel was incapable of sitting down, he could only rub his hands triumphantly, as though the lady from Paris were the big gun that was going to force me to surrender.

"Herr Doktor," I said, "I have no objection to visits from ladies, I merely repeat the warning I gave you before: I'm a hot-blooded man, unrestrained, as I told you, especially at this time of the year."

"So I told her."

"Well?"

"The lady insists," he said, "on seeing you *tête-à-tête*. She'll be here on Monday at ten o'clock. She is convinced that she knows her husband better than he knows himself, and there's no question of his being unrestrained, she says, that was always a wish-dream of her husband, says the lady, and she's quite sure she can manage him on her own."

Then he offered me another cigar.

"Monday at ten o'clock?" I said. "All right."

Knobel, my warder, is beginning to get annoyed with my questions about the lady from Paris who claims to be married to me.

"I told you," he grumbled, "she looks smart. And her scent fills the whole corridor."

"What about her hair?"

"Red," he said, "like rose-hip jam."

He is incapable of giving a real description, even when he answers my questions one by one; the more I hear the less I am able to visualize her.

"Now eat your dinner," he said. "You'll see her for yourself. Perhaps the lady isn't your type at all, although she swears she's your wife."

"My type," I laughed. "Did I ever tell you the story about the little mulatto girl?"

"No."

"She was my type," I said.

"A mulatto girl?"

"It was on the Rio Grande," I began in a tone of voice that made Knobel sit down. "Suddenly—haven't you got any bread?" I interrupted myself, whereupon Knobel jumped to his feet and placed half a loaf on the table; I cut a thick slice and took a bite, while Knobel sat down again and waited till my mouth was a little less full. Then I went on. "Suddenly—we were just crouching round our fire, for evenings in the desert are bitterly cold, naturally there was no wood anywhere around, we were burning cotton waste, which gives out more stench than heat, discussing with the smugglers how they could smuggle us over the frontier during the night, because there was another warrant out for my arrest—suddenly, he came round the red rocks."

"Who?"

Of course you can't talk with a mouth full of bread, not to mention the *minestra* I had to get down while it was still hot.

"Who?" asked Knobel. "Who came round the rocks?"

"A limousine," I said at last and could not restrain myself from taking another bite of the magnificent bread, "stolen of course. A splendid sight, by the way, like a banner of gold dust. Because of the last rays of the setting sun. A limousine streaking across the desert, pitching like a yawl, naturally, up and down over the waves of sand."

"Naturally."

"Of course he had seen our little fire."

"What happened?"

"Bang!" I said. "But the fellow drove straight on, and of course we thought it was the American police. So bang! bang! and again bang!—and who do you think was inside?"

"Who?"

"Joe."

I took a spoonful of my *minestra*.

"Who's Joe?"

"Her husband."

"The mulatto's?"

"Of course."

"Well I'm blowed!"

"A negro," I added, "a thoroughly nice chap, but not when you'd abducted his wife. So in the dark, when you could see the dazzling whiteness of his teeth—cheers!" I said, breaking off to take a drink.

"Go one."

"We were in love."

"You and the mulatto?"

"I asked her: 'Do you love me or him?' She knew exactly what I meant. And nodded. And bang. And not another sound from Joe."

"Dead?" he asked.

"On the spot."

"Well I'm blowed!"

"She kissed me," I said. "That's my type."

Thereupon Knobel ladled me out another plateful of *minestra;* he's as attentive as a waiter serving rich customers.

"I like negroes," I said, "but I can't stand married men, even if they're negroes. They expect you to lay off their wives, and that doesn't suit me. Of course we drove straight across the frontier—"

"To Mexico?"

"Without lights. To the left, the Rio Grande. To the right, the full moon."

"That was your third murder?"

"I believe so . . ."

It really wasn't right for Knobel to spend so long in my cell; the others always got cold food. My warder had already picked up the pail; I don't know what he was waiting for.

"Man is a beast of prey," I said in a general sort of way. "That's the truth, Knobel, and all the rest is humbug."

But he still waited.

"When I think how I first met Florence," I said, "— in the burning sawmill."

"Who's Florence?"

"My mulatto."

"I see."

"That was up north in Oregon," I said. "When I was fishing on the coast. I had no money for any other sort of food, and I hadn't yet sunk to stealing. I still thought I was an honest man, even when I didn't catch anything for days, not a thing; it's no easy matter fishing in the ocean, from the rocky shore, with the breakers splashing. It's a tricky business. You stand for hours on your reef, in the dry; the spray from the surf flies up and falls, but it never rises beyond a certain point, it never comes up over your reef; you feel as safe as a solid citizen, and suddenly a wave comes along that is higher than the rest, God knows why, fifteen feet higher; if you don't spot it in time, that wave, as it foams over the reef full of seals, then you're drowned, honest man or no, smashed against the rocks, a drifting corpse that is never identified . . .

"There was a cloudless moon as I stood there, deafened by the breakers, when suddenly I saw smoke billowing up over the shore behind me, so much smoke that it looked like an eclipse of the sun. That can only be the big sawmill, I thought at once, in this lonely neighborhood. You must imagine what it was like: not a single house within a radius of twenty miles, nothing but rocks and sheep and a wire-rope with which they lowered the logs from the wild forest, and when I looked up at the hill the sky was full of flying sparks; I've never seen such a fire and you should have heard it crackle; and not a trace of a fire engine, naturally, only the women standing round sobbing and biting their fingers, and praying to God to stop blowing with his wind; no water to put it out with and it was Sunday, so the men were off somewhere playing bowls, and here there was a flapping and slapping in the air like crimson banners—a glorious sight—flames flickered out of every window, there was nothing to be done; outside lay a whole ocean full of wind, and as it blew into the huge stack of dry timber the heat was so terrific it was unbearable at a hundred paces; and right in the middle stood a tank full of petrol."

"Well I'm blowed!"

"I asked her if she was crazy. The tank might go up at any moment. But just the same she rushed into her hut—"

"Who?"

"Right in the middle of all the clouds of smoke," I said. "The mulatto girl."

"Well I'm blowed."

"And I—ran after her."

"Naturally."

"What do you mean, naturally?" I said. "It was absolutely crazy, but I suddenly thought, perhaps she wants to save a child—I shall never forget how I stood there in the hut, a few roof shingles were already on fire, an old negro was running up and down on the roof like a monkey trying to put out the burning shingles with a ridiculous garden hose, one at a time, for his jet of water wasn't enough for any more, it was a joke, and inside the smoke was so thick I thought

I should suffocate. 'Hallo,' I yelled, 'hallo.' And there she stood, motionless and weeping, her hands on her hips, helpless, a young mulatto, a lovely creature, my dear Knobel, as beautiful as an animal, eighteen years old, a lovely creature—! Everything else was sheer rubbish, not worth saving, nothing but crockery and mattresses. I was so furious I just grabbed hold of her and shook her."

"Why?" asked Knobel.

"She wanted me to save the refrigerator. 'Like hell,' I shouted. And outside the old negro was still squirting with his thin garden hose so that drops fell on us. 'What do you want then?' she asked. 'You,' I yelled. And when I took hold of her she laughed so that all her white teeth showed. 'I've got a husband,' she said. 'Come on,' I told her. 'Have you a car?' she asked. There are plenty of cars about, I thought, and as she put her arms round me so that I could carry her better, the roof began to crack and set the sparks dancing. I carried her out like a casualty, dumped her in the first car I came on standing in the street, and off we went. It was a Plymouth. The owner, probably a commercial traveler, never noticed as I drove past him, everyone was staring at the petrol tank that was going to explode at any moment."

"So you were off and away, Mr. White."

It's wonderful how delighted Knobel is by other people's successes; he positively beams.

"Four hours later," I went on, "we were sitting in a quiet bay which is already inside California, fishing, where not a soul could see us. 'By the way, what's your name?' I asked her. 'Florence,' she said, and her eyes were like deadly nightshade berries, her skin like coffee. 'Joe will kill you,' she said, 'if he catches us.' I just laughed. 'We've got a car,' I said, and showed her how to open shellfish to get bait for fishing."

In the end Knobel was called from outside and had

to leave me. With his bunch of keys in his hand he asked me: "Did you catch anything?"

"And how!" I said, showing him the size with out-stretched arms. "This big."

My public prosecutor, at the moment the only person to whom I can disclose my real wretchedness almost undisguised, has said goodbye; he is going to Pontresina for ten days' holiday with his wife (who again sends her regards). We wish one another "All the best."

Her hair is red, very red in fact, in keeping with the new fashion, not like rose-hip jam, however, but like dry minium powder. Very curious. And with it a very fine complexion—alabaster with freckles. Also very curious, but beautiful. And her eyes? I should say they are glittering, somehow watery, even when she is not crying, bluish-green like the edges of colorless window-glass, and at the same time, of course, full of soul and therefore opaque. Unfortunately her eye-brows have been plucked to a thin line, which gives her face a graceful hardness, but also a slightly mask-like appearance, as though perpetually miming surprise. Her nose looks very aristocratic, especially from the side; there is a great deal of involuntary expression in her nostrils. Her lips are rather thin for my taste, not without sensuality, but they must first be roused; and her figure (in a black tailor-made costume) has some-thing spare and also boyish about it; it's easy to see she's a dancer; perhaps it would be more accurate to say there is something of the ephebe about her, which is unexpectedly attractive in a woman of her age. She smokes a great deal. Her very slender hand, when she stubs out the half-smoked cigarette, is by no means lacking in strength and a considerable measure of forcefulness, although she seems to see herself as com-pletely fragile. She speaks very softly, to prevent her interlocutor from shouting. She banks on being protected. I believe this little ruse, too, is unconscious. And she smells intoxicating, just as Knobel said; it must be a very high-class make, one immediately thinks of Paris, of the perfumeries in the Place Vendôme.

"How are you?" she inquired.

Her habit of always answering one question with another is something you find in many women, in fact in all women, and I'm quite familiar with it. This made it all the more necessary for me to guard against the insidious feeling of having met her before.

"Don't you recognize me?" she asked.

Her fixed idea that I am her missing husband was by no means assumed; it came out in even her most trivial remarks.

"Don't you smoke any more?" she asked.

Later—because you can't keep a conversation going indefinitely with nothing but questions, especially when they are not even genuine questions, since she would only accept one answer and simply ignored all others as being prevarication—I told her the little tale of Isidore, adapting it to the case of my beautiful visitor by omitting the five children and making free use of a dream I had recently: when Isidore turned up at home he did not fire at the birthday cake, but merely showed his two hands covered with scars . . . A crazy dream.

"Oh," sighed my lady, "you're still the same, one can't get a word of sense out of you, nothing but freaks of fancy."

First it was comical, then annoying, but somehow also touching. This lady from Paris sitting on my bed in her black costume, smoking one cigarette after another, was anything but a stupid person, and I could imagine spending a delightful afternoon with her, more than an afternoon in fact. Above all, her rather tired and for some reason bitter laugh was enchanting, making one curious about the experience that lay behind it, time and again I couldn't help looking at her lips and being conscious of my own. But it seemed she couldn't get away from her fixed idea that she knew me. She simply refused to believe I could be anyone else than her missing Stiller. She kept on talking about her marriage, which, I gathered, had not been all that a marriage should be. Several times I indicated my regret. When I finally got a chance to speak—she didn't talk incessantly, far from it, she interspersed her conversation with frequent pauses during which she puffed hastily at her cigarette, long minutes of bitter silence it would have required more courage to inter-rupt than a spate of words—when I finally got a chance to speak, I said:

"I suppose you've been told, Madame, that you are talking to a murderer?"

She ignored my remark as though it were a joke that had fallen flat.

"I'm a murderer," I repeated at the next opportunity, "even if the Swiss police can't establish the fact. I murdered my wife."

It was no use.

"You're funny," she said. "You're really funny, I must say. At a time like this, when we haven't seen one another for half a lifetime, you start with your freaks of fancy again, your childish freaks of fancy."

Again and again, I admit, her gravity made me mo-mentarily uncertain, not uncertain about the fact that I had murdered my wife, but uncertain whether I should succeed in freeing this unhappy lady from her fixed idea. What did she want of me? I also tried gravity as a means of convincing her that there had never been a marriage between us, remaining grave even when she jumped up from my bed, walked up and down shaking her red hair, stood in front of my barred window smoking, her slender hands in the scanty pockets of her tight-fitting tailor-made, not saying a word but staring out at the autumnal chestnut tree, so that I could not see her face.

"Madame," I said, taking one of her cigarettes, "you flew down here to forgive your lost husband; you have waited years for this grave, indeed solemn, hour, and I can understand that it's a blow for you to find that I'm not the man you have waited for with all your desire to forgive everything. I'm not the man, Madame."

Her only answer was to puff out smoke.

"I think," I said, now smoking myself, "that is obvious, there is no need to discuss it."

"What's obvious?"

"That I'm not your lost husband."

"Why not?" she asked without looking at me.

At least I could see the back of her shapely head.

"Madame," I said with undiminished gravity, "I'm deeply moved to hear you speak of your unhappy marriage, but, if you will forgive my saying so, the more I listen to you the less I understand what you want of me, in fact I don't understand at all. What can a lady like you, who, thank God, have so brilliantly recovered from the effects of your unhappy marriage, want with me—a man who murdered his wife. To be quite frank, I don't understand what it is you want to forgive me?"

Silence.

"You live in Paris?" I asked.

Then the figure turned. Her face, partially unmasked by quiet dismay and more beautiful than before, making one think that contact must be possible, contact in the realm of truth—her face had for a short space of time a look that made me want to kiss her on the brow, and perhaps I ought to have done so, regardless of whether she misinterpreted it or not; for a short space of time, then her face seemed to close again and back she came with her fixed idea:

"Anatol, what's the matter with you?"

Again I told her:

"My name is White."

She simply turned the tables, acting as though I were the one with the fixed idea. She threw her lighted cigarette out of the barred window (which is strictly forbidden, like so much here) and stood in front of me without taking hold of me of course, but knowing quite well that I should take hold of her and suddenly overcome by remorse beg her forgiveness. And in fact for a few moments we were quite defenseless, we smiled, although it wasn't funny at all. I might have looked like a gnome, a minotaur, anything you like, and it would have made no difference whatever; she was simply incapable of perceiving any other being than her vanished Stiller.

"I didn't think," she said, "you would ever go bald on top. But it quite suits you."

I was simply struck dumb. I was helpless. If I had taken hold of this lady and strangled her she would have gone on believing I was her lost husband.

"Why didn't you ever write?"

I said nothing.

"I didn't even know whether you were still alive—"

I said nothing.

"Where have you been all these years?"

I said nothing.

"You say nothing—"

I said nothing.

"Fancy disappearing like that," she said. "Going off and never writing me a line. And just at that time. I might have died."

Once I said:

"That's enough."

I don't know what else she talked about, she went on until I took hold of her, and even then she was unshakeable in her fixed idea, taking every reaction of mine, whether I laughed or trembled, as a confirmation. She didn't stop forgiving me, though I grabbed hold of her, shook her till her hair-combs fell in showers all round and flung her on the hard bed, where she lay with a torn blouse, crumpled costume, tousled hair and an expression of bewildered innocence, unable to rise because I was kneeling on the bed gripping her two hot hands in my left fist so that she shut her lovely eyes in pain. Her loose hair was gloriously silky and as light as gossamer. She was breathing heavily as though she had been running, her chest heaving and her mouth open. Her front teeth were splendid, not without fillings, but otherwise gleaming like mother of pearl. And since I had gripped her delicate lower jaw with my other hand, she was incapable of speaking. I looked at her as though she were an object, suddenly quite sober, as though she were just any unknown woman. If Knobel, my warder, hadn't come with the ash-tray—

It's no good running away. I know that and keep repeating it to myself every day. It's no good running away. I ran away to avoid committing murder, and now I've learnt that my very attempt to run away was the murder. There is only one thing to do: to take this knowledge upon myself, even if no one shares with me this knowledge that I have murdered a life.

Freaks of fancy! I'm supposed to tell my life story, and when I try to make myself understood they say, "Freaks of fancy." (At least I know now where my counsel picked up this expression together with the patronizing smile that goes with it.) He listens as long as I talk about my house in Oakland, about negroes and other facts; but as soon as I come to the real story, as soon as I try to tell him things that cannot be verified by a photograph—for example, what happens after you put a bullet in your temple—my counsel cleans his finger-nails and waits for a chance to interrupt me with some trifle.

"You had a house in Oakland?"

"Yes," I said briefly, "why?"

"Where's Oakland?"

"Opposite San Francisco."

"Ah," said my counsel, "really?"

It was thirteen feet wide and forty-two feet long (my counsel makes a note, that's the sort of thing he wants to know) and to be quite exact it was really more of a shingle hut. It once housed the laborers of a farm, but the farm was swallowed up by the town and only the now tumble-down hut remained, along with a giant tree, a eucalyptus—I shall never forget the silvery rustle of its leaves. Round about there was nothing but roofs, a sky filled with leaning telephone poles carrying the washing of my negro neighbors. To be precise again, there were Chinese living on my right. And the little overgrown garden must not be forgotten. On Sundays you heard the negroes singing in their wooden church. Otherwise there was silence, a great deal of silence, occasionally broken by the hoarse wail of sirens from the harbor and the rattle of chains that makes the blood curdle. Incidentally, I wasn't the owner of this little shingle-hut, only the tenant. I had absolutely no money at the time. The rent consisted in my having to feed the cat. I can't stand cats. But the cat's food stood ready in green tins, and in compensation I had a kitchen with a cooker and a refrigerator, and even a radio. In the hot nights the silence was often almost unbearable; I was glad to have the radio.

"And you lived there all on your own?"

"No," I said, "with the cat."

He had even got beyond making a note of the cat . . . Yet this cat, I now believe, was the first warning. Her owners called her Little Gray and had always fed her in the kitchen, a custom I was not inclined to continue, because of the smell apart from anything else. I opened the daily tin and tipped the revolting stuff on to a plate in the garden, an arrangement which on her side, spoilt as she was, the cat was not inclined to accept. She jumped up on to the sill of my open window and glowered at me with her green eyes, spitting. How could I read under such circumstances? I flung her out into the Californian night, a bundle with kicking paws, and shut all the windows. She crouched outside the pane and spat, she spat for hours at a time, for weeks on end, whenever I looked at her. I never failed to give her the tinned food, that was my duty, the only one I had at that time. And she never failed to slip into the house again through some open window (I couldn't spend the whole summer behind closed windows), unexpectedly rubbing herself against my legs just when I was feeling happy. It became a real struggle, a ridiculous struggle to see who could hold out longest, a horrible struggle; night after night I lay awake because she was howling round my hut, denouncing me to the whole neighborhood as a cruel man. I let her in and shoved her into the refrigerator, but still I couldn't sleep. When I took pity on her, she had stopped spitting; I warmed her some milk, which she vomited. She looked at me as though threatening to die. She was quite capable of ruining everything for me, the little shingle-hut, the garden—. She was there even when she wasn't there; she brought me to the point of going to look for her when it was time to shut up for the night. I asked the negroes sitting on the curb whether they had seen Little Gray, and they shrugged their round shoulders. She stayed away eleven days and nights. One hot evening, just when Helen had come to see me, she jumped on to the window sill. "My goodness," cried Helen; the cat was sitting there with a gaping wound in her face dripping with blood, and looking at me as though I had wounded her. For a week I fed her in the kitchen: she had brought it off. At least almost, for one night after midnight, when I had been dreaming about her, I went downstairs, took her out from among the warm pillows she had snuggled into, and carried her out into the garden—but not without first making sure her wound was healed. Everything began all over again; once more she crouched outside the window and spat. I should never get the beter of this animal—

My counsel smiled.

"But apart from the cat, I mean, you lived alone."

"No," I said, "with Helen."

"Who is Helen?"

"A woman," I said, angered by his knack of always entangling me in side-issues, and by his Eversharp, with which he immediately made a note of the name.

"Don't hold anything back," he said, and after I had served him up a pretty hot story of love and passion, he assured me: "Of course, I shall treat all this in strict confidence—anyhow, I shan't say a word about it to Frau Stiller."

I hope he talks!

Have been reading the Bible.

(The ghastly dream of the confrontation with Frau Julika Stiller-Tschudy: I am looking from outside through a window at a youngish man, probably the missing man, walking between the café tables and raising his outspread hands in order to display the bright red patches, hawking his stigmata, so to speak, which no one buys from him; embarrassment; I myself am standing outside, as I said, with the lady from Paris, whose face I don't know and who is explaining rather scornfully that the stigma-hawker is her husband, she also shows me her hands—also bearing two bright red scars. It is obvious, this much I can guess, that the point is to show who is the cross and who the crucified, though none of this is put into words; the people at the café tables are reading illustrated papers . . .)

My warder wanted to know who Helen was. He had
just heard the name in the public prosecutor's office.
My warder already knew she was the wife of a U.S.
sergeant, and also that the sergeant in question came
home on leave one morning and surprised us together
in the house . . . Too tired to make up another murder story, I merely added:

"He was a charming fellow."

"Her husband?"

"He wanted his wife to go and see a psychoanalyst,
and she wanted him to do the same."

"What happened next?"

"That was all."

My warder was disappointed, but I realize more and
more that this has its advantages; it's precisely the dis-
appointing stories, which have no proper ending and
therefore no proper meaning, that sound true to life.

Otherwise there's nothing new.

P.S. I don't know what they hope to gain from these
on-the-spot investigations. They've evidently abandoned, or at least postponed, their plan of taking me
to her lost husband's studio, because of my assurance
that I should smash to pieces everything belonging
to the fellow who had caused me so much trouble.
Now, I hear, they want to go with me to Davos. What
for?

You can put anything into words, except your own
life. It is this impossibility that condemns us to remain as our companions see and mirror us, those who
claim to know me, those who call themselves my
friends and never allow me to change, and discredit
every miracle (which I cannot put into words, the inexpressible, which I cannot prove)—simply so that
they can say:

"I know you."

My counsel was beside himself, as was bound to happen sooner or later; he did not lose his self-control, but self-control had made him white in the face. Without saying good morning, he looked into my sleepy eyes, silent, his brief-case on his knees, waiting till he felt I had sufficiently recovered my senses and was sufficiently curious to know the reason for his indignation.

"You're lying," he said.

Probably he expected me to blush; he still hasn't grasped the situation.

"How can I believe anything you say?" he complained. "Every word you utter begins to seem dubious to me, extremely dubious, now that this album has come into my possession. Look," he said, "just look at these photographs for yourself."

Admittedly they were photographs, and I won't deny that there was a certain outward likeness between the missing Stiller and myself; nevertheless, I see myself very differently.

"Why do you lie?" he kept asking me. "How can I defend you, if you don't even tell me the whole and complete truth?"

He can't understand.

"Where did you get this album from?" I asked.

No reply.

"And you dare to tell me you have never lived in this country, that you couldn't even imagine living in our town!"

"Not without whisky," I said.

"Just look at this," he said.

Sometimes I try to help him.

"Herr Doktor," I said, "it all depends what you mean by living. A real life, a life that leaves a deposit in the shape of something alive, not merely a photograph album yellow with age—God knows, it need not be magnificent, it need not be historic and unforgettable—you know what I mean, Herr Doktor, a real life may be the life of a very simple mother, or the life of a great thinker, someone whose life leaves a deposit that is preserved in world history—but it doesn't have to be, I mean, it doesn't depend on our importance. It's difficult to say what makes a life a real life. I call it reality, but what does that mean? You could also say it depends on a person being identical with himself. That's what I mean, Herr Doktor, a person has lived and his life has formed a deposit, however wretched it may be—it may be no more than a crime, it's bitter when all our life amounts to is a crime, a murder for example, that happens, and there's no need for vultures to circle overhead—you're quite right, Herr Doktor, those are just circumlocutions. You understand what I mean? I express myself very unclearly, when I don't just lie for all I'm worth for the sake of an outlet; deposit is only a word, I know, and perhaps we are talking all the time about things that elude us, things we can't grasp. God is a deposit! He is the sum of real life, or at least that's how it sometimes seems to me. Are words a deposit? Perhaps life, real life, is simply mute—and it doesn't leave photographs behind, Herr Doktor, it doesn't leave anything dead . . ."

But dead things are enough for my counsel.

"Look," he said, "just look at this photograph of you feeding swans. It's definitely you and in the background, you can see for yourself, is the Great Minster of Zurich. Just look."

There was no denying it. In the background (not very clear) you could see a kind of small cathedral, a Great Minster, as my counsel called it.

"It really all depends," I said once more, "what we mean by living—"

"Look at this," said my counsel, continuing to turn the pages of the album. "Just look: Anatol in his first studio, Anatol on the Piz Palu, Anatol as a recruit with cropped hair, Anatol outside the Louvre, Anatol talking to a town councilor on the occasion of a prize-giving—"

"So what?" I asked.

We understand each other less and less. If it were not for the cigar he had brought, in spite of his annoyance, I shouldn't have spoken to my counsel at all any more, and it would have been better, I think. I tried in vain to explain to him that I didn't know the whole and complete truth myself, and on the other hand was not disposed to let swans or town councilors prove to me who I really was, and that I should tear up on the spot any further albums he brought into my cell. It was no use. My counsel would not get it out of his head that I must be Stiller, simply so that he could defend me, and he called it silly make-believe, when I contradicted him and swore I was no one but myself. Once more it ended in our bawling one another out.

"I'm not Stiller," I shouted.

"Who are you then?" he shouted. "Who are you?"

P.S. His cigar makes me feel ashamed of myself. Just now I bit off the crisp tip, and then drew the first few puffs that are always so especially dry and especially fragrant. In a minute I was so amazed by the aroma that I took the cigar from my lips and looked at it carefully. Dannemann! My favorite brand! Really and truly? So he's once more—

Went to Davos yesterday. It's just as Thomas Mann describes it. Moreover it rained all day long. Nevertheless I had to go for a very special walk, during which Julika made me look at squirrels while my counsel kept handing me fir-cones to smell. As though I had denied the aromatic smell of fir-cones. Later, in a very special restaurant, I had to eat snails, which are a famous delicacy but make you stink of garlic afterwards. All the time I could clearly observe Julika and my counsel exchanging glances, waiting for me to let slip some admission, or at least burst into tears. None the less I greatly appreciated eating off a white table-cloth again. Since conversation flagged, I told them about Mexico—the mountains round about, though very small, reminded me of Popocatepetl and the Cortez Pass, and I have always found the conquest of Mexico one of the most fascinating stories.

"May be," said my counsel, "but we're not here for you to tell us about Cortez and Montezuma."

They wanted to show me the sanatorium where Julika lay during her illness; but it had since been burnt down, about which my counsel was heart-broken. After the meal there was coffee, kirsch and cigars ad lib. I wondered what they were spending all this money for. The little outing cost about two hundred Swiss francs; my counsel and I went in the State prison van (meals for the driver and the police constable were extra), Julika by train. In better weather it would have been a pleasant bit of country-side, no doubt about it. Once, down in the valley, we overtook the train, Julika waved.

My greatest fear: repetition.

Frau Julika Stiller-Tschudy discovered the old scar over my left ear and wanted to know how I got it. She kept on about it. I said to her:

"Somebody tried to shoot me."

"No," she said pressingly, "seriously—"

I told her a story.

P.S. Julika, now that I have seen her more often, is quite different from what I thought at our first meeting. Just what she is like, I should find it hard to say. She has moments of unexpected grace, especially when my counsel is not there, moments of defenseless innocence, a sudden blossoming of the childhood years that were never lived, a face as it must have been the first instant it was awakened by the breath of the Creator. Then it is as though she were surprised herself—a lady in a black tailor-made costume and a Paris hat, generally surrounded by a veil of smoke— surprised that no man has yet known her. I can't understand this vanished Stiller. She's a hidden maid waiting under the cover of mature womanhood, at moments so beautiful it takes your breath away. Didn't Stiller notice? There is nothing womanly this woman does not possess, at least potentially, smothered over perhaps, and her eyes alone (when she stops believing I'm Stiller for a moment) have a gleam of frank anticipation that makes you jealous of the man who will one day awaken her.

Repetition. And yet I know that everything depends on whether one succeeds in ceasing to wait for life outside repetition, and instead, of one's free will (in spite of compulsion), manages to turn repetition, inescapable repetition, into one's life by acknowledging: That is I . . . But again and again (here, too, there is repetition) it needs only a word, a gesture that frightens me, a landscape that reminds me, and everything within me is flight, flight without hope of getting anywhere, simply for fear of repetition—

While we were soaping down in the showers today the little Jew told me we were probably seeing one another for the last time, because he was shortly going to hang himself. I laughed and advised him not to. Then we marched along the corridor again one by one with towels round our necks.

The latest news:

"It won't be long now," said Knobel. "You'll get your whisky at last, Mr. White, perhaps this week."

When I asked him what he meant, he didn't answer;

I realized at once that he had heard something, but wasn't supposed to talk about it. At the end, when he had already picked up the soup pail, he nevertheless added:

"The lady seems to have taken a great liking to you."

"So what?"

"Anyhow she's gone bail for you," he said in an undertone, "a tidy sum."

"What for?"

"Well—for you, Mr. White," he grinned and winked his eye. "So that you can go for walks with her."

P.S. I have asked my counsel to bring me another notebook, because this one will soon be full. I haven't let him read it yet, and his earnest hope that this notebook will enable him, so to speak, to get my life into his brief-case, is gradually beginning to worry me.

Zurich could be a charming little town. It stands at the lower end of a delightful lake, whose hilly banks are not disfigured by factories, but by villas, and as we had such pleasant weather for our outing yesterday, a blue September sky with a thin silvery haze, I was really enchanted—not merely to please Frau Julika, whose generous bail makes it possible for me to go for trips like this every week, provided of course that I always return punctually to my prison. In this connection, I am less bound by my oath, which I had to swear to my counsel to prevent him from coming with us, than by natural consideration for Julika; if I made off she would lose a sum I could never restore to her. Moreover, I'm allowed one or two glasses of whisky! She looks simply magnificent, this woman, I think so every time I see her with her fiery hair in the sunshine, the white Paris hat on top of it and her willowy figure—I'm simply enchanted.

Once, when I caught sight of her reflection in a shop-window again, I couldn't help turning round, taking her by the chin and kissing her.

"Anatol," she said, "this is Zurich!"

I am particularly enchanted by the position of their little town, which is embraced on both sides by tranquil hills and natural woods that tempt one to go for country walks, while in the center there glitters a little green river that reveals the direction in which great oceans lie (as every watercourse does) and therefore always arouses a vital urge, a longing for the world, for seashores. It must be delightful to spend three weeks in Zurich, especially at this time of the year, if one is not in a prison. At this time of year, too, as you can hear in the street, there are all sorts of foreigners in the town. Not for nothing is Zurich's coat of arms blue and white; in the dazzling brightness of its windswept blue ornamented with the white of gulls—a brightness that is said to cause even the residents a great many headaches—this Zurich really has a charm of its own, a *cachet* that is to be sought in the air rather than anywhere else, a radiance that is in the atmosphere and stands in curious contrast to the moroseness that marks the faces of those who live here, and something positively festal, something neat and decorative like its coat of arms, something blue and white without many special characteristics. It is, one might perhaps say, a town whose charm lies above all in its countryside; in any case, one can understand the foreigners who get out and take snaps from the quay before going on to Italy, and one can also understand the residents who are proud when people take a lot of snaps. Their narrow lake, about as wide as the Mississippi, gleams like a curved scythe in the green, undulating countryside. Even on workdays it is alive with little sailing boats. In spite of all its bustle there is still something of the spa about this Zurich, this meeting-place of businessmen.

Fortunately the Alps are not so close as on picture postcards; at a seemly distance they crown the undulating foothills, a spray of white névé and bluish clouds.

Perhaps Julika hasn't shown me the right parts of the town; looking back it strikes me that we haven't met a single beggar, and also no cripples. The people are not smartly dressed, but their clothes are made of good material, so that one never has to feel sorry for them, and the streets are clean from morning till evening. We stroll along for nearly an hour, unmolested by beggars, as I have said, and also undisturbed by outstanding works of architecture, which would have interrupted our conversation. The way they try to regulate the modern traffic is not always comprehensible to a foreigner, though the Swiss police take the greatest trouble and look very grave, and above all it would seem that they are more concerned about justice than about the traffic; at every crossing you feel you are undergoing some kind of moral training. The closer you come to the lake, where the foreigners create their own atmosphere, which they take to be the atmosphere of Zurich, the less you make yourself conspicuous if you are gay and laugh in the street; even Julika, I notice, becomes freer in this part of the town, and I can imagine what she is like in Paris. Her mama was Hungarian, but Zurich is her native town, and Julika is angry out of all proportion when the town council of Zurich makes a *faux pas*, when it fails to welcome Charlie Chaplin, for example. She talks about nothing else for half an hour.

An Indian couple, probably attending a congress, look most attractive. There are a lot of congresses here, there is altogether something international about the place with its large, dusty coaches crowded with German leather shorts, and every waitress speaks American. A touch of universality forms part of the essence of this little town, which, as I have said, is very pleasant for the foreigner; it is provincial without being dull. It is provincial with concerts by Furt-wängler, guest performances by Jean-Louis Barrault, exhibitions from Rembrandt to Picasso, dramatic art by German émigrés, and Thomas Mann's new home, but also with all sorts of great men of its own who achieve things in the world outside, until their fame also gradually flatters their own country, which is incapable of bestowing fame itself precisely because it is provincial, in other words outside history. But what do I care about all that? For the foreigner it is a pleasure to stroll about this little town, especially when he has money, and, as I said, it might have been a delightful afternoon—if Julika had not slipped back into her fixed idea that I am her lost husband.

Once she came to a stop.

"Look," she said, pointing to a bronze figure that was no better for having been bought by the municipality, a type of sculpture which, to be quite honest, does not appeal to me at all; and when I started to walk on Julika took me by the sleeve and pointed to the plinth, on which was engraved in rather large letters, the name A. Stiller. (Fortunately, I made no comment, for as soon as I express any opinion about the work of their missing Stiller, they take it for self-criticism and as a further indication that I am Stiller.) . . . Another time when Julika felt the irritating need to tug me by the sleeve, I at least saw no sculptures, thank goodness, but swans, a flotilla of natural swans, their white plumage glistening in the sunlight and with down floating on the green water around them. And in the background, from the position in which Julika placed me, I could see the so-called Great Minster. I understood; just like in the photograph album! What she was trying to prove, I don't know. Finally I stopped dead in the middle of the street (inside the pedestrian crossing); it was no use her tugging at my sleeve, exasperated as though by a stubborn mule, when I asked:

"Where can we get whisky in this neighborhood?"

"We can't stop here."

The motor-scooters were already whizzing past us to left and right, a taxi hooted at me, then a lorry and trailer thundered by and Julika's face was as white as chalk, although the lights were now with us again. An unknown pedestrian, to whom I had done no harm, shouted expressions of moral indignation at me, as though, in a country that daily boasts of its liberty, there were a law against risking one's own life . . . Later, in a garden restaurant under gaily colored umbrellas, I asked Julika:

"How do you live in Paris, dear?"

I called her "dear," not because of the bail, God knows, but from a tender impulse, involuntarily. There is always something wonderful about this first touch of intimacy, something like a magic wand over the whole world, which suddenly seems to be floating, something very quiet which nevertheless drowns every other sound. Involuntarily, but then as though dazed by unexpected happiness, so that I was scarcely aware of anything but our little point of contact, I laid my hand on her shoulder. For a blissful minute, until the new "dear" has become a habit and, as it were, devoid of resonance, you feel that all men are your brothers, including the waiter who brings you the whisky; you have the feeling that there is no more need for disguise in this world, a feeling of peaceful elation. You laugh about your prison. In cases where this "dear" is a mature and no doubt enterprising woman I feel a natural urge, which in my state of elation, is not a very serious or pressing need, but rather a playful curiosity, to know what other men there are in the life of my "dear." No man ever appears in her stories of Paris and of the ballet school, which is presumably not a convent, no François, no André, no Jacques, nothing. A Paris of Amazons—what can that mean? Finally I asked her in a roundabout way:

"Are you very happy in Paris?"

"Happy?" she said. "What does happy mean?"

It's very curious: for some reason or other Frau Julika Stiller-Tschudy can't bear me to think of her as well and happy. She immediately gets back to Davos and the no doubt very terrible time she spent in that lonely veranda with the olive-green *art nouveau* windows, where Stiller, her missing husband, simply abandoned her. I listened to it all over again. Without doubting the frightfulness of the past, I saw her flourishing present with her strange face lit from below by the reflection from the tablecloth, like a face before the footlights. I longed for her. I waited for her to come out of her past, which she wanted to forgive and in order to forgive had to describe in detail, into the present of our short afternoon.

"My dear Julika," I said, "you keep on telling me how terribly your Stiller behaved. Who's disputing it? He made you ill, you say, mortally ill, he deserted you, you might have died; and yet, as I can see, you're looking only for him—do you grudge him his good fortune that you didn't die after all, that you're sitting here looking radiant?"

This was no joke, as I could see for myself. Without looking at me, Julika took from her white Paris handbag a letter yellowed with age, which was obviously intended to refute what I had said. It was a brief note Stiller had sent her while she was in the sanatorium at Davos, I was to read it, really just a crumpled scrap of paper, the leaf from a scribbling pad, ruled in squares, the message scrawled hastily in pencil and looking somehow objectionable, repellent.

"Well?" I asked rather awkwardly.

She hastily struck a match, so hastily that it snapped several times. This little text, the last she received from her missing Stiller, did not seem to her to require any commentary. She smoked.

"Julika," I said, giving her back the small sheet of crumpled paper, "I love you."

She laughed tonelessly, dully, unbelievingly.

"I love you," I repeated and tried to say something that did not have to do with her or my past, but with our meeting, my feelings at this hour, my hopes for the future; but she didn't hear me. Even when she was silent she didn't hear me, she was only adopting the pose of an attentive listener. Her mind was in Davos, you could see that, and while I was speaking she even began to cry. I also found it sad that two people could sit face to face and yet fail to perceive one another. "Julika?" I called her by name, and at last she turned her lovely face to me. But instead of seeing me, she saw Stiller. I took hold of her slender hand to wake her up. She made an effort to listen to me. She smiled whenever I protested my love, and possibly she was listening to me, but without hearing what I was trying to say. She only heard what Stiller, if he had been sitting in my chair, would probably have said. It was painful to feel this. Really it was no use going on talking. I looked at her hand lying close beside me, after I had involuntarily released it, and could not help thinking of the terrible dream with the scars. Julika told me to go on. What was the use? I, too, suddenly felt absolutely hopeless. Every conversation between this woman and myself, it seemed, was finished before it began, and any action it might occur to me to take was interpreted in advance, alienated from my present being, because it would in any case appear as an appropriate or inappropriate, an expected or unexpected action on the part of the missing Stiller, never as my action. Never as my action . . .

When I beckoned to the waiter, she immediately said with tender solicitude:

"You shouldn't drink so much."

At these words, to be frank, I winced and had to control myself. What was this lady thinking of? First, I had no intention of ordering another drink. And what if I had? She seemed to think she could treat me in the same way as her vanished Stiller, and for a moment I felt like drinking another whisky out of pure spite. I didn't do so. For spite is the opposite of real independence. I smiled. I felt sorry for her. I realized that her whole behavior did not relate to me, but to a phantom, and once confused with her phantom (for the man she was looking for probably never existed) one was simply defenseless; she could not perceive me. What a pity! I thought.

Unfortunately the waiter was a long time coming.

"I didn't intend to order anything," I said with rather tired rebelliousness—and Julika laughed, so that I added almost with irritation, "You're wrong, my love, I really didn't mean to order anything, I meant to pay—but unfortunately I have no money."

In the meantime, however, as though she never expected anything else, Julika had already slipped her red morocco-leather purse under my elbow, so that I could pay (as she must often have done with Stiller). What could I do? I paid. Then I gave her back the red morocco purse, pulled myself together and said:

"Let's go."

On the stroke of six I was back in prison.

P.S. That's the trouble—I have no words for reality. I've been lying on my bed without sleeping, hearing the clock strike one hour after another, trying to decide what to do. Shall I give in? I've only to tell a lie, a single word, a so-called admission, and I shall be "free"; in my case that means, condemned to play a part that has nothing to do with me. On the other hand, how can anyone prove who he really is? I can't. Do I know myself who I am? That is the terrifying discovery I have made while under arrest: I have no words for my reality.

The little Jew, with whom I had allied myself for purposes of back-soaping, was not at the showers today. When I remarked that I didn't grudge him his freedom, they merely raised their eyebrows. He was an intelligent man, and the rumor that he has committed suicide keeps occupying my mind. Of course, we are a group of ten, and if we hadn't soaped one another's backs I should probably never have noticed he had gone. It's not that I miss him, either. (I always found the back-soaping somehow embarrassing.) What is on my mind is the fact that it is always the intelligent people who can't wait for death, and when I think of his eyes that were not only intelligent but also full of the knowledge of mysteries, it seems incredible that this man did not know what was waiting for him. Now I even imagine that he was the only one to whom I could have communicated my experience— the otherwise almost incommunicable meeting with my angel.

Once more I have the familiar feeling of having to fly, of standing on a window sill (in a burning house?) with no possibility of escape unless I am suddenly able to fly. At the same time I know for sure that it is no use flinging myself into the street, suicide is an illusion. This means that I must fly in the confidence that the void itself will bear me up, that is to say a leap without wings, a leap into nothingness, into an unlived life, into guilt by omission, into emptiness as the only reality which belongs to me, which can bear me up . . .

2nd *Notebook*

My counsel has read the notes I have made so far. He wasn't even angry, but merely shook his head. He couldn't defend me with that, he said, and didn't even put it in his brief-case.

Nevertheless, I continue to keep the records.

(With his much appreciated cigar in my mouth.)

The relationship between the beautiful Julika and the missing Stiller began with Tchaikovsky's *Nut-cracker Suite* (to the young dancer's mortification, Stiller, who was still very young and felt obliged some-how to impress the lovely Julika, described this music as soap-bubble magic, impotent virtuosity, illuminated lemonade, sentimental rubbish for the elderly and so on), and to judge by Julika's most recent intimations a *Nutcracker Suite* hung over all the years of their marriage. Julika was in the ballet at the time. On an old photograph, which she showed me casually the day before yesterday, she appears as a page or a prince, blissfully happy in a costume that suits her down to

the ground; one could gaze for hours at the ephebe-
like charm she displays in this photograph. At that
time, unlike today, her large, exceptionally beautiful
and apparently frank eyes contained a strange shyness, something like a veil of secret fear, either fear
of her own sex, from which her delightful disguise
could protect her only part of the time, or fear of the
man who might be waiting somewhere behind the
scenes for the removal of her silvery disguise. Julika
was then twenty-three. Any reasonably experienced
man—which Stiller obviously was not—would immediately have recognized in this fascinating little person a case of extreme frigidity, or at least have guessed
it at the first contact, and adjusted his expectations ac-
cordingly. At this time a great future was predicted
for Julika in the ballet. How many men, reputable
citizens of Zurich, people of importance, Julika could
have married on the spot, if this strange and hence
fascinating girl had not put art (ballet) above everything, so that she regarded every activity outside art
as an unwelcome distraction.

Dancing was her life. She kept the gentlemen at a
distance with a giggling laugh, which discouraged
many of them and made all serious conversation impossible; and whether they would believe it or not, the
lovely Julika lived like a nun at this period, though
surrounded by rumors that made her out a vamp;
but at this, too, Julika only giggled.

Why didn't people let her be as she was? She
never left the theater without a bouquet of fresh
flowers nor without a slight but genuine fear that
her closest admirer, the donor of these flowers, a student perhaps or a gentleman with a shiny car, was
waiting outside. Julika was afraid of cars. Fortunately, they generally didn't recognize Julika as she
swept past with her beautiful red hair hidden under a school-girlish woolen cap, a very ordinary looking girl once she no longer stood in the glare of the

spotlight. Like a marine creature whose glorious colors are only visible under water, Julika's elfin beauty showed only when she was dancing; afterwards she was tired. Understandably: when she danced she gave her last ounce of energy. She had a right to be tired, and Julika told every waiting admirer she was tired. But Stiller always believed that Julika was only tired for him. What did he get out of it when he persuaded Julika to take a glass of wine or, since Julika did not drink wine, a cup of tea? Stiller talked a great deal on these occasions, it seems, like someone who feels it is entirely up to him to keep the conversation going; Julika was tired and said nothing. At that time Stiller talked a great deal about Spain; he had just come back from the Spanish Civil War and had already been condemned by the Swiss military court. Julika did not feel sorry for him because of his impending imprisonment, which he referred to with rather ostentatious pride, but for some other reason which she did not understand herself. She had only to smile and Stiller was afraid she was laughing at him and put his hands over his forehead or his mouth; and when she refused to walk arm in arm with him on the way home he was abashed and spent a long time outside the door of her house apologizing for his forwardness, which he too found objectionable. This made Julika like him better than anyone else.

Stiller was the first, or at any rate one of the few, who ever received a letter from Julika, a few lines in which she confirmed that she had been very tired and intimated that they might see one another again. She knew how much this young man desired her and also that Stiller would on no account take her by force; he was lacking in some quality without which such an action was impossible, and this made her like him all the more. And she liked the fact that this man, who had just been in Spain on some front or other, a man of slim yet powerful build and a head taller than

Julika, did not expect the least apology on her part when she had kept him waiting outside the theater for nearly an hour, but, on the contrary, apologized for his own importunity and was already afraid of being a nuisance again.

Julika liked all this very much, as I have said; at any rate, she always spoke very kindly of Stiller when she recalled these early times. It was March, and they were going for their first country walk, which was much too long for the delicate Julika, too exhausting and also too dirty; the ground was still very wet, although the warm sun was shining, and once her left shoe stuck in the mire when Stiller led her across the middle of a field, and he had to take hold of her to save her from treading in the mud with her stockinged foot; it was then that Stiller kissed her for the first time. Julika is firmly convinced that she kissed him too. Stiller soon stopped, not wanting to be a nuisance to Julika, but nevertheless he was extremely gay during the rest of the walk, breaking off willow rods like a boy and striking his open overcoat with them as he went along. Julika felt as though he were a brother. And she liked that too. He didn't mind the fact that even in the country Julika talked about nothing but the ballet, and in particular about the people connected with ballets, conductors, theatrical designers, hairdressers, ballet-masters—that was her world. Other admirers had reproached her with having nothing in her head but gossip. But not Stiller. He made a great effort to listen, occasionally pointing out a particularly beautiful view, which did not distract Julika's attention from her subject; then Stiller felt ashamed of knowing so little about the art of the ballet.

They ate bread and bacon in a simple peasant inn of the sort that obviously appealed to Stiller, and Julika enjoyed the sense that for the first time she had met a man of whom she did not feel afraid. Once again he talked about his Spanish war. A few days after this walk he had to report somewhere, with a woolen rug under his arm, to serve his few months inside.

For a long time they did not see one another. During this period Julika wrote several letters, in which, in keeping with her own shy way, she did not put her love for him into words; but Stiller, being a man of sensibility, could not fail to realize what the beautiful Julika, in keeping with her own shy way, perhaps felt without being able to put it into words—at all events, Frau Julika Stiller-Tschudy still appeals to those letters as unmistakable proof of how deeply and with what tender abandon she loved the missing Stiller.

They married a year later.

Looking at these two people from the outside, one has the impression that Julika and the vanished Stiller were suited to one another in an unfortunate manner. They needed each other because of their fear. Whether rightly or wrongly, the beautiful Julika harbored a secret fear that she was not a woman. And Stiller too, it seems, was at that time perpetually afraid of being somehow inadequate; one is struck by the frequency with which this man felt he had to apologize. Julika has no idea of the cause of his anxiety. In fact, Julika never mentions the word anxiety when she is talking about her wretched marriage with the vanished Stiller; but almost everything she says points to the fact that she felt she could only hold Stiller through his bad conscience, through his fear of failure. She obviously didn't credit herself with being able to satisfy a real, free man, so that he would stay with her. One gets the impression that Stiller, too, clung to her weakness; another woman, a healthy woman, would have demanded strength from him or cast him aside. Julika couldn't cast him aside—she lived by having a husband whom she could continually forgive.

But I want to try and record in these notebooks nothing but what Frau Julika Stiller-Tschudy herself told me or my counsel about her marriage; I am particularly anxious to be fair to her, for one thing so that she shall stop thinking I am her husband.

Several years before, the theater doctor had detected a mild attack of tuberculosis, but really only a mild attack; nevertheless, he always said Julika ought without fail to spend the summer in the mountains. This was good advice, but it needed money to put into effect, and Stiller, her husband, at that time earned nothing at all with his sculpture, almost nothing, anyway not enough to enable his poor wife to stop working. Julika never reproached him for not earning as much as a company director. Julika even went so far as to not to tell him what the doctor had advised, out of consideration, to avoid making him feel that he earned too little. All Julika asked was that he should also have some consideration for her. During these early years their marriage is supposed to have been wonderful. Julika earned six hundred and twenty francs a month in the ballet, and when Stiller was lucky and sold a figure, for a public fountain or the like, they were well off—Julika was satisfied with very little. She was too much of an artist seriously to ask a man she loved to betray his talent in order to look after his wife better; if she said anything of the sort it was only in jest. As to how talented her vanished Stiller really was opinions differed, and there were some people who did not consider him an artist at all. Of course Julika believed in him. Anyhow he worked unremittingly.

Julika's success as a dancer, against which Stiller could set no success of his own, troubled him and probably contributed to the fact that he was rather shy and unsociable; in every gathering when people crowded round Julika, he was greeted as her husband. In view of their earnings at that time children were out of the question; it would have meant a year's loss of work for Julika. Not that Stiller felt any overwhelming desire to be a father; it was merely that he had twinges of conscience about the fact that Julika had to go without children on his account, and he kept wondering whether it might not have been very important for Julika of all people to have a child. Why Julika of all people? Stiller thought that a child might have fulfilled Julika as a woman in a way that he was unable to do. This was an idea he could not be talked out of, and he was always bringing up the subject of the child. What did he want of Julika? She could see that somehow Stiller did not take her seriously as an artist, perhaps out of unconscious jealousy over her success; anyway, Julika was upset by his never-ending references to the child. Wasn't she sufficiently fulfilled already? He only stopped talking about it when Julika told him flatly that he was insulting her as an artist, but especially when she asked him, "Why have a child by a mother with T.B.?" After this the child was buried for ever. Instead he was always talking about her tuberculosis, admonishing her at appropriate and inappropriate moments to go and see the doctor again. Poor Julika didn't even dare to cough, so much did his admonitions get on her nerves. What did he want with her now? Stiller was sweet, but obstinately convinced that Julika was not living her life to the full. Julika was certainly no companion for endless walks, no comrade for nights of drinking with his friends; she needed looking after, God knows, but at that time Julika was really quite satisfied with her life. Why wasn't Stiller?

When the weather changed during a rehearsal, Stiller used to wait at the stage door with her warm coat, not forgetting her umbrella and scarf; his concern for her sadly precarious health was really touching, only his perpetual attempts to make her go to the doctor depressed Julika. She felt them to be a covert repudia-

tion of his tender solicitude, even as a sign that he
did not love her, and this made her stubborn. She felt
she was being sent, pushed, forced to the doctor
solely to salve his conscience, to free his masculine
egoism from the need to be considerate; she waxed
indignant as soon as Stiller asked if she had been to
the doctor yet. It may have been very silly of Julika,
but it was understandable; she had always been a sensitive creature. For years, therefore, she danced at the
risk of collapsing on the stage; everyone admired
Julika for her will-power, the producer, the whole
ballet company, the whole orchestra; only Stiller did
not. He called it idiotic. Probably for no other reason
than the fear of not being taken seriously, he had outbursts of vulgar rudeness that were only silenced by
her sobs. Everything about her was now wrong; he
nagged at Julika for not taking some dirty plates out
with her when she got up from the table to go into
the kitchen, and obstinately maintained that she could
live on half her energy if she had a little sense, if she
would learn a little from him. What could Julika answer? His pettiness only made her sad. Fancy a man
of intellect, such as Stiller claimed to be, talking for a
mortal hour about the fact that Julika did not take any
of the dirty plates with her when she went into the
kitchen to fetch something! Julika put her hands to
her head. He could practically evolve a philosophy
out of a thing like that, while Julika was so tired from
rehearsals and housework she could have dropped.

Then it seems he was charming again. But the out-
breaks of petulance became more frequent. Once,
when poor Julika refused to cancel her evening performance although she had a high fever, because she
knew how much depended upon her part on this particular evening, Stiller did it literally over her head:
he took the telephone from above the recumbent Julika and said that unfortunately his wife could not appear that evening, a high-handed action which the

dancer could not tolerate. What was Stiller thinking of! Snatching the telephone from her husband, she ordered a taxi so that she could drive to the theater in spite of his call. There was a row, one of the first in the marriage, and then the taxi arrived. Stiller shouted after her down the staircase: "Kill yourself if you want to, go on, kill yourself, but don't blame it on me . . ." At moments like this she was shocked by him; at such moments Stiller seemed to forget whom he had married. Her home background was not wealthy, but it was cultured; her Hungarian mother had moved in the highest society, she was somehow an aristocrat, and her dead father was at least ambassador to Budapest; whereas Stiller (it must be said) came from a lower-middle-class background, in fact he had hardly any background at all; he occasionally spoke of his stepfather, who was in some old age home, but never of his father, and his mother was the daughter of a railway-man.

It is curious and horrible that such things suddenly assume importance between people who love one another, but it is a fact. Naturally Julika never referred to it in words, or almost never. But she felt the difference between them, for example when Stiller shouted down the stairs. It must have been dreadful. He always regretted such outbursts afterwards. Stiller apologized and often thought of nice little ways of making up, either by preparing one of Julika's favorite dishes, which only he could cook, or by giving her a silk scarf because she had just lost the previous one, or by bringing her lilac, which he had stolen over a fence on his way to the theater to fetch her after the performance; everything always went well again, and it was really and fundamentally an extremely happy marriage—until the other woman cropped up.

That was seven years ago.

Julika suspected nothing. Julika would never have

considered such a possibility. As a young wife who
loved her husband above all else, it seemed to her
out of the question that Stiller could be capable of
such a betrayal; it simply never occurred to her.
Poor Julika, entirely devoted to her profession and her
husband, only noticed it through the fact that Stiller
began to pay no more heed to the fever she had now
had for years on end; true, he asked her every evening,
when she came home from the theater, how many
curtains she had, but always with a slight hint of sar-
casm. In the same tone he would ask, "How's your
T.B.?" Or when Julika spoke of the outrageous im-
pertinence of a critic who had completely omitted
to mention her, Stiller, her husband, adopted an attitude of positvely mean fair-mindedness and told Julika not to take it so much to heart, saying that perhaps the critic's omission was just a slip, no more. In
particular, however, Julika was upset because Stiller
too now began to place his work above all else, and
consequently felt it right to live for days at a time
in his studio, and once for a whole week, until one
morning Julika made up her mind to go and see him
in his studio. She found him whistling as he dried
glasses, immediately scented the previous evening's
visit, but was ashamed to ask. What proof was there
in a hair-slide on the floor, which Julika picked up
without a word and placed on the table? Julika wasn't
petty, she took no notice of the two empty bottles of
Châteauneuf-du-Pape—not exactly the cheapest of
wines—nor of a black hair on his light colored trousers. Stiller laughed. But it wasn't because of the
woman who had been with him the night before that
Julika broke down; his hollow, consolatory laugh, the
fundamentally sadistic tenderness with which he felt
obliged to comfort a jealous women, were out of place,
God knows, and so was the roughness with which he
forbade what he called hysterical scenes about a hair-
slide; all this was very out of place. For a long time

poor Juilka sobbed so much she couldn't utter a word.
"Julika?" he asked, as the suspicion dawned on him at
last that her sobbing had nothing to do with the
silly hair-slide. "What's the matter, Julika? Do say
something."

Julika had been to see the doctor.

"Have you?" he asked. She tried to get a grip on
herself. "Well?" he asked. Stiller sat beside her on the
couch, still holding the glass and the drying-up cloth,
while the despairing Julika, shaken by a fresh bout of
sobbing, clawed at the cushion with both hands so that
it tore. Julika had never wept like this. And Stiller, it
seems, was simply helpless; he put down the drying-
up cloth so that he could stroke her hair with his free
hand, as though her life could be saved by his affectation of tenderness. He seemed put out by the fact that
Julika had been to the doctor; it disturbed his merry
whistling. Julika tore the cushion, and Stiller merely
asked, "What did the doctor say?" His sympathy (and
Julika still thinks so today) was of a horrible kind—
his affectionate thoughtfulness, his friendly concern,
and all this with last night's glass in his hand. To begin
with, her stammered revelation, interrupted again and
again by choking sobs, that she must go as quickly as
possible to Davos elicited from him only a dry question, "How long have you known?"—"For almost a
week," she replied, imagining that Stiller would realize the full horror of that week, "—for a week!" Instead he merely asked, "Why didn't you tell me before?" Stiller was behaving outrageously. "Is it true?"
he went so far as to ask. "Is it true? . . ." At first
Julika laughed, then she jumped up and looked at him,
and saw the manner in which Stiller was looking at
her: as though it might be nothing more than a feint
on her part, a cheap exaggeration, designed to spoil
his recollection of the night before.

She shouted, "Go, go, get out of my sight." Stiller
shook his head. "Go away! Get out!"—"Julika," he

said, "this is my studio." His calmness was a bitter mockery, an inhuman attitude Julika would never have believed possible; while Julika was telling him that she might die, Stiller actually smiled. He smiled. And poor Julika, who had borne the affliction of the medical report alone for nearly a week, could scarcely believe her eyes and ears; Stiller began to dry the previous night's glass again, as though this glass were the most pressing, the most fragile thing, the true object of his concern; and then, adopting an affectionate tone, he wanted to know, not the terrors Julika had suffered, but what the doctor had told her, exactly, without embellishment, word for word. "I've told you. I have to go to Davos immediately, straight into the sanatorium," she said, "otherwise it will be too late."

It seemed to take some time for Stiller to grasp the full significance of this announcement. What was passing through his head, he did not reveal. He merely bit his underlip and went as limp as an empty sack, growing somehow smaller, and looked at Julika with eyes that were suddenly quite helpless. Hadn't he always wanted Julika to have another X-ray? Now she had done as he wished, that was all. Why did he stare at her so? It was her left lung. It seems the doctor had only spoken to her in consoling, human terms, without going into medical details. He mentioned cases of complete recovery he had seen himself. Humanly speaking, the doctor had been magnificent. Not that he made any wild promises; he took Julika too seriously as a personality for that. All the same, faced with her utter panic, he considered it quite possible that the beautiful Julika might one day return to the ballet. No promises, of course. The only thing he could promise, as a conscientious doctor, was her early death if she did not go into a sanatorium right away. Julika was now about twenty-seven or twenty-eight. She already knew the name of her sanatorium, its pretty position at the edge of a wood, as well as the approximate cost of treatment, most of which would have to be borne by the Health Service. If Stiller, her husband, had ever made enquiries and told her that this sort of thing could be paid by the Health Service, Julika would gave gone into a sanatorium long ago and probably have been cured by now. Stiller did not deny his negligence. To her surprise, Julika saw that her innocent remark had visibly touched and distressed him; Stiller seemed on the verge of tears. Had Julika now got to console him too?

She put her arms round his shoulders, which was a lot for Julika with her shy ways, especially as there were all sorts of other things to be done now. Ravel's *Waltz* and Da Falla's *Three-Cornered Hat*, two heavenly ballets, would be her last premières; the following day, Thursday the such-and-such, Stiller was to take her to Davos. Julika showed him her little calendar, where the date was already marked with a cross. What was it that didn't suit him? Stiller got up from the couch without really looking at her little calendar, flung his dry glass into the kitchen recess, where it smashed in pieces, stuck a cigarette between his pale, thin lips, and then stood as mute as a statue in front of the big studio window, with both hands in his pockets and his back to Julika, as though it were her fault that she had to go to Davos. In fact, as though she had upset his calculations with her understandable despair, and that was all there was to it.

"Why don't you say something?" she asked. "Sorry," he said, referring to the glass, which must have startled Julika; but that wasn't what concerned her. "What are you thinking about all the time?" Stiller went to the cupboard, filled two glasses with the last dregs and offered Julika a sort of consolation which she not unkindly, but firmly, declined. There were times when she found his way of trying to make amends with a friendly gesture, with gin or stolen lilac, intolerable. It seemed to her that Stiller

fancied himself in these warm-hearted gestures, seeing himself at a very cheap price as a solicitous friend,
a reliable protector, a wonderful husband—and yet in
all these years it had never occurred to her Stiller to
find out whether the Health Service would pay for
the sanatorium. "No thank you," she said, "not for
me."—"Why not?"—"Alcohol won't help." Stiller
tilted his glass. "No," he said at last, emptying Julika's
glass too at one gulp. "No, of course it's not your fault,
Julika, that you have to go into a sanatorium, there's
no question of that, of course it's my fault."—"I never
said that."—"It's all my fault," he went on obstinately.
"You've nothing to worry about, my dear, you're
going to Davos, you poor thing, and I'm staying here
in town, I the healthy one—my bad conscience will
be your soft pillow." So saying he gave a nasty laugh.
"What do you mean by that?" asked Julika. "You're
always coming out with these proverbs." Stiller
picked up the empty gin bottle, shook his head as
though over himself, but seemed quite composed, and
hurled the gin bottle into the kitchen recess, so that
splinters of glass spurted in all directions. This behavior was something Julika has not forgotten to
this day, the expression of an unrestrained egocentricity, as I fully agree, on the part of the missing man.

Stiller is reported to have once told a group of friends
when he was slightly drunk: "I've got a wonderful
wife, I'm delighted every time I see her again, and
whenever she's there I feel like a greasy, sweaty, stinking fisherman with a crystal water-fairy." And this
was shortly after his marriage . . . One gets the impression that there was something about this woman
which the vanished Stiller, fascinated as he was by
Julika, had simply not taken into account, had probably not even noticed, and this was her frigidity.
Julika herself seems not to have known that such a
thing existed, not merely as a pathological, but as a nat-

ural, phenomenon. Does she know now? Recently she was rather taken aback when I casually mentioned the scientific theory that in the whole of nature no female, except the human woman, experiences the so-called orgasm. We didn't discuss it any further. The beautiful Julika probably suffered in the most solitary manner, really suffered, from the fact that male sensuality always rather disgusted her, although that was naturally no reason for imagining herself a half creature, an unsuccessful female and even for thinking herself an artist.

So much about this woman, especially when she speaks of her lost Stiller, seems to be a touchingly obdurate self-deception, indeed one is half-inclined to doubt her tuberculosis, in spite of her medical certificate and the devastating effect this illness had on her life. Why couldn't Julika talk to anyone? Perhaps there are only a few women who experience without deception the overwhelming intoxication of the senses which they expect from their encounters with men, which they feel bound to expect because of the fuss made about it in novels, written by men; on top of this come the vain lies that women tell each other, and perhaps the lovely Julika was merely rather more honest and at the same time shocked, so that she kept her thoughts to herself, dressed up as a prince or a page and crept into a thicket of solitary misery where her husband could not follow her. It is not surprising, therefore, that she esteemed ballet and everything to do with ballet, even the mediocre sort of ballet usually performed in municipal theaters, above everything, and in any case above Stiller. A few unsuccessful ventures into Lesbianism seem not to have altered the situation; ballet remained the only outlet for her sensuality. Other women spare themselves the ballet by becoming mothers instead, by tolerating their husbands as necessary procreators and then disregarding them and being happy with their children, whom they prize above all else exactly as a ballet dancer prizes ballet; they can talk about nothing but their children, even when they appear to be talking about other children, and relinquish themselves, apparently, the better to be able to pet themselves in their children, calling it mother love, self-sacrificing devotion and even child education. Of course, it's pure narcissism. One might say that in the lovely Julika this narcissism of the frigid at least had the advantage of causing no harm to living human beings, but only to art, only to Tchaikovsky and Rimsky-Korsakov, not to mention Ravel and Stravinsky; her narcissism did not take as its victim a child who would have been dependent on her as its one and only mother.

I'm sure Frau Julika Stiller-Tschudy would flare up if I told her I am generally suspicious of women in art; it would be no use assuring her that this did not imply any contempt for women, nor, on the other hand, any contempt of art. The missing Stiller (I have little interest otherwise in being in agreement with the missing man) may unconsciously have felt the same thing; only it seems that he made a reproach, a reproach concealed in tenderness, of the fact that Julika never experienced voluptuousness with him, a reproach against Julika and an equally silly reproach against himself. As though every woman were made to be man's consort in this sense as well! As I have mentioned, it was a striking and typical characteristic of this man that he felt obliged to apologize all the time; he obviously took it as a defeat for his virility if the beautiful ballerina, perhaps only rather more honest than other girls, did not melt at his kiss. Her coldness was alarming, maybe, but genuine. She did not act cold in order to provoke him; on the contrary, Julika was more inclined to give way in order to avoid all provocation; but she soon found that when she gave way she very quickly felt disgust, that solitary disgust which she had at all costs to conceal.

She didn't want to hurt him. She didn't want to lose him. She preferred Stiller to any other man. Yet it went absolutely against the grain to sham the blissful and abandoned swoon which man in his vanity almost always believes however badly it is acted, the appearance of utter surrender which he must see in order to believe in a woman's love and above all in his masculinity. Oh, it was horrible! Compared with this it was a comfort to be on the stage, to feel thousands of strange eyes on her body, eyes of so many different kinds, the eyes of schoolboys and respectable married men, eyes that took in anything rather than her skill as a dancer; as a matter of fact this worried Julika less than when Stiller, her husband, laid his roughened sculptor's hands on her body. Her helpless excuse that she was tired annoyed him often enough. Stiller considered himself tenderness incarnate, but he could not understand that someone might be tired. Stiller took everything personally . . .

Somehow Julika was almost relieved when the theater doctor first told her that her lung was slightly affected and she must take care of herself. The dusty air on the stage was not at all good for Julika, but unavoidable in her profession, so she had to take all the more care of herself off the stage. That's what the doctor said. So it wasn't a caprice on the part of the lovely Julika, it was plain commonsense, when she asked for indulgence, consideration and plenty of rest. It was a question of her health. Julika was a delicate, an exceptionally delicate creature; Stiller loved her none the less for that. Only, as I have said, he had to have some understanding.

Stiller had less and less it seems, less and less understanding for his wife. His egocentricity went so far that he even took personally her fatigue, which was due to her state of health; he used to stalk out of the flat without a word, slamming the doors behind him— simply because Julika had said she was tired—and come home late at night reeking of the tavern, his stinking breath a positive insult. Or he would say, "I'd like to see you one day when you're not tired!" and his voice was full of reproach, full of animosity. What could Julika do? He never said, "You're simply not a woman," but Julika was perfectly well aware that he compared her with other women. Stiller drove her to desperation, she had no other means of proving the contrary to herself, to him and to the world in general than by indulging in the most blatant flirtation, something she had never done before in her life. Stiller drove her to it. Stiller found the way Julika encouraged every passing male to pay court to her—preferably men from whom fate soon parted her—in bad taste. Julika enjoyed hearing praise of her beauty combined with praise of her art; anything else was going too far. Stiller was by no means jealous, only shocked, when Julika said goodbye with kisses, kisses here and kisses there, for preference inside a restaurant or in the street outside the restaurant door. All he said was, "Are you sure you've kissed everyone?" He treated it as a childish game. On another occasion he was furious. It was after a dance: Julika, a graceful Bacchante, sat on the knees of one man after another and could not stop playing the "wild woman"; Stiller was waiting with her coat and told her, as he put it in his vulgar way, that it made him sick.

They must have been very intelligent and amusing gentlemen who paid court to Julika, not without wit and charm, which on her side she matched with her beauty; Stiller always maintained that they were all more or less homosexual, and his smile when Julika asked how you could tell a thing like that understandably offended her. It was this smile as much as anything that drove poor Julika further and further, further than she had any natural urge to go, and finally into the arms of a young publicity expert renowned for his virility who also had a charming little house near Ascona. Stiller probably never dreamed that Julika would dare; he knew quite well that the publicity expert, an acquaintance of his, had been in love with the ballerina for a long time, and something impelled him to introduce them to each other. Did he want to put Julika to the test and find out whether she was a woman? Anyhow, when it came to the point, the good Stiller almost went out of his mind; he took veronal, so as to sleep for days on end, and locked himself in his studio. Now it was Julika who found his actions in bad taste. He was probably afraid that the right man had now come along, and without knowing in the least what was happening Stiller threw down his weapons. In his pitiable letters he saw Julika, his ballerina, already with a pram, a mama by the Lago Maggiore.

The fuss he made must have been all the more burdensome for Julika because the affair itself, it seems, was short-lived, a week at Ascona perhaps. The young publicity expert was very hard-working, he flew about all over the place, while Julika, of course, still had her rehearsals. Stiller asked every other day why Julika didn't go to Ascona; while he asked he always looked at her as though she owed him an answer to some question, but what it was Julika quite genuinely had no idea. What did Stiller want to know? As far as Julika was concerned the matter was not worth talking about, quite apart from the fact that she was a reserved and shy being with no urge to put things into words, and anyway she thought that surely Stiller could see it was all over. Stiller didn't see this, it appears, or at any rate not for sure. In his eyes the publicity expert remained the great man who was able to make Julika happy; of this Stiller was certain from the first moment of terror on, blind to the fact that his Julika remained absolutely unchanged. He no doubt thought she was dissembling, concealing her happiness to spare his feelings, yet Julika, after all he had done to her, had not the slightest desire to spare his feelings. For months Stiller lived as though lying in wait; once he went so far as to search her handbag for some clue, a letter, a ticket to Ascona, an entry in her diary. But the only entries in her diary referred to rehearsals, the hairdresser, the dentist. It is easy to imagine what a burden it must have been to Julika that Stiller was still preoccupied by this business, if only in his thoughts; in particular what a burden it must have been that—without reproach, it is true—but with the look of a man who is being persecuted, Stiller was forever waiting for something, for a redeeming word. What was Julika to say to him? Once, when Stiller asked her openly what the publicity expert had meant to her, she said to him: "You brought me to despair, Stiller, let's say no more about it, I've come back, but you mustn't drive me to despair . . ." In any case, Julika was not conscious of any fault that Stiller was not guilty of many times over, and so it was really up to him to see that she, who had come back to him, was happy with him.

For a few months everything went splendidly.

Stiller, who had evidently heard by some roundabout route that the flying publicity expert long ago had another girl friend, waited for Julika outside the theater, cooked his Valencia rice and was not offended when Julika, tired after the rehearsal, could eat little or none of it; he entered into her terrible row with a producer and sided with her; he took care of her, as the doctor had ordered, or at least tried to—for a few months. Then, it seems, he relapsed into his self-centered outlook and expected Julika to give all her attention to him. Once again he left the flat without a word, slammed the doors and got drunk, for instance because Julika was too tired to take an interest in sculpture for hours on end. The next day she allowed herself the remark that his drinking cost a lot of money. Stiller took it ill when she said nothing, and he took it ill when she spoke. And how could Julika be affectionate to a man who at bottom, as she could feel, was seething with resentment?

One day, in the very middle of breakfast, Stiller asked why she had told them at the ballet that his new overcoat, an American army greatcoat, had been bought with her money. Julika didn't understand his question. "Why do you tell everyone in the ballet about it?" he asked, trembling with rage and making a mountain out of a mole hill. "What does it matter?" she asked. Stiller tore the newspaper out of her hand, and spent half an hour explaining to her what, in his opinion, it mattered. His explanation was infamous. Julika burst into tears, and when Stiller did not stop she cried, "Get out, please get out." Stiller didn't go, although he must have seen how much his infamous explanation had upset her. "Then I'm going!" said Julika, but Stiller didn't let her go. "I never want to see you again," she cried in her affliction. "That was a rotten thing to say, a dirty rotten thing to say!" Incidentally this seems to have been the only time, almost the only time, that Julika in her indignation expressed herself so forcibly. Did Stiller realize how unjustly he had behaved towards this woman? It never occurred to him to apologize. And the rift remained open. Now that she had learnt what an infamous construction Stiller was ready to put on the slightest thing, it henceforth cost Julika an effort to say anything at all. And the silence proliferated, a silence that was worse than quarreling. Stiller seemed to have no idea how deeply he had wounded Julika; he interpreted her acts and omissions as best suited his self-centered outlook, stubbornly incapable of learning.

Then there was something else.

At that time Julika had a dog, a fox terrier, of the sort that goes with childless couples. He was called Foxie or, in the language of this country—which, by the way, is an extremely pleasant language, not exactly melodious perhaps, but down-to-earth and, when you listen to it closely, not unmusical—Foxli. She loved him, naturally, otherwise they needn't have had him at all; that's the nice thing about dogs, you either love them or you needn't have them. Stiller could never understand how anyone could love Foxli, and he was scarcely able to read the message in Foxli's eyes. He sneered at Julika's motherly patience, when they arrived late wherever they went with Foxli, who ran sniffing from tree to tree. He referred to the dog sarcastically as the Sacred Beast. Everyone knew that Julika would arrive late and nobody took it amiss, Foxli was too amusing. In restaurants, thanks to the beauty of his mistress, whom no reasonably cultivated waiter dared gainsay, Foxli was allowed to sit on an upholstered chair just like Stiller. That Stiller could never get used to this was his own affair, his own pig-headedness. Why should Julika, who never ate much anyhow, leave half her excellent *filet mignon?* In any case—though no one mentioned it—Julika paid most of the bill and Stiller had his wine to make up for it. He said nothing, but Julika often felt obliged to stand up for Foxli. And Foxli felt just the same. Foxli was on her side. The fact that they formed a majority may have angered Stiller; Julika and Foxli, both of them admired on every hand, outvoted him on every decisive issue. Not that Stiller ever struck her sweet little doggie—I should hope not! But Stiller didn't like him; he acted as though Foxli didn't exist. No sooner was he in the hall of their flat, with Foxli jumping up and down in a cordial welcome, than Stiller busied himself with his mail, nothing but his mail, as though every letter came from a Maecenas with an offer of money.

Once someone said, "Oh, Julika, isn't he a sweet little thing," to which Stiller replied, "Yes, very sweet, we'll make jam of him before long." Stiller was simply jealous of her dog; he didn't admit it, but evolved a fresh theory, that had nothing whatever to do with the real live Foxli, and kept on talking about Julika's (not Foxli's) psychic life, about which he understood absolutely nothing.

Why, for instance, would Stiller never allow Foxli into his studio? And then he wondered why his wife did not come into his studio for months on end— once for almost a whole year—and was disappointed that she took so little interest in his creative work. Julika just didn't know where she could tie Foxli up without having to worry about him—or was she to let Foxli run about the unfamiliar streets, just to give Stiller another opportunity of showing her that his creative work, as he always complained, was making no progress? Stiller really seems to have been the quintessence of hypersensitivity. The fact that for years he had been coming to her ballet rehearsals, where he was allowed to sketch, was only to his own advantage. But what benefit, speaking objectively, could Julika derive from standing about in his dusty studio, where he worked for years on more or less the same undertaking, and perhaps catching a cold?

In his egocentricity Stiller was simply closed to all such considerations. What did he expect of Julika? His mortification, however politely he kept it to himself, was a burden for poor Julika. The fact that she, the ballerina, never spoke a word during the countless discussions about sculpture that Stiller and his companions often carried on until late at night saddened him; he interpreted it as lack of interest, never thinking that it was simply natural modesty on the part of Julika, who knew nothing about sculpture, quite apart from her whole reserved and shy attitude. When his companions had gone at last, he became rude as well. "At least you could have made us some gruel," he said morosely, "at least you could have done that." Julika had no intention of becoming his servant. And from the day when the other woman made her appearance his capacity for understanding ran completely dry. Believe it or not, Stiller was indignant because on her veranda it was not he, but Foxli, that Julika missed; and he was honestly surprised because the sick and abandoned Julika did not write him any affectionate letters from Davos, none at all, in fact, except for a note asking Stiller to get her something in the town; Julika simply couldn't write! And later, during the summer, when he himself stopped writing for weeks at a time, he did not shrink in his obtuseness from the cheap excuse that Julika never wrote to him either . . .

And so on.

I have no wish to play the arbitrator between the beautiful Julika and her lost husband; but since she is always talking about these unhappy times, one naturally tries to guess at connections, if only to pass the time as one might do a crossword puzzle. What else can I do in my cell? . . .

A little remark of Julika's, which must lie far back in the past, is difficult to guess but essential to the completion of the crossword involving the vanished Stiller. She doesn't mention it. A completely innocent remark. A remark of no importance. And yet I can hear that Stiller never got over it, in fact he got over it less and less. The fact that Stiller felt himself to be a stinking fisherman with a crystal fairy must have had something to do with this little, this positively tiny remark, which Julika had long since forgotten. The remark was made during their first night together. Stiller was evidently not only a man of morbid egocentricity and corresponding hypersensitivity, so that he took entirely personally a remark which Julika might possibly have made to any man; on top of this he was given to chewing things over, which was often simply unbearable for poor Julika. Years later a bagatelle of this kind would suddenly come to mind again. Meanwhile Julika, as she assured me, had long since forgotten that little remark made during the first night. Stiller simply couldn't get over it, he carried these few words like a mark of Cain behind his forehead, and it was no use Julika, tenderest of mortals, stroking his always rather untidy hair back from his brow. Julika was sweet to him. And she had probably only expressed what many girls may feel, amongst other things, when first embraced by a man. Stiller should have understood. And he did understand. What tormented him was clearly the fact that this was all his beloved Julika could say to him after the first embrace. Years later this trifle from the past suddenly rose to the surface again; you could see from his eyes how it was burrowing into him, how his soul was contracting as though to a single point, how this little, innocent and in any case completely dispassionate remark was beginning to echo in his memory, drowning every other sound. And it was just when Julika tried to be particularly affectionate that he was startled afresh by what her lips had once uttered many years ago. Stiller appeared to himself a polluter. He acted as though Julika were disgusted by him, and repulsed her, as I have said, precisely when Julika tried to be particularly affectionate; he withdrew. Stiller appears to have been a strong swimmer; for several years he swam across the lake and back every day, rain or shine, often right on into October; he was doing penance. Julika called this athletic performance his quirk. Stiller needed it in order to feel well. He needed a lake full of water, it seems. He felt terrible when he sweated. And at social gatherings when he was sweating, or felt that he might begin to sweat, he completely ceased to enjoy himself and sat in mute embarrassment, incapable of even following a conversation. At times like these he had such fear in his eyes that Julika was touched.

He frequently imagined he had a rash. It was generally pure imagination. Then again he raved about a lady who had kissed him on his sweaty face at the top of the Piz Palu; this event became for him the Piz Palu—unforgettable, unique, magnificent. His hostility towards the body related, it seems, only to his own. Stiller was enchanted by the children in the lakeside bathing-place, by the children's skin; and the human bodies in the ballet, for example, always delighted him. There was something painful about his enthusiasm, something of the hopeless longing of a cripple. Stiller was already a man in his thirties, but when a woman put her hand (or her glove) on his hand, without immediately withdrawing it again, or stroked the mousy hair back from his forehead not only to make him look tidy, but also to feel his hair, to feel his narrow forehead, he was as edgy as a boy, and on this account particularly attractive to certain women. He was a man with opportunities, as the saying goes, but he didn't believe in his opportunities. And what irritated him most, no doubt, was not the opportunity, but the fear that he was merely being made a fool of; he was suspicious, lacking in confidence, unwilling to believe that a woman who put her hand on his was free from a feeling of disgust. We may assume that at times, not often, but occasionally, after the daily shower perhaps, which made him only temporarily clean, this unhappy man stood in front of the mirror to see what it was that repelled Julika, his crystal fairy—and Stiller could see nothing that he himself did not also find repulsive. Stiller thought men very beautiful, he was always drawing them; women too. Only he himself, Stiller by name, had the misfortune to dwell in a male body which soiled his beloved; Julika, that honest person, had told him so innocently, so impartially and it had only hurt because it was her sole comment . . .

In short, Stiller really did have a quirk, and poor

Julika, for her part an exceptionally sensitive being, shy by nature and given to maidenly restraint in her speech, defenseless against arguments that simply misconstrued her true nature, must have had a hard time with her neurotic husband. Other people evidently thought so too, thought that Stiller misconstrued her true nature, and there was no lack of friends who warned Stiller, but received no thanks for their pains. Stiller couldn't tolerate their advice. "Oh," he said, after one such conversation, "devil take people who interfere in a marriage just because they think they mean well, and they imagine meaning well is enough even if they know less than a fraction about the affair in which they mean well." And that disposed of the most friendly counsel: Stiller always knew better. People told him that Julika not only loved him, but loved him more than he deserved, and the most Stiller answered was, "I'm glad you told me." But in reality it never occurred to him to take any of their advice to heart. His suspicion that Julika stirred up their mutual friends against him was unjust, like so much in his attitude towards this woman, who, I believe, was far too bashful to confide in a third party. People could see with their own eyes. And this was something Stiller couldn't stand.

For a long time they had been acquainted with a very pleasant married couple; he was a veterinary surgeon, she a well-known children's specialist; two people full of culture in a vital sense, full of heart and intelligence, friends to whom Stiller owed a great deal, not only a number of excellent dinners, but stimulus of all kinds, introduction into Zurich society, and once even a commission. Stiller liked them enormously, this children's specialist and this veterinary surgeon, until the wife, who occasionally had a *tête-à-tête* with Julika, once said in a *tête-à-tête* with Stiller what she really thought, namely that Frau Julika was a quite wonderful person, such a fine and profoundly decent being as she, the children's specialist, had never met in her life. Stiller immediately interrupted: "And why do you tell me that?" She answered jokingly: "To be frank, Stiller, I often wonder what this Julika has done to deserve you for a husband," and she smiled, to make it quite clear that she was joking. Stiller was merely chilly. "Seriously," she added—and really meant it in the most friendly spirit —"I hope you'll realize before it's too late, before you're an old man, Stiller—I hope you'll realize what a wonderful wife you have, what a grand person she is. Quite seriously, Stiller, I hope so with all my heart, for your sake."

But Stiller, it seems, couldn't bear seriousness either; they were in a restaurant at the time; Stiller beckoned the waiter; and while his friend, the children's specialist, went on talking about Julika, he paid, without contributing a word to the subject. And then his only reply was never to have time when this splendid couple, the children's specialist and the veterinary surgeon, invited them over—the cheapest kind of reply. Julika quite rightly defended herself, and took to inviting the children's specialist and the veterinary surgeon over to them; when Stiller came home in the evening and heard from the passage the voices in the flat, he wanted to turn round and leave again. With great difficulty Julika managed to prevent this piece of rudeness; Stiller stayed to dinner, but then he "had" to go back to his studio. He simply made off.

At times it really bordered on persecution mania. No doubt Stiller tried to be nice to her friends, but of course they felt that he was on the defensive and tense. And the good Stiller was surprised that a vacuum began to form round him. Nobody likes visiting a married couple in a state of crisis, it's in the air, even if you know nothing about it, and the visitor has the feeling of being present at an armistice, he feels himself somehow misused, employed for a purpose; conversation becomes dangerous, jokes suddenly begin to fly that are somewhat too sharp, that carry a touch of poison, the visitor notices more than the hosts intend to give away; a visit to a married couple in crisis is as jolly as a mine-field, and if nothing blows up it smells all the time of hot self-control. And although you can quite believe it when the hosts say it was the nicest evening they've spent for a long time, your tongue isn't exactly hanging out for the next invitation; obstacles involuntarily pile up, in fact you hardly have a free evening. You don't break with a married couple in crisis, certainly not. You just see one another less often, and consequently you forget the couple when you are sending out invitations yourself, involuntarily, unintentionally.

That's what happens; Stiller had no reason to be surprised, considering the way he behaved towards all well-meaning people. Fortunately, one can only say, Julika at least had her friends in the ballet, and above all the work itself. On the stage, in the flood of the footlights, she was set free from everything, another person, a happy person, happiness incarnate. Stiller even stopped coming to rehearsals. He took refuge in his work. And it did no good when her friend's husband, the veterinary surgeon, came into his studio one morning to talk to Stiller man to man, without reproaching him, of course. One sentence was enough: "You know, Stiller, I think you're doing your wife a great wrong." Stiller replied: "Sure!" in a tone of pure mockery. "What else did you expect?" he said. "Have you ever known me do anything but wrong?" The veterinary surgeon tried everything, but Stiller just left him standing, cleaned his spatula and said goodbye without accompanying his visitor to the door.

It was really a kind of persecution mania, the way he regarded anyone with whom Julika became friendly as his own secret enemy. What could Julika do? She was sorry for Stiller. He was simply making himself lonely. She tried everything. She treated it as a joke when Stiller posed as the misunderstood husband, and often, when he was brooding, as inactive as a paralytic, so sulky and silent you could have died of boredom, unsociable, joyless, indifferent, the very reverse of a man who could make a woman happy, Julika put her hand on his shoulder for a moment and smiled:

"Yes, yes—you're a poor fellow! . . ."

Her summer at Davos, her life in the *art nouveau* veranda, where you smelt hay and saw squirrels, was certainly not easy. Julika went through the same phases that most of the new arrivals seem to pass through: after an initial horror, after two or three nights when she made up her mind to run away at once, after the ghastly feeling that every time she was wrapped up in a rug and rolled out on to the veranda she was being prepared for death, Julika unexpectedly grew accustomed to this new everyday life, even enjoying the fact that there was now nothing she had to do, nothing at all. Rest was the only thing asked of her. Julika enjoyed being alive as she had not done for a long time. Davos wasn't so terrible at all, it was a valley much like other valleys, green, peaceful, a bit dull perhaps, a valley with steep woods and flat meadows and here and there a stony rivulet, a landscape, nothing more. Death did not stalk about in the guise of a bony reaper, no, only the grass was mowed, the scent of hay drifted up, and of resin from the nearby wood, somewhere or other they were scattering manure, and in the larches in front of her veranda a mischievous squirrel was doing gymnastics.

During the day, perhaps, it was like being on holiday. A neighbor who used to sit on the end of her bed every day for a quarter of an hour, one who was saved, who could go for walks and brought her wild flowers, a young man, younger than Julika, but a

veteran of the sanatorium, who used to give a helping
hand to newcomers, seems to have cheered Julika up
considerably. It was he who brought her books, different from any books Stiller had ever brought, a new
world. And what a world! Julika read Plato, the Death
of Socrates—difficult, but the young sanatorium veteran helped her without any trace of didacticism,
cheerfully casual like those people who pick things up
extremely quickly and never imagine we can't understand something, because our brains aren't up to it.
He was enchanting with his narrow, always rather
shrewd face and big eyes, but they were not in the
least in love. For her part Julika probably told him
about the ballet, and the young sanatorium veteran,
who wore suits that had belonged to those who had
died, told her a bit about all the people whom Julika
heard coughing without ever catching sight of them,
no life stories, just tittle-tattle, no indiscretions. Julika
was delighted; at the beginning she had been rather
put off by his "frivolous" tone, until she realized that
a sharp wit does not rule out deep feeling, but is
merely another form of deep feeling, a cleaner,
chaster form perhaps.

In short, Julika enjoyed these quarters of an hour
and missed the young sanatorium veteran profoundly
when he failed to appear one day. What was wrong?
Nothing at all; a visit from his family, nothing more.
The next day he came back and gave Julika an explanation of an X-ray photograph. His own? He
didn't answer this question, showed her what is
called a "shadow," and gradually led Julika to find a
skeleton like this beautiful, to look at it as a drawing,
to be enchanted by the transparency of the heart,
which was not to be seen, and fascinated by the
mysterious clouds between ribs and spine; if you
looked at it long enough it was positively seething
with forms, all of them lost in a dreamlike twilight.
Finally, when the rascal revealed that it was she per-

sonally, Frau Julika Stiller-Tschudy, illumined by the
X-rays, she was no longer shocked. How did he get
hold of it? Stole it yesterday, while waiting for the
doctor; mischievous pranks were called for in the
sanatorium, but perhaps elsewhere too. Julika couldn't
help thinking of Stiller.

Naturally these visits at the end of her bed interested her more than Stiller's dutifully regular letters, which, as Julika felt very strongly, illumined
nothing, just the opposite. His letters were a voluble
concealment. What could Julika have answered? The
letters had only one good result; the mere sight of
them pacified the head physician and the nurse. The
fact was, they found it odd, putting it mildly, very
odd that Herr Stiller never visited his wife. Julika
had to speak up in his defense. "My husband will
come," she said frequently. "About time," said the
head physician, "otherwise I'll send the gentleman a
list of trains, in case he hasn't got a timetable! . . ."

Everyone was very fond of Frau Julika and during
the day, especially when the weather was fine, the
time passed almost without strain. The young sanatorium veteran, a student from a Catholic seminary,
was really a gift from heaven. Julika would never have
believed that so much culture and so much boyishness could be found together. He was the most
learned man Julika had ever spoken to, and often
enough she felt like an illiterate; but on the other hand
like a mature woman; for he was a boy, as I have said.
Anyhow, Julika greatly enjoyed his conversation, his
knowledge and his boyishness at the foot of her bed.
If you asked him something he didn't know, he was
delighted, just like Foxli when you threw a stone or a
fir-cone for him to run after. A few days later he
would come back knowing where and what you could
read on the subject. He gave Julika a general outline
of modern physics; it was really exciting; and all
with a scientific exactness such as Stiller never had,

even when he came straight from a lecture, bursting with enthusiasm, but incapable of explaining to Julika so much as the structure of an atom. Here, for the first time, she understood everything, almost everything.

Or Julika learnt about the Mother of God and the sanctification of woman, things about which—as a Protestant—she hadn't the slightest idea, all of it expounded with a mastery of the subject and carried only so far as the uninformed listener could follow, at least in essentials. Indeed, for the very first time, although her Stiller had once fought in Spain on the Communist side, Julika was objectively and dispassionately instructed as to what the Communist idea really consists of, how much of it stems from Hegel, how much is a misunderstanding of Hegel, what is meant by dialectics, what part of Communism is thoroughly Christian and what anti-Christian. Secularization, transcendence—there seemed to be absolutely nothing this young Jesuit with the narrow face and rather skull-like eye sockets could not think with ease and expound in a concise, unrepetitive, dispassionate manner, which was amusing, so that Julika often had to laugh, irrespective of whether he was talking about the Mother of God or the absolute speed of light, and his dispassionate way of expressing himself seemed never to force a point of view on her. Stiller was always forcing points of view on her, which he later refuted himself; but while his enthusiasm for them lasted he advanced them in such a way that Julika did not dare to contradict. It was quite different with this young Catholic. Julika felt no desire to contradict. She lay on her veranda and absorbed his words like the air from the nearby wood.

From this daily visitor, it seems, Julika heard the not unknown idea that it is a sign of non-love, that is to say a sin, to form a finished image of one's neighbor or of any person, to say "You are thus and thus, and that's all there is to it"—an idea which must have touched the lovely Julika very closely. Was it not true that Stiller, her husband, had formed an image of Julika? . . .

In a word, Julika was not bored, and as long as she looked out into daylight, rain or shine, her illness caused her little suffering.

But her nights were different.

Julika doesn't talk about them much, but it is evident that sometimes in the morning, when the nurse came into the room, the light was still burning and an utterly exhausted Julika, bathed in cold sweat, was found sleeping heavily among wildly disordered bedclothes. Her temperature chart showed clearly enough how little poor Julika was obeying the pious admonition to avoid excitement at all costs. Julika denied everything when talking to the rather stupid nurse who washed her and brought her fresh bed linen, an electric blanket, or tea before it was due, only so that her first walk, which had been promised weeks ago, should not be again and again postponed. During such awful nights as these Julika may sometimes have seen her Stiller as he stood drying last night's glasses, putting the hair-slide of last night's visitor in his pocket so that Julia should not continue to be offended by it, and reacting to the news that Julika was mortally ill by smashing last night's glass against the wall—and by nothing else . . .

Now Stiller wrote no more letters.

One naturally wonders whether nobody (if poor Julika couldn't write herself) ever told this Stiller in confidence what his wife, and after all she was his wife, whom, in spite of the other woman, he still loved sufficiently to want her to miss him, was going through up there in Davos. But that was just it, Stiller wasn't willing to be told anything in confidence; the few friends who had once tried to do so gave it up as a bad job, and the new friends Stiller had made since knew as little about Julika's awful nights as Stiller himself . . .

Who did know? Poor Julika unbosomed herself to nobody. One person seems to have known about them, however, and that was the young sanatorium veteran. And this too he talked about in the same light-hearted tone as about his Fathers of the Church, about the absolute speed of light (which is not doubled when two rays of light are speeding towards one another) and about the classical law of the addition and subtraction of velocity, which just does not apply to light, or about Buddhism. He was once again sitting on the foot of her bed, full of knowledge, and the exhausted Julika was making an effort to listen to him. He had just read in a paper an aphorism of Professor Scherrer, Zurich, which delighted him, namely: Mass is energy in a blocked account. "Isn't that witty?" he asked. "Yes," said Julika. "It is indeed," he then continued without any change of tone and still turning the pages of his newspaper, "—during the day people play chess and read, and during the night they cry, you're not the only one in the place, Julika, you mustn't think that. It's the same with everyone here. At the beginning, for the first few weeks or months, you're amazed how pretty it is here with the hay and the pinewoods and the squirrels and so on, but then horror comes over you just the same. You sob into your pillow without really knowing why, it only does harm, you know your fevered body will fall to pieces like tinder. And then, sooner or later, every one of us here thinks of breaking out. Especially in the night, when we're alone; our heads seethe with the craziest plans, each one becomes his own Napoleon, his own Hitler, neither of them got to Russia, and we don't even get down into the valley, Julika, four hours by the little train, change at Landquart, there's nothing to it. A few try every year, they secretly pack their toothbrushes, tell the nurse they've got to go to the

toilet and set off in the little train for the valley; they
get so far or so far, depending on luck and the
weather, and they have their breakdown and imagine
they're suffocating, and come back here in the ambulance without a word.

"*Et après?*" he smiled. "We don't even feel sorry
for them, you know, it's too stupid. I know from experience. Our comradeship is limited to acting as
though we'd heard nothing about it. Swear to me, Julika, that you'll never get up to that silly trick?" Julika
swore. "No," laughed the sanatorium veteran, "not
under the camel's-hair rug, my dear, the good Lord
wants to see too." Julika swore on top of the rug.
"*Ecco!*" he said and added, once more sunk in his
paper: "And you'll see, Julika, that even when somebody dies here it doesn't create much of an impression. Anyone who hopes to impress us that way is
dying in vain. The only thing that impresses us here
is life! Incidentally, most people die around Christmas, I've noticed—out of pure sentimentality."

(He died in late September himself.)

In August Stiller turned up again, unannounced and
altogether in a way that Julika felt must surprise the
head physician even more than his long absence. The
fact was that Stiller behaved as though his beautiful
Julika were being kept on this *art nouveau* veranda
quite wrongly, straight away demanding of the nurse
that his wife should go for a walk with him, for an
hour at least. The reason: Stiller wanted to talk to
Julika. What had happened? The veranda, where he
guessed there were ears listening to right and left,
didn't seem to him the place even to start. He took
off his cap, but not his American army greatcoat,
which he wore in summer and winter, because it was
the only coat he had. Julika asked:

"Well, how are you?"

Stiller was very much on edge; he twisted his cap in
his hands agitatedly, as though the only person in the

sanatorium entitled to consideration was himself, who wanted to talk confidentially to his Julika. He ignored her friendly enquiry after his health. When the head physician arrived on his usual round, he immediately reiterated his request that Julika should go for a walk with him. The head physician was somewhat taken aback. Should he say outright in front of the patient that walks were out of the question in her condition? Julika had been waiting months for permission to go for a walk. A downright No, such as Stiller himself deserved, was prohibited by consideration for the already despondent Julika. Really, what was the head physician to say? In an undertone and looking the other way, as though he would rather not have heard the request at all, he agreed to half an hour, or three-quarters of an hour at most, but asked Stiller to wait outside in the corridor, because he wanted to speak to him first . . .

For the first time in months Julika went out of the sanatorium, which had become something like a snail's shell to her, strangely perplexed at suddenly being without her veranda. She felt weaker than she had expected. Arm in arm, Stiller giving her some support, without actually treating her as an invalid, they walked slowly along the path that Julika had so often seen from her veranda (when she sat up in bed for the purpose). It was such a moving experience for poor Julika that her eyes filled with tears, tears of joy. To have earth under her feet, to be able to grip a fir-cone, to smell resin on her fingers—all this was such a delight for her that Stiller may have felt it; in any case, he did not come out with what was on his mind.

"What did the head physician say to you?"

Stiller tried to keep it to himself.

"Go on, tell me," she bade him.

Stiller seemed confused.

"What did he say to me?" he remarked at last. "I'm

to spare you any excitement. That's all. He was very brief, your head physician. You shouldn't really be going for a walk at all, he said, your condition is much more serious than I seem to think."

"So," she said.

"Yes."

"They never tell me anything."

"Yes," added Stiller, to divert the conversation from the medical information which he probably ought not to have imparted to Julika, and smiled, not maliciously, but oddly, sadly: "—and then of course, he told me you were a fine and wonderful person, frail and very much in need of looking after, a grand person. Everybody finds it necessary to give me instruction. I must be an idiot."

"But Stiller!" she laughed.

"No," he said, "perhaps I really am. It's good to see you again. It's so easy for specters to come into being when people don't see one another. Anyhow, in my case."

Julika repeated her question:

"What do you do with yourself all the time down there?"

"Oh—nothing special," he murmured.

"Have you seen Foxli at all?"

"No."

"Are you still working?"

Stiller wasn't exactly talkative.

"Yes—," he repeated, "that's about all he had to tell me. That you are a superior person who deserves to be treated with great consideration by her husband. And anyhow we must see that you're not excited in any way. It only does you harm, and your condition is pretty serious, Julika, he told me that three times, I believe."

And so they walked along arm in arm, a thing Stiller and Julika seldom did, silent, as though everything of importance had already been said, as though the only thing that mattered now was to enjoy this cloudless August day and the celebrated air; they went for that classic walk with pine-cones and almost importunate squirrels which my counsel and Julika showed me recently, really a very pretty walk, partly through woods and partly through meadows. Down below in the town it was frightful, continuously sultry as though before a thunderstorm, but the thunderstorm never came and it remained so hot that everyone sweated; up here one didn't sweat. Stiller enjoyed it. And the meadows were fragrant.

Meanwhile they were not getting along very fast, because of poor Julika. Stiller took off his brown U.S. army greatcoat, a really practical garment, and sat on a dry, soft carpet of sun-warmed pine-needles. It was simply glorious. Why talk? thought Julika. And they scarcely said a word. To talk about matters of indifference before the important thing had been said proved impossible. Finally Julika asked, "What is it then? You wanted to talk to me about something." Somewhere out of the noonday blue echoed the rumble of an invisible fall of stones. Insects were buzzing. The mountains were wrapped in silvery gray silence. Julika waited in vain for Stiller to speak. Stiller crumbled red earth between his fingers, until Julika—not out of pettiness, heaven knows, but simply for the sake of something to say—drew attention to his rather long nails, which this earth had made dirty, an absolutely innocent remark which the good Stiller, that masculine mimosa, once more took very much amiss, without saying so (it came out later, in a letter). Now he merely dropped the crumbled earth without a word, picked up a dry twig from the ground and cleaned his finger nails, which Julika had not actually requested. At the same time, he asked her a strangely unexpected question, "Did you ever really love me?" What could Julika reply to that? But Stiller, cleaning one finger nail after the other, insisted on an answer to his odd question, which had come upon Julika out of the blue. "What's that got to do with your dirty finger nails" she asked more or less jokingly, and then saw his lips trembling with agitation. "Did you come here to ask me that?" This tone, they both found, was not happy, not promising, not in keeping with the splendor of the silent wood. Stiller seemed unable to appreciate fully what it meant to poor Julika to see this wood otherwise than from the veranda, to be outside its *art nouveau* windows at all, to be able to pluck wild flowers with her own hands instead of merely receiving them from her young Jesuit, to be wearing her almost forgotten coat and skirt instead of being wrapped up in camel's-hair rugs. Half an hour had already passed. Stiller was smoking, not without having first asked her permission, and Julika was drawing grass stalks through her teeth.

"How's your—lady?" she asked.

"Whom do you mean?" he asked.

"Are you still in love with her?"

In fact Julika made it as easy as possible for him, but Stiller was an utter coward, not a word about the fact that he was seeing the lady (as it later turned out) almost every day. He merely looked at Julika and said nothing. What did he expect of her? Julika was lying in the warm grass, tired after the short walk, understandably tired, but still propped up on her right elbow in order to see more of the view, a long swaying stalk between her lips. She could feel Stiller scrutinizing her, her red hair, her slender nose, her now suntanned skin (her usual alabaster pallor probably suits Julika better) and her lips without lipstick, also her bosom, in fact her whole body, which was, after all, the body of a ballerina; Stiller scrutinized her as though he had never seen a woman before. Was he comparing her with the other one? Stiller gave the impression of being very much in love,

Julika thought, in love with her, and at the same time desperate. Why?

Julika asked, "What's the matter?" Suddenly (Julika still can't help smiling slightly when she thinks of it) Stiller seized hold of her like a Tarzan, which, heaven knows, he wasn't, took her thin face in his rather hard sculptor's hands, kissed her with incomprehensible vehemence, to which she naturally couldn't immediately respond, and pressed her now enfeebled body to him as though he wanted to crush Julika. He actually hurt Julika a great deal. She didn't say so at once. Why did he stare at her so? For a while she put up with it. But what was he about? Julika took care not to smile, but the very fact that she was taking care not to became evident to Stiller.

"You?" he shouted, "you!" he really shouted as though Julika were lying on the opposite side of the valley. He tore the swaying stalk from between her teeth, though it was only a defense against her understandable embarrassment. Julika didn't even know she was still holding the stalk between her teeth. Why was he so indignant about this innocent stalk? His eyes actually began to glisten, to grow watery, and when he noticed that they were filling with tears Stiller buried his head in her lap, clung with both arms to Julika, who suddenly, as was to be expected, saw the open landscape in front of her, the sanatorium some distance away, the familiar little church of Davos village, and the little red railway that came straight out of the wood whistling. How could Julika help seeing all this?

Stiller sobbed in her lap, sobbed as a returned prisoner of war might sob at the station, sobbed so that she could feel the heat of his face. Julika wondered whether they could be seen from the sanatorium. Stiller had hands like claws, and Julika naturally found it funny, and even embarrassing, that he was clutching at her buttocks. Eventually, as he didn't stop sobbing,

she laid her hand on his neck, which was damp
with sweat, moved her hand a little further into his
dry hair and waited for Stiller to pull himself together. He didn't pull himself together at all. He
didn't want to. He even tried (ridiculous though it
sounds) to bite into her lap, to bite like a dog, but because of her thick corduroy skirt he couldn't.
"Come," said Julika, "stop it." Julika still doesn't
know what she should have done on the walk at
Davos. For the last two minutes she had been watching two unknown walkers coming along the path they
had followed, slowly to be sure, but coming closer all
the time, and it was embarrassing, quite apart from the
fact that Stiller's behavior seemed to her really rather
theatrical—Mortimer or Clavigo or someone like that,
Julika wasn't quite sure who it reminded her of—
but it was embarrassing anyhow, for now Stiller was
lying like a corpse in her corduroy lap, heavy and motionless, without sobbing, his arms by his sides, inert
like a gratified man.

"You!" said Julika kindly. "People are coming!"
The people had come to within a hundred yards of
them, Stiller couldn't deny it. He sat up with the
rather sleepy face of a diver returning to the surface,
without looking round, without even seeing for himself that the people were really coming nearer and
nearer. He put both hands over his face, until the people, two old ladies, had walked past and were behind
them; then he lowered his hands, let them dangle over
his knees and looked out into the valley, probably
feeling a very tragic figure. Anyhow the only thing
that occurred to Julika when she looked at him was to
stroke his always rather untidy hair back from his
forehead and to smile:

"Yes, yes—you're a poor fellow! . . ."
Stiller could say nothing, he just stood up, pulled
up his rather slovenly trousers and, after Julika had
had to rise to her feet without his helping hand,

picked up his crumpled U.S. army greatcoat, gave Julika his arm for support and took her back to the sanatorium, where he promised to wait in the corridor until Julika had been tucked in again and rolled out on to her veranda. This took scarcely twenty minutes. But when the nurse looked in the corridor, there was no Herr Stiller. He had simply gone off without saying goodbye . . .

This was their last meeting but one.

Knobel, my warder, is becoming a nuisance. He waits like a magazine reader for the daily instalments of my life story, and his memory is beginning to worry me.

"Excuse me, Mr. White, that can't be right. First you murdered your wife—"

"Yes."

"Then Director Schmitz—"

"Yes."

"That was in the jungle, you said, in Jamaica. And then came the little mulatto's husband, after which you fled to Mexico—what happened then?" he asked with the soup pail in his hand. "From Mexico you came here."

"Yes."

"But what about your other two murders? You told me there were five murders."

I spooned up my soup and said:

"Perhaps there were only three."

"Joking apart," said Knobel and over this point, as it turns out, he has absolutely no sense of humor; he's become a nuisance . . . I merely said:

"There are all sorts of ways of murdering a person or at least his soul, and that's something no police in the world can spot. A word is enough for that, plain speaking at the right moment. A smile is enough. I should like to see the person who cannot be killed by a smile, or by saying nothing. All these murders, of course, take place slowly. Haven't you ever wondered,

my dear Knobel, why so many people are interested
in a real murder, a visible and demonstrable murder?
It's quite obvious: because we generally don't see our
daily murders. So it's a relief when there's a bang for
once, when blood flows, or when someone dies of
real poison, not merely of his wife's silence. That's the
magnificent thing about bygone ages, for instance the
Renaissance—the fact that the human character revealed itself in deeds; nowadays everything takes
place inwardly—and to tell the story of an inward
murder, my dear Knobel, takes time, a long time."

"How long?" he asked.

"Hours and days."

To this my warder replied:

"Mister White, I've got next Sunday off."

Despite his silence, therefore, Julika knew about Stiller's summertime affair. Affair is not a very pretty
word, perhaps, but why should Julika (when she
thought about it) have wrapped it up in romantic
phrases? She knew about it, then. What could she, an
invalid in a glass-enclosed veranda, do to prevent it?
Nothing at all.

Nothing but put up with it patiently, patiently,
patiently . . .

Now more than ever, thought poor Julika at times,
there was nothing left for her but her art, and she
gazed at the cover of a Swiss illustrated paper (recently sent by her friends) bearing a picture of beautiful Julika, the dancer, Julika all by herself. It seems
to have been a spectacular photograph, almost rem-
iniscent of Degas with the magical lights flitting in
the ballerina's gauze skirt. It had been taken the
previous winter and Julika had given up all hope that
the photograph, which had been so much trouble to
take, would ever appear. But now, at the end of
August, it had been printed to coincide with the opening of the new season. The picture showed Julika

from the back view, her left leg swung up, her face in luminous profile; the fluid and yet definite poise of the arms with the hands emerging from the ends like buds—everything was faultless. The caption underneath was rather silly, as usual, but at least not an outright distortion of fact, which Julika thought was quite an achievement for this paper. Incidentally it was a periodical of some importance; Julika gave a slight shudder when she read the number that had been printed. There were so many Julikas now, Julika on the newspaper kiosk, Julika in the train, Julika in the privacy of the home, Julika in the café, Julika in the overcoat pockets of well-dressed gentlemen, Julika beside the soup plate, Julika everywhere, Julika in a tent on some beach, Julika in the halls of the best hotels, but above all Julika on the newspaper kiosk, on all the kiosks in the country, and some abroad as well, for a whole week: then later, Julika in dentists' waiting rooms, but also in the New York Public Library, available for the asking, and Julika here and there in a lonely room over the bed. Julika was not proud, oh no, just dumbfounded every time she picked up the rather cheap paper this magazine was printed on, but above all glad it was such a spectacular photograph and that her pose was quite faultless from the dancing point of view.

Julika felt very lonely.

A hitherto unknown and bewildering longing for her husband, the more she felt her slender body burning like tinder, a desire that from dreams at least could not be banished, and added to this the perpetual knowledge that in these same nights Stiller was deceiving her—all this compelled poor Julika to write letters which could never be sent, no, not under any circumstances. Strictly speaking, it was not of Stiller she dreamed, but of head physicians, baker's boys and men whom she had never seen. The young sanatorium veteran treated Julika like a nun, not even

like a nun, but like a neuter being, even if he sat
every day on the end of her narrow bed, so that her
feet felt his warmth. Not even the most restrained act
of tenderness escaped him. When Julika asked him
to, he straightened her pillows without so much as
touching her by mistake. On the other hand he talked
to Julika about Eros with just the same light-hearted
objectivity as about Communism, or Thomas Aquinas,
or Einstein, or Bernanos, he spoke in exactly the same
way about Eros—with an openness that is only possible when there is no possibility of translating words
into deeds. Julika didn't know what to say. So this
was the tone in which the young man spoke of the
singular phenomenon of Eros, to which, to Julika's
surprise, he attached enormous importance. Yet he
never did more than touch her hand in greeting or
parting. Was Julika a leper? And yet this same man, for
all his staggering knowledge, was not above flirting
with a person who beat mattresses in the meadow
opposite, flirting in the most shameless fashion. Julika
couldn't understand him.

Altogether, there arose shortly before his death a
painful estrangement, to which Julika does not like to
refer. The young sanatorium veteran had gone rather
too far with the remark that it was time Julika stopped
seeing her own behavior towards her husband, and
towards people in general, as only a reaction, never
regarding herself as the initiator, in other words it
was time she stopped wallowing in infantile innocence.
That was too much! Moreover Julika didn't quite
understand what he meant. He had to explain, though
reluctantly.

"Well," he smiled. "I have the feeling, my dear and
respected Julika, that you don't want to grow up, you
don't want to be responsible for your own life, and
that's a pity."

"What do you mean by that?" she asked.

"Anyone who is always seeing himself as a victim, it

seems to me, never gets wise to himself, and that's not healthy. Cause and effect are never divided between two people, certainly not between a husband and wife even though it may sometimes look like it, Julika, because the wife apparently doesn't act. It just strikes me that you explain everything you do or don't do by something your husband has or has not done. That, if you will forgive my saying so, is infantile. Why do I say that? You know perfectly well, Julika, that it isn't like that and never has been in the history of the world, and you mustn't lead me by the nose simply because I'm younger than you, really only a boy. In the long run this way of looking at life is tedious for you too, Julika."

After this she kept teasing him, calling him "The Sage," and he didn't like it. He stayed away for two or three days, just because Julika had told him not to meddle in matters which at his age, clever as he was, he simply didn't know by experience—matters concerning marriage, for example, and in particular marriage with Stiller, whom he didn't even know by sight—in short she told him to stick to his Fathers of the Church and the theory of relativity, and so (says Julika) no real contact developed out of this acquaintance either. To be sure, the young man kept on coming to see her, sat on the end of her bed, and chatted wittily, recklessly, more and more extravagantly the nearer drew his death, which he certainly did not expect during that mild September.

Julika simply couldn't believe her ears when the furniture was moved as quietly as possible out of the next room. They had thoughtfully given Julika a sleeping pill, which she had spat out. A whole night long they fumigated the room. Julika was flabbergasted. This was not how she had expected death to be here, so casual and invisible, so silent, so indulgently sudden and unannounced, so unfair, so like the chance extinction of a bedside lamp just when one is reading.

And in fact people simply never spoke of him
again. The nurse and the head physician just ignored
Julika's repeated questions, as though her young
neighbor, the young Jesuit with the big eyes and the
always rather shrewd face, had been guilty of some
indecency. Everything else went on as before, the little railway whistled in the valley, newspapers arrived.
A few days later, while Julika was lying as usual in
her silent veranda, somehow still waiting for his
daily visit, she heard the dry cough of her new neighbor. It was a blue September day. She shuddered.

As far as Landquart, the station where she had to
change, everything went off as though Julika were on
an ordinary journey, not in flight; nobody stopped
Julika, nobody stared at her, or at least no more than
people always did stare at her because of her beautiful hair. A short halt at Klosters, about midway,
seemed to her endless, as any four-minute wait before a closed barrier is bound to seem like eternity to
a fugitive. Julika hid behind a newspaper, but she
was terrified every time anyone passed through
her second-class compartment. The little train remained stationary; why ever were they stopping so
long? Julika couldn't understand why no one recognized her, no one tapped her on the shoulder and said,
"What's all this about, my dear Julika, what's all this
about?" Uninitiated in the mysteries of the railway
system, Julika could only suppose that this long halt
was due to a call from the sanatorium and that they
were searching for her, going from carriage to carriage looking for the unfortunate fugitive. Julika
pulled her hanging coat down over her face, as people do who want to sleep in a train. Someone sat opposite her, a gentleman; she could see by his shoes.
Her head physician? In her mind's eye she could already see his compassionate smile, his friendly but

inexorable, "Frau Julika, Frau Julika, we'd better drop this little scheme."

At last, when the little train started to move off, Julika had to find out who it was that had caught her; she pushed her overcoat camouflage a little to one side, as though she urgently needed to look at the scenery. It was a German gentleman, who, the moment he saw Julika's red hair, politely took his cigar out of his mouth and inquired whether his smoke was inconveniencing her. Did he think Julika was a lung patient? "Oh, not at all, not at all," said Julika with rather gauche over-emphasis, "please don't mind me." Stupidly enough she had taken a seat in a smoker. Julika, the fugitive, couldn't even indulge in the sort of pleasant light conversation which the German gentleman, without any effort, just started quite naturally, no, she could already hear in imagination the pointless, but in such conversations inevitable, inquiries: "Do you live in Zurich? Are you coming home from your holiday? Do you live at Davos?" Julika brought the conversation to an end by turning away towards the window in repugnance, as though this German gentleman had looked shamelessly down her bosom. Yet in reality he had merely referred to the rather mild October. Now thank God, he picked up his book again, but continued to smoke his still almost complete cigar—*Marmorklippen* by Ernst Jünger, a book the deceased young Jesuit had never recommended to her, *Marmorklippen*, a word that irritated Julika when she heard it recently—and his smoke was horrible. Julika asked if she might open the window a little, oh no, not because of the smoke, just so that she could get a better view of the scenery. Julika leaned out of the window, her flaming hair streaming in the wind, and felt short of breath, as even a healthy person might have done. Above all, however, she saw a dark-colored Citroën, just like the head physician's, following the little train at a pretty breakneck speed; it was left behind owing to bends in the road while the little train shot through a short tunnel, caught it up again, drew closer and closer, stopped at a lowered barrier, sped on and caught up again. The head physician?

Julika withdrew her flaming red hair from the landscape and the German gentleman had to shut the window at once. The dark Citroën was just overtaking the little train; at Landquart, thought Julika, her head physician would be standing on the platform, he would take her bit of luggage from her and smile: "Frau Julika, Frau Julika, we'd better drop this little scheme, my Citroën is over here."

But there was no one waiting at Landquart, not even a porter. The *Marmorklippen* gentleman, his politeness unimpaired by Julika's attitude of repugnance, carried her luggage across the little square and asked, "Do you live in Zurich?" Thereupon Julika took a porter after all.

Then, on the spur of the moment, Julika went into a call-box—perhaps merely for the sensation of entering a call-box as any free person can do anywhere—and tried to ring Stiller, but in vain; no one lifted the receiver. So it simply isn't true that Julika was planning to take him by surprise. During the whole of this journey, strangely enough, it never occurred to Julika for a second that the other woman was still there. She tried a second and then a third time to ring Stiller; likewise in vain.

The German gentleman was now rather offended; he kept to the far end of the platform, where he sat on a bench with crossed legs reading his *Marmorklippen*—now, at last, without a cigar. Unfortunately the Zurich-Paris-Calais train was a bit late, otherwise Julika would probably have managed to board it.

It began (she told me) without a cough, simply with a growing feeling of being short of breath; she tried to persuade herself that this might merely be due to excitement, the natural excitement of a fugitive, to joyful anticipation, and natural disappointment that Stiller was not in the studio and not in the flat. She breathed deeply, slowly, calmly. She had sent her porter to buy some magazines, in particular the Swiss illustrated paper, as though despite everything there was a fairy-tale possibility that Julika was still dancing on the cover, and had to sit down on her little suitcase. Nobody noticed that Julika felt giddy. Julika thought she was suffocating, but just heard the chugging of the approaching Zurich-Paris-Calais train, she even saw the board with these names on, but after that nothing. At this moment people were naturally busy with their own journeys, they stormed the nearest footboards with cases in both hands and acted as though this were the train to life, while the platform was certain death. Julika remained on the platform . . .

Three hours later, after a journey in the ambulance, she lay in her white bed again, shivering in spite of all the hot water bottles, glad not to have to say a word. The nurse did not say a word either, she carried out the head physician's instructions, but you could see from her face that it hadn't been a dream, this journey down to Landquart, but an entirely real act of madness. And it was clear to the head physician why the unhappy woman had committed this act of madness. His displeasure was not directed against the patient, naturally, nor even against the stupid nurses who hadn't noticed the flight for hours; the head physician tried to telephone Stiller. Without success. Later he sent a telegram asking Herr Stiller to come at once to Davos. And no sooner had poor Julika recovered consciousness than she had to keep defending her husband. He didn't even answer the telegram. Julika had to give the addresses of his friends, of Sturzenegger for example. When it turned out Stiller was on a visit to Paris, without having said a word to his wife, it made an odd impression in the sanatorium, a painful impression; people were highly indignant, and although they didn't talk about it to the poor patient, Julika could see it in their faces.

Stiller in Paris! Everyone else was all the kinder to her, Julika, the unhappy Julika, received presents from all sides—flowers, sweets, even a brooch, signs of a heartfelt solidarity running from veranda to veranda. She couldn't help thinking of the young sanatorium veteran, who had predicted a universal silence of contempt in a case like this; it turned out that he had been wrong not only with his impertinent assertion that Julika had an infantile attitude to the world, but also over this point. On the contrary, how sweet everyone was! And only he himself, the young sanatorium veteran, remained silent . . .

Her condition was calamitous.

And then, yes, then, came Stiller's monstrous letter from Paris, the note which Frau Julika Stiller-Tschudy recently took out of her hand-bag and showed me, a note hastily scribbled in pencil, seven or eight lines, not a word of sympathy, no, the whole thing in an icy and heartless tone, as though Julika had only carried out her ill-fated flight in order to collapse at Landquart, and as though Julika was only ill at all in order to give Stiller a bad conscience, mortally ill, so that only injections kept her alive. The note was simply grotesque; for there was not a trace of bad conscience to be seen in these lines, merciful heaven, every word in the note was imbued with shameless egocentricity and a cynical self-righteousness.

(Unfortunately I haven't got Stiller's letter here.)

Injections kept Julika alive, as I have said, and nearly three full weeks passed before Stiller really appeared on her veranda, where he talked exclusively about himself, about his defeat in Spain, that's to say about an event which had taken place ten years ago, and even now not a word of comfort, not even an enquiry about her condition, which was calamitous, not a glance at her temperature chart, no, Stiller merely talked about himself: as though he were the patient, he Stiller, the healthy one!

Here we must go back a little.

Stiller, as we know, took part in the Spanish Civil War, while still a very young man, as a volunteer in the International Brigade. It is not clear what impelled him to this militant gesture. Probably many factors were combined—a rather romantic Communism, such as was common among bourgeois intellectuals at that time, also an understandable desire to see the world, a desire to subordinate his personal interests to some higher historical force, a desire for action; perhaps too, at least in part, it was flight from himself.

He passed his ordeal by fire (or rather, he failed to pass it) outside Toledo, where the Fascists had entrenched themselves in the Alcazar. Young Stiller was set to guard a small ferry across the Tajo—owing to the shortage of troops, entirely on his own. For three days nothing happened. But then, when four Franco Spaniards finally appeared on the opposite bank at the break of day, Stiller allowed them to use the ferry without firing, although it would have been easy for him, from his perfect cover, to have shot the four enemies dead on the ferry. He had eight minutes in which to do it. Instead he let them reach his bank waiting for the others to open fire, in other words, ready to be shot. To avoid giving away their presence, the Franco Spaniards did not shoot either, but disarmed young Stiller, threw his Russian gun into the Tajo, tied him up with his own braces and left him lying in the gorse, where he was found two days later by his own side, faint with thirst. When he was called to account, he swore to the commissar that his Russian gun had failed to go off . . .

As a matter of fact, this little story was the very

first thing Julika ever heard from his lips, and she clearly remembered the evening in his studio, the fateful evening after Tchaikovsky's *Nutcracker Suite*, when a rather wild band of artists and art-lovers forcibly carried off the beautiful Julika and, with a few bottles under their arms, made an equally forcible night attack on young Stiller in his studio. It was past midnight, all the taverns in the town were closed; but the light was still burning in the studio occupied by Stiller, who had just got back from Spain. So up they went.

That evening Julika and Stiller saw one another for the first time. In the middle of the high-spirited company, which now filled his studio, Stiller was so still that to begin with Julika imagined his name to be a nickname. Then someone called on him to tell his "great story of Toledo." Stiller didn't want to at all. He wasn't shamming; he really didn't want to, and his embarrassment was obvious when a friend, a young architect named Sturzenegger, began to tell it himself. Now, of course, Stiller had to interfere, to fill in the gaps and finish the story. I don't suppose the young ballerina was particularly interested in this tale of a Russian gun that didn't go off; she paid less heed to the tale than to the teller, the young sculptor who kept working his fingers all the time he was talking, twisting a piece of wire this way and that, then threw it away, but still couldn't leave his fingers in peace; she felt somehow sorry for him.

As he spoke, all the life drained out of his face. The story the young sculptor was telling sounded somehow second-hand, not a recollection of his own experience, but a mere anecdote. His lengthy account was followed by an embarrassed and uneasy silence. Stiller put his glass to his lips, and no one uttered a word. Then a pleasant, but pale and soft and extremely unmartial-looking opera singer asked the naive question, "And why didn't you fire?" The others wanted to know the same thing. All respect for his boldness in stepping out from his hiding-place, all respect for the torment of lying for two days tied up in the blazing sun; but why indeed, the opera singer had spoken for all of them, why hadn't Stiller fired?

The explanation advanced by Stiller also sounded somehow second-hand, worn by repetition: He hated the Fascists, otherwise he wouldn't have volunteered to fight in the Spanish Civil War; but that early morning on the Tajo, when Stiller first came face to face with the hated foe, he saw the four Fascists as human beings, and he found it impossible to shoot at human beings, he couldn't do it. That was all . . .

Again there was silence, again the artists and art-lovers puffed at their pipes and shot out clouds of smoke into the studio. The opera singer was satisfied with the reply, highly satisfied; he couldn't have fired either, he thought. Others emptied their glasses without speaking. And simply to talk about something else, the *Nutcracker Suite* for example, wasn't possible either. A stillness spread over the gathering, until his friend, the young architect named Sturzenegger, expressed open-hearted admiration for Stiller. He called it a victory for humanity, a victory of concrete experience over ideological rigidity and so on; he found all sorts of words for it. No one contradicted this flattering interpretation, and Stiller himself, visibly ill at ease, had for his part no desire whatever to delve deeper into this story; he was all in favor of more life and gaiety, uncorked the next bottle and made sure in his charming way that everybody had something to drink, including the lovely Julika in the corner, who on this first visit to the studio, looked round with her great big beautiful eyes, without drinking much, without saying anything; her contribution, as so often, was her glorious hair with its reddish glow . . .

Stiller's anecdote, it seems, was always a great success. Later, when she was friendly with Stiller and then married to him, Julika had to listen to it very often. It was one of the duties of a loving wife not to yawn and not to interrupt when her husband came out with his hit number again. It was a hit number, Stiller with his ferry on the Tajo. Only the Communists wrinkled their noses when the victory of humanity over ideology was talked about, but they kept quiet out of friendship for Stiller; at most they asked the listeners how they would feel about a victory of humanity over ideology if it didn't happen to concern Fascists. But such conversations had nothing further to do with Stiller. And anyway, the Communists became rarer and rarer—at least among Stiller's acquaintances.

In all other company Stiller always emerged with honor from his Spanish anecdote. Why did he tell it so often? And in any case, Julika still can't understand why Stiller, her missing husband, suddenly talked about a "Spanish defeat" on the occasion of their last meeting at Davos. Why defeat? Julika had no explanation for this. Hadn't he demanded of Julika for years that she should find his behavior in Spain magnificent? And now it was suddenly a defeat, a thing that weighed in the scales as the beginning of all evil, as a curse, an ill omen, by which Stiller also explained the unhappiness of their marriage. Why?

Their last meeting was in November. It was desolate enough without Stiller's visit. There was already snow again. Julika lay in her *art nouveau* veranda more muffled up than ever, even her arms were under the camel's-hair rugs and she looked like a mummy. She could just move her head sufficiently to look out into the gray mists, where she saw the spectral skeletons of the nearest larches, which reminded her of her X-ray photograph, also a bare skeleton in clouds of gray mist. And this was now her only view. The sky was like lead, and trails of dirty mist were creeping down the hillsides. It was impossible even to guess whereabouts in the sky the sun was. The familiar mountain peaks seemed to have dissolved like a tablet in a glass of water, all that remained was an opaque gray broth. Julika had always thought that only stupid people could be bored, so she couldn't be. But it had nothing to do with stupidity, on the contrary, perhaps this unspeakable tedium, when one really didn't know what to do with the next hour, this hellish taste of eternity, where one couldn't see beyond time, was the most genuine form of suffering of which Julika was ever capable . . .

Stiller was sitting mutely on the veranda railings looking out into the driving snow. He was unshaven and pale, exhausted by a sleepless night, with a haze of alcohol in front of his mouth, and in addition he smelt of garlic from a distance. "What did you have to eat?" asked Julika. "Snails."—Stiller didn't make the slightest enquiry as to how she was. Moreover he hadn't come from the town, but from Pontresina; Stiller announced this spitefully, as though it was poor Julika who had compelled him for a whole summer to indulge in subterfuges; there was almost a malicious glee in his voice. Stiller had come from Pontresina: that is to say, he came from the other woman.

After this almost sneering opening, he fell silent again, without looking at Julika, lit a cigarette and smoked out into the gray whirl of snow. His lips were trembling. Julika didn't know why. "How was it in Paris?" asked Julika. His only answer to this was that in Paris (as though it had been a plot on Julika's part) he had dreamed of her. Julika had always hated his habit of relating his dreams, which might mean anything, and naturally it wasn't his dreams in Paris she had asked about, but his real activities. Nevertheless Stiller recounted his dream—in great detail.

"We were in company," he began, "and somehow I

was beside myself, I don't know why. I wanted to say something but I had no voice, the louder I tried to speak the less sound I made, and it had to be said. It was enough to make one cry. But it had to be said, even if I perished in the attempt. I could see your smile and I yelled; you were smiling just as you are now, like someone who is entirely in the right, and when I yelled in spite of it you walked out, I couldn't stop you, and no doubt the company also thought one really shouldn't yell so; I was behaving in an impossible manner, I knew, I ought to have some sense, they said, and run after you to comfort you, to make amends. I felt how wrong I was, oh yes, and I went out; I looked for you in the streets and found you in a public park, the Jardin de Luxembourg or something like that, it doesn't matter where; it was spring and you were sitting on the green lawn smiling, I tried to strangle you, yes, with both hands and with all the strength of my life, but in vain, and I knew all the time that people were looking at us, I strangled you into a little ball, but you were too elastic—you merely laughed . . ."

Julika said nothing, of course. The nurse appeared soon afterwards to inquire whether Frau Julika was really not cold. Julika thanked her in the nicest way; you could see your breath before your mouth, but Julika with her hot water bottles and rugs was really not cold. When the nurse had gone, Stiller said:

"Yesterday we made an end of it—Sibylle and I—yesterday in Pontresina."

"Who's Sibylle?" asked Julika.

"Now it's all over between us as well, Julika, and for good, you must see that."

Julika said nothing.

"For good," he repeated.

The whole thing must have had its comic side: first, the way Stiller blamed his Julika, who in reality was lying on this veranda, for having smiled in his Paris dream, and secondly the tone in which he delivered his message made it sound as though this were the first love affair in human history that had come to grief, indeed his attitude suggested that dying in a sanatorium was nothing compared with yesterday's burial at Pontresina of his seven-month love affair; there was a comic side, also, to the retrospective frankness of his revelations concerning his love for the lady—whose name turned out to be Sibylle. Julika could read in his face how she was annoying him by blowing snow crystals off her camel's-hair rug while he spoke. What could Julika do? What he now told her was pretty much in agreement with what she had feared during the summer, so it was not now too severe a shock for poor Julika. Stiller on the other hand, in his desolation, enjoyed going into quite uncalled-for details as he walked up and down on her *art nouveau* veranda, simply in order to cling for as long as possible to his lost summer.

"Yes," he said at last, "that's how it is."

"What now?"

It is not true that Julika displayed a smile of secret glee, or that she smiled at all. Stiller was no doubt dreaming again. On the other hand, no one would have expected poor Julika to burst into tears because there was no longer any "Sibylle." What did Stiller expect of her? She blew the snow crystals from the camel's-hair rug, nothing else, and she had by no means failed to hear the dry remark he passed before, namely that it was also all over now with Julika, his legal wife, only she didn't see the logical connection.

But when Stiller tried to explain it, sitting on the railing again and for the most part staring out into the driving snow, as though he were talking to the ghostly larch trees, his vehemence did not spring from this time and place, it did not spring from the presence of his poor Julika; the observations Stiller now made with brutal determination, the more brutal the better, sounded as though they had been conceived in solitude and long bottled up inside him, now they were all trotted out with no living thread running through them, as though under the compulsion of an alien command which Stiller had given himself on his journey to Davos, or perhaps during his meal of snails, a grisly masculine command.

Julika listened, but could not rid herself of the feeling: "Whoever told you to talk such brutal nonsense, my good Stiller, that's not you speaking!" He was behaving with the brutality of a wretched executioner who, at the instant he sees his victim with his own eyes, dare not soften but has to carry out his orders; that was why Stiller scarcely looked at Julika, but gazed instead out into the snowstorm and at the gray larches. And the more he talked the more clearly did Julika have the feeling: "It's not like that, my good Stiller, it's all quite different!" . . .

Stiller talked and talked. "If it hadn't been for that defeat in Spain," he said, "if I had met you with the feeling of being a complete and proper man—I should have left you long ago, Julika, probably after our first kiss, and we should both have been spared this whole miserable marriage. That's the bitter thing, you see; we might have known it wouldn't work out. And there was no lack of signals along the whole line, only of the courage to see them. Today I know that fundamentally I never loved you, I was in love with your shyness, your fragility, your muteness, which set me the task of interpreting and expressing you. What a task! I imagined you needed me. And your perpetual tiredness, your autumn-crocus pallor, your sickliness, that was just what I unconsciously needed, someone in need of care and protection to make me feel all big and strong. To have an ordinary sweetheart, you see, a healthy, normal girl who wants to be embraced and herself is able to embrace, no, that I was afraid of. I was altogether full of anxiety. I made you my test. And that's why I couldn't leave you. My crazy idea was to make you blossom out, a task no one else had undertaken. To make you blossom out! That was the responsibility I took on myself—and I made you ill, of course, for why should you become well with a husband like that; the fear that you were unhappy with me chained me faster than any kind of happiness you're able to give."

Once Julika asked:

"What do you mean, defeat in Spain?"

No answer.

"And did you know it!" exclaimed Stiller. "How well you knew it! That's quite obvious. From the very first evening on; you were in love with my secret anxiety. You liked that, my dear—a man who didn't just come and embrace you, but trembled, an anxious man, a somehow broken man, who thought he had to prove himself with you, a man with a bad conscience from the start, an idiot who always thought it was his fault when something went wrong. Wasn't it like that? I was even responsible for the weather. I can just see you, Julika, as you suddenly stretched out your hand and said, not looking at the sky but at me, 'Now it's raining!' And I put up with the look—"

Julika let him go on talking.

"Wasn't it like that?" asked Stiller. "Why did you never go to a doctor all those years? You wouldn't be lying on this wretched veranda, Julika. Why didn't you want to be a healthy woman? It's ridiculous but true, Julika, you didn't want to be healthy. You thought me heartless because I once found to my delight that you had no temperature for a change. It annoyed you. Think of the countless evenings when you disappeared into your room to lie down, just so we shouldn't forget to think, 'poor Julika,' and so you didn't have to compete with all those healthy

women. You were dead scared of that. I know—you
had very strenuous rehearsals, yes, yes, and I had an
easy time with my clay bashing, where it didn't matter whether I worked or not, living like a pasha; I
know—your work was not to be compared with any
other, not to be compared with the work of a children's specialist, for instance, and it was quite unfair
even to hope, or wish, that you should not be more
delicate than other women. Your consumption of consideration (from all sides) was shameless. And how
everyone gave in to you, not only your idiot, everyone, even those who were not in love with you,
heaven knows why they apologized to you, and when
you fell asleep in company, because your ballet was
not being discussed, they simply thought you a brave
woman, covered you up so you shouldn't be cold, because you couldn't even cover yourself up, a company of Good Samaritans, and we all whispered, for
who didn't know that Julika had a strenuous rehearsal next morning? They were all at your beck
and call, Julika, just like me. And when I didn't understand why you couldn't slip out and make our
friends a bowl of gruel, it was my fault, of course, you
have to take your wife as God gives her to you. Again
and again I forgot how frail you were, how much in
need of looking after! And no sooner had our friends
gone than you pulled yourself together, exhausted as
you were, and made Foxli some warm milk. For Foxli
was yourself!"

Once in his stride, Stiller brought out a whole
string of complaints like this, mere trifles, each more
petty than the last; Julika could only feel amazement.

"You just lie there and say nothing as usual," he
said. "I know, you think you're love and devotion
personified, but I think you're narcissism personified.
And arrogance personified—that above all. I've gone on
my knees before you, Julika, I've wept before you, as
a man does weep under certain circumstances. I've felt

ashamed before you. I've repented before you, and you forgave me, certainly, you forgave me non-stop, I know, without a moment's emotion, without really thinking for a moment that perhaps you too were destroying me, and trembling. Why should you? You are the patient sufferer, all our friends know that, a noble being, who never shouts reproaches, no, I had to reproach myself. You never lowered yourself to such an act. But just think it over: Did you ever set me free from my guilt, when I thought I had to reproach myself? You forgave me. And that confirms the reproach, more than anything else. There is a satanic quality about feminine forgiveness, my dear, which is alien to you, of course, anything of that kind is alien to you; I just took it like that because I'm so hypersensitive, and you can perish of hypersensitivity just as well as of tuberculosis . . . I talk and talk, Julika, and you blow the snow off the rug!"

Stiller went on:

"Yes—I sometimes ask myself why I never jumped up and simply boxed your ears in all those years. Seriously, that was a mistake that can never be made good now; a mistake, of that I'm convinced. How much it would have spared us both! For instance, your ill-fated journey to Landquart, I believe. Of course you knew from the start that you would collapse somewhere along the line, but you no longer shrink from paying any price to make sure of my bad conscience. You're mistaken! But the terrible thing is that in a different sense it's really my fault you're in this sanatorium. But there you've got nothing more to forgive me. I often think, if I hadn't made you my test the idea of fettering me with your ill health would never have occurred to you, and we should have loved each other in a natural manner, I don't know, or parted in a natural manner. You ought to have met a man who had no guilty conscience and yet plenty of patience, free patience, anyhow a man who could only be won and held by natural love. Who knows, my dear Julika, how healthy you might have been—all the time . . ."

Stiller fell silent.

"Go on," she said. Stiller merely gaped at her.

"So that's how you see me," said Julika. "You've made an image of me, that's quite clear, a complete and final image, and there's an end of it. You just won't see me any other way, I can feel that. Aren't I right?" Stiller lit a cigarette. "I've also done a good deal of thinking lately," said Julika, continuing to blow the snow crystals from her rug even though it was now her turn to speak, "—not for nothing does it say in the Commandments 'Thou shalt not make unto thee any image' . . . Every image is a sin. All those things you've been saying are exactly the opposite of love, you know. I don't know whether you realize that. When you love someone you leave every possibility open to them, and in spite of all the memories of the past you are ready to be surprised, again and again surprised, at how different they are, how various, not a finished image such as you have made of your Julika. I can only tell you, it's not like that. You always talk yourself into believing things—Thou shalt not make unto thee an image of me! That's the only answer I can give you."

Stiller smoked away to himself.

"Where did you get all that from?" was all he asked. It was impossible to talk to Stiller any more, it seems he only listened to himself. He had come from Pontresina with the fixed determination to tear everything to the ground. "Love?" he laughed, "let's not talk about love, not in our case, and not about fidelity either—you too would probably have left me long ago, Julika, you never lacked opportunities, I know, merely confidence in your ability to hold a real man. Let's be frank. Our comparative fidelity was fear of defeat at the hands of another partner, such as I have suffered now, nothing else. Don't let's kid ourselves. It's all over now between us also. I think, Julika, we're seeing one another for the last time."

Julika wept.

"It's horrible," remarked Stiller very soberly, "that it has to be in this sanatorium. You're by no means past the crisis, your head physician tells me. But perhaps it's a good thing, Julika, that from this day on you should know, without any shadow of doubt, that your illness no longer impresses me. That may sound thoroughly mean to your ears. Look, the truth is that I was always full of secret reproach towards you, that's why I was so ridiculously considerate: I was forever trying to make amends for something, something unspoken, you understand; and now for the first time, it seems to me, I stand before you without being angry with you. The fact is, I know now that it isn't you who have hindered me up to the present from really living. Thank God, I know at last! The tears in your eyes, Julika, are a threat that no longer works. The fact is, we've all got to die."

At this Julika said:

"I'd like you to leave me alone now."

Stiller stood a little while longer beside her bed, his hands in his overcoat pocket after he had thrown his cigarette over the railings, rather embarrassed. And then, as though Julika were already in her coffin, he merely kissed her on the brow, without waiting for her arms, and quickly left the wintry veranda . . .

Since then (says Julika) he has disappeared from her life. Stiller was still seen in the town during December. Only then, after a varnishing-day followed by a midnight carouse, did he also disappear for the others, imperceptibly at first, not from one day to the next; people only noticed gradually that he was not to be seen in the coffee-bar and other places where they used to meet him, and each one shrugged his shoulders when the other casually inquired after Stiller. They waited well on into January before someone, worried by Stiller's permanently closed studio, informed the police, who began with a fruitless search of all the drawers and today, six, nearly seven, years later, know as little as they did then.

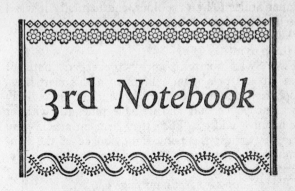

3rd *Notebook*

YESTERDAY (among other things) paid a visit to a Swiss quartermaster's stores to look at the military equipment of their missing man. A long wait in a Nissen hut. No smoking. I sat down on a bundle of Swiss trousers. Couldn't I stand up? The place smelt of leather and camphor and of horses from the stables next door. Just for something to say, I asked the young lieutenant, who looked rather awkward in his shining boots and found this waiting just as tedious as I did:

"Do you still have cavalry?"

"No," he answered curtly.

Finally they brought me a packet tied with string, which contained the ragged uniform of their missing man, and told me to undo it. Of course I should have refused; every act of politeness on my part, however minor, confirms them in the opinion that they can do what they like with me, as they could with Stiller. As I unpacked the mildewed and, at its best, rather ridiculous kitbag, all the property of Machine-

Gunner Stiller fell on the floor, and naturally it was I who had to pick it up. I said:

"What has this to do with me, gentlemen?"

"Jump to it."

Two Swiss quartermaster's storekeepers, both of them fat and pale from a lifetime in this martial atmosphere, tried to counterbalance their unsoldierly appearance by a curt and irritable tone. All without any form of address. Then they held up a field-gray greatcoat against the rainy light, looked at the lieutenant, who examined the garment conscientiously, and waited for my dismay.

"There—don't you see anything? Eh?"

Cockroach holes, admitted, a positive Milky Way of cockroach holes. I felt the material and said:

"It isn't waterproof anyway."

They all looked at me as though I were a Communist, just because I had uttered this simple truth. I took hold of the raincoat worn by the young officer, who was standing nearby in the rôle of silent supervisor.

"Here," I said, "that's the proper stuff."

Later I had to look down the barrel of a Swiss rifle. They compelled me. For some strange reason I let them compel me. I wonder why. I looked into the foreign rifle as though it were a telescope, but I couldn't see anything, a small hole full of gray light, nothing else. And all the time they were waiting for me to sink through the concrete floor with shame. A little mirror was attached.

"Can you see anything?"

I saw rust, and as I hadn't asked how much the barrel of a Swiss rifle cost I wasn't in the least interested in the young officer's lecture, to which I listened out of politeness. I hadn't dreamed of buying a Swiss rifle. A revolver, yes, or a sub-machine-gun; but what could I do with a rifle as long as a walking-stick? The young lieutenant seemed somehow ill at ease, as though he thought I might also be an educated man; he kept on saying:

"I don't have to explain that to you."

Then, purely from a sense of duty, as though he himself were being put through an examination by the two storekeepers, he explained it just the same, embarrassing though he found it. Somehow I had the feeling he was trying to show me that he too had higher interests, but the only way he could do so in this quartermaster's hut was now and then to look out of the window at the pouring rain—while the two storekeepers, who now regarded me with ever growing hate, were not prevented by my manifest indifference from laying on the table everything they considered necessary for waging war. To wit: two brushes, knife and fork, a reel with field-gray thread, leather soap, a very exact number of buttons, each one of them bearing the Swiss cross, a mess tin, a water-bottle, of which the cork ought not to stink, shoe laces, a paint brush with a case, a steel helmet, a so-called tie, a bayonet with a sheath, as well as two needles, which the missing Stiller had also irresponsibly allowed to rust. In short, there was a whole table full of stuff, at which I stared in amazement, though keeping my hands in my trouser pockets.

"I don't need to give you a lecture," said the young lieutenant. "You know that you will have to pay for the damage."

"I?" I laughed. "Why ever should I?"

"Who else do you think is going to?"

I didn't get a chance to speak. I even had to put on their missing man's battledress tunic. I simply didn't get a chance to speak; therein lay part of their power, and to my surprise I actually knuckled under, although reluctantly. It didn't occur to them to hold the tunic for me, and when I couldn't find the attachment on the collar they just exclaimed, "Jump to it." Nor did they pay any heed to my innocent remark that in a tunic like this a soldier would be exhausted before he ever caught a glimpse of the enemy. I had to turn round like a tailor's dummy.

"You've grown thinner," affirmed the young lieutenant, who was seeing me for the first time in his life. "It's baggy everywhere."

In the meantime one of the storekeepers had stepped over to a rack and dragged out another tunic, which he threw to me:

"Try this one?"

"What for?" I asked. Again I received no answer, but only another tunic of a different size and a lecture from the young officer: up to the age of forty-eight I was a member of the Swiss militia, and I was liable for military service until the end of my sixtieth year; of course I was entitled to go abroad, but it was my duty first to ask the State for leave and to report my departure to the local command, as laid down in standing orders; furthermore, in the event of such leave being granted, the military equipment issued to every male Swiss citizen should not be left lying about in a loft, but handed in, so that the quartermaster's men could guard it from moths; and furthermore, on arriving in a foreign country it was my duty to report immediately to the nearest Swiss legation, so that I should not evade the military tax, and also to report my departure from there and so on . . .

"My compliments on the efficiency of your Swiss organization, Lieutenant," I said. "But as far as I'm concerned—"

They didn't let me go on. There was only one idea in their three heads: Stiller must be in fighting trim. I couldn't escape trying on a pair of army boots as well —first-class goods, incidentally. And I didn't only have to try them on; the young lieutenant said:

"You must feel comfortable in them too."

There was nothing for it.

And then right at the end, they became furious. I had to sign my name, to confirm receipt of a rifle and the new army boots. Everything must be in order, I quite understood that. I allowed the young lieutenant, who was obviously yearning for more important employment, to lend me his fountain pen and filled in the form: White, James Larkin, New Mexico, U.S.A.

"White—what do you mean White?"

I returned the fountain pen.

"My name is White," I said in English.

They looked at one another reproachfully.

"Aren't you Machine-Gunner Stiller?" asked the young lieutenant holding my binding signature in his hand and half shaking his head over the two store-keepers, who were really not to blame. They had simply been sent this man. Who? Why? I tried to elucidate, to explain.

"There is a suspicion," I said, "that I am the missing gentleman, but this suspicion—"

Obviously they couldn't arm a man on the strength of a mere suspicion. The lieutenant explained this to them, while I had to take the boots off again, just when they fitted me.

"Why the bloody hell," swore the storekeepers, "didn't you tell us that at the beginning?"

In view of their rage, which unfortunately they let out on the helmet and mess tin, I refrained from justifying myself. They simply hadn't given me a chance to speak. Their anger was understandable; for now I wasn't allowed to touch anything, neither the rifle nor the army boots, which latter I should have been glad to keep, and they had to repack the whole kitbag themselves. I merely said, "Sorry!" But the young lieutenant found it very embarrassing; he felt obliged to chat with me for a while. He had a lively interest in America. He apologized several times; it upset him that a thing of this sort should have happened to an American in Switzerland, and he said good-bye to me with a military salute. To avoid waving, I also put my hand to my cap, and the two prison van attendants, whom the young lieutenant's civility had not escaped, received me as they had never done before, as polite as though there were a prospect of a tip; one of them even held the gray van door with the barred window open for me, while the other gave me a light, and the only thing missing was an inquiry as to where they could drive me.

Wilfried Stiller, the brother, is apparently very disappointed because I haven't answered his brotherly letter. I shall do so as soon as I have a moment to spare.

My second afternoon out on bail with Julika.

The moment I saw her again I received the vivid impression: This isn't she! This woman has nothing to do with the dreary story I have partially recorded during the last few days, nothing at all. There are two different Julikas. It isn't her story at all. And so on.

"You," she asked me several times, "what's the matter with you? Why do you look at me like that all the time?"

Today she was more at ease than I. My suggestion that we should hire a sailing boat delighted her. We went along arm in arm. I didn't know what to talk about, and was glad to be able to busy myself with the halyards and the rudder, while Frau Julika Stiller-Tschudy, dressed today in a banana-yellow frock—after some anxiety as she jumped into the rocking boat and some concern as to where she could stow her white handbag and her butterfly-like Paris hat without getting them dirty or damaged—sat on the other seat in charming indolence, propped up by her outstretched arms. Julika had only to change seats when I put the boat about. Then she abandoned herself to repose again and her lustrous hair to the wind. How different she was! Out there on the lake, whose hilly shores, packed almost solid with houses and always very close, were lost in an autumnal haze, giving one a certain sense of distance, we were more or less alone together for the first time. Did she realize the fact? Anyhow, we didn't have to reckon with the warder, my good Knobel, appearing at any moment with the ash tray . . .

Now (back in my cell) I try in vain to see her laughing face; I only know very vividly that whenever it laughs I want to take it in both hands like a gift from heaven that cannot be grasped with the hands, but only believed, and then I have the alert, sober feeling: there is nothing that could not be melted away in this laughter. In a context which I forget, she said:

"The trouble is that when I'm all by myself and think about everything, alone, I can't laugh about it, or if I do it's such an angry and bitter laugh that later on I howl over the very things I laughed about."

We seized the opportunity of a rather lengthy calm to whip off our clothes and jump into the green water, which was sparkling in the sun but already pretty cold, and then swam round the rudderless, drifting boat, kicking like children. When we were back in the boat, lying dripping wet and with goose flesh in the blessed sunshine, Julika said:

"You're thinner."

Thinner than who? For the sake of our idyl I did not take her remark as referring to the missing Stiller, but to the still unmentioned gentlemen in Paris, of whom I was less jealous than of her Stiller, funnily enough. Since little steamers were cruising by on all sides, we had to dress before we were quite dry. A change in the direction of the wind, as the result of which I had to sail into the wind almost all the way to the shore, very nearly made me late back to the prison. Julika had to take me there in a taxi . . .

Now (in the evening on my bed) I can still see the beads of water on her arms and her alabaster brow, and also the antique curls of her wet hair round the nape of her neck.

P.S. In the near future she is going back to Paris for a week, to see her ballet school; I shall miss her.

A dream:

I'm wearing Stiller's battledress tunic, together with helmet and rifle. I hear a command: "Battery, atten-shun! Shoulder arms! By the left, quick march!" It is hot and the ground is very stony and bumpy. War has broken out. I know quite clearly in my dream that the date is 3.9.1939. But I don't feel that it is the past, any more than you feel it is the past when you are sitting in a dream at your school desk. I hear a voice behind me, screeching with exasperation. Someone wasn't marching in step. Why doesn't the man step forward? We stand stiffly at attention. A captain's face is white with rage. "You there," he shouts, pointing to me and I can actually hear myself calling out, "Gunner Stil-ler." It's funny, even in the dream I don't feel myself to be "Gunner Stiller," but I call straight out in the landscape, "Gunner Stiller." The captain's lips trem-ble. There are very special positions for people like me in wartime—understand? And when things started humming he'd deal with me (Gunner Stiller) without much ceremony—understand? I stand stiffly to atten-tion, with rifle at the shoulder, and have understood that the Swiss captain, who has a perfect right to do so, hates Stiller for some reason and, thanks to the obe-dience we have just sworn to the fatherland, can kill me: without much ceremony—with a command . . .

P.S. When I mentioned this dream casually to my counsel, he was visibly indignant. We talked about the army. It wasn't enough for him that, for the sake of peace (peace between my counsel and me) I accepted it as a necessary evil. The army seems to be sacred, even in Switzerland, and my counsel could not tolerate someone dreaming badly about it. In reality, he asserted, no Swiss officer could ever utter such an unseemly, such a positively criminal threat. "I guarantee that," he said with the pride of a Swiss officer, a major I think. "I guarantee that," he said several times.

Answered Herr Wilfried Stiller, brother of the missing man—unfortunately again forgot to make a copy—roughly as follows: "Your cordial letter to your missing brother moved me deeply, dear Herr Stiller, it reminded me of my mother, so that I too shed tears, and I apologize for not having replied to it sooner. My life is one single act of neglect. I am not annoyed that you do not ask me about it, on the contrary, I am grateful to you for this, as for your brotherly invitation; it reminds me of my brother and of the fact that I also neglected my brother. We rarely had a quarrel, and never a long or important one, for we never had anything important to do with one another, it seems to me; we used to go on walking tours together, simply because we were brothers, and spend peaceful nights under canvas and hours round the camp-fire without speaking a word. Why did I also neglect my brother? Friends have to understand one another in order to be friends; brothers are brothers in any case, and in the last resort, you're quite right, it doesn't matter who I am as long as I am a real brother. In this sense . . .

The latest news: the American passport, with which I have been half way round the world, is a forgery.

Didn't I tell my counsel so weeks ago? I can't communicate, it seems. Every word is false and true, that is the nature of words, and anyone who wants to believe all or nothing—

My public prosecutor (who returned from Pontresina yesterday) isn't interested in Mexico, but he's very interested in New York, and whenever he talks about it he slips into a very unofficial and familiar tone. He said:

"My wife was very fond of New York."

"Really?" I said.

"She lived on Riverside Drive."

"Did she?" I said.

"You know where that is?"

"Of course," I said.

"Near Hundred and Eighth Street."

"Oh," I said, "that's almost next door to Columbia University—"

"That's right," he said.

"A very beautiful district," I said, "looking out over the Hudson, I know—"

And so on.

To begin with, it seemed as though all he was trying to do during these chats was to test whether I really knew New York, whether I had really lived in New York. I passed this test long ago. Times Square and Fifth Avenue, Rockefeller Center, Broadway, Central Park and the Battery, these are the sort of places my public prosecutor saw for himself during his week in New York about five years ago.

"Do you know the Rainbow Bar?" he asked.

I nodded and let him give vent to his enthusiasm, for I like men who can be enthusiastic; I didn't correct him, didn't tell him that the Rainbow Bar, where my public prosecutor obviously spent an unforgettable evening, is not the highest bar in Manhattan, that the Empire State Building is taller; I didn't interrupt him. I could see that for my public prosecutor it was a highlight of his life; in the Rainbow Bar he met his wife after being separated from her for years. Then I asked in my turn:

"Did you also know the Bowery?"

"Where's that?" he asked.

"Third Avenue."

"No."

The Bowery, an originally Dutch name, is a district into which even the police no longer venture, fields of the lost, though right in the middle of Manhattan; you go round the marble corner of a palatial law-court and after a hundred paces you are in the fields of the lost, of drunkards, failures, degenerates of all kinds, people on whom life itself has passed judgment. There's no need even to put them in prison; no one who has landed in the Bowery ever gets out again. In summer they lie in the gutter and on the pavement; you have to move like a knight on the chessboard in order to get along. In winter they crouch round the iron stoves of the doss-house, dozing, quarreling, snoring, telling the same stories over and over again or fighting, and it reeks of booze, petrol and unwashed feet.

Once I saw a figure I shall never forget. It was three o'clock at night, as I was going home from Blacky as usual; it was a short-cut for me, and there would be nobody in the street at this time of night, I thought, especially not in this frightful cold. The old-fashioned overhead railway rumbled past up above, its windows filled with warm light; in the street filthy litter was being whirled round by the wind and dogs were snuffling about. When I saw him coming I hid behind one of the iron pillars of the overhead railway. On his head he wore a black bowler like diplomats, bridegrooms and gangsters; his face was smeared with blood. In addition to the hat he wore a tie, a whitish shirt and a black jacket, but that was all; the lower half of his body was stark naked. On his thin, grayish-purple old man's legs he had sock-suspenders and shoes. He was obviously drunk. He swore, fell down and crawled along the icy roadway; a car sped past with its headlights blazing, thank God without running over him. At last he found his trousers, tried to shin up a streetlamp and climb into his trousers, slipped and lay once more full length in the roadway. Of course I wondered whether to go to his assistance, but I was afraid of becoming entangled in something that would get me into difficulties. Meanwhile the old man had succeeded in sticking his left leg into his trousers; I wished him luck and was about to move off. From somewhere or other I heard voices, though I could see no one, voices full of scorn and hate that were no doubt directed at this unfortunate. I immediately retired into the concealing shadow of my iron pillar; up above rumbled the overhead railway. When he tried to get his second leg into the trousers he slipped again, and once more stark naked he lay where he was, rattling in his throat. His black bowler rolled along in the wind. He made no movement of defense when a dog sniffed at him.

My limbs were shaking and I decided to retreat from pillar to pillar. People passed by on the other side who didn't go to his assistance either. You never know what you may be letting yourself in for! In the end the Good Samaritan has to prove he's not the murderer, with an alibi and so on. I couldn't do that to Blacky. One block further, and I could get into the overhead railway; in twenty minutes I could be at home, where I was sure Blacky was already ringing up to say goodnight. I could just see him in the distance as a dark heap on the ground, about the only thing the savage wind wasn't whirling along. All of a sudden there was a chap standing next to me, with his hand on my shoulder; a stubbly beard, a bald patch, red fishes' eyes—not at all an unsympathetic face, incidentally; he asked for a cigarette. And a light. With that he was satisfied, left me and walked down the avenue, saw the dark bundle in the roadway, stepped over to it, as I hadn't dared, and walked on. Up above the overhead railway rumbled again. Finally I also dared, and went back to the drunken man, who was no longer moving. He lay on his belly, blue with cold, and his colorless hair was also matted with blood. I saw the wound on the back of his head, I shook him, I raised his arm; he was dead. I was so horrified by his face that I ran away, and I didn't report the matter to the police, although it was my own father.

"Your father?"

My public prosecutor was smiling. He didn't believe me, it seemed, any more than he had believed that I murdered my wife. He asked, as though he hadn't heard properly:

"Your father?"

"My stepfather," I said. "All the same—"

But even then, when he can't believe me, my public prosecutor is a great deal nicer than my counsel; he doesn't become indignant if our conceptions of truth don't always agree.

He tapped himself a cigarette and said:

"Of course, my wife didn't get to know districts like that."

He's always talking about his wife.

"Do you know Fire Island?"

"Yes," I asked, "why?"

"It's supposed to be very pretty, according to my wife, all the country round New York in fact."

"Very pretty."

"Unfortunately my wife didn't have a car of her own," he declared, "but she often used to drive out —with friends, as far as I know."

"One has to do that," I said.

"Did you have your own car?"

"I?" I laughed. "No."

Somehow this statement seemed to please him, to relieve him, to cheer him up and free him from some idea which I couldn't quite guess.

"No," I confirmed, "I didn't have my own car, the whole of that summer I drove poor old Dick's car, while he was ill."

He didn't seem to like this either, and I could feel that he was rather interested in my week-end trips.

Then he came out with his question:

"Whom did you take out with you on these trips? I don't suppose you went by yourself?"

"No."

"May I ask—"

"Mr. Public Prosecutor," I said, "it wasn't your wife."

He smiled and looked at me.

"Word of honor," I said.

These are strange interrogations.

Wilfried has answered:

Dear Sir,

Your letter of yesterday came as a great shock to me, as you may well imagine, since Herr Dr. Bohnenblust, who came here to fetch a photograph album of my brother's for his file, assured me that you were definitely my brother and that your release was only a matter of days, provided you, or as the case may be, my brother, had nothing to do with the Smyrnov affair, I told Herr Dr. Bohnenblust at once that as far as I knew my brother had not been politically active since his return from Spain, and in any case was certainly not a political agent. I apologize for the inappropriate letter I wrote you previously. As regards my visit, which you asked me to drop for the present because of possible misinterpretation, I must unfortunately let you know that I have been officially requested in writing by the examining magistrate to come for a meeting with you, but I suppose you have been informed of this. I am sure you will understand our first excitement and forgive my over-hastiness. At the same time I should like to thank you for your short, but in spite of my misunderstanding, so understanding letter, which it was probably not easy for you to write. I hope you will not think me impertinent if I repeat our invitation to come and live with us after your release, even if you are not my brother.

"With kindest regards both to you and to Herr Dr. Bohnenblust and good wishes for the solution of your present problems,

Wilfried Stiller, Dip. Agric."

Julika knows nothing about any Smyrnov affair, nothing precise. It seems to have been a political affair, which a few years ago raised a great deal of dust, as the saying goes, so much that in the end the general public couldn't see what had happened at all . . .

Unfortunately it rained today.

We passed my afternoon out on bail in her hotel. In any case Julika had left something in her hotel, an extremely urgent letter to Paris, and naturally I accompanied her. When the concierge, with a look that couldn't have been more equivocal, tried to make me wait in the vestibule, Julika said without a blush, "The gentleman is my husband." At this the concierge blushed and personally conducted me to the lift as though I were an honest man. I regarded it as a white lie, and hence with approbation. In the lift, alone with Julika, I expressly congratulated her on her quick-witted rejoinder; but later, when we were in her room, I said nothing more about it, which was probably a mistake. Does Julika really love me? It would be the last straw if I started getting jealous! The person in Paris, to whom Julika writes such urgent and such very thick letters, is called Dmitritch, doubtless one of the old Franco-Russian émigrés, Jean-Louis Dmitritch. She didn't tell me: I saw it on the

envelope which she put underneath her white handbag as we entered, so as not to forget it a second time,
and which I looked at secretly, while Julika was giving her hair a thorough combing in front of the mirror, after which she powdered her face and put on
rouge.

Dreamed about the uniform again.

A walk in the prison yard, whose square reminds me
of the cloisters of old monasteries. Is there anyone
who doesn't wish at times that he could become a
monk? Somewhere in Siberia or Peru, it makes no
odds, the same sun shines on us everywhere, and
the fact that it makes no odds is freedom; I know.
And then again the square of the prison yard with the
autumn branches, the cooing pigeons and particularly the idle figure which I contribute, reminds me
of the garden courtyard of the Museum of Modern
Art, New York, which is certainly larger and decorated with pieces of sculpture, but also enclosed by
façades and party-walls. Was I freer than now? I
could go where I liked, and yet it was a ghastly period;
it really isn't true that I yearn for those times or for
any period in my past life.

P.S. Julika: Either the vanished Stiller was simply mistaken when he compared this woman to a cold sea-
beast, or else it was his fault that Julika was not a
woman. Or else Julika has been through some experience since Stiller vanished that has fundamentally
changed her. What?

P.S. Perhaps he is an agent, this Jean-Louis Dmitritch,
or the caretaker of her dancing school, a general
factotum of seventy-seven, and her recent letter was
so thick because it contained forms Julika had to sign

—or what shall I say?—or he's a ladies' tailor, this Monsieur Dmitritch, or a subtenant, to whom she was sending the Agreement, or her doctor, her lawyer— there are thousands of possibilities . . .

My friend the public prosecutor is a gift from heaven. His smile takes the place of whisky for me. It is an almost imperceptible smile, which frees his interlocutor from a great deal of fuss and bother, and lets him be. How rare such a smile is. Such a kindly smile— very precise in its knowledge and by no means vague, yet not scornful—blossoms only where a person has once wept and admits to himself that he has wept.

Of course Herr Dr. Bohnenblust, the defending counsel provided for me by the State, is right: If I tell him a hundred times what a fire in a Californian redwood sawmill looks like, how the American negress makes up or how colorful New York appears during an evening snowstorm accompanied by lightning (it does happen) or how to land without papers at Brooklyn harbor, it doesn't prove that I've been there. We live in an age of reproduction. Most of what makes up our personal picture of the world we have never seen with our own eyes—or rather, we've seen it with our own eyes, but not on the spot: our knowledge comes to us from a distance, we are tele-viewers, tele-hearers, tele-knowers. One need never have left this little town to have Hitler's voice still ringing in one's ears, to have seen the Shah of Persia from a distance of three yards, and to know how the monsoon howls over the Himalayas or what it looks like six hundred fathoms beneath the sea. Anyone can know these things nowadays. Does it mean I have ever been to the bottom of the sea? Or even (like the Swiss) almost up Mount Everest?

And it's just the same with the inner life of man. Anyone can know about it nowadays. How the devil am I to prove to my counsel that I don't know my murderous impulses through C. G. Jung, jealousy through Marcel Proust, Spain through Hemingway, Paris through Ernst Jünger, Switzerland through Mark Twain, Mexico through Graham Greene, my fear of death through Bernanos, inability ever to reach my destination through Kafka, and all sorts of other things through Thomas Mann? It's true, you need never have read these authorities, you can absorb them through your friends, who also live all their experiences second-hand.

What an age! It means nothing any more to have seen swordfish, to have loved a mulatto girl, it could all have happened during a matinée performance of a documentary film; and as for having thoughts—good heavens, it's already a rarity in this age to meet a mind that's molded on one particular model, it's a sign of personality if someone sees the world with Heidegger and only with Heidegger; the rest of us swim in a cocktail containing pretty well everything and mixed in the most elegant manner by Eliot; we know our way about everywhere and, as I have said, not even our accounts of the visible world mean anything; there's no *terra incognita* nowadays (except Russia). So what's the point of telling all these stories? It doesn't mean you've been there. My counsel is right. And yet—

I swear:

There was a mulatto named Florence, a docker's daughter, I saw her every day and occasionally talked to her over the fence, a fence made of tar barrels and overgrown with brambles that kept us well apart. There was Florence with her gazelle-like walk. I dreamt about her, certainly, the wildest dreams; but nevertheless she was there next morning in the flesh. There was a tapping of high-heeled shoes on the wooden porch, and I immediately looked out through the holes in the curtains of my shingle hut hoping to see Florence; I was generally too late. But then I waited until she came out again with a bucket, emptied the frothy contents against my fence, and nodded; for at this moment I rushed impetuously out into the garden. She said, "Hallo," and I said, "Hallo." And I daren't describe her white smile in her brown face. People are familiar with this smile too from documentary films, from the newspapers, and even from a variety show in this very town, I know, and her singular voice can be heard on gramophone records, almost her voice . . . Then, as I "happened" to be in the garden, Florence would ask, "How's your cat?" The fact was that once, months ago, I had asked Florence after my hated cat, the agile beast which I once shut up in a refrigerator because of its reproachful spitting; I have referred to the incident already. Of course Florence knew nothing about this refrigerator intermezzo, but she must have guessed at my inner conflict with this black cat (she was gray, her name was Little Gray, but at night outside my window she was black) and thought I ought to show her (the cat) more love. But it was Florence I loved and the cat was perfectly well aware of the fact. So was Florence, in all probability . . . When Florence was not at home and I could not hear her singular voice, I used to go round the district from bar to bar looking for her. Once I actually found her.

Everyone knows how negroes dance. Her partner at the moment was a U. S. Army sergeant. The couple danced so well that a circle of spectators formed round them, and the enthusiasts in the circle began to clap their hands in an ever faster rhythm, and finally in a frenzy. The U. S. Army sergeant—a tall fellow with the slender hips of a lion, with two legs of rubber, with the half open mouth of pleasure and the sightless eyes of ecstasy, a fellow who had the chest and shoulders of a Michelangelo slave—reached the end of his strength; Florence danced alone. Now I could have taken over—if I'd been able to. Florence was still dancing alone when another came and spun her around, scarcely touching her fingers, circled around her, then took hold of her with the palm of his hand and swung her almost to the parquet floor, and then picked her up by the waist and lifted her so that her head almost struck the low ceiling; as she was poised in mid-air Florence made such a regal gesture with her arms, a gesture of such joyful triumph, that I felt like a cripple with my inexpressive white man's body; then she landed on the parquet floor as weightless as a bird. Now there was nothing to be heard but a dull jungle drumming, a soundless tremor, a kind of frenzied silence, while she went on dancing. A third partner was used up, and a fourth. Then suddenly, without being in the least exhausted, Florence laughed and stopped. As unself-consciously as a child, a very happy child, who has been allowed on the roundabout and is still beaming with pleasure, she made her way out between the little tables, no doubt to powder her nose, and saw me. "Hallo," she said, "Hallo"; she even added, "Nice to see you," and it almost consoled me for the bitter-sweetness of my confusion. For I knew very well that I could never content this girl.

This filled me with all the greater longing.

And then, one hot Sunday, I heard the long missed tapping of her high-heeled shoes again and dodged behind the curtains. I saw her father, the docker, in a black suit that made him look like a cross between a waiter and a clergyman, walking round with a broom tidying up the back garden; the bushes were decorated with colored ribbons, so was my tar-barrel fence, and Florence, dressed in an exaggerated evening dress, as gaudy as a parrot, was carrying armchairs out of the house. Florence's mother, a kind of mother earth, came with a gigantic cake, put it on the table with the white cloth, raised a black umbrella over it to keep it from being ruined by the sun, and placed flowers all round it. From behind my curtains I shared her excitement. While the docker was only concerned to have clean stairs and no litter in his garden and no dry twigs and certainly not an old tin (he threw it over my fence) and not even a match, in short, while the father was exclusively attendant upon his broom, mother and daughter had all four hands full; a great bowl of punch came out on to the table and under the umbrella, also glasses of every shape and size, and gradually the guests arrived too, families with children of all ages, all the women in gaudy evening dress, so that the back garden soon looked like an aviary, but all the men, of course, were in black with white shirts. One of them drove up in a Nash, and not a model from the year before last either; he also wore horn-rimmed spectacles. It was very hot.

Once the first greetings were over, the clan did not seem to have much to say to one another. The U. S. Army sergeant was also standing about. Even the tiny tots with their fuzzy hair and big eyes, the boys in white shirts, the girls with colored ribbons round their short pigtails, all behaved with model good manners. The grownups sat down and crossed their legs; some of them were smoking cigars. Besides a few ladies who were no longer negresses in color, who were recognizable as negresses only by the modelling of their faces, by their teeth, by their improbably slender fetlocks, but above all by the animal grace of their movements—the hand never moves without the movement flowing out of the arm, the head never turns without the movement rising up out of the back and radiating out into the shoulders; whether slow or quick, it is always a perfect movement, unconscious and without fidgeting, without rigidity in some other part of the body, it flows or hurries or rests, it is always in harmony with itself—in short, besides girls like Florence, who had already rid themselves of the frizzy hair, this clan also contained others, Africans with gray-black skin and grayish-purple lips, with hands like boxing gloves, fathers to whom their de-frizzed daughters were an embarrassment. The man with the new Nash no doubt set the tone; it was very hot, as I have said, but no one took off his black jacket, and this tediously conventional conduct, the standing around with cigars swapping small talk, the perfect behavior of the countless children which reminded me of performing animals in a circus, the stiff politeness between relations, the general uneventful-ness, the restraint and a joyless effort on the part of every family to keep its end up, despite unequal abilities, in the whole clan's demonstration of refined comportment, this utter caricature of white middle-class respectability without the faintest hint of Africa, was itself the great event for them, I believe: now they were really acting like white people.

When my doorbell rang and the docker invited me over for some punch, I went across, naturally not without first also putting on a white shirt and the darkest jacket I had. Everyone said, "Nice to see you," and in more personal conversation, "How do you like America?" The U. S. Army sergeant with the slender loins of a lion and the shoulders of a Michelangelo slave, I learnt, was only here on leave, normally he was in Frankfurt, so that the Russians shouldn't come too close to America. I asked in return, "How do you like Frankfurt?" and I could see from his studied ex-pressions of admiration that he lumped all us Euro-peans together. Then, at last, came my glorious Flor-ence, who gave me a glass of punch and said:

"This is Joe, my husband—!"

I congratulated them.

"And how's your cat?"

They were married that Sunday, and Joe remained on leave another three full weeks, that is to say Flor-ence was not to be seen in her father's house for three more weeks . . .

In love as I was, I couldn't let these weeks slip past without seeing Florence at least in church. I knew now which church she belonged to. It was called the Second Olivet Baptist Church and turned out to be a hut that was almost indistinguishable from the rest of the storage sheds, except for a wooden Gothic front dating, I should say, from the twenties of this century. On the stage inside, to left and right of the microphone, hung two large flags, the Stars and Stripes and a white flag, while for the rest, apart from a black piano, the room was as bare as a drill hall. The large congregation was murmuring in a curious fashion, and right at the front stood a negro in a light-colored Sunday suit, asking questions that always contained the word "sin." The congregation nodded, one or two called out, "Oh yes, my Lord, oh yes." The questions, begun in a casual, matter-of-fact tone, were repeated with slight variations, sounding more and more urgent with every repetition, although the voice grew no louder. Somewhere a young woman cried, "I know, my Lord, I know." Most people murmured, a few gazed indifferently into the air, but the woman yelled out and began to shout whole sentences and to moan so that you felt you ought to go to her assistance.

The questioner in his light-colored Sunday suit, unflinching in the repetition of his questions, was no longer a person but only the human repository of a voice that poured out over the congregation, his questions were calls, songs and finally yells that pierced me to the marrow, loud and agonizing. As though from a distance, like an echo, the murmuring congregation answered with lowered heads, some with their hands over their faces. The moaning woman had jumped up from her bench, a young negress with a ladylike hat, with white gloves which she stretched up towards heaven and holding a red handbag. "My Lord," she screamed, "my Lord," and then, unhin-

dered by anyone, she fell on her knees, disappeared
from my sight and whimpered as perhaps people
whimpered in a torture chamber, sounds of extreme
agony that were now indistinguishable from the
sounds of voluptuous delight; her voice melted into
sobs.

The prayer, the general prayer, came to an end as
the questioner, after becoming more and more pressing, died away into a voiceless ecstasy. Then came a
moment of breathlessness, of exhaustion; then relaxation, the heads in front of me bobbed up again, a matron at the piano played a few lazy rhythms, ushers
came round distributing gaudy fans, presented, as you
could read on them, by a hairdresser "around the corner," and everyone fanned himself . . .

I couldn't see Florence, but I caught sight of Joe in
his uniform; he was leaning against the wall, his arms
crossed, unmoved, as though looking down on these
people from the heights of Frankfurt. It was frightfully hot. During this pause a jovial priest at the microphone reminded us that the Lord had also saved
the poor children of Israel and the Lord knew very
well how hard it was nowadays to earn a dollar, therefore the Lord was not angry with the reluctant, for
the Lord had infinite patience, therefore the reluctant
would be given another chance to put something in the
bowl. Meanwhile the congregation was chatting gaily
and freely, like a social gathering in which everyone
feels at ease. When the collection had reached a point
where the Lord could feel satisfied for today, the
matron at the piano played an electrifying prelude, as
though in a dance hall, softened the tone as soon as
there was silence in the room, and accompanied the
sermon with almost inaudible, almost soundless jazz
that was just a low rhythm and fell almost imperceptibly but effectively silent when the preacher made
solemn pronouncements: "The Lord knows we are
poor people, but the Lord will lead us into the Prom-

ised Land, the Lord will protect us from Communism . . ."

All around the fans presented by the hairdresser as an advertisement were waving and the dust dancing in the rays of the sun. It smelt of gasoline, sweat and scent, I sat stewing in the sunlight that glared in through a torn blind, next to a lady in black silk, next to an old negro with ashen hair, an Uncle Tom, who restrained with trembling hand a lively grandchild who found it difficult to get used to me, the stranger. In front of me sat a young workman; he listened to the sermon as a soldier listens to the latest bulletin from the front. Beyond him I looked straight at the back of a very pretty girl's neck smothered in white powder. (Oh, this yearning to be white, this yearning to have straight hair, this lifelong striving to be different from the way one is created, this great difficulty in accepting oneself, I knew it and saw only my own longing from outside, saw the absurdity of our yearning to be different from what we are.) . . .

After the prayer, as we sat down again, the side doors opened and from the courtyard, from which came the horrid stink of gasoline, there appeared the choir of angels, some twenty negresses in white dresses. Florence among them. As well as some twenty negroes in white shirts and black ties, each of them carrying a black book. Now the stage was full. They started off triumphally, as though we had just entered the Promised Land, first the piano and then the voices; softly to begin with, a hum like a hot summer field, as though we were hearing from a distance a primeval river of lamentation, dull and monotonous as waves, then the sound slowly swelled until gradually it flooded everything, a cataract of voices, half anger and half exultation, a mighty song that sank again and trickled away without really ceasing, an endless river of longing, as broad as the Mississippi; a male voice rang out above the rest like a fanfare, hard, loud and lonely; then there was only the strange buzz, the voiceless hum as over a burning hot summer field, the heat in the hall, the dancing dust in the sunlight that glared in through the torn blind, the smell of gasoline and sweat and scent.

After three weeks Joe disappeared.

Once more I heard the tap of high-heeled shoes, Florence was back, even though married, and she actually called up to my window; I rushed down the steep stairs, miraculously without stumbling, although I wrenched a newel post out of the banister, and over to the tar barrel fence, where Florence was already standing on the other side of the brambles.

"What's happened to your cat?" she asked.

She was even holding the creature in her arms.

"D'you know she's hurt?" she said. "Awfully hurt."

That was the wound on the snout.

"And you don't feel any pity for her?" she said. "You are cruel, you just don't love her."

And with that she handed the beast over to me.

"You should love her."

"Why should I?"

"Of course you should."

That was my affair with the mulatto girl called Florence, and even now, I think of Florence whenever I hear high-heeled shoes; unfortunately the cat always comes to mind as well.

Julika has postponed her trip to Paris, so that we shan't lose our afternoon out on bail and because it would be a sin, she says, not to take advantage of such a golden October day.

Not another word about her former marriage.

Somehow it worries me.

Smyrnov was a Soviet agent passing through Switzerland. Personal description unknown. On the other hand, the Swiss Federal Police seem to know that this Smyrnov, known as The Boss, had the job of organizing the murder of a popular ex-Communist then living in Switzerland. Helpers and helpers' helpers were, as usual, known by code names: one was called "the Hungarian," another "the Swiss," and the latter is supposed to have negotiated with Smyrnov in Zurich on 18.1.1946 and may possibly also have done intelligence work. Shortly after the date in question, the Zurich municipal police reported Stiller's mysterious disappearance. Stiller seems to be something like the last hope of the Federal Police. Didn't he once fight against Franco? And since anti-Fascism, although it was once a Swiss virtue, is now enough to put a person under suspicion of being a Fellow Traveler—

What do I care!

P.S. My counsel has absolutely no sense of humor regarding the fact that Switzerland is not only a small country, but is being made even smaller by world events. This frequently makes our discussions difficult. He is (understandably) opposed to the future. Any change frightens him. He pins his hopes upon the past; but at the same time he knows that it is not the past but the future which is coming, and that makes him more hostile than ever towards the future. How far my counsel is representative of the national outlook in this respect, I don't know. He always feels assailed, even when I have no intention of attacking him, and this leads to severe bouts of self-satisfaction.

"A country's greatness," he says, "is not to be measured by its area nor by the number of its inhabitants; our country's greatness lies in the greatness of its spirit."

This is quite true, and what irritates me into contradicting him is only the unquestioning, self-satisfied assumption that the Swiss do not lack spiritual greatness. I become argumentative, you can't do justice to the self-righteous, I ask for manifestations of this spiritual greatness and bow before a storm of historical personages which my counsel lets loose on me every time this subject crops up. But when I point out that I didn't ask for historical, but only for contemporary manifestations of Swiss spiritual greatness, my counsel becomes thoroughly personal.

"Your hatred of Switzerland is pathological!"

"What do you mean, hatred?"

"You're trying to pretend you're not Swiss and therefore not Stiller," he says. "But you won't fool me; your hatred of Switzerland certainly doesn't prove you're not Swiss. On the contrary," he shouts, because I laugh, "it gives you away."

My counsel is mistaken: It's not Switzerland I hate, but untruthfulness. That, though it may often come to the same thing in the end, is fundamentally different. It may be that as a prisoner I am particularly sensitive to their slogan of freedom. What the devil do they make of their legendary freedom? Whenever it becomes in the least costly they are as submissive as any bootlicking German. The truth is, who can afford to have a wife and children, a family with dependents, as is right and proper, and at the same time a free opinion in anything but minor matters? For that you need money, so much money that you don't need commissions or clients or social goodwill. But anyone who has piled up so much money that he can really afford a free opinion is generally in agreement with prevailing conditions anyhow. So where is their glorious freedom, which they hang up on the wall like a desiccated laurel wreath? Where is it in their everyday existence? My counsel shakes his head.

"If you talk like that before the court," he says quite hopelessly, "before the assembled Press—"

There we have it.

"You'll only do yourself harm," he says.

Probably the sort of freedom that people here claim to possess cannot exist at all; there are only degrees of bondage, and I willingly admit that theirs is a comparatively mild form of bondage. I am very grateful to them for this, but I am not on that account obliged to like their national untruthfulness. I know he gives another name to this untruthfulness in its most dangerous form—when it is bound up with a flag and the claim to be sacred and inviolable: he calls it patriotism. It's stupid of me to get so excited that I take the whole thing seriously. You can't talk to these Swiss about freedom, simply because they can't bear to have freedom questioned, to have it regarded not as a Swiss monopoly, but as a problem. They are altogether frightened of any open question; they think just so far as they have the answer in their pockets all the time, a practical answer, an answer that is useful to them. Which means they don't think at all—they merely justify themselves. Under no circumstances dare they cast doubt upon themselves. Isn't this the very hallmark of spiritual bondage? They can imagine France or Great Britain perishing; but not Switzerland; God would never allow that, unless He turned Communist, for Switzerland is innocence. Incidentally, I have noticed how frequently my counsel justifies Switzerland by pointing to the misdeeds of the Russians, but prefers to say nothing about Hitler's; I have observed how flattered he is as a Swiss by the terrible fact that elsewhere there are concentration camps. What is he actually trying to prove by this as regards his own country? Once I ventured to say:

"You are lucky, Herr Doktor, that Hitler threatened your sovereignty and hence your trade; that stopped you from developing towards Fascism yourselves. But surely you don't believe that the Swiss bourgeoisie, alone in the world, would show no tendency towards Fascism if it happened to be good for trade instead of harmful? The test will come, Herr Doktor, make no mistake about that; I shall be interested to see what happens."

At this he packed his brief-case.

"As a free Swiss—," he said and seemed to be offended again. "Why are you laughing?"

Free! Free! Free! In vain I tried to make him tell me, free from what? And above all, free for what? He simply told me he was free, and I too, sitting on the bed and shaking my head, would be free, if only I had the sense to be their missing Stiller. With his hand on the latch, ready to step out into his freedom, he said in a tone of mild concern:

"Why are you shaking your head?"

One ought to be able to think. And one ought to be able to express oneself in such a way that they have nothing left but their truth. I merely see that even their civil liberty, of which they are so proud, as though it were human freedom pure and simple, is really pretty worthless; and I can deduce that their whole country, as a State among States, enjoys just as little freedom as any small power among great powers; it is only thanks to their unimportance (the fact that today they lie outside history) that they can delude themselves they are independent, and also thanks to their commercial good sense, which forces them to be polite to the mighty for the sake of trade, and anyone who has no complaint to make against the mighty, because he lives so well on them, will always imagine himself free and independent. But what has all this to do with freedom? I see their faces: Are they free? And their gait, their ugly gait: Is that the gait of free people? And their fear, their fear of the future, their fear of one day being poor, their fear of life, their fear of dying without life insurance, and finally their fear that the world might change, their absolutely panic fear of spiritual audacity—no, they are no freer than I am, as I sit here on my bed knowing that the step into freedom (of which no ancestor can relieve us) is always a tremendous step, a step with which we leave behind everything that has previously seemed like solid ground, and a step that no one can hinder once I have the strength to take it. For it is the step into faith, everything else is not freedom, but empty chatter. But for this very reason, perhaps my counsel is right once more: Why should I say this before the assembled Press. Why offend people? In the last resort it is my own business whether I ever become free, free of them as well—a very lonely business.

Again and again I observe that I can talk to my public prosecutor, my accuser, better than to my so-called defending counsel. This leads to confidences that are not without danger. Today he showed me a photograph of Sibylle, his wife, who always sends her good wishes. We spoke for a long time about marriage—of course, quite generally. My public prosecutor considers marriage (certain experiences have manifestly given him cause to doubt it) quite possible, though difficult. Naturally he means a real, living marriage. Among the prerequisites he numbers: the knowledge on both sides that we have no claim to our partner's love; life-long readiness for living experience, even if it endangers the marriage, in other words an ever open door for the unexpected, not for little adventures, but for the risk—the moment two partners feel sure of each other, they have generally already lost each other. Further, equal rights for man and woman; renunciation of the view that sexual fidelity is enough, and equally of the other view that without sexual fidelity there is no marriage at all; the most far-reaching and honest, but not reckless, frankness over difficulties of this kind. It also seems important to him that both should face their environment courageously—a couple has already ceased to be a couple when one or both of the partners conspires with those around them to put pressure on the other; further, the courage to be able to think, without reproach, that our partner might be happier without us; further, the fairness never to persuade the partner verbally or otherwise cause him to believe that his withdrawal from the marriage would kill us, and so on . . . All this, as I have said, he put in general terms while I was looking at the photograph of his wife, a face that was not at all general, a unique face, lively, lovable in the highest degree, much more enthralling than his words, though the latter were perfectly true, as he referred to his unspoken experience with this face. Then I returned the photograph.

"Yes," said my public prosecutor, "what were we actually talking about?"

"You were saying that your wife is expecting a baby."

"Yes," he said, "we're very happy about it."

"Let's hope all goes well."

"Yes," he said, "let's hope so."

Jean-Louis Dmitritch is the pianist in her dancing school, half Russian and very sensitive, a gentleman between forty and fifty, unmarried, gifted—and Julika is delighted with this jewel, she says, and calls him her right hand man in Paris. Perhaps I shouldn't have asked. Perhaps Julika now imagines I'm jealous.

My friend and prosecutor asked me whether I knew *Anna Karenina*. Then, whether I knew Effi Briest. Finally whether I could not visualize a quite different attitude from the one adopted by the deserted husband in this masterpiece. A more generous attitude, he meant—and then he began to tell a story . . .

My public prosecutor seemed very much preoccupied by the fact that he himself found great difficulty in taking this more generous attitude, which he could imagine a deserted husband adopting. I listened to him the whole afternoon. Somewhat bewildered by his own frankness (he didn't really want to be frank, but felt increasingly compelled to be precise in order to dispel all sorts of misunderstandings and keep to the concrete example within his own experience) he asked from time to time, "Can you understand that?" It was a story like a thousand others, and therefore easy to understand. I could also understand his need to see that missing Stiller whom his wife, as I heard, had loved to the very limit of the (for him) bearable.

Knobel, my warder, has been behaving rather oddly for some time, he's always in a hurry to leave my cell. It didn't escape my notice. Today he said straight out:

"Herr Stiller—"

I just looked at him.

"Heaven above," he said, turning away in shame like a traitor, "I was the only one who believed you—"

Julika has convinced them all.

"Herr Stiller," he said, "I can't help it being like that, heavens above, I don't blame you for having told me all that rubbish, but I can't help it—"

I ate and said nothing.

4th *Notebook*

I CAN'T get out of my head the little story about the flesh-pink cloth at Genoa, which my friend and prosecutor told me yesterday. I see him—we'll call him Rolf—in the night train which he boarded blindly, not caring where it was going, as glad as a fugitive that any train was still leaving at midnight. He thought it might be easier to bear while moving, and then he wanted at all costs to avoid meeting his wife again, after having stood up quite well to the first shock. It may be, too, that he expected to gain some advantage from crossing the frontier. The further the better! So he was sitting in the night train, a gentleman without any luggage, alone in his second-class compartment. The train stopped at daybreak at Milan, in an empty station. An Italian railwayman tapped the wheels with a hammer; otherwise the whole world seemed to be sleeping like Sibylle, who now, having told her husband, had nothing more to worry about. Puerile plans for revenge passed through his head; the wait in this station made him all the more aware of his lack of any goal. Suddenly a cock crowed somewhere, quickly followed by a second and a third; finally a whole goods train of fowls waiting here for the morning market was crowing. And then, when at last the wheels turned again, Rolf slept in spite of everything, only occasionally waking to the consciousness that one looks stupid with one's mouth open; yet he was just as alone in his compartment as ever. He did everything in his power to sleep, for the longer he slept the greater the chance that when he woke up it would all turn out to have been nothing but a bad dream.

In Genoa the sun was already shining. Rolf stood in front of the station arcade, so tired he would have liked just to sit down on the steps like the beggars, a gentleman with no luggage, but with a superfluous overcoat on his arm, rather unshaven too; he stared at the hooting traffic, the rattling and tinkling tramcars in the shady canyons of the narrow streets, the crowds of people, all of whom seemed to have a goal —so this was Genoa. He had already lit a cigarette. What next? He noticed that someone was slipping along between the arcades watching him, probably a moneychanger, and he strolled away. In a cheap bar, surrounded by porters and taxi drivers and therefore solicited from all sides, while a scruffy individual washed down the stone floor between his far too perfect shoes, he drank black coffee and observed his total lack of any feeling.

"Whether we get a divorce, or what we're going to do about it," she had said, "I don't know myself yet. For the moment all I want is for you to leave me in peace."

Another thing his wife had said was:

"You don't have to give me my freedom. What do you mean by that? I can take freedom for myself, if I need it."

It was this remark in particular, it seems, which so infuriated the husband that in the broad daylight of Genoa he talked aloud to himself and walked along without really knowing where he was. It didn't matter anyway. Somewhere among warehouses, railway lines and tar barrels. Yes, there were even moments when he loudly cursed his wife beyond the Alps, with words that did him all the more good the more vulgar they were. He used expressions (so he says) of such crude, unvarnished obscenity as he had never before heard from his own 'lips. When someone unexpectedly addressed him he was completely taken aback. He hadn't the slightest wish to see the sights of Genoa. Never in his life had he felt so defenseless —as though anyone could read his jumbled thoughts. At this moment he was incapable of saying No to a boatman, and let himself in for a trip round the harbor. The sea turned out to be gray lead flecked with iridescent patches of oil. Rolf sat on a seat covered with worn cushions, as tense as Rodin's *Thinker* and quite unable to take in the running commentary provided by the Italian oarsman sitting behind him, which was included in the price. Hot galley water spurted from the side of a ship. At one point they rowed over a sunken merchantman; its seaweed-covered iron plates rose threateningly up out of the filthy depths. Riveting hammers echoed in the distance. For Rolf, of course, it was all like a film, in color and even with smells, but a film—visible but unreal. From time to time there was a thin siren-wail, carried away by the wind and split up into echoes, impossible to tell where it came from or what it meant, since none of the great steamships actually put out to sea. It was hot. Trails of bluish stench hung over the harbor water. Only a large fishing vessel chugged by, and the buoys, whose mildewed chains faded away into the murky depths, rocked hideously. They rowed on past wharfs and jetties, everything, whether of wood or stone, was smothered in greasy black grime. At least time was passing. Here and there the belly of a dead fish or sailor's washing flashed white; the sound of singing came up out of a cabin; everything a trip round the harbor could offer was there, even a gray battleship with mantled guns and mountains of coal with white seagulls on top of them. In the distance the city of Genoa rose in tiers up the hillside, almost real again . . .

Sibylle had also said: "I'd rather you didn't ask me any more questions now. He's a man, that's all I'll tell you, and he's very different from you. I can't say any more. Perhaps I really love him, I don't know yet. All I ask now is that you should leave me in peace."

. . . Rolf finished his trip round the harbor with the look of a man who has been hit on the head by a falling plank, and paid what the rogue demanded of him. Wine was now his only wish, a great deal of wine. The story about the cloth—of course my public prosecutor told it far more graphically than I can—began outside the restaurant, when an American sailor asked him the way to a certain street. How was Rolf to know? But the sailor trotted along beside him. His American sounded genuine, and therefore almost incomprehensible to Rolf. But this much he did grasp: At two o'clock, in other words pretty soon, the sailor had to leave port—there actually was a ship lying with steam up—and the parcel was a present for a wartime Italian comrade. Rolf had his own troubles, God knows, but the despondent sailor clung to him like a leech with his extremely confused story and the parcel tied with string, which, since he could not find his wartime Italian comrade, he now had to sell before his ship, which was indisputably under steam, left port; for there was no sense in taking this magnificent piece of cloth back to America with him.

Rolf wasn't interested. To rid himself of the fellow and get to his wine, he beckoned to a passer-by, a youngish and quite ordinary-looking Genoese, who might perhaps know the street the sailor was looking for, or want the cloth. And so *basta!* Only the Geno-

ese, visibly annoyed at being delayed in his purpose-
ful walk, knew no American and the sailor no Italian.
Rolf had to act as interpreter. It didn't suit him at all;
that wasn't what he had traveled through the whole
night to Genoa for, and naturally the suspicion that
he had fallen for some sort of racket also crossed his
mind. But where was the catch? His Italian was just
as inadequate as his American, and since the young
Genoese had no more desire for cloth than Rolf and
was very reluctant to have anything more to do with
the matter at all, there seemed no prospect that the
two of them would ever strike a bargain. Rolf had already started walking away twice, but he had been
fetched back by the excited sailor, who was simply
lost without an interpreter. After a great deal of haggling (while this was going on, Rolf at least forgot
his wife), the Genoese led them with a wink—a sign
that one is willing to engage in an illegal transaction—
through ever narrower alleyways full of steps and
children, through crooked chasms filled with multi-
colored washing and hullabaloo, until in the half-light
of a passageway between two houses he was ready to
inspect the cloth that was for sale.

Rolf smoked a cigarette, temporarily relieved of his
duties as interpreter; no words were exchanged at this
stage. The Genoese, a less sympathetic character than
the sailor because of his air of contemptuous superiority, pulled two or three threads out of the parcel,
licked them and held them up against the dim light of
shady backyards, while the sailor kept glancing at his
watch. It wasn't wool, he said. Anyway, not pure
wool—half and half, perhaps. Rolf returned to his interpreting, toning down the Genoese's remarks a trifle.
All right, thirty thousand lire, that was his last word!

When it came at last to paying, the Genoese unfortunately had only ten thousand lire on him, the rest
was at home of course, while the sailor couldn't wait
a minute longer. What now? Perhaps the interpreter

could help out. Now they had come to the point, Rolf knew this in spite of all his abstraction; and despite his suspicions he put his hand into his not particularly well-filled wallet—not out of pity for the supposed sailor, but (so he says) merely out of a fear of seeming narrow-minded. The sailor, half grateful and half angry at having been beaten down so far, bundled together the thirty thousand lire, of which twenty thousand were Rolf's, and hurried off with a curt farewell. It was one-thirty! Notwithstanding the objectionable way in which he had behaved towards the sailor, the Genoese acted like a gentleman as far as Rolf was concerned. He refused to take the cloth, insisting that Rolf should keep it until he had the lire. As security—he could feel Rolf's distrust. Again they passed through the back streets of poverty, Rolf with the parcel tied with string under his arm, until the Genoese—too offended to speak as they were walking along—finally said, "*Mia casa, attenda qui, vengo subito.*"

Rolf saw a dilapidated Renaissance gateway; he had no idea where he was—somewere in Genoa. In the nearby harbor a ship's siren droned dully. Overcome by the noonday heat even in this shady alley with its damp and moldy walls, by the silence, for it was far from the traffic, his fatigue after the night in the train —and that wasn't all: twenty-four hours ago Rolf had still been in London taking part in an international conference of lawyers, and then (yesterday) the rather bumpy flight, the supper with his strangely elated wife, then the closed door of her bedroom, then its opening and so on—then daybreak at Milan with crowing cocks (all this in twenty-four hours—it was rather much) and now to find himself in this back street of mildewed poverty where slops trickled down the walls—and back came the knowledge that a fact does not cease to be a fact because you forget it for a time, no, it kept returning again and again, her face full of happiness with another man, it wasn't a bad dream, but more real than this Genoa with its alleys and children and these tangible walls, and on top of it this heat that made you tear off your tie, and this parcel that Rolf had to carry—overcome by it all Rolf simply couldn't help falling into a heavy sleep, in spite of the danger that the Genoese might do the dirty on him . . .

It was almost four o'clock when Rolf, my public prosecutor, woke up again sitting with his back to a wall and on his knees the damned parcel that had served him as a pillow. Naturally there was no trace of the Genoese waking him up with lire. Children were playing in a courtyard, mothers were shouting, "Ettore, Ettore," and in between, a tone higher, "Giuseppina, Giuseppina," and there below in the alleyway sat a strange gentleman with gold wrist-watch waiting in vain for his twenty thousand lire. Rolf stood up. On closer inspection, the rather mossy Renaissance gateway, through which the Genoese had disappeared, did not lead to a house at all, but simply to the next street. And there stood Rolf as though only now grasping for the first time the fact that Sibylle was in another man's arms. And during the haggling over the cloth, he had half-consciously looked at this young Geneose from time to time and asked himself whether Sibylle could have loved hair like his, ears like his, lips like his, hands like his; anyone might be the other man. Rolf only knew, "He's very different from you," and this might apply to several million men. As he stood in front of the empty Renaissance gateway, Rolf was really almost glad not to see the slick young Genoese again. But he had lost pretty well all his ready cash. Worse still, it was a discomfiture, just when he would have liked to cut a dash because of his wife; the blow to his pride was incomparably more serious than the loss of twenty thousand lire, irreparable. He dared not look at the parcel tied with string and supposed to contain gent's suiting cloth, which was his security. In any case he could only go to a cheap hotel, where the fact that this bundle was his sole luggage would not arouse too much comment. He stood in a hotel room with flowered wallpaper, bathed in sweat and at a loss what to do next in this city of Genoa. He threw the parcel into the wardrobe, picked up the jug, filled the basin and tried to wash without soap, without a toothbrush, without a comb—

He stayed in Genoa four days.

Rolf (so he says himself) had never foreseen that his marriage, his own, might go on the rocks like so many other marriages around him. He saw no reason why it should. He loved Sibylle and lived in the belief that he had found his own solution to the marriage problem. It had long since ceased to be a marriage in the classical sense of monogamy. But that was how it was, and to make up for it Sibylle had the child, a boy named Hannes, who made up for a great deal during the first few years of his life. It wasn't the life Sibylle had dreamed of, but it wasn't hell either— just a marriage like so many others, and every year they went for a fine trip together, to Egypt for example. The idea of separating had never occured to them, and in all the troubles they had passed through up to now both parties had obviously felt at bottom absolutely sure of one another. A fancy-dress ball flirtation, of which Sibylle made a demonstration, he granted his dear wife with magnanimity. He had other worries just then: the problem was whether to become a public prosecutor or not, a crucial decision, and it occupied his mind a good deal more than the fact that Sibylle was going for walks with her fancy-dress pierrot. Rolf didn't even ask his name. And then he had always been of the opinion that one shouldn't be narrow-minded about marriage; he evidently had a very serious theory as to how much free-

dom should be introduced into a marriage—a man's
theory, Sibylle called it. She couldn't stand this theory,
it seems; and yet it was based on the knowledge afforded by various sciences. And naturally this theory
presupposed complete equality of the sexes. It wasn't
simply a clever male excuse, as Sibylle frequently said
—not merely a clever excuse. Rolf was really perfectly serious about it: his profession had shown him
the misery, the hypocrisy, that springs from a view of
marriage which has nothing to do with reality, and
what he cared about was the idea of a viable marriage
and avoiding the indignity of a life of self-deception.
Rolf had a great deal to say on this subject; Sibylle
called these talks his "lectures," but when asked for
her opinion—and she was asked very often, because
Rolf didn't want to entrench himself in a private doc-
trine—she merely answered with the feminine argument that life couldn't be solved with theories . . .

It seems that the fancy-dress pierrot was still on his
mind, even if this preoccupation was unexpressed and
perhaps even unconscious. Rolf had suddenly decided
to build his own house—a house of their own had
been Sibylle's fondest wish from the beginning, and
Rolf, a man of action, had already bought the land.
Sibylle was strange. She knew the land, they'd been
after it for years; now he had bought it, and Sibylle
showed no sign of jubilation. A week later he brought
the young architect to black coffee, a certain Sturzenegger, who raved about consistent modernism and
called upon Rolf's obviously abstracted wife for an exact statement of her requirements. A double bedroom
or two single bedrooms, for example, and everything
was now extremely urgent. In the middle of the discussion (says my public prosecutor) came a telephone call, Sibylle answered it as usual, fell silent,
said No and Yes and No, quickly hung up again, asserted it was a wrong number, and was very jumpy.
Well, well, thought Rolf, the fancy-dress pierrot; and

the discussion of sketches proceeded. Sibylle took refuge in a studied interest, and everything seemed all right to her, whether like this or like that, as though she were never going to live in the projected house at all.

At the end of the black coffee (my public prosecutor cannot remember how the subject cropped up) the young architect talked about an Eskimo who offered a white stranger his wife, in order to be hospitable, and was so offended when the stranger did not make use of her that he seized his guest by the throat and banged his head against the wall of the igloo until he was dead. Everyone laughed, of course. Thereupon the young architect came out with another funny story of something that had happened to a friend of his called Stiller during the Spanish Civil War. This was the first time my public prosecutor had ever heard Stiller's name. He remembered little of the story from the Spanish Civil War—only something about a Russian gun that failed to go off. On the other hand he clearly recalls that his wife, who had previously been so abstracted, showed a boundless interest in this Russian gun. And when the architect had gone, she went humming through all the rooms. Rolf imagined her joy was connected with the new house, but could not refrain from remarking, "It sounds as though you're in love." And as she didn't deny it, he added, "You like the young architect, eh?" It was a joke. "Do you think so?" she asked. "Admit it!" said he. "You're hurting me!" said she. "I admit it, but let go of me!" It was a joke, as I said, and Rolf had to get back to work; Sibylle put the three coffee cups on the tray, and that was that . . .

The four days in Genoa:

This (so my public prosecutor says) was the most ludicrous ordeal of his life, but not the most useless. He learnt a number of things about himself: First, an unsuspected amount of sentimentality, of which he had previously had no inkling—he drank and drank, until he had to leave the restaurant because he was crying; then the primitive nature of his reactions—he stared after every reasonably clean skirt and took refuge for hours at a time in thoughts of the cheapest sort of revenge; then the shallowness of his emotions —in four days and four nights (so he says) he only achieved a few minutes of real suffering that threw him to his knees in the flowery hotel bedroom, without it being a pose or the effect of alcohol, and consumed the last residue of reproach and the last residue of self-pity; but above all, his inability to love a woman if he was not her idol, to love her without claiming gratitude, consideration, admiration and so forth. It was an ordeal.

Lying fully dressed on his iron bed smoking, he tormented himself with shamelessly precise imaginings of his wife giving herself to the other man. This was not the ordeal, but the relaxation he allowed himself. The ordeal was the realization, the involuntary admission, that up till then he had been very much mistaken about the level of his emotions, about his maturity. Not even his will (so he says) stood up to this test: he had gone off without a word, but was later unable to restrain himself from sending his secretary a sealed letter to be handed to his wife if she asked for news of him, a letter with his address in case of need. For four days no such case of need seemed to have arisen. He wasn't missed! Day after day, always half an hour after the arrival of the northern trains, he asked for *posta restanta*, in vain. In between there were hours of solemn dignity, certainly: he managed to read Churchill's memoirs in English, he sat in the guise of a neatly shaved man of leisure in the morning sunshine, drank his red campari and learnt what went on behind the scenes during the Second World War— and without looking at the clock; but at bottom he was only waiting to be missed and sought with every

possible means, indeed, he wouldn't have been surprised to meet the ruefully searching Sibylle somewhere in the streets of Genoa. Her "contemptuous"
silence, which presented itself to him in the shape of
the marble hall of an Italian main post office, made him
turn pale every time. How often did this woman force
him to the same discovery—how incapable he was of
living according to his own theories.

On the fourth day, at last, there was a telegram.
With the typical collapse of the man who has been
saved, who is at first completely overcome by the relaxation of tension, he sat for a while before opening
it, wearily calm with relief, whatever his wife might
have written. But it wasn't from his wife at all: his
secretary merely had to know when he was coming
back. That was enough. He laughed. It affected him
(so he says) like a very cold shower. He stuffed the
telegram into the wastepaper basket and resolved without further reflection to take the next train. Only
he hadn't got the twenty thousand lire with which to
pay the hotel bill.

What was he to do? He must see how and where
he could sell his security, the American gent's suiting
cloth, and as quickly as possible. The best train went
at noon. At all costs not another night train! It was
about ten in the morning when Rolf went out through
the vestibule of his hotel, feeling rather embarrassed,
because the parcel under his arm was very tattered,
and determined despite his inhibitions to find a clothes
shop—not too high-class of course—and try his talent
as a salesman. It was very hot again; but he kept his tie
on in order to make a better impression. He gathered
from the half insolent, half pitying way in which he
was turned away from the first shop, that he would do
better to find an even poorer district. It was already
striking eleven o'clock when he entered the fourth
shop, where at least he was not immediately shown the
door, but allowed for the first time to untie his parcel.

He was lucky, there were no customers in this shop. A corner of his American gents' suiting was enough: the owner of the shop, a pale dandy with a thin mustache, laughed in his face. Rolf didn't want to make a profit, but just to recover some of the money he had lost, so that he could pay his hotel bill; he was cheap, perhaps too cheap, to judge by the treatment he received. The dandy with the thin mustache went on reading his paper as though Rolf were no longer there. In this shop, for the first time, he didn't talk about a unique opportunity, but about his actual situation. The man behind the counter just turned away and yawned into his rustling paper, without showing the slightest interest even of a purely human kind, without even showing any sign of a sympathy that would have cost him nothing, till Rolf went away of his own accord with his parcel under his arm.

He felt rather dejected even without imagining his wife's expression of happy superiority. In fact, to judge by the corner, it was a pretty lousy piece of cloth, rough, anything but wool, no question of half and half, and on top of that a pattern such as he (my public prosecutor) wouldn't have worn at any price, a loud, vulgar pattern—and pink!

He sat down on the steps of an old church, surrounded by cooing pigeons with rings of blue, green and violet iridescence round their necks, and considered—or tried to consider—what was to be done under the circumstances. Behind him stood a delightful baroque façade—Sibylle understood more about these things than he did. Now there was nothing to prevent him from taking off his tie and rolling up his cuffs (which were probably pretty dirty anyway) under his coatsleeves. He was glad that at least his wife couldn't see him—the rest of mankind could stare if it wanted to. Up above, in the baroque façade—the sun was shining on the upper volutes and their glaring ochre yellow stood out against the noonday blue of the sky—it struck twelve. His train left in two hours. His gold watch also had to be put out of sight, that was it, before he went to the old-clothes-men in the back streets round the harbor, where the goods hung on the peeling walls—shirts, trousers, socks, hats. He was no longer concerned (so he says) about the lire, but about his bare self-confidence, which he was carrying around under his arm in the shape of an increasingly tattered parcel. Why hadn't he gone to these old-clothes-men in the first place!

He felt more confident than at any other time that morning, positively exhilarated by the thought of what a story this would be to tell at parties. He whistled, or rather he heard himself whistling, although he was well aware that he did not feel at all easy. It was a back alley near the port, a district where first law prevailed. For fear of being beaten up as a swindler, here where there were no police, he undid his parcel for the first time in a side-alley to make sure there was really enough of the material for a gentleman's suit. Yes, it was quite long enough. So Rolf rolled the cursed material up again, which was no easy matter if it was not to touch the pavement and so stink of urine. Then he approached an old-clothes-man and opened the conversation by asking the way to the station, offered him a cigarette, chatted good-humoredly and referred in a casual way to a piece of suiting he had bought yesterday to have made up by an Italian tailor, but you know the way it is, he'd just received a telegram and had to leave in a hurry, then he cursed the customs who wouldn't let a length of cloth through—a long and stupid story which he thought crafty, positively oriental. But his own suit with the unmistakable traces of trouser-creases, his all too faultless shoes, not to mention the golden seal ring, which had naturally been carefully noted, were not calculated to arouse comradely trust in this neighborhood. There was nothing to stop him unpacking his wares in the open, however. A few women with babies at the breast and glances which Rolf did not consider impartial, followed the transaction with suspicious curiosity. The secondhand-clothes dealer, an old man with brown teeth and garlicky breath, felt the cloth very fully, which gave Rolf a faint hope—so faint that he dared not quote a price, but asked how much the dealer would give for it. "*Niente.*" Rolf would have been satisfied with a thousand lire, a thousand lire for his self-confidence. In order to get at least that much, he said two thousand was his rock-bottom price. "No." One thousand then? "No." Very well, how much? "*Niente.*" The women with the babies grinned and walked off. Rolf rolled the cloth up again. For the seal ring, however, said the old-clothes-man, he would give thirty thousand. Rolf laughed. For the faultless shoes the old-clothes-man, without having to feel them, offered seven thousand lire, as though he (my public prosecutor) could walk home bare-foot. He was spared nothing in this city of Genoa!

Finally there was only one thing left for it: to give the parcel away. As quickly as possible. For instance to a young man standing beside an advertisement pillar playing a mouth-organ, obviously out of work, his empty cap lying on the pavement. At the last moment, however, when Rolf noticed his black wooden leg, he couldn't do it. Forward once more. A young ragamuffin begging for cigarettes, and an old grandfather with a pram held together with wire didn't seem the right people either. To give away a piece of material one would under no circumstances wear oneself wasn't so easy, and Rolf wandered in all directions through a neighborhood whose poverty was anything but picturesque. It's always a shock to see the ragged condition in which the majority of all mankind lives. Rolf came to a halt. He felt how bourgeois was his desire to be fair, to find the person who most deserved his gift; he made up his mind to turn down the next street and present the first person he met with the material for a gent's suit. The first person he met was a young woman shuffling along in her slippers. Forward once more. The next was a whistling policeman, and then the street came to an end. In a small square with a tree they were playing football. Rolf was only in the way and through standing in the goalkeeper's line of vision the obvious cause of one side shooting into its own goal, as the result of which a violent quarrel broke out between the youthful teams. Forward once more. He was utterly exhausted again. His train left in forty minutes. But where could he get rid of his gift? A drunken man staggered out of a noisy tavern, but he was too truculent, too dangerous to be given it. Of course Rolf could simply have thrown his parcel down in the street—but that would have been capitulating. Later, he circled for some time round a blind beggar with outstretched hand. That wouldn't do either he thought.

In the last resort he could pay his hotel bill by post later on—besides, his overcoat was still at the hotel. But of course it wasn't a question of whether he could pay his hotel bill at all. It was a question of how he was to rid himself of this parcel. What real reason was there why he shouldn't throw it away? Rolf tried. Nothing could be easier, he thought, than to lose a parcel; nevertheless, his temples were pulsing when, pushed by his commonsense, he put the project into execution. He dropped it in the crowd in front of a red traffic light, squeezed across the street in the general crush and thought he was saved—for just then the policeman blew his whistle, the traffic changed and the street behind him was temporarily blocked. To have his hands free at last gave him a feeling of relief, a new *joie de vivre*, as though nothing had happened to Sibylle either.

Rolf lit a cigarette, without looking back to see

what had happened to the nightmare parcel, and he didn't need to, for a poorly dressed but attractive young woman pulled at his sleeve and handed back to the absent-minded gentleman the parcel which she had picked up. Rolf dared not deny that it was his, this shabby parcel with its dirty paper and cheap string that scarcely held the pink cloth together any more. Was he condemned to carry this pink cloth through the rest of his earthly life? Ten minutes before the train left, he was still standing helplessly with the parcel under his arm—five minutes before it left. He put off the capitulation (as he calls it) until the last minute. The carriage doors were already shut when Rolf stepped on to the footboard, and the train was just starting. As though the empty seats were not for him, not for defaulters and deserted husbands, Rolf stood outside in the corridor as far as Milan. What would Sibylle say to him? Naturally he still grossly overestimated her need to concern herself with him. After Milan he was not alone in the corridor: a Swiss got into conversation with him, talkative as most people are when they run into a fellow-countryman abroad. Fortunately they soon reached the frontier.

After the train left Chiasso he sat in the dining-car, staring out of the window all the time, so that no one passing along the train should recognize him. It never struck him how noticeable he was gazing out of the window all the time, regardless of whether the train was passing through a tunnel or not. With the active imagination that accompanies self-pity, Rolf, more than ever before on a journey, was gazing into the past, and as he looked back he could remember no happiness without Sibylle, not a single significant hour without Sibylle. Everything else was chaff, not worth a thought. Rather suddenly Sibylle had become the whole meaning and content of his life, and now this meaning had passed over to another man, had been.

transferred to a fancy-dress pierrot, or a Genoese with jet black hair, or a young architect, or whoever it was, had simply been transferred. From Göschenen on, rain splashed diagonally across the window-panes.

The best thing, thought Rolf, would be not to let her notice anything: his detachment should annihilate her. Rolf had only to remember her shameless face and the detachment came of its own accord, in response to her face that was not only happy and estranged by happiness, but scornful, insolent, arrogant, triumphant over him, and it would have been the last straw if he, Rolf, with his theories, had started reproaching her: she would have laughed out loud and her contempt would have been plain to see. Detachment seemed to him now the only reply, detachment that was free from indignation, free from accusation and complaint, but a detachment that would bring this hussy to her knees. He had made up his mind to this and his hometown lake was already in sight. In preparation for the future with his hussy, Rolf even began whistling in the restaurant-car, but he stopped, of course, the moment he heard himself, and called urgently for the bill, as though this would get him to Zurich quicker.

But suppose there wasn't any future at all? Suppose Sibylle no longer lived with Rolf at all, but with the other man? In other words, if Rolf was left alone in the house, alone with his detachment? He was sitting like this as the train entered the station, with his hand on the glass and still afraid that someone might pull him by the sleeve and hand him the tattered parcel containing the flesh-pink material again—

Shortly after midnight yesterday, Sibylle (my prosecutor's wife) gave birth to a girl weighing almost seven pounds. He was speechless with joy. I asked him to send flowers, which I would pay for later. He will probably forget.

To continue my notes:

When Rolf came back from Genoa he got out at the central station without overcoat, and therefore conspicuous, so that Sibylle could not miss him if she was waiting for him at the station—though he told himself she could not possibly be waiting for him at the station: she knew nothing of his arrival, and Rolf didn't imagine she would come to meet every international train on the off chance. Just for safety's sake, because it would have been too stupid to miss one another, he looked about among the waiting people. In Zurich it was raining. He had to look into his purse, standing under a penthouse, to see whether he could afford to beckon a taxi as usual. And then, when this taxi stopped outside their flat, it was worse than he had expected. The uncertainty as to whose home it was, his or hers, made him hesitate to get out. As he turned up the collar of his jacket ready to run through the rain, he looked up at their flat, and all the humiliations of the journey were nothing compared with this moment when he saw there was no light in the window. It was late, but a long way off midnight. Perhaps she was already asleep. Anyhow, Rolf didn't get out, despite the taxi-driver's pressing inquiry as to whether they had come to the wrong address. Rolf also felt too unshaven to appear before a wife who now loved someone else. Had he forgotten the fact that Sibylle loved someone else? Now, after a chaos of feelings of all kinds, which, although they had tormented him, had kept his mind distracted, the whole thing had once more acquired the bleak actuality of a grave; and Rolf could not face being told by their Italian maid that the *Signora* had gone away for a few days. For now anything was possible. Perhaps there was a note lying in the flat: "Probably back on Monday. All the best, Sibylle. Please don't forget to pay the rent." Or perhaps only: "Please don't forget to pay the rent. Best wishes, Sibylle."

Rolf drove back to town in the same taxi, and didn't even dare to ring up that evening. There is always a certain sensation to be derived from sleeping in a hotel in one's own town, and Rolf enjoyed it through all his gloom; but the sensation was bound up with uncertainty and agitation—and his dreams were a turmoil.

The following day, a Sunday, the rain had stopped and Rolf went first on a pilgrimage to the building site, shaved, but still without an overcoat. The building site was situated on an eminence outside the town; hitherto Rolf had always gone there by car. On foot it was quite a trek. The brickwork was not yet roofed over. At Rolf's last visit they had just concreted the upper floors, and his wife had not been to the site once. Now he understood her lack of interest in the house. With his hands in his pockets, taken aback when people out for a Sunday morning stroll wandered across the building plot, and not looking at all like the owner of the building that was going up, Rolf stood in the future rooms that were already recognizable in the rough—the garden room with big French windows and the five steps to the loggia, his study looking out over the lake, the bedroom on the same level, everything as planned, and the terrace had now also been paved with concrete. Building material lay everywhere—rolls of tar-board, firebricks, sacks of Portland cement, a tank for the oil heating, bricks for the small dividing walls, lengths of cast-iron piping and all sorts of objects whose purpose could not be guessed at—there were signs of activity on every hand. Nevertheless Rolf felt as though he were standing in a ruin.

Then, to his embarrassment, Sturzenegger, the architect, arrived carrying a folding rule open in his hand. Sturzenegger was so full of enthusiasm for his building that he couldn't stay away from it even on Sunday morning, and, as always happens, his enthusiasm made him look more handsome and charming than ever. Rolf eyed him from the side. No doubt about it, this Sturzenegger was very different from Rolf—and younger. They trudged along over boards and pipes, ducked under the dripping plank linings of the concreted terrace and jumped over brown puddles. Rolf had to feel various kinds of sandstone to decide which one he wanted, and young Sturzenegger explained and explained relentlessly. Rolf examined especially his ear, his hair, his nose, his lips (this he couldn't bear) and his hands. Why not? he thought, and in spite of everything, decided in favor of the cheaper type of sandstone. Didn't this young man see that the house was already for sale? He didn't see it, but spoke enthusiastically of spatial effects and even expected enthusiasm from Rolf, who now suddenly remembered his last evening with Sibylle: Sibylle had met him at the airport, the hypocrite, and the only thing she talked about to her homecoming husband during supper was the good fortune of this young Sturzenegger, some long story about a marvelous contract somewhere in Canada. Wasn't that a clue? Of course Rolf said nothing, but let the architect explain the serpentine piping of the ceiling-heating to him and enjoyed (he now had an exceptional need for inner enjoyments) the thoughts of leaving Sibylle in the dark long after he himself was perfectly clear about everything. He wasn't clear about anything yet, but this young architect was under suspicion, however serenely he now walked around with his yellow folding rule. Sturzenegger was not to be dissuaded from driving his client home. When he himself chatted about his fantastic good fortune in getting the chance to build a large factory over in California, Rolf interrupted:

"My wife told me Canada."

"No," said Sturzenegger, "California."

There was something wrong here; but Rolf had resolved to wear a mask and no one should see him as he had seen himself at Genoa. Whether for fear of meeting Sibylle alone, or to keep himself in countenance, he insisted on Sturzenegger coming in for an apéritif that Sunday morning. Sibylle was there—and so were Cinzano, gin and even salted almonds. His wife, this hussy, who immediately put on the quiet-Sunday-morning-at-home act, and his architect, this young fellow with a fantastic commission in Canada, where Sibylle would no doubt accompany him, seemed to Rolf an entirely possible couple, indeed a convincing couple, a well-matched couple. The formal manner in which they spoke to one another did not fool him for a moment. And anyway, what difference did it make whether it was this Sturzenegger or another man who embraced his wife? All that mattered to Rolf was to see his wife with some gay and lively young man and not to go mad on the spot at the thought of Sibylle embracing this young man or another like him . . .

As I've already said, my public prosecutor told this story much more graphically. When I asked him what finally happened to the pink cloth at Genoa, his reply was reluctant and vague. If I understood correctly, he eventually threw the tattered parcel down a station lavatory.

"Believe me," laughed my public prosecutor, "it was years before I stopped dreaming about that parcel."

(I wonder why he speaks so frankly to me?)

"It's not right," I said, "for me to interrogate my public prosecutor—but if you will permit me to ask one more question: Didn't your good wife tell you who her friend was?"

"Not till later. Very much later."

"When?"

"When it was all over," he said. "When he had disappeared."

"Bit queer, wasn't it?"

"Oh well," he smiled, "we were both of us extremely queer just then, both my wife and I."

Throughout a whole harrowing summer Rolf tried to prove that, true to his theory, he granted Sibylle complete independence. The resulting risk of an equally complete estrangement was something that Sibylle herself had to face up to. It went with her proud assertion: "You don't have to give me my freedom, I can take my freedom for myself if I need it." His theme song was "All right, darling, have it your own way." At the same time, they spent delightful evenings with mutual friends, who didn't show they had noticed anything and perhaps really didn't notice anything. Then again there were nervous outbursts over trifles. Nevertheless, they went to the International Musical Weeks at Lucerne together, just as they always had done, walking arm in arm through the foyer; and it wasn't hypocrisy, either towards the outside world or themselves—suddenly they were on such good terms with each other. Rolf was the husband, and even if he didn't make any mean use of the fact, he still had certain advantages, for example that he could show himself arm in arm with Sibylle at any time. Sibylle even attached great value to the fact that Rolf, now a public prosecutor, strolled through the foyer arm in arm with her. The fancy-dress pierrot, on the other hand, had to contend with the handicap that accompanies all illicit activity, and for the first time in Rolf's life this handicap rested upon his opponent. When he was in a particularly good mood he may occasionally have let fall an ironic allusion that flickered like a distant beacon, warning them both, in case they should forget it as they went arm in arm, where the dangerous reef lay.

It seems they never had any arguments. And yet it must have been a summer that neither of the partners would care to repeat. Sibylle continued to live in the house with Rolf: anything else would have upset their relatives, a catastrophe which Sibylle, although free from any pangs of conscience, could not contemplate. This was her express wish after his return from Genoa, an outright demand in fact—that for the time being everything, as she put it, should remain outwardly the same. Consequently there were only a few hours every day during which she escaped from his supervision, and a horrible incompleteness was unavoidable. The fact that she blamed this incompleteness, this stifling incompleteness, which may in time have become more unbearable than the bitterest quarrel, upon no one but Rolf was too stupid to be put into words. But her feminine mind did blame it on him: there were times (so he says) when she looked at him as though she could no longer stand the sight of him. Then she would go into her room and cry behind a locked door, whereupon Rolf would go down into the cellar and fetch himself a beer. Why didn't she really take her freedom, if she wanted more of it? Rolf was not being sarcastic at all. Why didn't the two of them simply go away together, his poor wife and the fancy-dress pierrot? Why didn't they dare? He couldn't understand it. It couldn't be such a grand passion after all, he thought, and towards autumn, Rolf actually felt that for his part he had got over the affair.

In September he took up his duties as public prosecutor.

In October the house was finished, and the young architect by and large very satisfied. One or two things, said the young architect, he would do differently today—the very things, incidentally, which his clients, Sibylle as well as Rolf, liked best, whereas other things displeased them; but it was the very things which they did not like that were particularly emphasized in the photograph which was to appear shortly in an architectural journal. As Sturzenegger had promised in that first discussion over black coffee, it was a house of consistent modernity. Not that Rolf really disliked it, but you couldn't say he liked it either. Rolf felt constrained in his attitude towards this young Sturzenegger, and almost grudged him all the praise bestowed on his house, Rolf's house. Once, in a café, someone came up to Rolf, introduced himself as the editor of the architectural journal and congratulated Rolf on the courage he had shown as the architect's client, congratulated him in the name of modern architecture as a whole; and not enough that young Sturzenegger was praised as an architect, Rolf also heard the praises of this young man's human qualities, his charm, his audacity, his forcefulness, his ruthlessness, his verve, his vitality, his sensibility, his intensity in the sensual sphere, as well, and all the other things that may distinguish both an architect and a lover. At such moments Rolf had the feeling that everybody was laughing at him, felt as though he were a character in a Molière comedy. Sibylle was sitting with him in the café. Vitality, sensibility, intensity in the sensual sphere as well—yes, she thought so too, and asked Rolf whether he didn't think so too, and Rolf, a man of wide personal and professional experience, didn't know how much perfidy to attribute to his wife. At certain moments he felt her to be capable of anything precisely when she seemed so innocent, as women in love always consider themselves innocent and one with everlasting nature, which in their simplicity of spirit they then regard as God Himself . . .

It was more or less with this feeling of being the town idiot that Rolf drove out one autumn morning for the final check-up on the building. With a few exceptions, trifles which the young architect pointed out himself, everything was in order. A sunblind did not go down, due to faulty installation, nothing more; a large pane of glass had cracked; the last workmen on the premises, decorators, had stupidly blocked one of the toilets with rubbish; in addition, all the cellar keys were missing; a power point beside the client's bed, clearly shown in the plans, had been forgotten; the bathroom mirror had for some inexplicable reason been placed four inches too high; a few slabs of the wrong stone—granite instead of quartzite—had been laid outside in the garden at the last moment, likewise a trifle that could be rectified; and of course the decorators had not quite finished. But that was really all; anyhow Rolf couldn't see any other faults. Whether the great catalpa would flourish or die, only time could tell. A word of cordial gratitude on the part of the client was now due. As it was not forthcoming and as Rolf, the client, simply left the locked house and looked round the neighborhood as though saying goodbye, or as though he were standing on his plot of land for the first time, the young architect—doubtless for the sake of saying something—mentioned the fact that the work was guaranteed, as though Rolf knew nothing about this. Then they sat side by side in the public prosecutor's car, while the latter, his thoughts still far away, inserted the ignition key but did not drive off.

"I didn't want to talk to you," began Rolf, putting on his gloves, "until I was quite calm. But now I have got over this whole business—" Sturzenegger probably had no idea what he was talking about. "No," said Rolf, "of course you're quite right, at bottom it's all simply prejudice. I thought a lot about the little story of the Eskimo, which you told my wife and me when you first came to see us. Do you remember? The Eskimo offers his wife and kicks up a fuss when the guest doesn't take her, and we imagine we can't bear it when the guest does take her. At bottom it's all prejudice . . ."

Rolf had not propounded his theory for a long time. Also it met with less opposition among men. The architect, this young man with vitality, sensibility, intensity and so forth, was full of understanding, though he had no idea what this conversation was in aid of. Meanwhile they had driven off, but they had to stop and wait again at a level crossing. "I can quite understand your embarrassment," said Rolf. "In cases like this I too always avoid discussions. What's the use of them? Only it seems to me that since we're sitting here in the car together—you know, it's just that I don't want you to think I'm a fool." At last the train rumbled past. "You're in love with my wife," said Rolf, unshakable in his delusion and at the same time with admirable detachment, "I can understand that. And my wife is in love with you. That's a fact, and it won't make any essential difference if you fly to Canada next week or the week after."—"To California," corrected Sturzenegger. "My wife told me Canada." —"I'm sorry," laughed Sturzenegger, "but nevertheless I'm going to California. To Redwood City. I'll send you a card as soon as I get there, Herr Doktor, so that you will at last believe me."—"That's not necessary," said Rolf. Someone behind was hooting. "—That's not necessary," said Rolf again. "Canada or California, you know, that makes no difference to me, if my wife intends to go with you, and I suppose she does." The barrier had gone up again long ago, but Rolf, deaf to the hooting behind him, did not start up. The young architect had doubtless cottoned on at last and tried to say something, for instance: "Your good wife and I—" Rolf interrupted: "You might as well call her Sibylle."—"Certainly," said Sturzenegger, "from the very first visit there was a kind of sympathy, on your good wife's part too, I can well believe . . ."—"You can well believe!" It angered Rolf that his wife's lover was so cowardly, it offended him; on the other hand it also made him arrogant. "I'm a man of forty-five," said Rolf, looking at the little architect. "You're not yet thirty." To which Sturzenegger quite rightly replied: "What about it?" The discussion, which had started on a dignified note, seemed to be going off the rails, Rolf realized this and also noticed that the barrier had been raised. The cars which he had held up drove past on the left, and, since it was a narrow country road, half on the grass verge; naturally the drivers looked at Rolf full of reproach and contempt, and one of them bored with his finger into his temple to show Rolf what he thought of him . . .

One must suppose that young Sturzenegger assured Rolf several times that there must be a mistake: either Rolf didn't hear or didn't believe him. Without speaking, as one doesn't speak to a worthless ninny, he drove down into the town and stopped outside the home of the young architect, to whom all this was very painful. Sturzenegger sat by the open door with his brief case, his gloves and the rolled-up plans bundled together under his left arm, so that his right hand was free to say goodbye: he couldn't think of the right remark, the joke that would carry conviction and yet wound no one's feelings. "Don't say now," said Rolf, "that you're sorry or anything like that."—Rolf wouldn't learn. "Don't misunderstand me," he said. "I'm not blaming anyone. I understand perfectly well. I can even approve. Sibylle knows what I think about these things and I expect she's told you. I must approve. And yet—quite simply," he said throwing his cigarette out of the window "—I can't bear it." Sturzenegger seemed to pull himself together. "Have you ever known a man," he asked in a tone of a young man speaking to his senior, "who really could bear it, I mean, who didn't just pretend to—?" Rolf smiled: "I thought I was that man."

Soon afterwards they said goodbye. The architect had suggested a glass of wine together, but Rolf refused, partly from an aversion to entering a dwelling where Sibylle perhaps had spent her hours of happiness, partly from the sudden conviction that this was not the right man after all. He started the engine, thanked Sturzenegger for his kind invitation and asked him to slam the door hard. Sturzenegger hurried away as people do after accidentally entering a strange room that does not concern them, without looking back when Rolf opened the car door again and wished him a good flight to Canada. Then Rolf drove on, simply to avoid standing still, as aimlessly as before in Genoa —anything rather than return home. Anything rather than see Sibylle just now. Nothing had been settled, nothing at all.

That was in October.

Like every man of action who cannot deal with an awkward part of his inner life, Rolf did not plunge into introspective brooding, but into work, into useful and impersonal work, of which there was naturally no lack now that he was a public prosecutor. He dealt with everything that was in any way subject to his competence, he dealt with it from morning till late in the evening, until his last secretary was worn out, then he carried on alone. He dealt with things in the manner of an Orlando Furioso. His colleagues assumed that he was wildly ambitious. His colleagues had no idea what impelled this self-possessed and reserved man, well known for always keeping a cool head, to perform these prodigies of effort. All his life he had enjoyed the reputation of leading a regular and therefore happy existence, a reputation, incidentally, which he in no way fostered—not in the least, Rolf could show himself in front of the Doge's Palace feeding pigeons with another woman without giving rise to any talk in his little town: there are such men, phenomena of good reputation, whose reputation is as impervious to talk as a gull's feathers are impervious to water, and then nobody—even in a little town like Zurich—has any urge to gossip, for trying to wet a gull's wings is a tedious occupation. And it seems that this phenomenon also extended to his wife: in her case, too, the thought simply never entered people's heads. So who was to guess the real reason for a new public prosecutor's zeal? Moreover, in all the various cases he had to deal with, Rolf made every effort not to regard all women as being tarred with the same brush: where other people were concerned, at least, he retained his power of discrimination: he could see that in some cases it was the man's fault. He was considered very understanding, and he did everything in his power to spare the prisoner at the bar humiliation. His successes grew again like plums on the plum-tree, but they made not the slightest impression on Sibylle; worse still, she found exactly the same satisfaction in Rolf's professional success as in a toy water-wheel which she knew would keep little Hannes happy and busy for the next few days . . .

Rolf dreamt once more about a tattered parcel containing flesh-pink cloth . . .

Then came the move into the new house, and Sibylle had the effrontery to go and stay with a girl friend at St. Gallen, this week of all weeks. Rolf reminded her of the imminent move; but the girl friend at St. Gallen could not be put off. Rolf did not believe in this girl friend at St. Gallen for a moment, but all he said was "All right, have it your own way." And Sibylle actually went. To be in a rage for a precise reason, a rage there was no need to sublimate, a real tearing rage, such as Rolf was in during that week, was a positive treat. It released him for once from his admirable detachment, and he went around the new house in a way that made the men with leather belts who asked from underneath their burdens where they were to put the carved wardrobe, or the sewing machine, or the cutlery case, or the dressing table, surprised at the language of an educated gentleman. "Go to the lady!" said Rolf. "Go to the lady with the whole damn lot, or chuck it out of the window!" And as he left: "It's a bloody scandal the bitch isn't here, a bloody scandal." The honest workmen dared not ask any more, for fear the irritable gentleman should make a spectacle of himself again: they examined the stuff on the van, looked at one another, and anything that didn't obviously belong in the garden or the cellar, or wasn't recognizably an educated gentleman's desk, they silently piled up in the lady's room. At the end, when the chaos was complete, the honest workmen received a tip that embarrassed them: it verged on hush money.

Rolf found himself alone in his much-praised house, alone with little Hannes and an Italian maid who didn't know where the bed linen had got to. The lady was badly missed. Only little Hannes was not in despair, was blissfully happy in this chaos—where everything commonplace suddenly became a sensation—and asked a thousand questions. "Handle With Care," was written on the boxes. The place did not look like home at all. Rolf didn't know how he was to live here and found it senseless for the maid to begin opening the boxes, or at least premature: it was less certain than ever whether the marriage that would make it worth while opening the boxes and unrolling the carpets would take place at all. He simultaneously hoped and no longer hoped. What did independence and freedom in marriage really mean—quite practically, what did they mean—? What was left was common property with all sorts of goods and chattels and a maid to keep them clean. And what about Hannes? It couldn't go on like this. Should Rolf simply tell his wife to drop it, using threats, an either-or, and give her till Christmas to think it over? It was a possible way of bringing this impossible situation to an end, but not a possible way of preserving or regaining her love. Should he simply wait? A provisional, haphazard life, perhaps she'll come, perhaps she won't, perhaps he'd get used to it, perhaps he'd fall in love himself, and since everything passes, who knows, per-

haps a divorce would be premature—a life of blind
patience—was that the solution?

He stumbled from decision to decision, first one
way, then another. How often had Rolf given advice,
and where other people were concerned, with all due
precaution, it was always much clearer in which direction effort should be exerted. In short, Rolf found
himself at that dead point where with the greatest effort one can only tear oneself apart, but not turn the
wheel either forwards or backwards, and yet whether
the wheel turns forwards or backwards depends on a
trifle, perhaps on chance; and that was the bitterest
thing of all, the thought that everything might be decided as though of its own accord by a single word, a
good or a foolish word . . .

During that week he not only received Sturzenegger's promised card from Redwood City, California,
but also a very queer telephone call from Paris. A
manifestly agitated gentleman, who introduced himself as Stiller, talked some muddled nonsense and
seemed to think Rolf was bound to know where his
wife was, a man who absolutely refused to believe
that Rolf was not well acquainted with his name. The
excitable individual whose voice came to him over the
telephone was undoubtedly none other than the fancy-
dress pierrot. (So what my public prosecutor stated
earlier on is not quite true: he did know the name of
Sibylle's friend, even if not through Sibylle herself,
before Stiller's disappearance. I only mention this as
an example of the fact that even a public prosecutor,
in an entirely voluntary statement, does not manage
altogether to avoid contradicting himself, as they expect us to do during an interrogation.) A very queer
telephone call indeed; for Rolf had assumed that Sibylle had gone off with her fancy-dress pierrot. Had
the two of them missed each other in Paris? He rejected the thought that this call was an exceedingly
cunning attempt to put him on a false scent; but once

in his mind the thought would not let go of him. He couldn't credit Sibylle with such a plan. No! he said out loud, No! And from the very back of his mind came the echo, Why not? He tried to throw off this suspicion, felt ashamed of himself and with the same breath as he felt ashamed of his mean suspicion he thought himself ridiculous for feeling ashamed, a fool. Wasn't anything possible now? His reason revolted at the idea. Was it possible that he would one day hate Sibylle, the mother of his son and moreover closer to him than anyone else he could imagine? He was afraid of meeting her again.

It seems that this meeting, when it did take place, was an unfortunate affair. One morning in his office —it was November—he was told his wife wanted to speak to him, no, not on the telephone: she was sitting in the ante-chamber. Now he really was in conference, and she had to wait nearly an hour. It was eleven o'clock; couldn't they have simply lunched together? Rolf gave word for her to come in and went to meet her at the door with the mute question, What's wrong? Sibylle was rather pale, but cheerful. "Ah," she said, "so this is your office?" and went straight over to the window to look at the modest view. Rolf didn't ask, How was it at St. Gallen? nor, How was it in Paris? It was for Sibylle to do the talking, he felt, not for him. She acted as though nothing had happened and was more on edge than he had ever known her, chatting as though she had only come to see his new place of work and smoking hurriedly. Rolf might have rung St. Gallen; he wisely hadn't done so. Was this what she wanted to find out? Sibylle thanked him for seeing to the move. What else? She had a secret in her eyes, fear too, though she didn't speak of it and didn't want to speak of it. The situation seemed to Rolf farcical, unbearable—Rolf behind his wide desk, Sibylle sitting opposite him in the armchair like a client. Did she want a divorce?

Suddenly he said against his will, "A Herr Stiller phoned, obviously your lover." He was sorry he had used this word, and at the same time he felt indignation that on top of everything else he now ought to apologize; instead of doing so, he added with a freedom from rancor which he knew very well to be full of condescension, "I suppose you met in Paris after all, the call came on Wednesday." At this Sibylle rose as though after a fruitless discussion, which in fact had not taken place at all, slowly and without speaking, and went over to the window. Rolf could see by her shoulders that she was crying, sobbing. She could not endure his hand on her shoulder, nor even his gaze. "I'm going," she said. "Where to?" he asked. She crushed out her half cigarette in his ashtray, picked up her handbag, took out a small cloth and powder with which to put her face in order, and said with the most shameless levity, "To Pontresina." After a deep breath, during which Sibylle painted her lips, Rolf said once more, "As you like." Then came her foolish question, "Do you mind?" Then his equally foolish reply, "Do as you please." And so he let her go . . .

And she actually went to Pontresina.

At the beginning of December, when she returned bronzed by the sun, he suggested a divorce. She left the necessary steps to him. Rolf didn't know what to make of it all when she told him young Sturzenegger had written to tell her he urgently needed a secretary, and she had decided to go with Hannes to this Redwood City, California. Once again Rolf said, "As you like." He didn't believe it. The whole thing was just a childish farce. And even when she went to the American consulate to have her finger-prints taken, he didn't believe it. Was it up to him to make the first gesture of reconciliation? It wasn't in his power to make the first move, considering that he didn't even know what really had happened. It seemed to him that no marriage could be built on blind reconciliation. Was she waiting for him to tell her to stay? Her passage on the *Ile-de-France* had already been booked, as Rolf knew. Perhaps Sibylle had completely deserted him during the past summer, but even that wasn't the point: without a word from her that she wanted to stay, it was simply impossible for him to ask Sibylle without becoming ridiculous in his ignorance and thereby rendering ridiculous the marriage that was perhaps still possible between them. It was truly not possible, not like that anyhow. He felt he must not give way to her threats. A few days before Christmas Sibylle actually went to Le Havre with Hannes, who did not yet attend school, to embark for America.

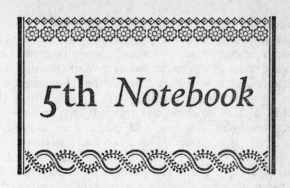

5th *Notebook*

THE show put on today by my defending counsel,
that diligent man who continues to defend the
missing Stiller, was a total failure from his point of
view—and yet this apéritif-confrontation with the
leading critics of the little town was most enjoyable.
A young gentleman's request that I should not take
personally certain biting comments written seven
years ago was touchingly superfluous. There was also
a lady present, a mature personality, in character a
"guardian of the temple," yet possessed of a human
modesty that was apparent at the first glance. My assurance that I was not the Stiller they took me for
visibly relieved the little gathering of critics, and on
top of that came the whisky. I asked the lady why
she had refused to shake hands with me at the beginning. The situation became embarrassing again, but
only for a few moments. If she had known it was
about Stiller, the lady would not have come to this
coffee-house table at all. Stiller must have behaved in
an absolutely scandalous way towards this lady. My
counsel looked at me, and my own curiosity was also
aroused: the lady's silence provoked all sorts of con-

jectures. Stiller had once written this lady a letter, I heard, calling her a "school-marm," just because she had been compelled, and would always be compelled, in the name of the spirit, out of love of the spirit and a profound sense of duty towards the art of all epochs, to deny him a place among true artists. I took the hand of this gracious and spirited lady, which was perhaps going too far, and said, "Frau Doktor, I couldn't agree more." The subject of discussion was a piece of sculpture I had recently seen in a public park. True, the lady's objections were not quite the same as my own, they were more subtle; but we conversed about strict criteria of judgment, and as a result we were very soon no longer concerned with the missing Stiller, who could not stand up to such criteria, but with the lady herself, with criticism as such, about which the lady knew a very great deal. I could understand her resolve never to write about Stiller again, simply to consign Stiller to oblivion: what better could I wish in my position, when the missing man gets in my way at every turn? And the gentlemen, too, were very pleasant. You only have to assure a critic perfectly frankly that you are not an artist, and immediately he'll talk to you as though you knew as much about art as he does.

Julika has gone away. Unfortunately when she came to see me before leaving, I was just being interrogated by the psychiatrist, who wouldn't allow the door to be suddenly opened for fear my soul might escape him. Her little good-bye present of cigars touched me precisely because they were the wrong brand again. As far as she is concerned, cigars are simply cigars, and as they are very expensive she's sure I'll like them. I do like them too—because they come from Julika.

Julika has written from Paris. The letter was addressed to Herr A. Stiller, c/o Remand Prison, Zurich. And it arrived—unfortunately. It began, "My dear Anatol." She had a good journey and in Paris the sun was shining. The letter was signed "Your Julika." I slowly tore it into a hundred pieces; but what difference does that make?

Today it was perfectly clear once more that we cannot bury the failure in our lives, and so long as I try I shall never get out of the failure, there is no escape. But the bewildering thing is, other people take it for granted that I have no other life to produce, and so they consider what I take upon myself to be my life. But it was never my life. And I know that only in so far as it was never my life can I take it upon myself—as my failure. This means one must be capable of passing without spite through their confusion of identities, playing a part without ever confusing oneself with the part; but for this I must have a fixed point—

My public prosecutor admitted he had forgotten the flowers for his wife; to make up, he suggested that I should visit his wife in the nursing home and take her the flowers myself (at his expense). His wife, he thought, would be delighted.

Dreamed about Julika. She was sitting in a boulevard café, perhaps on the Champs-Elysées, with writing paper and a fountain pen, looking like a schoolgirl who has to write an essay. Her eyes beg me urgently not to believe what she writes me, for she is writing under constraint; her eyes beg me to set her free from this constraint . . .

Went to the nursing home today.
   Sibylle (my public prosecutor's wife) is a woman of about thirty-five, with black hair and very bright, lively eyes, beautiful in her happiness at being a

mother, combining youth and maturity in one person.
Women in this condition have something like a nim-
bus round them, which tends to embarrass the man,
the stranger. Her face is brown and when she laughs
one sees a mouth full of enviable teeth, a very powerful mouth. Fortunately her baby wasn't in the room,
to be quite honest I'm rather at a loss with babies.
When the sister led me through the double padded
doors, she was sitting in a blue cane chair out on the
balcony. The lemon-yellow dressing gown (Fifth Avenue, New York) suited her admirably. She sat up in
her chair, took off her dark sunglasses, and as the
sister had to go and fetch a largish vase, we were immediately alone together. I felt somehow very comical
with my flowers. And then she unfortunately put
her dark glasses on again, so that I could not read her
eyes. Her husband, my prosecutor, had kindly lent
me twenty francs, so that I appeared before the happy
mother with an armful of long gladioli that quivered
as I mounted the linoleum-covered stairs and rustled
in their tissue paper. Thank God, it was not long before the sister returned with a rather cheap and nasty,
but capacious vase. It was no easy matter to arrange
the stiff gladioli in a reasonable cluster. (I should have
much preferred roses, only, in view of the fact that I
had to touch my public prosecutor for the money, I
found them too dear.) It was tea-time, the sister had
no idea that I had come straight from prison and asked
me with the greatest solicitude whether I preferred
rolls or toast. At last we were alone again, this time
without any prospect of an early interruption.

"Stiller," she said, "what's all this nonsense?"

I took her remark to refer to the gladioli. But it
seems that she was referring to my denial that I
was the missing Stiller. She removed her dark glasses,
and I saw her bright, calmly affectionate eyes. Even
though she had just borne a child by her husband, the
thought of having been loved by this woman was

perplexing. Of course, I stuck to my denial. I sat facing her, my left foot crossed over my right knee, both hands clasped round my left knee, gazing out at the old plane trees in the park, while Sibylle sized me up.

"You've grown very silent," she remarked. "How is Julika?"

She asked rather a lot of questions.

"Why did you come back?"

It was a curious afternoon, we kept on drinking tea when it was already cold, and the toast and rolls remained untouched. My silence (what was I to say?) drove her to talk. At six o'clock, on the dot, she had to pacify her baby.

I can now see their missing Stiller pretty clearly. He seems to be very feminine. He feels he has no will power, and in a certain sense has too much—he employs it in willing not to be himself. His personality is vague; hence his tendency to radicalism. His intelligence is average, but in no way trained; he prefers to rely on hunches and neglects the intelligence; for intelligence sets one before decisions. At times he reproaches himself with cowardice, then he makes decisions which he later cannot keep. He is a moralist, like almost everybody who does not accept himself. He often runs unnecessary risks, or puts himself in mortal danger, to prove that he is a fighter. He has a great deal of imagination. He suffers from the classical inferiority anxiety that comes from making excessive demands on himself, and he mistakes his fundamental sense of shortcoming for depth of character, or even for religious feeling. He is a pleasant person, he possesses charm and doesn't argue. When he can't get his way by charm, he withdraws into his melancholy. He would like to be truthful. In him, the insatiable longing to be truthful is partly due to a special kind of untruthfulness: he is truthful to the point of exhibitionism so that he can use the consciousness of being particularly truthful, more truthful than other people, as a means of skirting round a sore point. He doesn't know just where this point lies, this black hole, that keeps cropping up again, and he is afraid even when it doesn't appear. He lives in anticipation. He likes to leave everything in suspense. He is one of those people who, wherever they are, cannot help thinking how nice it might be somewhere else. He flees the here-and-now, at least inwardly. He doesn't like the summer, or any other state of present fulfillment; he likes autumn, twilight, melancholy; transience is his element. Women very quickly have the feeling that he understands them. He has few men friends. Among men he feels he is not a man. But in his fundamental fear of being inadequate he is really afraid of women too. He conquers more than he can hold, and when his partner has once sensed his limits he completely loses his nerve. He is not willing, not capable, of being loved as the person he is, and therefor he involuntarily neglects every woman who truly loves him, for if he took her love really seriously, he would be compelled as a result to accept himself —and that is the last thing he wants.

No sooner is one in this country, than one has bad teeth. And no sooner did I report my toothache, than they wanted to take me to Herr Stiller's dentist. As though there weren't any others here! His name, by the way, was quickly traced through an unpaid bill which my counsel carries round in his folder. They phoned him at once. Fortunately (and to the visible regret of my counsel) this dentist turned out to have died recently. They made an appointment with his successor—that is to say, with a man who has never seen Stiller and cannot claim that he recognizes me.

6th *Notebook*

THE missing Stiller's studio—as described by Frau Sibylle, the wife of my public prosecutor—must have been a big, light room, a garret somewhere in the Old Town, a room that looked even larger than it was through the lack of furniture, even of useful furniture on which Sibylle could have put her hat and handbag. Her estimate of thirty by forty-five feet is probably an exaggeration, but how clearly Sibylle remembers this studio in other respects. You walked on old, creaking pinewood planks with holes where the knots had been trodden out; and under a sloping roof, against which she had more than once bumped her head, there must have been something like a kitchen, containing a sink of red terrazzo, a gas cooker and a cupboard filled with all sorts of odd crockery. There must have been a couch too, for Stiller lived in the studio; also a bookcase, where Sibylle, the daughter of a middle-class family, first saw the *Communist Manifesto*, next to it Tolstoy's *Anna Karenina*, something by the oft-mentioned Karl Marx, then Hölderlin, Hemingway, also Gide, and Sibylle herself from

time to time gave Stiller a book, which contributed
to the motley character of this library. There were no
carpets. On the other hand, Sibylle remembers all five
bends in a long stovepipe that appears to have been
very romantic. And best of all, one could step boldly
out on the parapet (no doubt she had to lift her narrow skirt to do so) which was surrounded by a rusty
iron balustrade and covered in moss-grown grit and
tar that stuck to her white shoes and was also very
romantic—with pigeons cooing in the gutter, with
gables all round, with dormer windows and chimneys
and party-walls, with cats, with courtyards where people were fiercely beating carpets, with geraniums,
with flapping washing and sounds from the Cathedral.
An easy chair bought in a Salvation Army jumble
sale was by then, unfortunately, already beyond use;
the upholstery was moldy and it was better to sit on
the garbage pail, which for Sibylle, my prosecutor's
wife, evidently also possessed a quite special charm.
At all events, one has the impression that in spite of
everything she likes to remember that studio. Inside
there was a grandfatherly rocking-chair, on which
you could let yourself be rocked, which inevitably
produced a mood of exhilaration, and everything here
possessed for Sibylle, when she came from her tidy
household, the magic of the provisional. The rubber
tube on the tap was always attached with nothing
more than a piece of string, a curtain hung on drawing pins, behind this stood an old trunk with heavy
hinges that was now used as a linen press. Wherever
you looked in this studio, you had the feeling you
could depart at any time and start a completely different life—that is to say, precisely the feeling Sibylle
needed just then.

Her first visit took him by surprise.

"I've only dropped in for a moment," she said and
wouldn't have believed herself that she was going to

stay till midnight. "I must just see where you live and work . . ."

Stiller was unshaven and rather embarrassed about it. He gave her a Cinzano. And while he shaved at the sink behind the curtain, Sibylle looked around at the things hanging on the walls: an African mask, a fragment of a Celtic axe, a portrait of Joseph Stalin (which later disappeared), a famous poster by Toulouse-Lautrec—and two once brightly colored but now faded *banderillas* from Spain. "What are these?" she asked. "They're used in bull-fighting," he explained briefly, still busy shaving. "Oh yes," said Sibylle casually, "you've been in Spain, Sturzenegger told us a crazy story about you . . ."

She sat in the rocking-chair and laughed, "You and a Russian gun." His silence showed she had offended him, which she naturally regretted. "Sturzenegger is an idiot," he said from behind his curtain. "He hawks that silly story around everywhere."—"Isn't it true, then?"—"Not the way Sturzenegger tells it, anyhow," he answered so irritably that Sibylle asked no more questions about the story of the Russian gun. She was trying to change the subject when she said, "But you were in Spain—" Sibylle was annoyed at herself, anyone would have thought she had come to pump Stiller about Spain . . .

They had met at an artists' fancy-dress ball, when they did not know one another's names and were therefore free from all sorts of inhibitions; they had exchanged caresses, and that was scarcely three weeks ago, caresses which later, when they met in reality, seemed almost unbelievable, hardly different from secret memories of a dream about which the other knew nothing. After Sturzenegger, his friend, had revealed her name, it had become inevitable that they should meet again, if only out of curiosity to see what the face each one had kissed looked like without a mask.

They met over an apéritif; and since they found that they had much more to say to one another without masks, they went for a walk afterwards, and this in turn was hardly a week ago; this walk, it seems, also led to caresses which, now that Sibylle was in his studio, seemed almost unbelievable, very little different from her memory of the fancy-dress ball—like a secret memory of a dream about which the other knew nothing. Hence this embarrassment, this difficulty in keeping up a conversation . . .

"So this is where you work?" asked Sibylle, and she herself found it a stupid, really quite superfluous question. She wandered about among the pieces of sculpture, resigned with some trepidation to the prospect that Stiller would show her his work. "You know," she said, "that I understand nothing about art?" —"That's good," he said from behind his curtain and changed the subject himself. "You'll help yourself, won't you? The Cinzano is there to be drunk." Sibylle helped herself. She was standing glass in hand in front of a plaster cast, when Stiller, now shaved, stepped out and said, "That's my wife." It was a head on a long, columnar neck, more of a vase than a woman, strange, and Sibylle was glad that she wasn't expected to say anything. "Isn't that terrible for your wife?" she asked nonetheless. "I should find it terrible if you turned me into art like that!" As a topic of conversation his art was now exhausted, and no other subject suggested itself. Now they stood as though they were only there to taste Cinzano, both of them one degree more stupid than they were in reality—all because of an understandable fear that at the least contact they might relapse into caresses again, without really getting to know one another.

"Why are you interested in that?" asked Stiller. "That story about the Russian gun?" It interested Sibylle no more and no less than anything else out of his unknown past. It was Stiller, it seems, who couldn't get away from Spain, from the faded colorfulness of the *banderillas* with their sharp barbs. To avoid having to relate the story of the Russian gun, which was manifestly painful to him, Stiller now began describing a Spanish bullfight in great detail, putting down his Cinzano to free his hands. He did not take the two crossed *banderillas* down from the wall, however: he seemed to be afraid of them. "Yes, yes," said Sibylle every now and then, "I understand—" Stiller seemed to be fascinated by bullfighting, and enthusiasm, thought Sibylle, suited him admirably, better than any mask. "And now," explained Stiller, "now comes the matador." In Sibylle's eyes the bull was dead long ago. "Why only now?" she asked. "When the bull's dead?" She hadn't been paying attention, at least not to the bullfight, but only to his face; Stiller had to begin the whole description again. "Watch out!" said Stiller, "—I'm the bull."

He stood in the middle of the studio, and Sibylle had to rise from the rocking chair to play the part of the torero. She laughed at their respective rôles. Sibylle had absolutely no desire to kill a bull. Stiller found this casting of rôles perfectly in order. There was no need for Sibylle even to take her hat off, on the contrary, a torero cannot look too elegant. First of all, then, the bull comes into the arena, and Sibylle had to imagine the dazzling brightness of the sunlit sand all round, the arena is divided between life and death, light and shadow, and all round are stands filled with people, as colorful as a flowerbed and buzzing with voices that now fall silent as Sibylle, the torero, comes a little closer. Really there are several toreros who irritate the bull with their red cloths, but Stiller had to be content with Sibylle. The bull, as black as pitch, stands in the center like a gigantic funnel, and the combat begins playfully, almost like a ballet; the waving cloths are not very red, but bleached by the sun and more of a pink; still, the bull

doesn't quite know what to do and defends himself
only casually, jabbing his horns into the void and pulling up sharp in his charge, so that the dust rises in
clouds. Up to now it has all been teasing, a flirtation,
and they could perfectly well stop, the black bull is
uninjured and still capable of pulling a plough across
some Andalusian field.

Sibylle was horrified when he told her about the
picadors who now come along on their broken-down
nags and jab their spears into the bull's neck to rouse
him into a fighting fury. Sibylle involuntarily took
off her hat; the fountain of pulsing crimson blood that
was now streaming and gleaming across the panting
bull's black hide made her quite nervous. Sibylle assured Stiller she could never watch a real bullfight.
But this made no difference to Stiller, veteran of the
Spanish War, and now the wounded bull attacked;
when the broken-down nag was drawn out of the
arena with its belly slit open by the bull's horns and a
garland of entrails dragging behind it, Sibylle had to
sit down.

"Stop it!" she cried with both hands over her face.
But now, said Stiller, comes the incomparably beautiful and elegant phase with those gaily colored *banderillas* about which Sibylle had inquired, and as Sibylle remained seated on the couch, Stiller had to
change rôles and leave the bull to her imagination, so
that he could demonstrate the use of these *banderillas*.
But, as I said, Stiller did not take the darts from the
wall, he seemed afraid of them, as though he had personally experienced the lot of the bull. He made the
demonstration without properties—both arms raised,
as gracefully as possible, the body stretched and on
the very tips of the toes to gain height, the stomach
drawn in to avoid being slit open by the sharp horns
of the charging bull, and then—now Sibylle had to
watch closely—then in with the two gaily colored
darts like a flash of lightning, into the neck, not just

into the bull, but exactly in the neck, with grace and precision. Sibylle found difficulty in sharing his admiration; he kept saying, "That really is something!" and wouldn't let the matter rest until she had acknowledged, at least with a nod, that grace in the face of mortal danger was indeed an achievement.

"And what about the bull?" she asked with an undertone of partiality. "What about the bull?" He knows by now that it is a matter of life and death and that he will never again plough an Andalusian field. Smothered in blood and with a quivering sheaf of six *banderillas* hanging in his flesh by their barbs, the bull stands still, showing the first signs of exhaustion, and tries to rid himself of his pain by shaking off his sheaf of gaily colored darts, but in vain. Stiller showed her the barbs on the two *banderillas*. "And you call that beautiful?" she asked. Stiller didn't call it "beautiful," but there was something about it, apparently, that fascinated him, something painful too, almost something personal. In contrast to the lady, he was emphatically impartial; but he experienced it all very much from the bull's angle, once clutching at his neck as though he had felt this sheaf of gaily colored *banderillas*.

"And then," he remarked dispassionately, "the last round opens." Sibylle watched it from the couch, incapable of lighting the cigarette she had long ago placed between her lips. "Thank you," she said, showing her silver Dunhill lighter, "I've already got a light." Well then, the last round. Stiller dubbed it grace versus crude force, light against darkness, spirit against nature. The spirit appears in the guise of a silvery white matador, his naked sword under a red cloth, not to kill, oh no, but to conquer, to perform the figures of deadly peril, one after the other, without retreating a step, elegance is all, cowardice is worse than death, the aim is a victory of the spirit over animal life, and only when he has withstood these dangers, withstood them according to all the rules of the art, only then may he use his sword. Silence fills the arena, with all the rage of exhaustion the bull perceives the red cloth again and charges; the silvery white matador stands firm and the sword plunges, the audience go wild with acclamation and the bull stands with outspread legs, waiting, and suddenly he collapses to the front or falls sideways and dies. His eyes roll, his legs stretch out, the rest is an inert lump, a black mass. Hats spiral down into the arena, flowers, ladies' gloves, cigars, wicker bottles, oranges . . . Then at last Sibylle used her Dunhill lighter, and the conversation was open again—

There was no lovemaking.

"Your wife is a dancer?" asked Sibylle at one point, but she learned little about this woman whom Stiller had turned into a vase; in fact, to judge by his attitude, she was really only a beautiful, rare, dead vase, to which Stiller was married, an object that was only present when Stiller thought of it: and at the moment Stiller had no real wish to think of it. On the other hand, were Sibylle's comments on her Rolf any more informative? Anyhow, there was one thing she did not tell him: that Rolf, her husband, was spending the night in London and would not be back until the following day. Why should she bother him with that? She was quite bothered enough herself by the thought of this "freedom" . . .

"Did Sturzenegger ever show you our plans?" she asked, and this question led all of a sudden to a sensible conversation, for Stiller turned out to be an ardent champion of modern architecture, about which he knew something, enough, anyhow, to make Sibylle interested for the first time in her own building, to make her enthusiastic in fact, enthusiastic about her own house. It was (so she says) such a pleasant, matter-of-fact, sensible conversation that Stiller had no difficulty in saying, "You'll stay to supper, won't you?"

Actually, of course, it had never occurred to Sibylle to stay to supper; at most she had reckoned with the possibility of having a meal together somewhere in town. "Can I help you?" she asked rather awkwardly, as Stiller filled a saucepan with water and, still talking about architecture, set it on the old-fashioned gas stove. "Do you like rice?" he inquired casually, lighting the gas. Of course, Sibylle had made up her mind to leave around nine o'clock, or ten o'clock at the very latest. "Rice," she replied at last. "That'll be lovely." Stiller had to get the garnishings for a Spanish rice dish, and after the bullfight a Spanish dish was the only possible choice; he had to hurry, otherwise the shops would be shut in his face. After a quick glance into his purse, which was obviously not always full, Stiller went out and left his visitor alone in the studio . . .

During this half hour, Sibylle felt rather strange. What did she want? And what didn't she want? Now she had time to think it over. She stood at the big window that looked out on the Great Minster, smoking and trying to remember where she had parked her car, Rolf's car, and couldn't remember because there was so much else going through her head. Ridiculous! Supper in a studio—what did that amount to? Sibylle was then twenty-eight. She had loved twice in her life, no more and no less, and both times it had been an incursion into a life, into the other person's life. The first man she loved, a teacher to whom she owed her school-leaving certificate, divorced his wife, and the second man married her. She had no talent for mere philandering. Or could this be learnt? A jolly fancy-dress ball pierrot, such as Stiller had seemed to her three weeks ago, and on top of that an artist, in other words a man without moral scruples, an impudent and experienced rascal who was yet enough of a gentleman to mention no names afterwards—that might be just the thing to give Rolf, her self-confident husband, the fright he had been needing for a long time. Only it seemed that Stiller was anything but an impudent rascal. The closer she came to know him the shyer he was, the more sympathetic, and in reality, here in his studio, there was nothing much left of the jolly pierrot. Stiller was a witty, but secretly very depressed man, a man who had invisible *banderillas* in his neck and was bleeding. Also he was married. Why didn't they live together, Stiller and his ballerina? It was all very unclear. Was it a marriage that had failed, or a perfect marriage? In no case was it simple. What would happen if Sibylle really loved him? And this danger existed. Then again Sibylle said to herself, Nonsense! and turned down the gas flame a little because the water with the rice was already boiling. How different men could be. Sibylle had never met a man who shopped for her and cooked, all without the slightest inquiry as to what he should buy or how he should cook. Once the telephone rang. Naturally she didn't lift the receiver. The ringing had given Sibylle a disproportionate fright. Was it his wife? There was no reason why Sibylle should not have frankly introduced herself to his wife. Ridiculous! Sibylle positively wished that his wife would come in now. Or was it a sweetheart, who had rung so shrilly, so obstinately?

His spatula on the big table, the full ashtrays everywhere, which Sibylle would have liked to empty, all sorts of unfamiliar tools, the rather grubby drying-up cloth, newspapers all over the place, a tie on the door, all this was very masculine, his library rather boyish compared with Rolf's academic bookshelves, and Joseph Stalin not quite so frightening as usual, but nevertheless alien, not her type. Sibylle was pleased with everything that appeared to her strange. And his sculptures (I believe) seemed to her even stranger than Joseph Stalin. Was Stiller a real artist? She admitted to herself that in an exhibition she would have passed by such things. She forced herself not to pass them by, but to form an opinion that would preserve her from love. This wasn't difficult: she didn't love Picasso either, not yet. And these things were much the same. Sibylle couldn't remember ever having read his name in the *Neue Zürcher Zeitung;* but even if Stiller were not a real artist, did this preserve her from loving him?

She felt a great temptation to open a drawer here and there, but of course she didn't do so. Instead she turned the pages of a sketchbook, staggered by the feeling that she had fallen in love with a master, to judge by his sketches. Why was he so long? She hoped nothing had happened to him. A drawer that was almost open anyway contained all sorts of things, but no clues to Stiller's innermost life; it was an attractive, almost boyish muddle—shells, a dusty tobacco pipe, electric fuses, wire pipe-cleaners, which her little Hannes would have so much liked to have, and all sorts of coins, receipts, overdue bills, a dried starfish, a bunch of keys that made one think of Bluebeard, an electric bulb, an army pay-book, rubber patches for repairing bicycle tires, sleeping powder, candles, a rifle bullet, and also an old, but perfectly preserved brass plate bearing the name STILLER-TSCHUDY . . .

When Stiller entered, carrying paper bags, Sibylle was just standing in front of a photograph of the Acropolis with storm clouds. "Have you been to Greece too?" she asked. "Not yet," he answered gaily. "But we can go there, the frontier is open again now." He had managed to get his tinned crab and also paprika, instead of rabbit some fowl, tomatoes, peas, sardines instead of some other small fish, and he was ready to start cooking. Sibylle was allowed to lay the table, rinse the glasses and warm the plates. Even the salad he had to make himself; Sibylle was only permitted to taste, express delight and wash the wooden dish. When the telephone rang again, Stiller did not lift the receiver, and for a time his gaiety seemed to have vanished. When the Valencia rice stood on the table smelling delicious, Stiller washed his hands and dried them with manly composure, as though there were no cause for festive animation. They sat down to their first meal together. "How do you like it?" he asked, and Sibylle stood up, wiped her mouth and gave him the kiss he had earned by his masculine culinary skill. (Rolf couldn't even make himself a scrambled egg!) They set to. "Your health!" he said rather awkwardly. There followed a matter-of-fact conversation about the great difference between tinned crab and fresh crab—

And so on.

When ten o'clock struck from the nearby Great Minster, loud enough for Sibylle to hear it distinctly, she couldn't think of leaving, despite her resolution— "You mustn't forget," Stiller was just saying, "that I was frightfully young. One day you wake up and read in the newspaper what the world expects of you. The world! In actual fact, of course, it was only written by a well-meaning snob. But suddenly you're a white hope. And along come those who have already arrived, wanting to shake your hand and make themselves pleasant, simply out of fear, as though they were Goliaths scared of young David. It's ridiculous. But there you stand with your delusions of grandeur —until, thank God, a Spanish Civil War breaks out." Sibylle understood. "Irun," he went on, "that was the first cold douche. I shall never forget that little commissar. I was no white hope in his eyes. He didn't say anything, but the way he looked at me showed that he considered me a dead loss. My idea of Marxism was sentimental twaddle. All the same, I had a training school for recruits behind me, I had learnt how to throw hand grenades and operate a machine gun. And then, too, I had a friend, a Czech, who vouched for me—" Stiller spoke very slowly, filled his glass with chianti and held it, without drinking.

"Saragossa," he went on, "that was the second blow. I volunteered, we were cut off, and someone had to try and break through the enemy lines, I was the first to volunteer. But they didn't take me! There I was, a volunteer who was left standing . . . Can you imagine how I felt?"—"Why didn't they take you?"—"They hemmed and ha'd until someone else stepped forward, my friend the Czech, he wasn't a man looking for death, but a real fighter . . . That was the point," remarked Stiller, "I was really only looking for death. Without realizing it, may be; but people could smell it. During air raids, I was the one who refused to take cover, and I thought I was being brave! And that's how it happened later on the Tajo —" Now Sibylle naturally hoped she would hear the true story, but in vain. Stiller kept beating about the bush, losing himself in side issues, then in a detailed topography of Toledo and finally in a political commentary.

"To cut a long story short," he said eventually, "there we were in this rocky little valley, and I had to guard prisoners. I don't suppose they trusted me to do anything else. Out in front they were fighting for the glorious Alcazar, and there I was in this hot little valley guarding prisoners, in small groups. Fortunately I had Anya at that time—" Stiller filled his glass with chianti again. "Who was Anya?" she asked, and once more they did not come to the ferry over the Tajo, but this time the digression interested her a great deal more directly. "Anya?" he said. "She was my first love. A Polish girl. She was our doctor, a medical student, I mean she worked as a doctor . . ." Stiller drank from the glass in his hand, holding in his left a cigarette that had long since gone out; sitting like this he told her a few things about this Polish girl, describing her as a person who had always impressed him, not by her beauty, but by all sorts of other things—a clear mind and at the same time plenty of temperament, a trace of Tartar blood, a born fighter, and at the same time a person with a sense of humor, a rarity among revolutionaries, as Stiller explained, "the daughter of educated parents, the first Communist in her family, a Good Samaritan who seemed herself to be invulnerable, moreover with an exceptional gift for languages, an interpreter in Spanish, Russian, French, English, Italian and German, all of which she spoke with the same accent but with faultless grammar and a considerable vocabulary, and in addition an entrancing dancer—that was Anya," he broke off. "She used to call me her German dreamer." To judge by his expression, this was still a bitter pill for Stiller, one which he had not yet digested after ten years. "Did she love you?" asked Sibylle. "Not me alone," answered Stiller, and suddenly jumped:

"What's happened to your coffee?"—"Forgotten!" she laughed. "In your reminiscence of Anya!" Stiller apologized profusely. "Never mind," she said. "I don't want any coffee."—"You're not drinking any wine either," said Stiller. "What would you like?"—"To hear your story about the Russian gun," she replied, and Stiller, who had already got up to make the coffee, shrugged his shoulders. "There's not much to tell," he said. "My Russian gun was faultless, of course, I only had to press the trigger . . ."

There followed the final digression, an impartial and quite superfluous description of the tactical position, which Sibylle couldn't follow anyhow. "—well, there it is," he broke off, "Sturzenegger has told you the rest."

It was now eleven o'clock, Sibylle could hear the hour striking on the Cathedral clock, with which she had become quite familiar. She didn't understand why this story was such a burden to Stiller; she only felt

(so she says) that this hour was to him a confession,
a confession which not Sibylle, but Stiller himself,
had sought. "I don't understand" said Sibylle at last;
but Stiller immediately interrupted her, "—why I
didn't shoot?" That wasn't what Sibylle had meant.
He laughed, "Because I'm a failure. Quite simply, I'm
not a man."—"Because you didn't fire, that day on
the Tajo?"—"It was treachery," said Stiller with im-
patient emphasis. "There's nothing to explain. I had a
job to do, I'd even volunteered for it, I had orders to
guard the ferry, perfectly clear orders. What more do
you want? It wasn't I that was in the balance, but
thousands of others, a cause. I had to fire. What was
I in Spain for? It was treachery," he concluded.
"They should really have put me up against the wall."
—"I don't know about that," commented Sibylle.
"What did Anya, your Polish girl, have to say?"
Stiller didn't answer this question at once, but explained how he had later talked his way out of the
difficulty by telling the commissar the lie about the
gun not going off. "What did Anya have to say?" he
now smiled, twisting a cigarette until there was almost
no tobacco left in the wrapping, and shrugging his
shoulders, "Nothing. She looked after me until I was
well enough to go home. She despised me."—"I
thought you said she loved you?"—"It was treachery," insisted Stiller. "Love makes no difference to
that. It was a failure." Sibylle let him talk, let him repeat himself first in different words and then in the
same words, until he refilled his glass and drank.
"Have you never talked to anyone about it?" she
asked. "Not even to your wife?" Stiller briefly shook
his head. "Why not?" she went on to ask. "Are you
ashamed to talk to her about it?" Stiller evaded the
question, "Probably a woman can't understand what it
means. I was a coward."

The bottle was now empty, a liter bottle of chianti:
Stiller didn't give the impression of being drunk, he

seemed to be used to drinking. Was his drinking also somehow connected with this Tajo affair? Of course Sibylle couldn't simply take him in her arms; Stiller would have felt himself misunderstood as all men do when their seriousness is countered by a different seriousness, indeed, Stiller seemed already to be aware that Sibylle was permitting herself thoughts of her own, and he reiterated with apodictic melancholy, "It was a failure."—"And you imagined," smiled Sibylle, "that you were never going to fail in your life?" She had to make her meaning clearer: "You're ashamed of being as you are. Who demanded of you that you should be a fighter, a warrior, someone who can shoot? You feel you didn't prove yourself there in Spain. Who's denying it? But perhaps you were trying to prove yourself someone you just aren't—" Stiller wouldn't swallow this. "I told you already," he remarked, "probably a woman can't understand a thing like that." And Sibylle thought, perhaps better than you like. But she only laughed, "You men, why do you always try to be so grand? I don't want to hurt your feelings, but—" Involuntarily she took hold of his hands, a gesture which Stiller apparently misunderstood—anyhow, he looked at her with covert contempt, it seemed to her, not in an unfriendly way, but Stiller didn't take her seriously: he took her for a person in love expecting caresses and nothing else. She was a burden to him, a burden. He stroked her hair, the misunderstood man weighed down by tragedy, and now Sibylle, as though frozen by his tender condescension, couldn't utter a word. Stiller (she says) fancied himself in the rôle of a man with a wound; he didn't want to get over it. He took refuge behind it. He didn't want to be loved. He was afraid of it.

"Now you know," he said, clearing the glasses away, "why I didn't shoot. What's the point of this story? I'm not a man. I've dreamt about it for years: I

want to shoot, but the gun doesn't go off—I don't
need to tell you what that means, it's a typical impotence dream." This remark, which he made while
standing in the kitchen recess, upset Sibylle and she
stood up. She was sorry she had come to his studio.
She felt a sadness, which she concealed, and at the
same time she was sorry for Stiller. Why didn't he
want to be loved, really loved? There was nothing
left for her but to play the part Stiller forced upon
her and chatter with uncomprehending, inquisitive
gaiety, until Stiller had to leave the room for a moment.

She hoped she would never see Stiller again.

When he came back from the landing, accompanied
by the inevitable swishing of water, Sibylle had already combed her hair and her lips were freshly
rouged. She had already put her hat on, too. Stiller
was completely dumbfounded. "Are you leaving?"
he asked. "It's almost midnight," she said, picking up
her gloves. Stiller didn't reply. "You silly fellow," she
exclaimed suddenly. "Why?" he asked from the sink,
where he was washing his hands. Neither of them
knew what to say next, and Stiller went on drying
his hands. "Come," said Sibylle, "let's go away"—
"Where to?"—"Away from here," she said. "I've got
the car downstairs, I hope nobody's noticed, but I think
I forgot to lock it." Stiller smiled as though over an
ingenuous girl. The meaning of his decision could not
be seen in his face; anyway, he opened the little window of the kitchen to let the smoke out of the studio,
and without a word took his brown coat from the nail,
banged the pockets as one does to see whether one has
the front-door key; then he looked at Sibylle, uncertain
in his turn what she really had in mind, and switched
off the light . . .

The next day was not easy for Sibylle, or easy in a
perplexing way. Some country inn by night, where

there were no *banderillas* on the wall, but instead
probably a text from the Bible or some other saying
embroidered in cross-stitch—"Faithful and true," or
"Honesty is the best policy," or whatever people do
embroider on these things—in short, a country inn
by night that may have smelt of dried pears and where
cocks crowed outside the little window early in the
morning, and on the other hand her familiar home
with little Hannes, who hadn't died of his sore throat;
both were such wonderful worlds, and the bewildering thing was that she could go from one to the other
without any bridge. Around midday she rang up to
find out whether Stiller really existed. And then, we
may imagine, she went downstairs and out into the
garden . . .

It was spring, there was a lot to be done, digging,
planting, raking, hoeing, and the ground was as dry
as in summer. Sibylle took out the lawn-spray, set it
up in the little meadow and let it patter on the budding shrubs. A neighbor told her this was bad for
the buds, so Sibylle dragged the spray off somewhere else where its swishing would do no harm, but
she had to have the swish of water and her respected
neighbor, who also knew better about the weather
forecast, could jump in the lake if she didn't understand. She should mind her own business, anyway.

Little Hannes hadn't forgotten the promise she
gave him yesterday to buy cane and blue tissue paper
and make him a kite; she regretted her omission and
promised to go into town tomorrow, and to make
up for having forgotten, she also promised to take
him to the circus, when it came, and today he was allowed to go with Sibylle to meet Daddy at the airport. Altogether, Sibylle had an urge to see everyone
happy, including Carola, the Italian maid, who was
given the day off—the family could have a meal in
town. What a wonderful spring day! Even the neigh-

bor agreed about that. The forsythia was ablaze with yellow, the magnolia was beginning to blossom, and on top of this the lawn-spray conjured up a little private rainbow. And then, after four hours of valiant labor in the garden, Sibylle took another shower before once more changing her clothes.

They reached the airport much too early. Hannes got a bowl of ice cream for his disappearing sore throat, but on no account was he allowed to take off his jacket, for fear the silly sore throat should come back again. There were aeroplanes everywhere. They could have flown straight to Athens, Paris or even New York. Sibylle had no doubt that Rolf would see it in her face at the first glance. In any case, he was the person closest to her, the only one in whom she could, or wanted to, confide.

The plane was forty minutes late, time enough for Sibylle to say in imagination everything that was never said in reality. For the moment the echoing loudspeaker announced the landing of the plane from London, and a crowd of unknown people descended from it and were shepherded towards the customs by a stewardess, and Sibylle, looking down from the terrace with little Hannes's hand in hers, saw Rolf gaze round, catch sight of his family and wave to them with a newspaper—at this moment Sibylle suddenly went mute inside, in fact she didn't even wave. She didn't realize it, but Rolf swore later that she didn't even wave, didn't even nod. She suddenly felt: What's it to him? And as she waited and waited for him to go through the customs, she even experienced a slight feeling of anger at the way Rolf took it for granted she would be there to meet him at the end of every journey. Somehow Sibylle needed this armor of anger now. A wave with a newspaper, yes, but not a trace of delighted surprise; he simply considered it his right to find a waiting wife at the airport. This annoyed Sibylle so much that when he came out of the customs shed and kissed her, she gave him both cheeks, but not her mouth . . .

"What's new?"—his usual question. On her way to the car she felt a trifle weak at the knees after all. During supper in town, in order to have some news to give him, she talked about young Sturzenegger, their young architect, and his fantastic luck in getting a commission in Canada or somewhere. Furthermore, young Sturzenegger had recommended a film they ought not to miss, and today was the last performance. As a rule Rolf was always very cheerful and gay after his trips, as though he came straight from the fountainhead of life. Now, overshadowed by her gaiety, he actually complained of feeling tired, spoke of heavy squalls over the Channel and wanted to go home, acting as though he came not from London, but from the front, a hero with a right to be coddled at home. Sibylle was also a trifle surprised, without letting it show, to discover how differently she regarded Rolf—not without love, but without the fear that he was hiding something, and free from the illusion that she couldn't live without him, not without warm and sincere affection either, but the affection was mixed with compassion so that it contained an element of condescension which Sibylle did not want, but suddenly it was there, a subtle change in the tone of her voice that was more evident to her than to him. In order to show that his fatigue was not her fatigue, she proposed that she should go to the recommended film alone. Rolf raised no objection. She dropped the idea—not because of a bad conscience, which she did not have even now that she was face to face with him, but rather out of a motherly feeling. In the car, which Sibylle drove, it was not Rolf who put his hand on her arm, but the other way round, even though Sibylle was at the wheel.

He said, "You look magnificent." She said, "Yes, I

feel fine." And she thought with relief that now he knew everything. She probably looked at him a few times, finding it hard to believe that a man could take it so calmly. It was almost funny. It must have been a difficult moment (for Sibylle) when Rolf, the father of her child, put his luggage in the hall and hung up his coat with the intention of staying the night here. A monstrous idea! Sibylle thought she was going to burst into tears; he didn't notice that either, but talked about the frantic impoverishment of the British Empire. Little Hannes had already said his prayers and been put to bed; Sibylle no longer had any convincing reason for running away from the frantic impoverishment of the British Empire. She wouldn't have revoked anything, anything at all, even if she could; but how was she to get through this evening, when his blindness, which Sibylle could not understand, made it so easy to remain silent, and yet impossible?

Rolf was standing in the kitchen by the refrigerator, drinking a glass of beer, and asking the distant Sibylle whether she had been to the building site in the meantime. Sibylle had made up her mind to slip quietly out of the house while Rolf stood in the kitchen drinking his beer, to go off somewhere, not to Stiller, but somewhere. Rolf must have heard the latch click; he came and found her in her overcoat, key in hand, pale or blushing, but with a strange presence of mind. "The dog," she said, the dog had to be let out. And Rolf put down his glass to take the dog out, more helpful than usual. Had he really no inkling? Was he shamming? Did he really not care? Or was he stupid, quite incredibly stupid, or so hugely conceited that he imagined no other man could possibly compete with him, or what did it all mean?

Sibylle sat there in her overcoat. And yet in a way Rolf was right, it didn't make any difference, it seemed to her: it took nothing away from him. But he must know. Every hour more, every quarter of an

hour, poisoned everything that had been between
Rolf and her. She was crying. Did she really regret
it after all? And she felt ashamed before Stiller, who
was now so far away, she was afraid that in the moment that was drawing ever closer when Rolf brought
the dog back and she told him, she might diminish the
night that was past, diminish it to the point of betrayal, betrayal of Stiller and herself. She could see
it already: Rolf would put his arm round her shoulders with a kind of understanding and consideration
that buried everything; he wouldn't take her rather
silly little intermezzo seriously, and she, the be-
trayer, would hate him because of her own betrayal.
Wouldn't it be more honest in the end to say nothing
about it? And suddenly it seemed to her as though
everything that went to make up a home had the sole
purpose of rendering honesty impossible. Why wasn't
Stiller there? Her husband appeared to her so strong,
so invincibly strong, not because he had "right" on
his side, but simply through his personal presence: it
was as though Stiller were hidden by a hundred
things, by this piano, by furniture and carpets and
books and the refrigerator and a mass of things, mere
things, that seemed to come to Rolf's aid, obstinate, irrefutable. A home like this was a bastion, she thought,
an elegant but underhand trick. On the point of
ringing Stiller, just to hear his forgotten voice, she
heard the dog barking and hung up; at last she took
off her coat, utterly exhausted and ready to capitu-
late in the typical woman's way—to let everything be
decided by which of the men conquered the other and
thereby Sibylle. Rolf found her busy with household
tasks. Not unreasonably, he found it unnecessary for
Sibylle to check the monthly bills from the milkman
and the butcher at this particular moment, he thought
it unfair to a husband who had just arrived from London, and showed his ill-humor, yes, it looked as
though the evening would go off in a state of marital

ill-humor of an everyday kind, in other words pretty well.

That this was not the case, seems to have been due mainly to Rolf. He flung his beer glass into the sink. "What's the matter?" she asked. He deduced from her unfriendliness that Sibylle, his dear wife with her old-fashioned ideas, once more suspected him; Rolf had had enough. He found it so petty, so narrow-minded; once more (but with a clear hint that it was for the last time) Rolf delivered his "lecture" and re-fused to be interrupted, no, Sibylle must really de-velop a more generous conception of marriage, she must have confidence, must grasp the fact that Rolf loved her, even if he did occasionally meet another woman while he was traveling; besides, that hadn't even happened this time, but like all men he was par-ticularly concerned about the principle of the thing, and he hoped to bring Sibylle to a more mature con-ception of marriage, to the realization that there must be a certain amount of freedom even in marriage. He forbade fits of jealousy. But this chance passed too. Sibylle wanted to assure him that she understood him as never before, that she felt no trace of jealousy; it would have been the truth but at the same time down-right mockery, and she couldn't utter a word, not a word.

Sibylle's only wish was to be alone as quickly as possible. It was horrible, it was becoming farcical. When Sibylle gave him a hearty kiss on the forehead, she felt superior in a way that made her feel ashamed. Involuntarily, she locked her door. Her happiness wasn't a dream. As soon as Sibylle found herself alone, it filled her again in all its reality. Tact alone prevented her from singing. But her silent happiness was apparently audible through the walls, and her husband, although he had said everything that needed saying, could not rest. The locked door took him aback; he insisted on coming into her room, and only when he was sitting on her bed ready to play the Good Samaritan, having obviously expected a tear-stained face and dumbfounded to see a happy one, did the truth begin to dawn on Rolf. He asked, "What's happened?" Sibylle couldn't find the right words in which to tell him a thing like that; she said, "You know quite well." Rolf's choice of words wasn't particularly fortunate either, "You've been with a man?" Sibylle said Yes and was glad to be rid of her silence, relieved and now completely happy for the first time. Rolf stared at her. She begged him to ask no more questions now and to leave her alone. Rolf (says Sibylle) took it with remarkable composure. He even went away for a few days in order to leave Sibylle in peace, for which she was grateful to him from the bottom of her heart. After his return he was also (says Sibylle) remarkably composed.

It would ill become me to describe the lovers' happiness which Sibylle, my public prosecutor's wife, experienced or hoped to experience during the following weeks. Whether this happiness was as great as the other two partners—Frau Julika Stiller-Tschudy on the one hand, and my friend and prosecutor on the other —imagined, seems to me dubious. A homeless love, a love with no dwelling-place in everyday life, a love that depends on hours of enchantment, we know what that amounts to; sooner or later it is a despairing affair, embraces in the growing corn or the nocturnal darkness of a wood—for a time it's romantic, exciting, then ridiculous, a humiliation, an impossible business all their joint sense of humor could not save, for they were no longer a couple of secondary-school children, but grown-up people, a man and a woman, both of them already married . . .

Sibylle (so she says) understood his hesitations about receiving her in his studio, where everything reminded him of his sick Julika. She regretted it, because, as I have said, his big, light studio appealed to her, but she understood. What would Sibylle not have given to have a healthy rival, a woman who was her equal, to whom she could have offered friendship or open conflict, yes, even a fury of jealousy who laid moral mines for her everywhere in society, or a crazy woman who made ridiculous threats with the gas oven, a gallant fool who headed straight for counter-adultery—she would have preferred anything to this sick woman who retired to a sanatorium at Davos and immediately put the healthy ones in the wrong, and on top of this a woman Sibylle had never seen face to face, a phantom! But that's how it was, and so his studio was out of the question. Where else could they meet than in God's open air and a few inns? A rainy week was as disastrous for their love as will o' the wisps and midsummer night's dreams are for other people's; the inns began to repeat themselves; the roads round the town began to lead nowhere; their conversations began to grow melancholy, witty, but melancholy—in a word, it couldn't go on like this . . .

And yet they really loved one another.

"Come," said Sibylle one day, "let's go to Paris." Stiller laughed uncertainly. "Don't worry, I've just been to the bank," she said. "All we have to do is to find out when the train leaves." Stiller asked the waiter for a timetable. There was no lack of trains to Paris. And one day, it was in July, they actually got as far as the platform and sat on a bench underneath the electric clock, the tickets in their pockets and equipped with toothbrush and passport. "Are we going or aren't we?" asked Stiller, as though the inhibitions were all on her side, not on his. The porter was already going from carriage to carriage. "Take your seats," he shouted. "Take your seats please." She felt sorry for Stiller. There could be no doubt about his resolution to put her wishes into action at last, but suddenly Sibylle found she had lost all desire to go; she was upset by the grimness of his determination. "What about Julika?" she asked. Meanwhile the hand of the electric clock was jerking on from minute to minute. At bottom (so she says) Stiller was glad that the hesitation, in appearance at least, came from her, whereas he, with her suitcase in his hand, represented masculine ruthlessness personified. The doors were being shut of one carriage after the other. Sibylle sat where she was, she felt so clearly that the phantom was already sitting inside, and Sibylle had no desire to wander about Paris with a phantom . . .

The train left the station; they remained on the platform with the resolve that Stiller would first go to Davos and speak quite openly to the sick Julika—there was nothing else for it.

Stiller went to Davos in August.

For her part Sibylle felt perfectly free, even if her husband's remarkable composure (as she says) got on her nerves. Every time they sat down to black coffee, when little Hannes was no longer there, she waited for the heart-to-heart talk. In vain, Rolf merely said, "If you're free on Thursday evening, there's that organ recital in the Fraumünster . . ." Sibylle saw to the percolator. "I'm not free," she said, and that was the end of the organ recital. She could have killed Rolf: he allowed her a freedom, an independence that was downright insulting. It wasn't Rolf, but Sibylle, who burst out: "I don't understand you, you know I love someone, that I see him practically every day, and you don't even ask what his name is. That's ludicrous!" Rolf smiled: "What is his name then?" In response to such condescension Sibylle naturally couldn't tell him, and they waited silently for the coffee. "I think I told you," remarked Rolf chattily, "that they want to have me as public prosecutor . . ." Rolf always had something with which to evade the issue, something important, something objective.

At last the coffee boiled in the glass sphere, the

steam whistled. It couldn't go on like this with Rolf either, she thought. Amongst other things, money was suddenly beginning to assume an importance: not for Rolf, but for Sibylle. She was secretly hurt at the way her dear Stiller took it as a matter of course that every stitch Sibylle wore had been paid for by Rolf; Stiller earned almost nothing, true, and he couldn't go and fetch money from the bank, she realized that, and yet it secretly hurt her, against all commonsense. The most Stiller ever did was to call her a spoilt darling, feel the quality of her new material and praise her choice of colors; but the idea—which Sibylle would straight away have affectionately talked him out of, that goes without saying—the idea that Stiller ought no longer to let Rolf buy her clothes for her, never so much as crossed his mind. It didn't worry Stiller, no, and it didn't worry Rolf either. Often (so she says) she found both men impossible. Then she felt an itch to take it out of him. "By the way," said Sibylle, "I need some money, but rather a lot. The fact is, we are thinking of spending this autumn together in Paris—" She looked at him out of the corner of her eye after this remark; Rolf said nothing. The one thing she hadn't expected happened, to wit, nothing. She filled his cup and set it down in front of him. "Thanks," he said. Either Rolf, her husband, was opposed to her going to Paris with another man (and with Rolf's money), or Rolf wasn't opposed to it; there was no third alternative that she could see.

Sibylle filled her own cup. "So you want to go to Paris," was all he said. Sibylle didn't leave him without further explanation: "I don't know for how long, maybe only a few weeks, maybe longer—" Rolf didn't jump up from his chair, he didn't smash a cup against the wall, this Rolf with his ridiculous composure, to say nothing of falling on his knees and beseeching Sibylle to come to her senses and stay

with him. Nothing of the sort. Rolf blushed slightly
for an instant; he had probably imagined that the
affair with the fancy-dress pierrot was finished, and
now he had to get used to the idea of her happy
adultery all over again. But why did he have to, in
heaven's name? Rolf stirred his coffee. Why didn't
he throw a flowerpot at her, or at least a book? When
she saw his cup trembling slightly, it aroused no remorse in her, not even pity, but rather disappointment,
bitterness, scorn, sadness. "Or have you anything
against it?" she asked, passing him the sugar and explaining her reasons: "You know what it's like here,
there will only be gossip if people see me. It makes no
odds to me. But it's unpleasant for you. Especially
now that they want you for a public prosecutor. I'm
sure it will be much better for you, too, if we live in
Paris . . ." She looked at him. "What do you think,
Rolf?"

He took a sip, stirred, sipped, blew and stirred, as
though nothing else was so important at the moment
as drinking this hot coffee. Quite casually came his
matter-of-fact inquiry: "Yes, well roughly how much
money do you need?" Cowardly as men always are
when they are not doing the attacking themselves,
he immediately sought refuge in practical matters,
whereas Sibylle wanted to hear what he felt, what he
hoped. Was Sibylle in Paris with another man a matter
of indifference to him? Did he find it quite in order?
Did he find it unbearable? Sibylle asked him straight
out: "What do you think of it?"

Rolf was now standing at the big window, showing her his broad back, with both hands in his pockets
like a bystander watching a fire. His back seemed to
her so broad, his head so round and fat. She shot at his
tranquility: "I love him," she said unasked. "We really
love each other," she added. "Otherwise we wouldn't
be going to Paris together, you'll believe me when I
say that, I'm not irresponsible." And then men al-

ways have to get back to work, yes, yes, it was already ten minutes past two; a sitting, the bastion of their indispensability, Sibylle knew all about that. If Rolf didn't go back to work now, law and order would break down all over the world. "You must know yourself," he said briefly, "what is the right thing to do." And then, after he had put on his overcoat and forced the buttons into the wrong holes, so that his wife had to button it up properly, he added in rather a melancholy tone, "You must do what you think right," and left . . . And Sibylle, alone in her room, wept.

In this sense, then, Sibylle was free.

Stiller, on the other hand, came back from Davos having settled nothing and acted as though his ballerina were on the point of death; under these circumstances a trip to Paris was out of the question. Once more they sat at the edge of a wood—all round the ripe corn had already been cut, summer was passing, thunder clouds were gathering above the blue lake, a bumblebee zigzagged humming through the summer stillness, the heat haze quivered over the fields, hens were cackling in the farmyards, and the world was a faultless, perfectly arranged, positively inspiring affair. Only their happiness (or what they expected from their love) was very complicated. They sat silently on the ground, two adulterers with their hands tenderly interlocked, each with a blade of grass between lips stretched tight with care, and the only thing in this world that was not complicated seemed to them to be marriage, not marriage with Rolf and not marriage with Julika, but marriage to one another.

In the entirely rancorless recollection of this magnificent woman—I can see her before me while I write, in her blue wicker chair as she was the other day in the nursing home when I brought her the gladioli, with her lemon-yellow dressing gown and black hair—there is one point that would cause the missing Stiller no little astonishment, namely the fact that this summer or autumn, without ever saying a word to Stiller, she expected a child by him (it would now have been six years old) . . .

I will record the facts:

It was in September, and Stiller was very busy with all sorts of arrangements for an exhibition; important personages considered it desirable, indispensable, that Stiller should make another public appearance. "Am I in the way?" asked Sibylle, as Stiller, after greeting her with an almost perfunctory kiss, went on sawing at a stand. She looked at him. A man never looks so handsome, she thought, as when he is working with his hands. "I don't want to hold you up," she said, "but I just had to see you today . . ." She gave away nothing else, especially as Stiller did not inquire why she felt this need. The important things now were the stands. "When is he coming," asked Sibylle, "this man from the art gallery?" She tried to take an interest. Outside it was a mild, blue September day. There were at least nine more stands to be made and then painted or varnished—quite an undertaking; the wrong stand can make a great deal of difference, and what a lot of stands still needed varnishing, while from others, which were fortunately already varnished, the varnish had to be removed! That was the job at the moment.

"What about your wife," asked Sibylle, "are you going to exhibit her?" She had put on a kettle for tea and it was already boiling, so she was also occupied. "I've brought you something," said Sibylle. "I've been baking." And she showed him a fresh cake, a so-called seed cake; Stiller was touched, without looking at it, and talked about humbug. Sibylle couldn't see any difference in his sculptures; so why had they suddenly become humbug? And there was a letter from a curator, a hymn to Stiller, so that one might almost feel afraid Stiller would disappear in a cloud of fame.

"The tea's ready," she announced and waited; she would never have thought that an art exhibition called for as much preparation as an invasion (Rolf had been talking to her about Churchill's memoirs over coffee), and she was sorry for Stiller. "How do you like the poster?" he asked, rubbing away at a stand with glass-paper. Sibylle hadn't even noticed the sketch on a piece of packing paper. "There's to be a poster as well?" she exclaimed in astonishment, and true enough, it was a proper poster like they have for Furtwängler or Persil. She thought it frightful—A. Stiller, his beloved handwriting on every hoarding, enlarged as though under a microscope. Hadn't men any shame? If he'd enjoyed it, at least; but Stiller cursed the whole exhibition. Then why did he do it? He drank his tea standing up and ate her cake while he talked, not even noticing the showers of crumbs that were falling everywhere . . .

Sibylle soon left him; it seemed to her that this was no moment to win him over to fatherhood, and she was glad he hadn't simply let her go, but had arranged to go sailing with her at five o'clock. She was happy to be able to meet him again that day. Merely to pass the time, she strolled along the Bahnhofstrasse in the September air, from window to window, from shop to shop, until she had found the nicest tie in Zurich. Unfortunately, it struck her, Stiller had no shirt that would go with this tie. She bought a shirt to go with it.

When sailing (says Sibylle) Stiller was always like a boy, so serious, without brooding, so relaxed, so happy with his toy; he handled the tiller and rope, while Sibylle lay in the bows, a hand or a foot in the rippling water. Here on the lake she was free from the phantom. The shores were lost in the autumn mist, their sail gleamed in the pale light of the declining sun, in the east the sky was already turning to purple dusk, and the water beside their gliding boat was shadowy, almost black under a light surface. Sibylle rested her head on her elbows so as to have the ever more oblique rays of the sinking sun full in her face, heard the gurgling under the boat when it rocked in the waves of a steamer, and looked at Stiller, her busy steersman, out of screwed-up eyes—his face, his narrow head, his pale hair in the wind, yes, she liked him very much, this man who was perhaps already the father of her second child. How would Rolf take it? Actually she felt quite indifferent. Apropos Rolf: tomorrow he would take up his duties as public prosecutor. How able they were! Each in his own way. And Sibylle made up her mind to be sensible, to be content. In spite of everything. She was still young, and there was plenty of time. Something would happen. Perhaps she would have a child, perhaps Julika would die, perhaps a star would fall from heaven and straighten everything out.

As always when they were sailing, they spoke little. Above the lake hummed the town with its traffic, schoolchildren waved from a homeward-bound steamboat, and seen like this with one's head lying flat the world consisted entirely of colors, of highlights, reflections and shadows, of sound and silence; this was not the moment to reach decisions. Why shouldn't it be possible to love two men? Stiller was her intimate friend, he was not a man who subjugated. Rolf subjugated. That could be terrible, but in many respects it was simpler. Rolf didn't make sisters of women. At one point they scraped against a buoy, so that there was a grating noise, and Stiller, who had been talking about his exhibition and not watching out, apologized. Rolf never apologized; Rolf was self-righteous. One could be frightened for Stiller—not for Rolf. Both of them rolled into one, that would have been the ideal! Rolf often seemed to her like a big dog, a St. Bernard, which it was better not to put on the lead for fear of being pulled over. Stiller seemed to her like a brother, almost like a sister . . .

It had imperceptibly grown cool, and Sibylle stood up, walked along the swaying boat to Stiller, took his head between her wet hands and kissed him over and over again. He let go of the rope, so that the sail flapped, and asked, "What's the matter?" Sibylle didn't yet know herself.

"Men are funny," Sibylle still thinks so today: "You with your seriousness! For hours and days, sometimes for weeks, one could imagine you want nothing else than the nearness of a woman you love, you seek this nearness thoughtlessly, you'd shrink from nothing, one supposes, from no danger, from no ridicule and certainly not from brutality, if anyone stood in your way, there is only the woman, it seems, the woman you love—and then, in the twinkling of an eye, it's quite different, suddenly it turns out that a sitting is important, so important that everything has to be fitted in with it. You suddenly become edgy, you find the woman a fond burr that you can't shake off. I know this silly consideration for all sorts of strangers, for everyone but the woman who loves you. You and your serious affairs of life! An international conference of lawyers, the curator of an art gallery—suddenly there are once more things that must on no account be neglected. And woe to the woman who doesn't understand that, or even smiles! And then, in a twinkling of an eye, you're like little Hannes during a thunder storm again. Isn't that true? These same men have to put their heads on our shoulders, so as not to despair, to feel that they are not entirely lost in this serious world, not entirely superfluous with all their legal eminence and art exhibitions . . . God knows," she laughed, "you're a queer lot!"

One day at the end of September Stiller said over the
telephone, "Get ready, we're going to Paris." She
couldn't believe her receiver. "Are you serious?" The
cheerful voice answered, "Why not?" Still half in
doubt whether Stiller was not joking, already half
joyously serious she asked, "When?" The cheerful
voice answered, "Tomorrow, today, when you like."
(They knew the trains to Paris by heart; there was a
night train that came in through the suburbs of Paris
at first light, then breakfast with the early workmen
in a bar at the Gare de l'Est, coffee and brioches,
followed by a stroll through the great covered market
full of vegetables and fish—and suddenly, as in a fairy
tale, all this was within their grasp?) "I'm coming
over right away," said Sibylle; but it wasn't as simple
as that, for in the morning Stiller was receiving another visit from his curator, and in the afternoon
Sibylle had to take little Hannes to the circus. "After
the circus then," she said and put down the receiver,
as dizzy as a person who has just won a prize, empty
with happiness . . .

At last things seemed to be moving.

"What shall we say," asked Rolf over coffee, "we
must order the removal van, when would it suit you?
I've no intention of making the whole move by myself. Will you be here next week?" Sibylle quite understood his urgency, troublesome as she found it.
"Yes, yes," she said, "I know, but I can't tell you today."—"When will you be able to tell me?"—"Tomorrow."—"Why are you so on edge?"—"I'm not on
edge," she retorted. "Why should I be on edge?"
Sibylle had hoped she would be able to let her decision mature; now she suddenly had a twenty-four hour
ultimatum. After all, it concerned everything in the
world that mattered to her, Stiller, Rolf, Hannes, it
concerned a life that was not yet born, people to
whom her heart was bound, it concerned herself, it
involved the question whether Sibylle would be capa-

ble of choosing her life for herself. All this was in the balance. And Rolf wanted to know by tomorrow, so that he could order the removal van, tomorrow over coffee . . .

The children's performance at the circus (says Sibylle) was anything but a distraction for her; on the contrary, this was where she reached her decision—for Paris, for Stiller, for the risk. By daylight, thought Sibylle, these circuses look much shabbier, downright pathetic; the dilapidation behind the showy façade is visible everywhere; this makes the light under the tent with the sun shining on it all the lovelier, a light like amber, and on top of this the estrades filled with a motley crowd of children and the buzz of their voices, and then the brass band, the stench of beasts, and every now and then a roar as though from the jungle. Sibylle found it magnificent. In Paris, she thought, there would be some kind of a job she could do, any sort of job, that was part of the risk. Sibylle was not afraid. The clown who opened the performance evidently took the children for stupid adults, his success was meager, and little Hannes, at the circus for the first time, stared at the silly man without smiling, only glad when he stumbled, and didn't want him to come back. Sibylle was to tell the clown not to come back. But then came the leaping tigers! The crack of a whip and hoarse growling—Sibylle was fascinated, and for a few minutes she even forgot Paris, while Hannes sucked a sweet and asked why the nasty animals had to keep jumping through the hoop. He couldn't see any proper point in it. The seals, on the other hand, enchanted him, and on top of all the decisions she had to make, Sibylle now had to decide whether she wouldn't like to be a seal. While the horses were waltzing Hannes wanted to go home. Now Sibylle could easily have gone to Stiller. She didn't do so. Not yet. And then, as the lives of seven men hung from the smiling teeth of a girl on the

trapeze, Hannes spotted down below through the
estrade a scruffy-looking man in boots, who was dressing up all kinds of dogs in quaint little jackets, black
dress suits and white bridal veils, and the dogs could
scarcely wait. After this, Sibylle had to take little
Hannes on her knees, so that he shouldn't fall down
between the scaffolding. By this time, it seems, she
had made up her mind. And yet all her attention
was on the daring act on the glittering trapeze. She
would manage somehow, she thought. Suddenly
the children all round yelled their approval with a
single voice: the silvery trapeze lady had just left her
celestial swing with a *salto mortale*, bounced up and
down in the net, and just look, she hadn't broken
her neck, and the orchestra blared out Verdi. Interval.
Hannes wanted to go outside like all the other children, but Sibylle sat as though spellbound: A person in
fancy dress, who obviously earned her living like this,
was selling chocolates, and this was doubtless the
biggest attraction of the afternoon for Sibylle: an independent woman—

Just before seven o'clock, after bringing Hannes
safely home, she came to Stiller, who was whistling in
his studio like a reed-sparrow, the trunk with the
hinges pulled out and already packed. Of course he
was quite serious about the trip to Paris. Why had
Sibylle come without her luggage? Now it turned out
that Stiller had to go to Paris "anyway," not today,
not tomorrow, but soon—on account of a bronze that
could only be cast in Paris and was absolutely indispensable for the forthcoming exhibition, as the curator
agreed. What about Julika? He had such a magnificent
pretext for going to Paris, and Julika had no excuse
to excite herself and send her temperature curve up
on account of this trip. Sibylle understood. She said
simply:

"No."

Stiller was offended.

"I'm going—"

"Yes," she said. "Do."

He thought her queer. For months they had been talking and dreaming of Paris, and now—

"Do that," said Sibylle. "Go to Paris."

Stiller went (he had to, anyway) in the hope that Sibylle would regret her passing mood and follow him. Sibylle was no longer interested in his hopes. The following day over coffee, she said to Rolf, "I'm not going to Paris." Rolf made an effort not to lose his remarkable composure in his joy. Then she said, "But I'm going for a week to my friend at St. Gallen." And now, would you believe it, the cup was shattered against the wall. When Sibylle was alone, she took the telephone book on her knee, crushed her cigarette in the ashtray, looked up the number of the doctor, the only one who could be considered for the purpose, immediately dialed the number and waited without hearing the pulsing of her heart. She was only astonished by her calmness. It had to be, and the quicker the better.

Rolf naturally didn't believe in the girl friend at St. Gallen for a moment. He felt tricked, fooled, and as far as he was concerned that was the end. The unfortunate meeting in his office—after her discharge from the nursing home—looked quite different through his wife's eyes from the way Rolf, my public prosecutor, described it; the stubborn silence was not of her making (Sibylle assured me) but of his.

I record the facts:

Sibylle had to wait for nearly an hour in his antechamber, until the secretary came, "Will you step this way please?" After a handshake, after a moment in the doorway when Sibylle felt she would sink into the floor if his hands did not bear her up, she walked past Rolf (that is true) straight to the window, as though she had come to see the view. "So this is your office?" she said in a tone as though nothing had happened. "Magnificent." It was pure embarrassment. "Yes," he replied, "this is my office." He looked her up and down as though she had returned from a lovers' trip. "I want to talk to you," said Sibylle categorically. Rolf motioned her into the lounge-chair like a client and offered her a cigarette from a large box on the desk, official cigarettes, so to speak. "Thank you," said Sibylle and inquired, "How are you?" And Rolf, without altering the intonation, simply echoed, "How are you?"

So they sat facing one another and smoking, Rolf behind his big desk, while Sibylle felt as though she were in an open field. Did he want to hear at all how much she felt she owed him? He didn't even ask ironically, What was it like at St. Gallen? "You must forgive me," said Rolf, "in half an hour I've got a case." And of course Sibylle didn't utter a word. Why didn't he ask her straight out where she had been? Or quite simply, Why are you lying? Instead he merely announced: "The move is finished. Fortunately we had fine weather . . ." His report of the move was completely matter-of-fact, without a hint of reproach for Sibylle's absence. "For the moment I've just had your things put in the room," he explained. "I don't know how you want to arrange your room, or even whether—" Unfortunately they were interrupted by the telephone. (From the nursing home Sibylle had gone first to their old home. The echo of her footsteps in the empty rooms, the faded wallpaper with the darker rectangles due to the now vanished pictures, the dilapidation everywhere, the impossibility of believing that she had lived between these walls for six years, and all this after her easy, secret, necessary loss, which had nevertheless cried out to heaven through all her narcosis, all this was horrible, and Sibylle had wept, as though she saw in this empty and dilapidated, unspeakabl shabby home that was no longer a home the graphic symbol of her whole life. She had tried to phone Rolf, but in vain; the telephone had already been disconnected. Then she went to the new house to see the lady's room— an utter muddle, a furniture warehouse, the epitome of meaninglessness, a heap of pictures and mirrors, books, hat boxes, vases and shoes, sewing things, faultless goods, but goods, nothing but goods, a heap to set on fire. Hannes had left her no peace, and when he wanted to show her Daddy's new room Sibylle had stopped still in the doorway. Then she had come here . . .)

At last the telephone was dealt with, Rolf replaced the receiver and seemed to be recalling the interrupted conversation. But then he said: "Someone rang up from Paris, a certain Herr Stiller, your lover I suppose—" Sibylle only looked at him. "I imagine," he added, "that you met the gentleman in Paris after all . . ." This last straw wasn't even necessary, Sibylle had already picked up her handbag and involuntarily risen to her feet. "Where are you going?" was all he asked. "To the mountains," answered Sibylle shortly, thinking with presence of mind of a poster she had seen on the way, "to Pontresina." And Rolf, that dunderhead for whom it wasn't yet enough of a farce, actually accompanied her to the door. "Do as you please," he said, picking up the glove she had dropped. "Thank you," said Sibylle and she could really have gone now, indeed, she didn't know herself why she went over to the window again instead of out through the door.

"I think it's ridiculous," she remarked, "completely ridiculous, the way we are behaving, childish . . ." Rolf said nothing. "You're wrong," she said and had to go on speaking somehow, "—you've no right to treat me like this. Did you think I would come and ask your forgiveness? We were never a marriage, Rolf, not even before. Never. That's the point. At bottom it was never anything for you but an affair, no more, you never believed in marriage—" Rolf smiled. Sibylle was surprised herself at her speech, at her accusing tone. It was not at all what she had really intended to say. "Rolf!" she said, sitting down on the edge of a chair without putting down her handbag, ready to go the moment she felt she was in the way. "I didn't come to reproach you. Only—" Rolf waited. "I don't know," she said half to herself, "what's to happen now."

Rolf stood and said nothing. Why doesn't he help me out, she thought, forgetting that there was a great deal which he simply couldn't know, that he had no idea where Sibylle had come from and what had happened. "I never thought," went on Sibylle, "that we should come to this. I imagined something different by marriage. You and your lectures! I thought you were speaking from experience . . ." She looked at him. "I don't know," he said, "what you want." Sibylle really had to collect her thoughts. "I'm not complaining, Rolf, I've no right to. It just happened like that. You're free, I'm free, and yet everything is so wretched . . . What do I want?" She asked back, "Don't you know?" A rather mocking smile, may be, even a contemptuous smile came on to her face, the sort of expression with which one does look at a person who is shamming. For so much blindness, it seemed to her, could only be a sham. What was the point of this comedy?

Then suddenly Sibylle wanted to throw herself on to his breast, but remained standing a few paces away from her husband, as though she could not get through the look in his eyes. "Do you hate me?" she asked with a faint, involuntary laugh. When a person with whom we are intimate hates us for the first time it seems almost like bluff, but it was his real face, there was no getting away from it, and her laughter froze. He hated her. He looked quite different, too.

Sibylle no longer recognized him; he was only outwardly like himself.

". . . Lover!" she went on somewhere in her own
thoughts. "I wasn't looking for a lover, you know
that very well."—"What then?"—"I don't need 'a
man,' any man. That's your theory. You weren't just
'a man' for me. Why did you marry at all? For you
it's just 'a woman,' an affair with 'a woman,' any
woman. That's why I say you're a bachelor, a married bachelor. Go on, smile! Either marriage is a
destiny, I believe, or there is no sense in it at all, it's a
piece of humbug. I've behaved stupidly, I know.
It hurt me when you fell in love somewhere, that's
true, and perhaps I was petty. Latitude in marriage—
what does that mean. I don't want latitude, I want to
be more than just 'a woman' to my husband. Why
can't you understand that? My father isn't just 'a
man' to me. And Hannes isn't just 'a child,' whom
we happen to love because we feel like it . . . Oh
Rolf," she interrupted herself, "that's all nonsense!"—
"You mean," concluded Rolf, "that we've never been
married?"—"Yes."—"And that consequently there's
no reason why you should tell me where you've been
these last few days," he said, lighting himself a fresh
cigarette. "I don't understand why you came to me at
all."—"When you talk like that, I don't understand
either," said Sibylle. "I came to have a real talk with
you. You've got no time now, I know. You never have
time when it doesn't suit you. And then I really come
at the stupidest moments."

Rolf smoked. "What did you really want to talk to
me about?"—"I'm naive, you're right. I'm still naive.
Only I don't care about your superior smile any
more," she said. "Somehow I find you simply stupid."
She specified: "It's only that you can express yourself
better than I can, that's why I always let you talk. Did
you think I regarded you as the only man in the
whole world I could love? I realized that you felt so

certain of me, Rolf, but in a quite different sense
. . . Do you remember my British officer in Cairo?"
she interpolated. "You never took him seriously, I
know. He had a lot of things you haven't got, Rolf,
things that I miss. And yet it would never have occurred to me, in fact the idea would have seemed
absurd, that I should travel on with another man instead of you. I wonder why? I don't know where I got
my ideas about marriage from, but I still have them—
even now . . . Perhaps it would be best," she concluded after a moment's thought, "if we got a divorce." As she said this she gazed out of the window
and did not see his expression; anyhow, he said nothing. "Think it over," she said. "I never imagined it
would be possible for us to divorce. I approved of
all the divorces among our acquaintances, I always
thought that in these cases it had never been a marriage at all. They were just affairs, legalized to satisfy
bourgeois taste, but invalid from the outset. Why
should they stay together? That would have seemed to
me like putting up a scarecrow and then being afraid
to go into your own garden. They just weren't marriages, but only 'bourgeois' affairs. You always
called me 'bourgeois' when my feelings didn't suit
you, but now I think you are much more 'bourgeois'
than I am, seriously. Why else did you legalize our
affair, if you didn't believe in marriage? Just because
we were expecting a child . . ."

Rolf let her talk. "I know," smiled Sibylle, "you
like to be composed. Whether I want to go to Paris or
to Pontresina, you're always composed. And you think
it's your magnanimity. Isn't that so? Your magnanimity is supposed to coerce me. Fundamentally, I
often think, you only want my obedience. So as to
have your freedom! That's all. You're waiting for
my 'lover' to leave me, as you leave your women, and
then there'll be no one but you; that's all your love,
all your composure, all your magnanimity amounts to

. . . Oh Rolf," she repeated, "that's all nonsense."—
"And where do you see sense?" asked Rolf, but the
telephone rang again and he had to go over to the
desk. "I don't know," said Sibylle, "why I tell you all
this—"

Rolf picked up the receiver: it was the secretary,
ringing through to remind him, as instructed, about
the sitting, a so-called summing-up for the jury. "I
won't keep you any longer," said Sibylle, watching
him fill his brief-case with papers. "Are you angry
with me?" she asked. "Why don't you answer?" Rolf
hunted for his ballpoint pen on the desk, then in his
pocket, then on the desk again. "I see," he said,
"you're disappointed that I didn't forbid you anything—" His smile showed that he was making an
effort to find the whole thing humorous. "No," said
Sibylle, "you're really not in a position to forbid me
anything, Rolf, that's the miserable thing about it,
from the beginning you merely had an affair with
me, to be exact, and therefore no right to prevent me
from having another affair—" Meanwhile Rolf had
found his ballpoint, and there was no further reason
why they shouldn't say goodbye. Rolf's hand was on
the door-handle; if it had really been her Rolf, she
would have thrown her arms round his neck and
wept. It wasn't Rolf, it was a mask that seemed to her
ridiculous. "You must do what you think right," he
said once more, opening the door, ushering her
through the antechamber and politely accompanying her to the lift—

So now she had to go to Pontresina.

Pontresina greeted her with a shower of rain and a
feeling of shock, as though she had not imagined for
an instant that she would really arrive at Pontresina.
Pontresina consisted in the fact that the train simply
went no further; worse still—at this time of day there
was no train back. Sibylle felt trapped. Apart from
herself, only two local people had got out. She aban-

doned herself to some porter in a green apron, who had loaded her trunk and her skis on to a sledge; Sibylle followed through the mushy snow. The crazy poster—it might as well have been a poster of Capri or a North Sea spa—had naturally referred to February or March, not November. True, the porter asserted that there was good snow higher up. What was Sibylle to do in the snow? What was she to do in this old-fashioned first-class hotel? For half an hour, without taking off her fur coat, which now represented, as it were, her last habitation, she sat on the bed listening to a loud-speaker blaring Danubian waltzes over an empty skating rink lit by spotlights. Later she went down into the bar, ordered a whisky, and sought refuge in a flirtation with a gentleman who happened to be French and therefore witty . . .

A confrontation with Wilfried Stiller, Dip. Agric., has been fixed for Friday week: "possibly accompanied by a joint visit to his mother's grave," as I learn from my copy of the instructions.

The end seems to have been very unpleasant, and her leave-taking from Stiller—however clearly we can see that something is at an end, the leave-taking still has to be performed—unfortunately (says Sibylle) was not accomplished without profound mortification, not without humiliating even herself.

I record the facts:

Sibylle, at that time passionately keen on sports, romped in Pontresina and was only glad that Stiller, now back from Paris, hadn't the money to come after her. Instead he pestered her with so many phone calls that the concierge in her hotel, who soon realized how unwanted these calls were, wore a grimace of sympathy every time he came to announce "Zurich." The only half-conscious hope that it might be Rolf prevented her from simply pretending not to be there.

Also the concierge went a little too far for her liking
with his shameless discretion: "I'm afraid not," she
heard him say, "Frau Doktor has just gone out, yes,
this very minute," as she stood in the hall, watching
the expression of this noble ponce, who was undoubtedly banking on an extra tip for special services. She
went straight into the booth and rang Stiller. But
Stiller, it seems, had taken leave of his senses. He was
furious, because he had had to beg her address from
Carola, the Italian maid, and now he mounted his high
horse. What was Sibylle to say to him? There was
snow, yes, pretty good snow, no, today the sun was
shining as well, oh yes, there was a very nice crowd
at the hotel, and then she chatted about the terrific
progress she had made in the skiing school, about
Rücklage and *Vorlage*, about swinging from the hips
and so on. Sibylle prattled like a bobby soxer: about a
"heavenly" dancer, yes, yes, the Frenchman, about
the "crazy" atmosphere, her room was "sweet," the
skating rink was "gorgeous," oh no, the Frenchman
wasn't the only one who wanted to marry her, as a
matter of fact they all did, a "jolly bunch" really, and
the skiing instructor, a Grison, was an "absolute
darling." From time to time, while Stiller said nothing,
the voice came through with, "Three minutes are up,
will you please insert the sum indicated. Three minutes are up, will you please—" and Sibylle inserted
the money, as though the conversation was not yet
childish enough. The devil had got into her, and this
was a thoroughly agreeable feeling, she found, at any
rate a feeling that suppressed many other feelings,
and there was nothing of which Sibylle was so afraid
as of her real feelings . . .

Rolf, her husband, remained mute.

When Stiller turned up at the hotel one day to find
out what was really going on, he obviously hadn't
strength enough to set this utterly confused woman
free from her childish tone; Stiller let himself be

hurt by this false tone, and this made the helpless
Sibylle pitilessly superior. It was as though a mecha-
nism was at work: no sooner did she feel that this man
felt sorry for himself than she couldn't help hurting
him. They walked across the plateau towards Samaden.
Sibylle in black skiing trousers, elegant, athletic, suntanned, while Stiller wore his everlasting U.S.
Army greatcoat and was as pale-faced as everyone
from the lowlands. "How's your exhibition going?" she
inquired. "Has your bronze been cast yet?" Her buoy-
ant tone rendered him dumb and dull-witted. He
could think of simply nothing to say. Then there was
her gentleman from Düsseldorf, a wonderful fellow
always shooting a line about his experience as a
fighter pilot on the Eastern Front and in Crete, a good
deal more amusing than Stiller! She told him straight
out. "And I can tell you," announced Sibylle, "he
knows how to live. He's rolling in money . . ." And
Stiller had to listen while she told him how impressed
she was by all the money he "made," this son of a
family in heavy industry who yet took life so lightly.
"But as a man he's not my type," said Sibylle, and
Stiller looked at her out of the corner of his eye, then
he relapsed into his mute melancholy. The most he
said was once: "Pontresina makes me sick!" Sibylle
had a twisted ankle and limped slightly. "But yesterday I went dancing again," she said.

Something was egging her on to delight in everything Stiller despised and to tell him all over again
how witty this gentleman from Düsseldorf was, a
knight of the Iron Cross, how manly and entertaining
and full of ideas; if he felt he had hurt somebody's
feelings, for example, whether it was a man or a
woman, he made them a present of a Mercedes. "Cross
my heart!" Stiller only said, "I quite believe you." Or
another example: There was a young girl in her hotel
who had fallen in love with a Swedish student, and
immediately this gentleman from Düsseldorf had the

charming idea of bringing the Swedish student over—
by aeroplane. "Simply enchanting," commented
Sibylle, to show her tedious mope that men who make
money are not on that account necessarily devoid of
charm. Perhaps Stiller said once, "Possibly." Or he
asked, "Why do you tell me that?" But he was hurt; he
had no means of stopping Sibylle. Moreover, on that
walk Sibylle noticed for the first time that Stiller
stammered, that there were certain words he couldn't
say, words beginning with M.

Once a young fellow passed them, a coffee-brown
face with the white poster smile of a Grison ski instructor; Sibylle greeted him with a Hallo, then she
said, "That was Nuot." He asked with tired obedience, "Who is Nuot?" So that was the skiing instructor who had actually carried her all the way to the
nearest rescue sledge when she twisted her ankle.
"Isn't he a darling?" she asked. The conversation
continued in this tone.

Of course Sibylle knew perfectly well what sort of
inn he would have liked, some country pub used by
the locals. But once the devil had got into her—and
she was enjoying this feeling, as I have said—she immediately thought of a "ripping" place. Why didn't
Stiller resist? His lack of confidence was an insult to
her; she felt shamed by it. Was this the man she had
loved? The "ripping" restaurant proved to be an orgy
of "ye olde" Switzerland such as Stiller couldn't stand
at any price, but they had already been relieved of their
wardrobe by at last six hands and the Frau Doktor had
been greeted as a regular customer. And all the rest
of it—the way they were shown to a particular little
table and handed two extensive menus printed in the
style of the Gutenberg Bible, the head waiter in tails
who was so kind as to recommend fresh lobster, a rec-
ommendation which he made in the most personal
manner—all this was compounded of precisely the
mixture of *noblesse* and blackmail that rendered the

lower-middle-class Stiller, when he was not at his best, completely defenseless. On the table stood three roses, all included in the price, and everything, naturally, by candlelight. Stiller didn't even dare to tell Sibylle that he thought the prices grotesque. "What will you have?" asked Sibylle in a motherly way, adding, "I've got money on me." A wine waiter was already standing there, dressed up as a cooper, and Sibylle was in favor of "her" Châteauneuf-du-Pape at sixteen francs the bottle, but ready chilled-off. "You'll see," she told Stiller, "the Châteauneuf here is a poem!" Sibylle listened to herself; the devil gave her the vocabulary of a person whom Stiller couldn't answer. And then, after she had ordered "her" *filet mignon* with little more than a nod, she compelled the helpless Stiller to eat snails, though Stiller was a trifle doubtful whether snails and Châteauneuf-du-Pape went together; Stiller had never eaten snails, as he was forced to admit; this made him feel inferior and therefore not entitled to a contradictory opinion. All right then, snails!

And then a gentleman nodded to Sibylle and told her very briefly, so as not to interupt, in French that he had passed his second-class test today; Sibylle congratulated him with a wave of the hand and informed Stiller that he had just been looking at "Charles Boyer." Stiller, who was nibbling with shy hunger at a roll, asked, "Who is Charles Boyer?" The heavenly dancer, the Frenchman, and while Stiller had to taste the Châteauneuf-du-Pape, she told him the "sweet" story of how she had humorously addressed this Frenchman—who, incidentally, was in the diplomatic service—while they were dancing, as Charles Boyer—and his name actually was Boyer. "Wasn't that funny?" she asked. Stiller looked at her like a dog that doesn't understand human speech, and Sibylle had half a mind to stroke him like a dog. She refrained from doing so in order not to arouse vain hopes. When she saw that Stiller had already drunk from his glass, she said gaily, "*Prosit,*" at which Stiller, filled with embarrassment, raised his almost empty glass, "*Prosit—*"

And all the time, Sibylle felt so rotten that she could eat hardly any of the *filet mignon;* Stiller, on the other hand, whether it turned his stomach or not, had to get down his twelve snails. Meanwhile Sibylle —who had to make all the conversation, so dull was he—lit a cigarette and gave him an additional piece of news: "Sturzenegger has written to me. He needs a secretary, what do you think of that, and me of all people." Stiller poked about in his snail shells. "He's in love with me," added Sibylle. "Even my husband noticed that. Seriously. And I like your friend . . ." In between she gave instructions; "You must eat the juice, old chap, that's the best part of it." Stiller obeyed and ate the juice. "Seriously," continued Sibylle, "Sturzenegger has invited me. Apparently he loves it over there in California. A hundred dollars a week, what do you think of that, and my passage paid. A hundred dollars is a lot, I think, and in a quarter of an hour you're by the sea—"

And so on.

Not until they were on the way back to the hotel did they have a rather more real, though short and one-sided conversation. They walked through crunching snow, a cloud in front of their mouths; it was bitterly cold, but beautiful, to left and right walls of snow, the houses as though covered in white featherbeds, stars up above, a night of porcelain. "Where are you staying?" inquired Sibylle when they stood in front of the ornate entrance to her hotel. "Will you be here tomorrow?" she went on, trying to introduce the farewell, if possible the final farewell. "—it was simply too much of a shock for me," she remarked, breaking into his silence. "All of a sudden it suited you, now that you had to go to Paris anyway, now you had a good excuse, now you wanted me to come, now our Paris was suddenly possible. At that moment

I felt like your mistress . . ." Stiller said nothing, and whether he understood what had snapped in her remained uncertain. What was he brooding over? And since she had no other declaration to make, Sibylle inquired the name of a constellation above the snow-covered entrance—she had to ask twice before Stiller told her.

"Yes," she said then, as though it had some connection with this constellation, "where shall I be in a year? I've no idea. Perhaps really over in California! . . . It's funny," she added, "with you one knows perfectly well. I don't believe you will ever change, not even in your outward life." She hadn't meant to be unkind, but felt the harshness of her words and tried to soften them: "Or do you think you will ever become a different person?" This sounded no gentler, on the contrary. All speech was simply out of place now. "Oh Stiller," she said at length, "I was really very fond of you—" A long-distance skier on a training run, somebody like Nuot, swept past the mute couple with vigorous movements of his softly pattering skis. They gazed after him, as though sport interested them above all else; unfortunately he soon vanished from sight and left them alone with each other again. And then no doubt the indecision simply became unbearable; they parted—not yet capable of saying farewell—after quickly agreeing to meet at breakfast next morning.

At breakfast Stiller did not appear.

Two days later, when Sibylle came out of the dining room accompanied by the gentleman from Düsseldorf, there he stood, without approaching Sibylle, like a ghost. "Why didn't you come before?" she asked at once, not waiting to greet him first; Sibylle was taken aback. "Have you already eaten?" he asked. "Haven't you?" she asked back. Stiller was pale with fatigue and unshaven. "Where have you come from?" she asked, and Stiller helped her into the fur coat which a bell-hop, a Grison boy in a circus livery, had carried after her. "I expected you for breakfast the day before yesterday," said Sibylle and repeated her question, "Where have you come from?" She nodded to the gentleman from Düsseldorf, who had waited by the lift, busy lighting a cigar, a cavalier skilled in self-effacement, so that Stiller hadn't even noticed him, the wonderful fellow . . .

Stiller had come from Davos. She learnt this just as they were passing through the revolving door out into the cold. "From Davos?" she asked, but the glass panel had already interposed itself between her and Stiller, who was following behind. "From Davos?" she repeated when he emerged from the revolving door. In the meantime Stiller had spoken to his sick wife in the sanatorium. His account was brief and bald. "That's all," he concluded. "Why are you so astounded?" It was true: the whole summer Sibylle had expected this, hoped for it and silently encouraged it. And now it was a shock. She felt guilty. "What about Julika?" she asked. "What does she say about it?" This didn't seem to interest him. "Separated?" she asked. "What does that mean? You can't just leave her—" Stiller appeared to her brutal, inhuman; his action horrified her. Now suddenly, for the first time, Julika was not a remote phantom, but a flesh-and-blood woman, a sick, unhappy, deserted woman, a sister. "Stiller," she said involuntarily, "you shouldn't have done that . . ." She corrected herself: "We've no right to do that. I'm to blame myself, I know that. It's madness, Stiller, it's murder . . ." Stiller was unperturbed, he seemed almost to derive a malicious satisfaction from her concern. Stiller fancied himself free, completely free, and for the moment it was enough for him that he had acted.

"I'm hungry," he said and showed clearly enough he had no wish to think any more about Julika, and no cause. They entered an inn full of locals, railwaymen enjoying a Saturday night out, each of them with a *Brissago* in his face and rather hushed by the lady's fur coat, till one of them said, "Are we going to play or aren't we?" There was no menu printed in the style of the Gutenberg Bible here, but instead a fat innkeeper's wife who greeted them with a rather damp handshake, and then wiped a few small puddles of beer and some crumbs off the varnished wooden table. The price of the wines from the cask—Veltline, Kalterer, Magdalener, Dôle—could be read on a blackboard attached to the wall, flanked by the laurel wreaths and cups of a rifle club and surmounted by the usual faded but colorful portrait of General Guisan. Stiller with his hunger was as confident as a woodcutter after a hard day's work, tired, unhurried, at one with himself; he immediately broke a loaf in two with his broad hands, while Sibylle, sitting on the bench by the tiled stove, suddenly found a purring cat on her lap waiting to be stroked. Stiller was delighted with the prospect of *Rösti* and *Bauernschüblig;* there was no salad here. While one of them shuffled the cards, the reveling railwaymen discussed the costly futility of a Big Four conference in a tone of conventional exasperation, without the least hint of real anger, and then became mute with concentration as the game started, diffusing a silence through the low bar-parlor that inevitably spread to Sibylle and Stiller. When the fat innkeeper's wife brought, not the impatiently awaited food, but the Veltliner, Stiller inquired about a room. "Single or double?" asked the innkeeper's wife, as Stiller went out with her to look at the room . . .

For a time Sibylle was alone, the only woman in the bar, she turned the pages of a cycling magazine without reading it; a workman had sat down at her table; he licked the froth from his lips and eyed the lady with undisguised distrust, with downright contempt, as though he knew what the good Stiller did not for a moment suspect. How would Stiller take her confession, which seemed to her, as soon as she tried to frame it in words, simply incredible, monstrous! Sibylle was surprised that she had been able to look him in the eyes—she had no difficulty in doing so, even when Stiller came back and sat down beside her, gay with hunger but not in the least put out by the fact that Sibylle, who had already eaten, only drank a kirsch. There had been an avalanche somewhere near Bergün, they heard from the railwayman. But the rumor was exaggerated; Stiller had seen the avalanche in question and told the rather pompous men with *Brissagos* in their brown faces that the line was already clear. Sibylle was surprised and somehow charmed, relieved, when she saw these reveling men, about whom there was something threatening in her eyes, disarmed by Stiller's nonchalant matter-of-factness. Sibylle felt protected. And the railwayman at their table had also stopped eyeing Sibylle with contempt; he even passed the ashtray without waiting to be asked. And later, after paying for his beer, he took off his cap and wished Stiller and Sibylle a good night "together." Once Stiller, as he ate, asked Sibylle: "Is anything the matter?"—"Why?"—"You're very quiet today."—"I'm glad you've come," said Sibylle. "I was so furious with you, I thought you'd just gone off and left me." She lifted the purring cat from her lap and dropped it to the ground, where it stuck its tail in the air. "Why didn't you leave me any message?" said Sibylle. "I did something stupid, I must tell you, something very stupid . . ."

Stiller went on eating and didn't expect anything serious. He had been to Davos, he had parted from the sick Julika; what could upset him now! He smiled: "What did you do?" But now the fat innkeeper's wife came with coffee in two glasses, and Sibylle was relieved. She hadn't wanted to talk about it at all. There

are things that happen and yet don't count, but once
they have been put into words they do count, and all
the time there is really no need for them to count.
The black coffee in the glasses was just as they had
feared, namely bitter, so hot that they burnt their
tongues and at the same time unutterably insipid, tasting of anything rather than coffee; they tried to make
it drinkable with humor and plenty of sugar, but the
sugar only rendered this brown and gray liquid
completely nauseating. Now he told her about Paris.
Why didn't she sink into the floor? She pretended to
be listening. When Sibylle thought about the last two
nights they seemed to her like a monstrous
dream . . .

"By the way, I've brought you something from
Paris," Stiller broke into his account. "Where on
earth did I put it?" Sibylle meanwhile filled their
glasses with Veltliner. "You know all those perfumeries in the Place Vendôme?" laughed Stiller and told
her the story of how he looked for her scent. The
famous Place Vendôme, a large square with arcades, is
the citadel of the French perfume trade, every firm
has its own shop there, so unless you know the maker
of the scent you are looking for, you have to go from
firm to firm having your fingers dabbed; Stiller had
imagined he would smell out her scent from among
hundreds. The young assistants were charming, dab-
bing their own little hands when Stiller had no more
free fingers. Naturally he became more and more uncertain. The young ladies did not laugh at him for a
moment, on the contrary, they were charmed by his
meticulous gravity, although his French was not adequate to describing scents. Stiller made a note of the
names. On his right index finger, for example, he had
Scandale. But in the course of the afternoon, his last
afternoon in Paris, even the names became confused
in his mind; he could only hold up his finger, *Celui
là!* Often even the assistants had difficulty in identify-

ing the perfume and had to call the *patron*. At one point every scent in existence reminded him of Sibylle, and then again none of them. And it's amazing how many perfumes there are; his hands were two palettes covered in scents, and Stiller walked with outspread fingers to prevent them from mingling. How much lay in the *nuance*, what bliss and what torment. And on top of everything else the assistants wanted to know whether the perfume he was seeking was for a blonde or a brunette, or even a redhead? It makes a great deal of difference—this was something Stiller didn't know before either—the same perfume smells quite different on a different skin. Then what was the use of these young ladies with all the samples on their alien skin? Shortly before closing time he gave it up. During the evening, watching Jouvet (*Ecole des femmes*) he almost forgot the whole business, Jouvet was so magnificent; but his hands hadn't left him, and during the interval Stiller started sniffing at one finger after the other once more. And again on the way home: he stopped in the middle of the street, took off his gloves and sniffed. His nose was now fresh again, but now there was no difference between one finger and another, it was all one and hence hopeless. Finally he washed his hands and was just as wise as before he started. The following morning, just before the train left, he bought a perfume at random . . .

"I've no idea whether it's the right one," said Stiller in some embarrassment, when he finally handed over the little packet, once very elegant, now a trifle tattered from its long stay in his trousers pocket, and waited for Sibylle to open it. "*Iris gris!*" she laughed. "Is that the right one?" he asked, while Sibylle immediately unscrewed the little bottle and rubbed a few drops on the back of her hand. "I think *Iris gris* is wonderful!" she said, and Stiller sniffed at her hand, the one and only hand at last, his disappointment growing at every breath. "No," he said, "that's not it."

Sibylle sniffed too. "But isn't it lovely?" she consoled him, without having to sham, and put the little bottle in her pocket. "Thank you very much!"

Soon afterwards Stiller paid, and they emptied their glasses, without having reached any agreement as to whether Sibylle was going back to her hotel or not. What did he intend? Stiller seemed to have completely made up his mind, but to what? "Drink up," he said, without impatience, still seated but taking her fur coat from the nearby hook. "It's not important," remarked Sibylle, "but I must tell you. It's really not important—" His lack of curiosity made it even more difficult to find the right words; Stiller seemed to suspect nothing yet, nothing at all. Or did he already know and really consider it unimportant? "I'm a goose," she smiled. "I took revenge, you see, took revenge in such a silly way, two nights in succession with two different men—" Stiller didn't seem to hear, didn't seem to understand, he said nothing and didn't even wince; and then the fat innkeeper's wife came back with the change and took the opportunity of asking whether the lady and gentleman would like breakfast in their room or not. She stayed by their table as a gesture of hospitality. The relentless conversation about avalanches, the weather in general, and hotelkeeping after a world war, lasted almost ten minutes.

When they were at last alone together again, Stiller asked with her fur coat on his knees: "What did you mean by that?" Sibylle looked at the beer mat he was twisting round on the table, and repeated it with a clarity which seemed to her now, however Stiller might take it, indispensable, her last chance to make a clean breast of things: "Two nights in succession I slept with two different men—that's what I mean . . ." Now he knew. And the future (thought Sibylle) now depended solely on Stiller's reaction to this monstrous trifle.

The reveling railwaymen threw down their cards, one of them wiped the slate clean with a sponge, now that it was settled who had to pay, and the commentary on the lost game, which there was no changing now, turned to yawns. It was eleven o'clock. With their railwaymen's caps already on their heads they, too, wished the couple, who were left alone in the bar parlor, a good night "together." Stiller went on fiddling with the beer mat. "I know that—," he said. "Only I never told anyone. Anyway, it was a long time ago. I knew perfectly well whom I loved, but all the same—! I was actually on my way to her, yes, it was the eve of our reunion. I suddenly went into a skid—in just the same way," he said putting down the beer mat. "I know that . . ." He had no more to say. "Went into a skid," this expression evidently consoled Sibylle greatly, it restored to her the possibility, even the certainty of afterwards getting back on the road. And that evening (so she says) she still believed it might be a road they could travel together.

This proved to be an error.

The following morning—after a wretched night—they said goodbye to one another at the little station of Pontresina. When the train at last began to move, Sibylle continued to stand like a statue on a plinth, and both of them, Stiller at the open window, Sibylle on the platform, waved a half-hearted farewell. (Since then Sibylle, my public prosecutor's wife, has never seen the missing Stiller again.) She herself walked slowly back to the hotel, asked for her bill, packed and left the same day. It was impossible simply to return to Rolf now, she felt, and Redwood City seemed to be the solution; she had to work, to be alone, to earn her own living. Otherwise she would have felt a helpless victim, not knowing where she belonged; the road from woman to whore had proved astonishingly short. In Zurich Rolf welcomed her with the opening remark that he was willing to have a divorce. Sibylle left it to him to make the necessary arrangements and asked his permission to take little Hannes with her to Redwood City. Their conversation was confined to the future, to practical problems. As regards Hannes, their joint son, it was difficult to decide what was best for the child himself: Rolf asked for twenty-four hours in which to think it over. Then to her amazement, he agreed. Sibylle thanked him by weeping on his hands, and shortly before Christmas, after being accompanied to the Central Station by her husband, left for Le Havre, where she embarked for America.

My friend the public prosecutor informs me that the final hearing (with the verdict) is fixed for Tuesday week.

America brought Sibylle a period of almost monastic solitude. She stayed in New York. When young Sturzenegger came over from California to fetch the secretary he really didn't need, Sibylle had already found another job—thanks to her knowledge of European languages, a pretty good job. She was proud. And Sturzenegger, who didn't take it to heart, went back to his Redwood City alone after entertaining Sibylle to a French supper in Greenwich Village. There was no more skidding. The road, her road, was pretty hard. For the first time Sibylle, the daughter of rich parents, found herself in the same position as other people, namely alone and responsible for herself, dependent on her abilities, dependent on demand, dependent on the moods and good faith of an employer. Strangely enough, it gave her a sense of freedom. Her work was dull, she had to translate business letters into German, French and Italian, always more or less the same ones. And the first home of her own she had ever had was such that even when the sun was shining outside she could scarcely read or sew without the electric light, hardly ever dared to open a window because everything immediately became covered in soot, and had to put wax in her ears in order to sleep. Sibylle was aware that millions of people lived in worse conditions than she and that therefore she had no right to complain. Complaint was altogether out of the question, if only because of Rolf. Fortunately, she was able to leave Hannes in a German-Jewish children's home during the day. She spent her free time, whenever the weather permitted, with Hannes in the nearby Central Park, where there were trees . . .

She began, as the saying goes, a new life.

Once, in February, Sibylle had a bit of a fright, though she doesn't know to this day whether the fright was based on mere fancy or on reality. They were sitting in Central Park again, Hannes and she, feeding the squirrels; the sun was warm, snow still lay in the shady hollows, the ponds were still partly frozen, but the birds were twittering and spring was on its way. The ground was damp; they were sitting on the slate-black Manhattan rock, and Sibylle was as merry as Rumpelstiltzkin, so secret and incognito did she feel in this huge city. Between leafless branches they saw the familiar silhouettes of the skyscrapers in the bluish haze; at the edge of the great park, beyond the silence, there was a ghostly hum and every now and then the hoot of a siren came from way over on the Hudson. A policeman rode along in the black dusty earth of the bridle path. Boys were playing baseball. Here and there on the long benches sat a man reading a newspaper, or a pair of lovers strolled past, then a lady leading her dog to one of the rare trees. Sibylle enjoyed the fact that she knew nobody. She only saw the man, who walked past behind her, from the back, but for a moment she was absolutely certain it was Stiller, and Sibylle was within an ace of involuntarily calling out. Of course she talked herself out of it. How could Stiller be wandering about New York? A trace of disquiet remained, nonetheless, half hope, half fear that it might really be Stiller. Sibylle took Hannes by the hand and walked through the park, not to look for him but rather to run away; all the same, she had to go in the same direction. Of course, as she expected, she did not see the man again.

She had completely forgotten this figment of her imagination (as no doubt it was) when, a few days later, as she was being carried down into the subway on the escalator, she saw him being carried upwards. It was impossible to alight. Had he not stared at her, even if he had made no sign of greeting? The unlikelihood was her consolation. Or was Stiller coming after her? In any case, when he reached the top of the escalator, the man she had taken for Stiller did not walk on, but immediately crossed over to the escalator coming down. There was a terrible crush, which made calm observation impossible, quite apart from her inner turmoil. What did a U.S. Army greatcoat mean in America? Later Sibylle talked herself out of it again; she had stared so hard at the man on the escalator that he might have fancied his chances, although he didn't know Sibylle, and that was why he had turned back. Could be. At the moment Sibylle acted completely mechanically: she forced her way into the nearest compartment of some underground train or other, the doors closed and off they went. For a few weeks she felt nervous every time she went out into the street, but in vain; she never again saw a man who might have been confused with Stiller.

Her work, as I have said, was dull. She sat in a room devoid of daylight, convinced after a week that she couldn't stand this unnatural state of affairs. No idea whether it was raining outside or brilliant sunshine, no awareness of the time of the day, never a breath of air that smelt of storm or people or leaves or even of rainwet asphalt—and it was all the more

frightful because Sibylle was absolutely the only one
who missed anything: she thought she would suffocate
with all the air-conditioning. The certainty that it
would be exactly the same in any better-class firm
rendered her utterly helpless. What alternative had she
but the diligence born of desperation? As a result, she
was highly valued, and when she gave notice after
a year they kept her on by doubling her salary.

Now Sibylle was able to afford another, more cheerful apartment, two rooms with a so-called roof garden
on Riverside Drive looking out on the broad Hudson. And here, on the eighteenth floor, she was blissfully happy. She and Hannes sunned themselves in the
shelter of a red party-wall, from where they could see
a great deal of sky and even some landscape—forest.
And to the east the sea. Even in the hazy distance
Hannes could already distinguish whether it was the
Ile-de-France or the *Queen Mary* coming into port.
And in the evening, when darkness fell, the curving
garland of lights on the George Washington Bridge
was right in front of their window. Here Sibylle lived
for almost two years. The idea of returning to Switzerland occurred to her less and less often.

She liked life in America very much (she says)
without being thrilled by it; she enjoyed its strange-
ness. Yet she had never seen the true America, the
West. Sibylle planned to travel across to the opposite
coast, to see Arizona, Texas, the flowers in California; but she was an employee, and that meant she
could live, live well even, just so long as she sat in
front of her typewriter and typed: in return she
had the freedom of her weekends, which covered a
radius of no less than a hundred miles. She loved
New York. During the first few weeks it seemed to
her that nothing was easier than associating with
Americans. They were all so open, so easy-going; she
made more friendships, or so it seemed, than at any
time in her life. She also enjoyed being so unmolested

as a woman, indeed, it was as though on landing in America she had ceased to be a woman; in spite of all the sympathy people showed her they treated her as though she were completely neuter. After her recent experience this was a boon, of course, at least at first. And even later (so she says) she had no desire for a man, certainly not for an American man. She had "friends," in the American sense; most of them had cars, and that was not unimportant, especially in summer, when it was so hot in New York. In time, however, this lack of any atmosphere, such as exists even in Switzerland, began to irritate her. It was not easy to say what was really lacking. Everyone praised her new spring dress, her look of good health, her son; compared with Switzerland in particular, it was simply delightful how lavish people were with praise. But suddenly Sibylle wondered whether they so much as saw what they were praising at all. It was remarkable to discover (she says) how wonderful and great was the diversity of erotic play; Sibylle had never realized it so clearly as here, where this diversity doesn't exist. When she left a restaurant, when she left a subway, when she left a social gathering, she never had the feeling of being missed by a man in that enchanting way which somehow uplifts both parties, without their making an effort to see one another again. Never, in the street, did she encounter that quick glance of purposeless delight, never in conversation was there any hint of the exciting realization that people are divided into two sexes. Everything remained on a comradely level and as far as it went very nice; but a tension was missing, a wealth of subtle radiations, a playful artistry, a magic, a threat, the exciting possibility of living complications. It was flat, not unintelligent, heavens alive, the place was seething with cultured people; but it was lifeless, somehow without charm, naive. Then Sibylle felt like a woman under a cap of invisibility: seen by no one, no, not seen, they heard what she said and found it amusing, interesting, may be, but it was a meeting in a vacuum chamber. It was funny: they talked about "sex problems" with such premature candor, with the enlightened frankness of eunuchs who don't know what they are talking about. Nobody here seemed to see any difference between sex and eroticism. And when they took their exuberant deficiency for health, no, it wasn't always funny, it was tedious. What had New York not got to offer! It was a shame to be bored here. The concerts alone! But life itself, everyday existence, shopping, lunch at the drugstore, traveling by bus, waiting at a station, the hustle and bustle that makes up nine-tenths of our life, was so immensely practical, so intensely lusterless.

Sibylle often went into the Italian quarter, to buy vegetables, she said; in reality she went to see, hungry for something worth seeing. Or did the fault lie with Sibylle? After about half a year she had the bitter feeling that she had disappointed everyone. She had a little book full of addresses, but she no longer dared ring anybody up. How had she disappointed all these friendly friends? She didn't know and nobody told her. She was seriously depressed by it. Meanwhile, and this perplexed Sibylle even more, she had forfeited nothing; if she met one of her friends by chance, they said Hallo Sibylle! just like the first time, and there was no trace of disappointment on the other side. Apparently all these frank and easy-going people did not expect anything else from a human relationship; there was no need for this friendly relationship to go on growing. That was the saddest thing for Sibylle: after twenty minutes you have got as far with these people as after half a year, as after many years, nothing more is added. Friendship stops at sincere good wishes for the other's well-being. People have friends simply to make life pleasant, and then there are psychiatrists, like motor mechanics for the

inner life, if a person has defects and cannot patch
himself up. Anyhow, you shouldn't burden your
friends with a gloomy face; in fact they have nothing else to give than a quite general and non-
committal optimism. It was better to lie in the sun in
the little roof garden. And yet, in spite of all the
trouble Sibylle had with this carefree lack of content
that characterizes the vast majority of Americans, she
was far from the idea of returning to Switzerland . . .

After a correspondence that had gradually died
away, after a mutual silence that threatened to become final, Rolf, her husband, rang her one afternoon
at her office. "Where are you speaking from?" she
asked. "Here," answered Rolf, "at La Guardia. I've
just landed. How can I meet you?" He had to wait till
five o'clock, since Sibylle couldn't simply walk out,
and in the end it was getting on for six when Sibylle,
the secretary, appeared in the agreed hotel lobby on
Times Square. "How are you?" they asked one another. "Fine, thank you," they both replied. Sibylle
led him across Times Square. "How long are you
staying here?" she asked; but naturally they could
scarcely talk in the crush. She took Rolf, the bewildered newcomer, to the top of Rockefeller Center
to show him something of New York right away. "Are
you in New York on business?" she asked and then
corrected herself: "I mean professionally?" They
were sitting in the famous Rainbow Bar and had to
order something. "No," said Rolf, "I'm here on your
account. On our account . . ."

They found one another pretty much unchanged,
only a little older. Sibylle showed him the latest snap
of Hannes. "He's no kid any more, no, he's a regular
guy already!" Rolf cut her short after a bit. "I've
come," he said, "to ask you—I mean, either we must
get a divorce or we must live together. But once
and for all." They didn't ask one another anything
else. "In which direction do you live?" inquired Rolf,

and Sibylle showed him the district, pointing out the play of lights, the incredibly colorful dusk over Manhattan; but not everybody finds the woman of his life again as he is looking at it . . .

"Babylon," exclaimed Rolf, who had to look down again and again at this net of shimmering strings of beads, this skein of light, this endless flowerbed of electric blossoms. One is astonished that in these depths down below, whose sounds are no longer audible, in this labyrinth of rectangular windows threaded by gleaming canals, which is repeated over and over again with no change, a person does not get lost every minute; that this never-ending movement from one place to another does not stop for a moment, or pile up into a hopeless chaos. Here and there it is dammed up into a pond filled with a white-hot glow —Times Square, for instance. The skyscrapers tower black all round, vertical, yet spread out from one another by perspective like a cluster of crystals, larger and smaller crystals, thicker and thinner. At times trails of brightly colored mist drift past, as though one were sitting on a mountain top, and for a while there is no more New York: the Atlantic has engulfed it. Then it is there again, half order as though on a chessboard, half confusion, as though the Milky Way had fallen down from the sky. Sibylle pointed out the districts whose names she knew: Brooklyn behind a curtain of bridges, Staten Island, Harlem. Later everything became even more colorful; the skyscrapers no longer rose like black towers before the yellow dusk, now it was as though the night had swallowed up their bodies, and what remained were the lights in them, the hundreds of thousands of electric light bulbs, a screen of whitish and yellowish windows, nothing else, thus they hovered above the bright haze that was roughly the color of apricots, and in the streets, as though in canyons, ran streams of glittering quicksilver.

Rolf could not get over his amazement. The ferries over the Hudson reflected in the water, the garlands of the bridges, the stars above a flood of neon lemonade, of sweetness, of sickliness, that attained the level of the grandiose, vanilla and raspberry, interspersed with the purple pallor of autumn crocuses, the green of glaciers, a green such as occurs in retorts, interspersed with the milk of dandelions, frippery and visions, yes, and beauty, oh, a fairy-like beauty, a kaleidoscope out of the kindergarten, a mosaic of colored fragments, but mobile, yet at the same time lifeless and cold as glass, then again the Bengal lights of a stage witches' sabbath, a heavenly rainbow that has fallen into a thousand splinters and been scattered over the earth, an orgy of discord, of harmony, an orgy of the everyday, technological and mercantile above all; you immediately think of the Arabian Nights, of carpets, but carpets that glow, of worthless gems, of a child's firework that has fallen on the ground and continues to flicker; you have seen it all before, perhaps behind closed eyes in a fever; here and there it is also red, not red like blood, thinner, red like the light reflected in a glass of red wine when the sun shines in, red and also yellow like honey, thinner, yellow like whisky, greenish yellow like sulphur and certain fungi, strange, but all of it possessing a beauty which, if it were to become sound, would be the song of the sirens; yes, that's about how it is, sensual and lifeless at the same time, intelligent and stupid and powerful, an edifice of human beings or termites, symphony and lemonade, you have to have seen it to imagine it, but to have seen it with your eyes, not merely with your judgment, seen it as one who is confused, benumbed, astounded, blissful, unbelieving, carried away, a stranger on earth, not merely a stranger in America; you can smile at it, shout for joy over it, weep over it. And far out to the east rises the bronze moon, a hammered disk, a silent gong . . .

But the most bewildering thing for Rolf was naturally Sibylle, his wife, who was at home here. They drank their martinis—rather mute—occasionally looking at one another, smiling almost with a touch of scorn as they realized that there was really no need to have an Atlantic between them. Rolf scarcely dared to take hold of her arm that lay so close to him; his tenderness stayed in his eyes, Sibylle, too, felt that the world, big as it was, held no one who could be closer to her than Rolf, her husband; she didn't deny it. Nevertheless, she asked for twenty-four hours in which to think it over.

7th *Notebook*

WENT to the dentist today.

They are trifles and the terrible thing is that you don't defend yourself against trifles. You get tired of it. At the very outset, the white-overalled receptionist came into the waiting room and said, "This way please, Herr Stiller." Was I to bawl at her in front of all the other patients? She couldn't help it, this nice little person—I was booked as Herr Stiller. So I followed her with a murmur. I owe all this to my defense counsel. They hung the white cloth round my neck, gave me a fresh glass, filled it with tepid water, all in the friendliest fashion, and the young dentist—the successor of the deceased dentist to whom the vanished Stiller owes an outstanding account—soaped his hands. He couldn't help it either: as far as the patient's name is concerned, he has to rely entirely on his receptionist, especially as he doesn't know the inherited clientele yet.

"Herr Stiller," he said, "you've got a toothache?"

I was just rinsing my mouth, nodded with reference to the toothache, and before I could rectify the mistake he had already found with his probe the spot where all discussion ended for me. The young man was very painstaking.

"Look," he said, showing me with his little mirror, "a crown like that, for example, left upper six—can you see?—I don't want to say anything against my predecessor, but one just can't do a crown like that."

He misunderstood the expression in my eyes, thinking I wanted to stand up for his predecessor. With my mouth full of cotton wool and matrix bands and saliva ejectors, so that I couldn't contradict, I listened to his no doubt very interesting exposition of the new advances in dental surgery. Although the young man had taken over his uncle's practice and clients, he had no intention of also taking over the mistakes of the generation that had just passed away; and my mouth seemed to contain very little else but mistakes. Only with helpless glances could I beg the young man not to regard my crown as the work of his deceased uncle, nor my teeth as those of the missing Stiller. He called out:

"Fräulein—give me Herr Stiller's X-rays again."

All this, as I have said, I owed to my defending counsel. Nobody believes me; every time the probe touched a certain spot, a few involuntary tears welled up from my eyes, and I couldn't think why he had to keep on probing this spot. At last he said:

"Yes, yes—it's alive."

The fact was, judging from the old X-rays which they had found in his predecessor's file, the young dentist simply couldn't understand how my left lower four could possibly be still alive, though in my opinion it was quite sensitive enough even if on the X-ray (they showed me Stiller's left lower four) it looked exactly like a dead root.

"Curious," he murmured, "curious."

Then he rang through to the receptionist.

"Are those really Herr Stiller's X-rays?" he asked. "Are you quite sure?"

"The name is on them—"

His professional conscience left him no peace: he made another tooth-by-tooth comparison, which showed that Stiller, the vanished patient of his deceased uncle, must, for instance, have had a perfect right upper eight, while in my case there was a gap. What had I done with (Stiller's) right upper eight? I shrugged my shoulders. I wasn't going to submit to an interrogation with a mouth full of cotton wool and matrix bands and saliva ejectors. Finally the X-rays disappeared and the young dentist reached for the drill. After an hour and a half, when at last I had no more clamps in my mouth and was allowed to rinse it, I naturally had no further wish to resume discussion of the old X-rays. I merely asked for Saridone. Knobel was sitting in the waiting room. The gray prison van was standing under an avenue of acacias. The drivers had been told to park it somewhere out of sight. But since the avenue belonged to a school, whose playground it bordered, and since the main break was just in progress, Knobel and I were naturally surrounded by all the children in the school when we returned to the van. A little fellow asked me shyly if I was the thief. A girl shouted in rapturous excitement, "Teacher, a criminal!" I waved, as well as I could from behind the little barred window. Only the teachers didn't wave back.

P.S. Perhaps—I wonder—one ought to defend oneself every time one is taken for somebody else, and I shouldn't have allowed any receptionist to book my appointment in the name of Herr Stiller—a labor of Sisyphus. Then again I believe it is quite enough if Julika, and she alone, doesn't take me for somebody else.

Mexico—

I can't help thinking (I don't know what makes me do so) of the Day of the Dead as I saw it on Janitzio, of the Indian mothers crouching all night long over the graves, everyone in their gala clothes, carefully combed as though for a wedding, although apparently nothing happens; the cemetery is a terrace overlooking the black sea and overhung by steep crags, a cemetery without a single tombstone or any other sign—everyone in the village knows where his dead lie, where he himself will one day lie. Candles are set up, three or seven or twenty, according to the number of dead souls, and alongside them the plates containing all kinds of foods and covered with a clean cloth, but the main thing is a strange object constructed with all the loving care of a Christmas present—a frame of bamboo on which are set the cakes and flowers, the fruits, the bright-colored sweetmeats. The dead are supposed to feed all night long on the scent of these foodstuffs, for the scent is the essence of things: this is the significance of the ceremony. Only women and children perform these nocturnal rites in the cemetery; the men pray in the church. The women, whose actions remain quite matter-of-fact and sober, settle down as though for a long rest, throwing a shawl over their heads so that woman and child, both under the same shawl, look like a single creature. The candles, lined up in rows between the living and the dead, flicker in the cold night wind, hour after hour, while the moon rises above the somber mountains and sinks again in a lazy arc. Nothing else happens. Every now and then the clanging of a bell is carried over by the wind, or the wailing sound of a dog howling at the moon; otherwise nothing. Nobody weeps, there is little talking, only what is essential is said, but then not in whispers as is the way in our cemeteries; this is no question of any special atmosphere here. The silence, to which even the children submit, as they gaze for hours on end into the candles or into the empty night over the sea, is not reverence, not depth of emotion as we understand it, neither in a good nor in a bad sense. It is simply silence. In face of the fact of life and death there is nothing whatever to be said. A few even sleep, while their dead, father or husband or son, feed soundlessly on the scent, on the essence of things. The last-comers arrive towards midnight; no one will leave the graves until dawn. The dead souls flicker in thousands. A shivering child, who is coughing very ominously, as though anxious to join the dead, is allowed to sample the sweatmeats already, although the food still belongs to the dead. On the whole, they are strangely patient. And it is cold, it is the night of the first of November. A little girl, whose mother is dozing, plays with a candle, making warm drops of wax fall on her hand until the candle goes out, and then relighting it. Every breath of wind is heavily laden with scent; the women pluck to pieces yellow flowers and scatter them in the direction of the dead—much as one prepares vegetables, not negligently, but without unnecessary gestures, with emphasis, with solemnity, without any dramatic expression to indicate that some symbolic significance is intended. The whole ceremony is not intended at all, but simply performed. And it is as though the silence grew yet more silent. The moon has gone down, the cold is cutting. Nothing happens. The women do not kneel, but sit on the ground, so that the soul of the dead may rise into their wombs. That is all, until day breaks, a night of silent patience, a surrender to the inescapable process of death and growth—

A conversation with the public prosecutor, my friend, about Stiller.

"The overwhelming majority of human lives are ruined by the fact that people make excessive demands on themselves," he said and explained what he meant like this: "Our consciousness has changed a great deal in the course of a few centuries, our emotional life much less. Hence there is a discrepancy between the level of our intellect and that of our emotions. Most of us have a parcel of flesh-pink cloth—namely, our feelings—that from our intellectual level we should like to ignore. There are two ways out of the difficulty that lead nowhere: either we kill our primitive and therefore unworthy feelings, as far as we can, at the risk of killing our emotional life altogether, or we simply give our unworthy feelings another name. We lie about them, disguise them as something else. We label them to satisfy the wishes of our consciousness. The more adroit our consciousness, the better-read, the more numerous and nobler-looking are our back-doors, the cleverer our self-deception. You can entertain yourself like that for a lifetime, excellently in fact, only you never reach life that way; it leads inescapably to loss of contact with your own personality. For example, we can easily call our lack of the courage to go down on our knees good breeding, our fear of self-realization unselfishness and so on. Most of us know only too well what we ought to feel in this, that or the other situation, or, as the case may be, must not feel, but even with the best will in the world we have great difficulty in finding out what we actually do feel. That is a bad state of affairs. A sarcastic attitude towards all emotion is its classical symptom . . . Excessive demands on oneself are inevitably linked with the wrong kind of bad conscience. One man blames himself for not being a genius, another blames himself for not being a saint in spite of his good upbringing, and Stiller blamed himself for not being the sort who could fight in Spain . . . It is extraordinary what we mistake for conscience, once we have begun making excessive demands upon ourselves and so losing touch with our own personalities. The famous inner voice is often enough no more than the coquettish voice of a pseudo-ego that does not allow me to finally give up trying, to recognize myself, and attempts with all the wiles of vanity, if necessary even with false voices from heaven, to bind me to my fatal habit of making excessive demands upon myself. We can see our defeats, but we do not understand them as signals, as the outcome of misdirected endeavor, of endeavor directed away from our self. Curiously enough the direction taken by our vanity is not, as it appears to be, the direction towards our self, but away from our self."

We then discussed the well known line: Him I love who craves the impossible. Without being able to recall just where this line occurs in *Faust*, Part Two, we agreed that it could only have been uttered by a demonic figure; for it is an invitation to neurosis and has nothing to do with any real endeavor (it doesn't refer to endeavor, anyhow, but to craving) that presupposes humility in the face of our limited potentialities.

"I don't see Stiller as an exception," said my public prosecutor. "I see some of my acquaintances and myself in him, although the demands we make on ourselves are of different kinds . . . Many know themselves, only few also manage to accept themselves. How much self-knowledge is limited to presenting other people with a more precise and exact description of our weaknesses—a form of coquetry. But even genuine self-knowledge, which remains mute and is chiefly expressed in behavior, is not enough; it is a first step, indispensable and laborious, but not sufficient in itself. Self-knowledge in the form of lifelong melancholy, of amused indulgence towards our early resignation is very common, and people of this kind may sometimes be very pleasant table companions; but what is it like for them? They have given up a false rôle, and that is certainly something, but it doesn't yet take them back into life . . . It is not true that self-acceptance automatically comes with age. It is true that when we are older our earlier aims seem more dubious and it is easier, cheaper, more painless to smile at our youthful ambition; but this is not the same as self-acceptance. In a certain respect, even, it becomes more difficult as we get older. More and more people to whom we look up admiringly are younger than ourselves, our allotted span grows shorter and shorter, resignation becomes easier and easier in view of our nonetheless honorable career, easier still for those who have had no career at all and can console themselves with the ill-will of their environment, cheering themselves with the thought of their unrecognized genius . . . To accept oneself calls for an extremely positive attitude towards life . . . The demand that we shall love our neighbor as ourselves contains as an axiom the demand that we shall love ourselves, shall accept ourselves as we were created. But even self-acceptance alone is not enough. As long as I try to convince those around me that I am none other than myself, I am necessarily afraid of being misconstrued, and this very fear keeps me a prisoner . . . Without the certitude that there is an absolute reality, I cannot imagine, of course," said my public prosecutor, "that we can ever succeed in becoming free."

P.S. Absolute authority? Absolute reality? Why doesn't he say "God"? It seems to me that he consciously takes care to avoid this word. Only when he is talking to me?

P.S. I am always hoping that precisely by recognizing myself as a negligible and unimportant man I shall cease to be a negligible and unimportant man. Fundamentally, to be quite honest, I am forever hoping that God (if I meet Him half way) will make me a dif-

ferent, namely a richer, deeper, more valuable, more
important personality—and it is precisely this, in all
probability, which prevents God from setting me on
the path to a real existence, that is to say from making it possible for me to experience existence. My
conditio sine qua non is that he shall revoke me, his
creature.

Julika is still in Paris.

The mother's grave. It is just like all graves in this
country: neatly enclosed by a granite border, every
grave a little too short so that you're afraid of treading on the dead people's feet, gravel paths in between,
evergreens round the edge, in the center of the grave
an earthenware vase containing a few withered asters,
behind the headstone a rusty tin for watering the
flowers. But today it was raining. We stood together
under the umbrella, and the church clock struck three.
The headstone was a bit queer, a typical piece of
tombstone art, some kind of allegory. Here and there
a small cypress towered above this gray Manhattan of
tombstones. Once Wilfried asked:
   "How do you like the stone, by the way?"
   "Yes," I said . . .
One would expect Wilfried to possess an umbrella.
I've never had an umbrella of my own in my life, but
now I was glad of an umbrella. It was a country cemetery, an insignificant church dating from the nine-
teenth century, situated on a hilltop and surrounded
by ancient elms. In good weather one would no doubt
have a pretty, quiet, wide view out over the lake towards the mountains. Today everything was gray, a
dripping autumn day with mist hanging round the
woods. We stood there for a long time, while the rain
drummed on the black umbrella, both of us without
speaking and without making a gesture, like any two
Protestants. The inscription read: Here rests in God.

Others had other inscriptions, Rest in peace, or else some vague lyric. The headstone, travertine, was slightly polished. The rain dripped audibly from the umbrella on to brown leaves. In the next row but one there was a fresh grave, a mound of loamy earth with wreaths on top of it. Then the church clock struck again. It was cold, wet, gray . . .

Afterwards we went to a tavern.

Wilfried Stiller, younger than I, is a hefty fellow with a tanned, rough and taut skin. You can see at once that he spends a lot of time in the sun and air. His black hair is cropped short like a peasant's or a soldier's. He brought me over in a jeep that belongs not to him personally, but to the Agricultural Co-operative. He is manager of the fruit section . . .

Naturally we talked about our mothers, while Wilfried smoked cigars all the time (except in the cemetery), the same brand as the inspector at the police station when I first arrived. Apparently his mother was extremely strict, mine not in the least. When Wilfried told me how his mother shut him up for a whole day in the cellar, because he had been pinching jam and she wanted to give him a lasting distaste for the place, I could laugh with the man who survived that day in a dark cellar with undiminished good health; but that wasn't my mother. She could never have brought herself to be so strict. His mother used to say: "Now pull yourself together, if you want to be a proper boy!" My mother used to say: "Leave the lad in peace, will you!" My mother was convinced that I should cope with life all right. I can remember listening at the keyhole as my mother told a group of friends all the witty and clever remarks I had made during the past week, enjoying a great success with them.

Nothing like that ever happened to Wilfried; his mother was worried that Wilfried would never achieve anything worthwhile, and the healthy man sit-

ting opposite me at the varnished tavern table smoking
a cigar, rather rough but cordial in his dullness, admitted himself that he was not a gifted child: he hadn't
even learnt to play the piano. My mother, I know,
saved on charwomen and washerwomen and did the
cleaning and washing herself, so that she could pay
for my flute lessons every month; for I was considered
gifted.

Both mothers were funny! Wilfried told me that his
mother, who was naturally just as respectable as mine,
loved raw liver above everything else, far more than
sweets. Now, no one could give her a packet of raw
liver for her birthday or mother's day, so she had to
buy her tit-bits for herself. And so she did. Once,
when a football had been kicked into some bushes
and Wilfried went to look for it, he found his mother
in the most hidden corner of a public park, eating raw
liver; the good woman was frightened to death, and
obliged to keep Wilfried at bay with any excuse she
could think of, until he believed anything of his
mother—except that she had been eating raw liver!

When Wilfried recalled incidents like this, it might
have been my mother too, and we laughed together.
Then again he described a mother whom I did not
know at all, a clear-thinking and incorruptible woman
whom you couldn't hoax, a practical woman who accustomed Wilfried at an early age to the idea that he
would never be able to marry a proper woman if he
didn't earn plenty of money. My mother wasn't like
that at all. She enjoyed it when I hoaxed her, and as
regards the future she attached more importance to
my inner qualities, convinced that I could marry anyone I liked, any woman whatever with the exception
of my fond mother herself, which when I was young
I regretted; my mother's worry was rather whether
the person I should one day bring home would really
be worthy of me. Once, I remember, I tried to spit
cherry stones on to our old neighbor as he sat reading

the newspaper in his little garden; my mother was so furious at his outrageous suspicion, that I swore black and blue I hadn't done it, so as not to show her up in front of the old gentleman. My stepfather used to say that my mother and I stuck together like burs. Wilfried had his own father. And my mother, I know, would never have cried in front of teachers; she would have denied everything or demanded a little understanding on the part of the teachers. I was a delicate child. When my mother, God knows how, paid the police fine, I brought her a whole lot of cowslips; that was when my mother cried, not before. His mother didn't expect any cowslips, but told Wilfried to apologize personally to the teacher he had been rude to. It's funny how different mothers can be! . . .

"Now she's been lying over there four years already," said Wilfried. "Anything rather than be buried in the town, anything rather than lie alongside people she had never seen while she was alive, she didn't like the idea of that—"

Once the taverner came, addressed Wilfried by name and then shook my hand too. Wilfried talks to people without the least trace of disguise. I can't do that. Why not? And then, when we were alone together again, I had to tell him about Julika—how she was getting on in Paris. Julika came here from Paris for the funeral with her red hair. Wilfried had not met her again since. Wilfried was wearing a knitted waistcoat. He was very interested in California; Wilfried once wanted to go and farm in Argentina, but couldn't because of his mother, so I talked about California, without thinking or seeing California; I saw rather the grave with the evergreens and polished travertine, without thinking or seeing my mother, and for Wilfried everything was fine.

His brother, the missing man, must always have been rather queer. He didn't say so, didn't even hint it. Wilfried is not ambiguous, not subtle, not inquisitive; he is a man of natural existence, not a man of expression. Even when I keep silent, I feel like a chatterbox beside him. Wilfried drank little and probably even that was only for my benefit, yet he found the wine good, which I for my part found touching, for it was a mediocre wine, with no body, really tasting only of cask. And all this was very normal, very strange, a conversation with many pauses, so that you could hear the cat purring, and when Wilfried once more repeated his invitation to go and stay with him and his wife I noticed I was very close to tears; and yet the whole time I had felt empty of all feeling. He was a brother, which I wasn't, and it didn't even worry him that I wasn't.

Was I also hungry? Wilfried didn't try to convince me of anything, and there was something disarming about this. And he wasn't afraid of silence, whereas I resumed the conversation about modern farms in California, a subject on which Wilfried was far better informed than I, through his reading. We made one amusing discovery: the illustrated paper that contained the article about the dancer Julika and her vanishing husband also carried a long report on modern methods of pest control, which set Wilfried laughing when I referred to it in conversation; even over this matter, the paper didn't have the facts right. This amused me.

Whenever anything we discussed (military service, for example) brought to light the fact that Wilfried was five years younger than I, it irritated me. I saw him as a small boy sees men, as ageless but under all circumstances superior. It also irritated me that this man, for his part, was not irritated by even the oddest diversity of our natures, but immediately took it for granted that my life, though incomprehensible to him, was certain to be perfectly all right in my own eyes; and somehow, by not poking his nose into my affairs, he maintained a respectful distance, which every time

I observed it made me feel ashamed and unsure of myself. But he was perfectly serious about this respect. I didn't dare order any more wine, any different wine, although I knew quite well that Wilfried would have raised no objection—after all, it was a special day that deserved a little celebration.

Of his children, I heard that they had got over the mumps one after the other; there was nothing left now but measles. When Wilfried, after first hanging his jacket over the back of the chair, ate bread and cheese to fortify himself for the long journey in the not exactly comfortable jeep, I wondered whether I should not, even unasked, declare myself—but I didn't know how, nor actually why either . . . Wilfried took it as a matter of course that we were brothers, and after standing under a black umbrella in front of a grave were about to part again.

Just before five I was back in Zurich.

Now (as I write these notes) I am sitting in a bar. Alone in the town! It is like a dream to me; and yet my immediate environment, a pack of freshly dolled-up Zurich tarts waiting for the first job of the evening, is anything but dreamlike. Nobody claims to know me. Supposing I don't return to my cell at six? Wilfried drove me to Bellevue; he still had a long journey in front of him and tomorrow another hard day's work, on the other hand I had another hour's parole provided Wilfried stayed with me. He shook hands.

"Yes," I said, "—and supposing I make a getaway?"

He laughed, his hand already on the brake.

"That's up to you," he commented, his jeep jerked and he was away . . . What should I have explained to him? There are many people to whom I am closer, in understanding much closer, than to this man; as a friend he is out of the question. He has his own friends, who are completely strange to me, and I don't think it would occur to him to number me among his friends. And yet he is the only person who can take it for granted that I am the missing Stiller, that is to say fundamentally misunderstand me, without my caring. What does understand mean anyway? Friends must understand one another to remain friends; brothers are always brothers. Why was I never his brother? Today's meeting has set my mind in turmoil. How do I stand in this world?

"You still deny it?" asked my counsel, the moment I was back in prison. "You still deny it?"

"Yes," I said, "I still deny it—"

"That's ridiculous," said my counsel.

"It's ridiculous," I said, "but if I were to admit what you want me to admit, Herr Doktor, that would be even more ridiculous."

"I don't understand you," said my counsel.

"I know that," I said. "That's why I have to deny everything you say about me, Herr Doktor—"

Yes—who is going to read what I have written in these notebooks? And yet I believe that no one writes without the idea that somebody is going to read what he writes, if this somebody is only the writer himself. Then I ask myself, Can one write without playing a part? One tries to be a stranger to oneself. My reality does not lie in the part I play, but in the unconscious decision as to what kind of part I assign myself. At times I have the feeling that one emerges from what has been written as a snake emerges from its skin. That's it; you cannot write yourself down, you can only cast your skin. But who is going to be interested in this dead skin? The ever-recurring question whether the reader is ever able to read anything other than himself is superfluous: writing is not communication with readers, not even communication with oneself, but communication with the inexpressible. The more exactly one succeeds in expressing oneself, the more clearly appears the inexpressible force, that is to say the reality, that oppresses and moves the writer. We possess language in order to become mute. He who is silent is not mute. He who is silent hasn't even an inkling who he is not.

Why doesn't Julika write?

Friends! Now they come in flocks, today no less than five—all at the same time. They all find me unchanged, almost unchanged, and address me familiarly. And the fact that I don't utter a word doesn't in the least prevent them from knowing me, oh yes, there's nothing better than an old friendship. One of them, an actor, just wouldn't let go of my hand; his eyes were full of profound emotion, and when he stopped talking he oozed deep understanding for Stiller. With a squeeze of the hand, a further intensification of the pressure and another shake of my crushed hand, which he had clasped in both of his, I let him say to me that which cannot be expressed in words. For my part, I merely said, "Take a seat, gentlemen." And one of them, I observed as time passed, considered himself my benefactor, because he hadn't taken the missing Stiller to court for the years of unpaid rent, as he would have been fully entitled to do. It appeared that my embarrassment was a sufficient expression of gratitude for him.

They are all of them very pleasant people, although on this visit, gathered together as probably never happens under natural circumstances, they were rather like a funeral party at the crematorium. The fact was that, apart from their connection with the missing Stiller, a connection with such various origins, they really had nothing in common with one another. Each of them had perhaps heard of the others in the past through Stiller, whose absence was now painfully evident. We should have got to know one another *tête-à-tête*. One of them, I learnt after a time, had in the meantime become a professor, a fine brain who must have had a lot of trouble with the missing Stiller, so vague in mind and temperament and so full of muddle-headed radicalism. That he had come at all, this young professor, who naturally had other friends than Stiller, was an act of true loyalty. His circumspection, the tender consideration with which he treated me, enabled me to guess how sensitive the missing Stiller must have been; and as a matter of fact I, too, felt inferior, felt the extent of my ignorance, relapsed into a kind of timid esteem and hence into a tone that must inevitably have reminded him of his vanished friend. He didn't want this tone or this silence of timid esteem; but it seemed as though he were used to it, and the queerer my behavior, the more certainly he must have seen in me the vanished Stiller, who had often enough struck him as queer and with whom he had kept faith, in spite of everything, more out of a desire for fair play than out of friendship, which never bore fruit with Stiller.

Why did it make me sad? They were all the sort of men one would like to have for one's friends. Why wasn't it possible? Incidentally, they were by no means agreed as to who Stiller was; and yet they acted as though they took me for one and the same person. A lively graphic artist already described the celebration that was to take place after my release, and the fifth, a compositor by trade, seemed to be a Communist who regarded the other four as arrant reactionaries and blamed me for talking to them, to judge by his expression. He was particularly annoyed with me over the friendly tone in which the property owner described the Sleeping-Beauty condition of Stiller's deserted studio; and at times, while they were talking, I seriously wondered what kind of person I must be to correspond, even in broad outline only, to the memories and expectations of these five visitors—something like a five-headed monster, I thought, and every one of them would have cut off my other four heads as not genuine, as superfluous, in order to produce the true Stiller.

The actor, I observed, had become a Catholic and looked down, not without respect, not without understanding, upon the composer, the Communist, whose views he had no difficulty in guessing, since they reminded him of the first intellectual adventures of his own youth. Apart from the Communist, it was obvious that none of them had stood still. The young professor assured me that, although he still valued the classics above all else, he no longer regarded modern art as purely decadent, and the graphic artist, manifestly converted by a considerable degree of success, had shaken off all pessimism concerning contemporary culture, pointed to the high level of Swiss graphic art and for his part, speaking frankly, had no need of either Communism or Catholicism in order to see his task in the world. The property owner, on the other hand, an antique dealer by profession, was more than ever attached to tradition, the more local the better, not a word against the European Defense Community, but for that very reason it was the antiquarian's duty to foster the sense of difference, for example the difference between the inhabitants of Basle and those of Zurich; for what were Europe's fraternal armies to defend if not the prerogative of being different, even over very short distances?

As I have said, they were the pleasantest of people. Afterwards, I asked myself why I couldn't really feel myself their friend. I have offended them, without saying anything. My cell grows lonelier after every visit.

Dreamed of Julika. Almost exactly the same again: She is sitting in a boulevard café among a crowd of people, trying to write to me, her pencil held to her lips like a schoolgirl in difficulties. I try to go to her,

but am arrested by three foreign (German) soldiers
and know that Julika has betrayed me. Our eyes meet.
The men in helmets drag me away, I want to curse
Julika, but her mute gaze beseeches me not to believe
what she has written, she was forced to write it, I
forced her. When I ask if I am going to be shot, the
three soldiers laugh. One of them says: No, we crucify now. After feeling very frightened I find myself
working in a camp. We have to pin photographs to
trees with drawing pins, that's what they call "crucify-
ing," nothing else. I "crucify" Julika, the ballerina . . .

It is hard not to tire in the face of the world, in the
face of its majority, in the face of its superiority,
which there is no denying. It is difficult, alone and
without witnesses, to know what one believes one
has learnt in a solitary hour, difficult to carry a knowledge that can never be proved nor even uttered. I
know I am not the missing Stiller. And I never was. I
swear it, even if I do not know who else I am. Perhaps
I am no one. And even if they can prove to me in
black and white that of all people who are registered
as having been born, only one is at present missing,
Stiller, and that I am not in this world at all if I refuse
to be Stiller, I shall still refuse. Why don't they give
up trying? My behavior is ludicrous, I know, my
position is becoming untenable. But I am not the man
they are looking for, and this certainty, the only one
I possess, I shall not relinquish.

Julika is still in Paris.

That's not true. I cannot be alone, strictly speaking,
and there has hardly been an hour in my life when I
was able to be alone. Most of the time, strictly speaking, there was a woman present. It began with my
dear, good mother. I just managed to scrape through
my school-leaving certificate and I was glad on my

mother's account, because my stepfather couldn't say, "Well, what about your precious son now?" Later I entered on my period of patriotic punishment with a federal blanket under my arm and spent nearly a whole summer in barracks, but I wasn't alone, because all the time I felt sorry for my mother, who was terribly upset by the whole thing. A host of hours, more hours than go to make a human life one would have thought, are on call in my memory, hours which I thought solitary—evenings in hotel rooms with a hubbub rising from foreign streets or a view into a courtyard, nights spent in railway stations, spring days in a public park filled with prams and a foreign language, then again afternoons in my usual pub, wanderings in rain and forest and in the certainty that I should never again speak to some person for whom I yearned, partings of all kinds, quick, clean and straightforward partings, but also pitiable, whimpering, dragged-out, cowardly partings—a host of hours, as I said, and yet I was never alone, strictly speaking, not for an hour. I always found some inner escape route, a tender or tormented recollection, a passionate conversation with an invisible person who generally didn't exist at all, but whom I invented in order not to be alone, or the hope of a magnificent encounter at the next street-corner or the next street-corner but one. Is that solitude?

Right at the beginning of my artistic activity, perhaps, I was alone or almost succeeded in being alone in a real sense in the hope of being able to realize myself in clay or plaster; but this hope did not last long before ambition raised its head, delight at the prospect of recognition, worry over possible rejection, for months all this clay and ambition and plaster kept me from seeing a single living soul, immersed in my art that never became real art, immured between the four walls of my studio, a hermit without a radio as in the Middle Ages, taciturn as a galley slave, a monk in relation to girls, but only in relation to them, a jubilant Rumpelstilz at the thought that nobody yet had any inkling of my genius; and I was as hard-working as a flogged beast, flogged by ambition. So I was not alone.

And I was not alone by my ferry across the Tajo; in the event of my death, I knew, Anya would not break down nor enter a convent, she would go on tending the living and go on letting herself be loved, but occasionally she would remember me. And when no one shot me, when they only tied me up with my braces, tied my hands and feet together and threw me into the gorse, I wasn't alone: I had my ignominy in front of Anya, I thought I should die miserably of thirst and never see Anya again; I shouted as long as I could, then I stopped shouting, but on the threshold of unconsciousness I had Anya, my searing ignominy in front of Anya. And I was not alone on my way back, although I already had a presentiment how foreign my homeland would seem to me; I spent whole nights on the march or in French waiting-rooms justifying myself to Anya, feeling ashamed before Anya, becoming indignant about her or piling up hostile thoughts about her. I wasn't alone.

And then, far away from her, I told my Spanish tale; my acquaintances believed it, more or less, but I knew who knew the truth—namely, Anya—so I wasn't alone. It's ridiculous but true: there was always a woman with whom I could delude myself. I had men friends, not many, sometimes one, sometimes others; that was friendship, but no delusion about our solitariness as individuals. I often thought of distant friends, curious about their ideas or glad of their contradiction or even in painful discord; but in the hour of horror, in the hour of inability to be alone, it was never with anyone but a woman, with the memory or the hope of a woman, that I escaped from my loneliness. Why wasn't I capable of being alone, why was

I compelled to bore myself with this ballerina, so much so that I even had to marry this sea beast? The fault was in myself, no doubt about that, time and again I was governed by an iron will operating in reverse. A thousand and one nights, at least, I took my head in my hands and fell asleep: even in marriage I couldn't be alone. I deserted her; she humiliated me and I humiliated her; but I wasn't alone.

And I wasn't alone stowed away in the after hold of an Italian tramp steamer, an emigrant without papers bound for America; only a bribed stoker knew I was down below among the barrels, and it was dark, stinking and so hot that the sweat ran out of my every pore (it would have run out of anyone's in my place!); I knew very well that the beautiful Julika would be disgusted by this sweat—so I wasn't alone. It was the chance of a lifetime to be alone, an opportunity of eighteen undisturbed days and nineteen nights with a calm sea most of the time, so I can't even make the excuse that I felt seasick. I was sick once, probably soon after we passed Gibraltar; the boat pitched for a few hours, then quieted down again. And what did I do with my chance, that was as big as the Atlantic? I lit a cigarette and saw by the flame of my lighter the labels on the nearest barrels, Chianti Italian Wine Imported, then nothing but blank darkness with a few slits of light between the planks and the throbbing of the propeller-shaft underneath me, day and night; it was enough to drive one mad; I didn't go mad, for in imagination I saw Julika on her *art nouveau* veranda and told her what still remained to be said. I was glad I should never see this woman again; that was my only pleasure down there in the hold. Was I alone? Every time I woke up after a longish sleep I was afraid the stinking tub was already homeward bound for Europe; it made no difference to my resolution not to see the beautiful Julika again. I had only to think, as I sat among the stinking barrels (I spent most of the time sitting down, because whenever I walked about in the darkness I kept stumbling over ropes and crane chains), of the letter she had sent me after her murder on the balcony, of the first sentence. "There is not much point in returning to the conversation we had last week, etc." I only had to think of this opening sentence and I regretted nothing, not even if this tub were to run aground on a sandbank the very next moment and fill up with water. I had only to think of Foxli! Or of the famous gruel which this woman couldn't be bothered to make, and a hundred other trifles, each more ridiculous than the last; but eighteen days and nineteen nights in succession in the darkness, with water dripping through some crack between the planks—an eternity of dripping minutes—were not enough to summarize the waste land between this woman and me, even in the rapid shorthand of thought; again I stumbled round and grazed myself on a piece of rusty sheeting, again I squatted on a coil of rope and licked the warm blood from my hand, squatted there stinking of stale sweat and fresh sweat, seen by no one and as blind as a mole, deafened by the throb of the propeller-shaft, and not a single waking hour went by without my thinking of something against this frail woman at Davos, and nobody heard my loudest curses. But I wasn't alone.

In Brooklyn harbor the propeller-shaft fell silent at last. My heart beat. First they discharged the forward hold. After ten hours my stoker came at last with the advice to remain hidden for another two or three days, because there was a dock strike. Five days passed, and naturally five nights as well, and then at last I heard my valiant stoker's whistle as agreed; but still I wasn't through with the waste land between this woman and me.

Now I had to go ashore. Was I alone in New York? I pushed my way through the antlike swarm in Times Square; for weeks my eyes were continually drawn to telephone booths, but I was resolved not to ring Sibylle. And I didn't ring, but boarded a Greyhound and headed west, no matter where to. The country varied, it was tedious and entrancing, repellent, delightful. I saw the prairie, the Chicago slaughterhouses, the Mormons, the Indians, the biggest copper mine in the world, the longest suspension bridge in the world; I talked to strange faces in a milk bar; I worked for a month in Detroit; I fell in love with the daughter of a conservative senator, who had a Cadillac, and we swam in Lake Michigan; I traveled on; I saw forest fires, baseball, sunsets over the Pacific and flying fish; I rarely had any money, but I whistled with joy at being so far from Davos, and slightly less far from Riverside Drive, New York; at this time I could have been as much alone as on the moon. They said Hallo! and I said Hallo! I listened to the last radio announcers after midnight, merely in order not to hear the silence, for in the silence I was not alone, so I preferred to listen to these ever-confident announcers telling me the best soap, the best brand of whisky, the best dog food, interspersed with symphonies or at least Tchaikovsky's *Nutcracker Suite*—so that I should not be so alone.

And it if wasn't my graceful ballerina, it was Little Gray, that graceful beast of a cat, that kept jumping on to my window sill although it had nothing to say to me. Haven't I written about that already somewhere in this heap of paper? I picked her up and shoved her into a refrigerator, then I tried to whistle and later on to sleep, but in vain; after a few hours I took her out of the refrigerator, well knowing that her death would prey on my mind; and when, after a while, she opened the slits of her eyes slightly, I was moved to tears that she hadn't inflicted her death in the refrigerator on me. I cared for her until she began to purr again and rub herself against the legs of my trousers, but at least she was alive, even if she bore herself like a victress and still had nothing to say to me; and then, as she began to exploit my bad conscience, I chucked her out into the not very cold night, where she hoisted her tail and spat; I shut the window, all the windows; she jumped on to the sill and spat, as though I had really killed her; I acted for a time as though I didn't see her, didn't hear her miauling, whereupon she maligned me throughout the neighborhood (especially to Florence, the mulatto girl). "Enough!" I cried, went to the window, took her by the scruff of the neck and flung the struggling bundle as far as I could. Catlike, she fell on her feet. To my surprise, she even remained silent and did not hop upon the window sill again. She left me alone, I admit, but every moment I knew that any moment she might jump back on my window sill. So I wasn't alone.

Am I alone now? I'm thinking of Frau Julika Stiller-Tschudy in Paris. I see her in her black tailor-made costume, which suits her so wonderfully, and her little white hat on her red hair. It must be cold in Paris now. She had in mind to buy a new coat. I see her (although I am not in the least acquainted with this autumn's models), in her new coat, which once again suits her splendidly. It may be that I fall in love very easily; but when I sit like this in my cell thinking of Frau Julika Stiller-Tschudy, it is more than being in love; I can feel it by my hopeless dejection; Frau Julika Stiller-Tschudy is my only hope. Quite apart now from her copper hair, her alabaster complexion, her greenish or water-gray or perhaps colorless, but anyhow exceptionally beautiful eyes—quite apart from all this, which anyone, even my defense counsel, can see, this woman (whatever the vanished Stiller may have against her) is a superb woman, not easy to love perhaps, a woman who has never been loved and has never loved. And for this reason, I believe, I am in no way deterred by what she and Stiller went through together. What has that to do with me?

I don't want to be high-falutin and declare, I love her! But I may say, I should like to love her. And so long as Frau Julika Stiller-Tschudy does not take me for her missing husband I dare to say, Why should it not be possible? On one of the next few days she will come back, according to her rather brief and reserved cards, wearing a Paris autumn model.

I shall admit to her that it is all untrue: I am incapable of being alone, I have tried, but in vain. I shall tell her openly that I have missed her. That is no exaggeration. And then, as soon as possible, I shall ask her whether she thinks she could love me. Her smile, the astonishment in her plucked eyebrows—I shall let none of this deter me; that's the way Frau Julika Stiller-Tschudy is. An orphan at eighteen, one quarter Hungarian, three quarters German Swiss, a tuberculosis that proved to be quite real, and then the marriage with a neurotic Spanish volunteer—all that wasn't easy; her childlessness, her art and the way she went through everything, not without self-pity, undoubtedly, not without a graceful kind of malice, but always with a head held high on her narrow shoulders—that is magnificent: a touch of arrogance (in the specifically feminine manner, namely as a tendency to "forgive") is only too understandable. My open question, whether she thinks she can love me, will not be answered by any maidenly Yes. Frau Julika Stiller-Tschudy is too experienced for that, and so am I; nor is this cell with a prison bed a green snuggery under blossoming apple boughs. I hope I don't become solemn! For when I become solemn I inevitably become cowardly, if only for stylistic reasons: certain unsolemn things are then almost impossible to say. If Frau Julika Stiller-Tschudy does not answer me with an outright No, I must talk something like this:

"The fact is, Julika, you are my only hope, and that is the terrible thing about it. Listen to me! There is no need for us to talk about Jean-Louis Dmitritch, perhaps he loves you much more than I ever can, Dmitritch is a sensitive man, I take your word for it, a faithful half-Russian and a bit of an invalid. You haven't improved, my dear Julika; you're forever keeping an invalid. And in fact there is no chance of our improving, neither you nor I. That is the choice that remains to us, I believe: either we smash ourselves to pieces on one another, or we love one another. So, to be perfectly frank, I don't imagine it's going to be easy. In fact it will get harder year by year. Don't you agree? But there is nothing else left to us. At all costs, I think, we must start from the fact that neither of us has ever loved the other. And that, you see, is why we can't even separate. That's a very funny thing! You have parted from Jean-Louis, you say. Out of loyalty to your husband, you say. Let us treat your husband as vanished! But you were able to part from Jean-Louis, you see, so why can't we part? Every couple who were once happy in their own way and realized their potentialities, can get divorced; it is sad, distressing, scandalous, incomprehensible, but neither of the two suffers harm to their soul: she has two sweet children, a recompense for her innocence that is visible from afar, and he becomes deputy chairman in spite of everything: who knows which of the two will be the first to remarry? And what about us, Julika, what have we got? The memory of Foxli, to put it in a nutshell. I know the little dog isn't personally to blame for the fact that we were never happy together. But you know what I mean. We were never through with one another. And I believe that is why, in spite of everything, we couldn't part. Poor Monsieur Dmitritch! He might possess every conceivable masculine quality, in vain, they would be of no avail to him against the vacuum that binds us together. I know that, Julika, I was loved as you know, and it was simple to love that woman, it was joy. But it didn't work out. It didn't work out because I wasn't through with

you, with us. She had a child recently, by the way, I
wrote and told you, and she is now once more the wife
of my only friend. That's another thing. I still love
her. That is why I ask you if you think you could
love me; it's anything but easy for you to love me
either. At times, to be quite frank, it's like trying to
walk on water, and at the same time I know, we both
know, that the water is rising to drown us, and will go
on rising, even if we don't try to walk on it. There's
not a great deal of life left to us. Everything, really
everything, that is left to us in life depends upon
whether we, you and I, can succeed in meeting one
another above and beyond all that has happened. That
sounds rather despondent, I know; but it is just the reverse, it is the hope, the certainty even, that there is
still a threshold for us through which we can enter
life, you into yours and I into mine, but there is only
this one threshold, and neither of us can cross it alone,
you see, neither you nor I—"

That roughly is what I shall say to Frau Julika
Stiller-Tschudy, so long as she—she at least!—does not
take me for the missing Stiller, and the rest my counsel can settle to his own satisfaction, I shall no longer
care about that.

In view of the imminent final hearing, my counsel was
very brief. He informed me that his defense (in case I
really didn't decide to make a confession beforehand)
was fixed and settled, already typed out. Further, my
counsel had also received a picture postcard (also the
Place de la Concorde?) with the message that "we"
could expect her tomorrow or the next day.

All I did was nod.

If I could pray, I should have to pray that all hope of
escaping from myself should be taken from me. My
occasional attempts to pray come to grief through the
very fact that I hope to be somehow transformed by

praying, to escape from my powerlessness, and as soon as I find that this is not the case I lose all hope of being on the road. By the road, I mean in the last resort nothing but the hope of escaping from myself. This hope is my prison. I know that, but my knowledge does not burst my prison asunder, it merely shows me my prison, my powerlessness, my insignificance. I am not hopeless enough, or, as believers say, submissive enough. I can hear them say: Submit and you will be free, your prison will be burst asunder, as soon as you are willing to go out from it an insignificant and powerless man.

They want to drive me crazy, merely so that they can make a citizen of me and have everything in order; they shrink from nothing now. Since yesterday there is not a single person who has not shamelessly betrayed me, with the exception of my public prosecutor. It was a bitter day. I will record the facts:

1. The Morning.
Around ten I was called to the public prosecutor. After eleven I was still sitting in the antechamber along with Knobel, who also had no idea what was going on. Knobel was worried that he might be in for a reprimand—because of the cervelat he had slipped me, for instance—and I was disappointed by the way the good Knobel reacted to the mere thought of a reprimand; he was afraid of losing his job. Of course he didn't say so, but felt obliged to drop the cordial tone that was usual between us as we sat in this antechamber. Knobel read a newspaper, to create an impression of independence, with an expression of ill-humor, as though churlishness provided some sort of guarantee that one was not crawling to one's superior. In Germany they click their heels, in the East they rub their hands together, in Switzerland they light a cigar and strain after a pose of surly equality as

though nothing could happen in this country to a man who behaved correctly. When a smart young lady came and said, "The public prosecutor will see you now," Knobel made no attempt to hurry: the public prosecutor is only human, we're all taxpayers! All the same, he forgot his pince-nez. Oddly enough (on purpose?) they left the doors open; without being able to see anyone, I heard the following conversation:

"I wasn't going to pay a fee for that!"

"By the way," said the public prosecutor, "don't be upset by the fact that the documents of the case are full of references to a hair-oil gangster. As you've seen for yourself, the phrase is put in inverted commas. It's an expression used by our prisoner—"

"So I suppose!"

"Everything else—"

"Hair-oil gangster!" said the indignant voice. "I shall bring an action for slander, no matter what it costs. You can tell the prisoner so today."

A short pause.

"Just one more question, Herr Direktor—"

"Certainly, Herr Staatsanwalt, anything you please."

"Have you any contact with Jamaica?"

"How do you mean?"

"I'm not trying to find out about your business contacts," said the public prosecutor. "Don't misunderstand me, Herr Direktor. All I want to know is: when this Herr Stiller was doing the plaster head of you, did you ever talk about Jamaica?"

"It's possible—"

"Aha."

"I have a house in Jamaica."

"Aha."

"Why?"

I heard the chair being pushed back.

"Once again, very many thanks, Herr Direktor," said the public prosecutor. "We are very relieved to see that you haven't been murdered."

"Murdered?"

"The fact is, our prisoner maintains positively that several years ago he murdered you with his own hands."

"Me?"

"In Jamaica—yes."

Now it was Knobel's turn, he was introduced as the warder and asked to relate everything I had told him. He was obviously unsure of himself. His story of the murder was poor, muddled and lacking in graphic quality.

"In the jungle!" laughed the company director. "Did you ever hear of such a thing, Herr Staatsanwalt? In the jungle! I've never seen a jungle in Jamaica, these are freaks of fancy, Herr Staatsanwalt, believe me—"

"I believe you."

"Freaks of fancy!"

Knobel seemed to have lost his nerve: he didn't dare describe the way the blood of the director, who was standing in front of him, mingled with the brown marsh water and how the black *zopilote* and the well-dressed vulture waited—just the things he should have told them now, when they asked him for more details. Instead, Knobel asked in return:

"Are you Herr Direktor Schmitz, then?"

"Answer my questions," said the director. "What does the prisoner claim to have murdered me with?"

"With an Indian dagger."

"Oh."

"Yes," said Knobel, "into the throat in front and then round to the left."

"So."

"Or else round to the right," said Knobel, losing his grip again. "I can't remember now."

"Thank you."

Then Knobel was told he could go.

"I'm sorry," said Knobel; and as he went through

the ante-chamber, cap in hand, his ears were lobster red; he didn't deign to glance at me . . . I didn't hear how the director felt about this murder because Knobel had tidily shut the door. Their conversation inside lasted another ten minutes. I was trying to read the newspaper my warder had left behind, a Social Democratic publication I should think, when suddenly the gentleman was standing in the doorway. He said:

"It's been a pleasure, Herr Staatsanwalt, to explain the true position to you personally. It's not a question of the money here, as I have said, I told him at the time that I was willing to pay half the agreed fee, the full half, I give you my word, but I wasn't going to be blackmailed, and if Herr Stiller wasn't satisfied he could have taken me to court, but he didn't care to, as you see. He had no money for litigation! They always say that, these psychopaths, and when I told him he could sue me for the money if he wanted to, he just called me a gangster. Now really, Herr Staatsanwalt, you wouldn't have put up with that either."

The gentleman who then put on his overcoat in the ante-chamber was a thoroughly worthy citizen, but no more striking than any passer-by in the Bahnofstrasse. Round his neck he wore a simple scarf of plain silk. He covered his bald head with an equally simple hat of plain felt, which, when he caught sight of me, he did not raise; instead he clutched at his throat, as though adjusting the scarf. I nodded. I wonder why? He left with the words:

"We shall see one another in Court."

Then I had to go to the public prosecutor.

"There is a type of millionaire," I said, "you can't get at in a state where the rule of law prevails, so it's no wonder they keep on being resurrected—"

The smart young lady was quickly got rid of with a job, a letter to be delivered to the Hotel Urban. I thought at once: I wonder whether Julika is back from Paris? Meanwhile the public prosecutor, whom I had hitherto only seen as a guest on my prison bed, invited me to sit down.

"Yes," he smiled, "my dear chap—"

He was interrupted by the telephone. He turned a little to one side with the official telephone receiver, as was proper for an unofficial conversation, listened with his hand on his bunch of keys and gazing out of the window, for his part said only that he would not be home for lunch, an on-the-spot investigation he had in the afternoon, and rang off rather abruptly, obviously bothered by a question he didn't want to have to answer in my presence. Then he turned to me again, not without a trace of embarrassment.

"Sibylle sends her good wishes."

"Thank you," I said. "How is she?"

"Thank you," he said, "she's glad to be home again."

Then—after the last smile had vanished from his face and a silence of unconcealed embarrassment had lasted long enough, a silence that seemed to imply it was now settled that I was the missing Stiller and therefore the former lover of his wife, who was now glad to be back home, and after he had put away his bunch of keys—he uttered his not very original remark:

"Life's a funny thing."

I couldn't think of anything either.

"If it's all right with you, Stiller, let us have lunch together. We've got until two o'clock—I suggest," he said as he stood up, "that we drive a little way out into the country."

2. Lunch.

A rather taciturn drive through fields and woods. Everything very autumnal. The sun was still just hot enough to sit out of doors, at least round midday. We sat in a rather quaint open-air restaurant which nevertheless had a wide and delightful view; above our

heads there were vine leaves and in front of us a few
straggling vines between which we looked out on the
lake sparkling under a hazy light; everything was as
though beneath a veil of blue smoke, including the
brown ploughed fields and the woods with their dying leaves glowing. Here and there ladders still leaned
against the trees and baskets stood down below. Wasps
even came at our campari. The mountains towering
up above the autumnal haze were as clear as glass and
somehow unreal; their snow gleamed dazzling white
from behind the spectral branches of leafless fruit
trees, like a monstrance behind a black rood-screen.

"It's beautiful here," I said, "very beautiful."

"Didn't you know this place?"

The food was excellent.

"What shall we drink?" asked my prosecutor and
friend. "They have a very good Maienfelder here, I
believe."

"That'll do fine," I said, "fine."

I couldn't help looking again and again at the landscape, which fell away to the lake in a magnificently
broad sweep. The autumn mist blotted out the pettiness of the housing development, which was neither
town nor village; there remained the hills covered
with trees, the gentle hollows filled with ploughed
fields and bogs, a landscape that preoccupied me precisely because it did not in the least surprise me. I
knew it. Did I love it?

"I've heard," said my public prosecutor, "that our
friends were rather disappointed the other day. They
found you cold."

"Perhaps I am."

"Why?"

I shrugged my shoulders. I felt about them as I did
about this landscape, which in fact, like almost every
landscape is worthy of affection. It must be my fault
. . . Once more everything was there, the wasps in
the bottle, the shadows on the gravel, the golden still-

ness of transience, everything as though spellbound, the crackling hens in the meadow, the brown and over-ripe pears littering the roadway, the asters leaning over an iron railing, their centers bloody stars that ran towards the edges, the bluish light under the trees. It was as though everything were bidding itself goodbye; the whispering foliage of a poplar, the metallic bloom on the fallen fruit, the smoke rising from the fields where they were burning weeds, the lake glittering behind a grille of vines. Soon the sun would be turning rusty in the haze of midafternoon, the time of walking home without an overcoat, hands in trouser pockets, the damp leaves that no longer rustle, the farmsteads with their wine presses, the dripping barrels in the dusk, the red lanterns of a lakeside landing-place in the mist . . .

That is autumn here, and I can also see the spring. I see a rather young couple: they are tramping across country and the fields, sodden with melted snow, squelch under their feet, dark and soft like a wet sponge; the Föhn blows above their heads and the sun gives warmth; they pick their route entirely by the inviting accidents of the terrain and always at a comradely distance from one another; all around is the smell of scattered manure, springs gurgle and comb the grass of the sloping banks and the leafless woods stand with arches of March sky between their trunks; two steaming brown farm-horses are pulling a plough over a gently sloping hillside; in black clods, the earth gapes hungrily after the light. A strange reunion after years apart! Young as they are, they are talking about the ages of man, and they already know that at every age, apart from childhood, time is rather horrifying; and yet every age is beautiful the less we deny or dream away what belongs to it, for death itself, which will one day be our lot, cannot be denied, nor dreamed away, nor postponed. How much the young man talks about the two conditions of his life, work and expiation, as he calls it; and work—that is the joy, the fever, the excitement, so that you cannot sleep for jubilation, a cry that rings out across hours and days, so that you feel like running away from yourself—that is work, the elation that wins people without wishing to, that puts no one under an obligation, ties no one and advances no one, that is not calculating and avaricious, but behaves like the angel who has no hands for taking; work is a grandiose fervor of the heart in which all human contacts are purely incidental, an extra, a cheerful squandering from excess of joy; later, of course, it always turns out to be the finest sort of contact that is possible between human beings, unattainable as soon as it becomes a goal, a need, an urgent objective. Again and again there comes this sudden outbreak of depression that does not develop because people stay away, on the contrary—people only stay away because depression is about to break out, they can scent weeks ahead, as a dog can scent an earthquake, that everything which has been built up will once more be reduced to rubble and smothered in ashes, smothered in melancholy like a flock of black birds flapping their wings over the scenes of past joy, the shadow of fear—that is the expiation, the afterpangs of doubt, the horror of uncreative solitude.

How the young man likes talking, and how beautiful the young woman finds it, nevertheless! The silveredged clouds melt before the sun and little woods rise like islands out of a metallic glitter; they wander through a reedy marsh and as she jumps across a murmuring rill her shoe sticks in the clinging morass; the young woman balances like a tightrope walker with one stockinged foot in the air, so that the young man has to hold her. They kiss for the first time. Behind the copses there are lakes of coolness with snow still lying in the shady patches between the red-barked willows. As they are leaving a wood they stand still, arm in arm; the lake lies before them again like a flashing scythe, and over the Alps froth the silent breakers of the clouds, a mass of luminous foam.

They stop at some peasant inn. A child with plaits serves them. Behind a row of low windows full of shoots and a tangle of plants and sun slanting into the stillness of the wooden room and gleaming on their waiting plates, they feel how far they have roamed; they enjoy the well-earned meal—bacon with bread, peasant bread, that breaks up into moist and delicious hunks. A fly is buzzing against the window pane. The moment is enveloped and borne aloft by the clouds of a happiness that is close to sorrow, a strange, an alert sense of existence, an unexpected community of sentiment, that was lying in wait for them in this work-aday peasant room, the knowledge that they have met one another. No question is yet raised as to what will come of it; there prevails only the complete sense of how much is possible in a lifetime . . .

That is spring here, and in summer the hens cackle under the wooden tables, the vine leaves overhead are green and dense, the sky whitish, the lake like dull lead, bees hum round the edge of the wood, the blue haze above the motionless stalks in the tall meadows is alive with darting butterflies, the mountains are lost in the glare of the sun, and now (almost before I have emptied my glass) it is already autumn again and once more all this: baskets full of leaves, the dampness of mist and suddenly it is midday, a midday as at this moment, with gold in the air and time passing like an invisible gesture over the hillsides and apples falling with a thud. If you walk through the woods now there is a smell of mushrooms. Here it smells of new wine. Wasps buzz round the sweetness of fermentation, returning again and again, and the summer sun comes back to us once more in the fruits that have reached their brief hour of ripeness, the sweetness of remembered days; people sit in their gardens and feel the cool of shadow on their skin, and the gardens suddenly appear surprisingly wide, vacant but serene, a bluish spaciousness fills the empty treetops, and once more the red glow of dying foliage climbs up the walls of the houses, the last leaves go up in flames. Who notices the passing of the years and all that happens? All things are one, space filled with existence, nothing comes back to us, everything is repeated, the span of our existence is but an instant and the day comes when we no longer count the autumns, all living things are like the stillness over the ripening slopes, the grapes of parting hang on the vines of our lives. Pass on! Once more on days like these the lake beckons; your skin tingles if you swim now, you feel the warmth of your own blood, you swim as though in glass, you swim above the shadowy deeps of cold, and the glittering waves splinter on the shore; far out a sail sweeps along in front of silvery clouds, a moth on a sparkling web, canvas steeped in the shimmering rays of the sun against a background of faint and hazy shores. There are moments when time seems to be standing still, dizzy with happiness; God gazes upon himself and the whole world holds its breath, before it crumbles into the ashes of twilight . . .

At one point my public prosecutor said to me:

"That's Herrliberg down there, you know, and that place you can see in the distance is Thalwil."

Then the peasant girl took our plates away and asked if we had enjoyed the meal, and after she had brought the box of cigars we were once more alone. Of course, I had felt long ago that my prosecutor and friend had something on his mind. Had I prevented him from coming out with it? When our cigars were alight, the moment had arrived. Our glasses were empty, the black coffee hadn't been brought yet, the wasps had disappeared and in some little country church a clock struck.

"I'm glad," he said, "I'm really glad that we have got to know one another at last. But that's not what I

want to talk about now. At two o'clock we have to be
back in town for an on-the-spot hearing, don't be
alarmed, an on-the-spot hearing in the studio—I can
understand," he immediately added, "your looking at
me as though I had behaved like an underhand perse-
cutor, a hypocrite who came uttering friendly words
and carrying a straitjacket, I quite understand your
fear of that dusty studio down there—altogether, my
dear Stiller, perhaps I understand you better than you
think."

My inquiry as to the purpose of this on-the-spot
hearing went unanswered.

"If you will permit me," he said, "I should like to
give you a piece of advice."

His cigar had gone out.

"Look," he said at last, after lighting his cigar for
the second time, "I'm not only talking to you because
Sibylle has asked me to. Sibylle wants to spare you
any unnecessary suffering, and I think she's right: the
court will not understand you at all, Stiller. The court
will quite simply treat you as a convicted swindler, a
figure of fun; the court is used to swindles, as you
may imagine, but only to swindles that bring some advantage, a fortune or a title or the like, in short you
will be condemned to some punishment. I don't know
what, or maybe they will dispense with the punishment, but not the shrugs, the headshakes and the
sneers. What will you gain by that?"

"What is your advice?" I asked.

"Stiller," he said, "speaking as a friend: spare us the
necessity next Friday of publicly condemning you to
be yourself, and above all spare yourself this ordeal.
A legal judgment will only make it more difficult for
you henceforth to bear the name of the missing man,
and that you are at least outwardly none other than
the missing man is something we need no longer seriously discuss. Admit it of your own free will! That's

my advice, Stiller, advice given out of sincere friendship, I believe."

Then the black coffee arrived.

"Fräulein," said the public prosecutor, "make up the bill please."

"Everything together?"

"Yes," said the public prosecutor, "please."

Then came my reply:

"I can't admit what isn't true."

But the peasant girl, evidently misconstruing our silence, did not go at once, but stood around on the gravel chatting about the weather and then about the dog, while we sipped taciturnly at our hot coffee; only when the public prosecutor asked for the bill again did she leave us in peace.

"You can't admit," reiterated the public prosecutor, "what isn't true—"

"No," I said.

"How do you mean, it isn't true?"

"Mr. Public Prosecutor," I began—

"Don't address me as your public prosecutor," he interrupted as I groped for words. "I should like you to think of me as a friend, if you can. Call me Rolf."

"Thanks," I said.

"I suppose," he smiled, "that must have been how you spoke of me in the old days—"

Now my cigar had gone out, too.

"I'm happy," I said, after lighting my cigar a second time, "that you offer me your friendship. I have no friends here. But if you are serious about not wanting to be my public prosecutor, and I believe it with all my heart—Rolf . . . why, then I can expect of you what one must expect of a friend: that you will believe what I cannot explain, let alone prove. Nothing else matters now. If you are my friend, then you must accept my angel as part of the bargain."

"What do you mean by that?"

"You must be able to believe that I am not the person people take me for and for whom you, as a public prosecutor, take me—I'm not Stiller," I said, God knows not for the first time, but for the first time with the hope that someone would hear it. "I'm not Stiller, seriously, and I can't confess what my angel has forbidden me to confess."

I shouldn't have said that.

"Angel—?"he asked. "What do you mean by that?"

I didn't answer. Then came the bill, which the public prosecutor paid, and as our peasant girl once more did not go, it was we who went. Our footsteps crunched in the gravel. In the open car, before the public prosecutor started up, we looked out once again over the noonday landscape, over the brown ploughed land with flapping crows, the vineyards and woods, the autumnal lake, and all the time I knew that my prosecutor and friend was waiting for the answer. As he started the engine I said:

"That's something one can't talk about."

"The angel, you mean?"

"Yes," I said, "as soon as I try to describe it, it leaves me, then I can't see it any more myself. It's very odd: the more exactly I can picture it, the nearer I come to being able to describe it, the less I believe in it and everything I have experienced."

We drove into town along the shore of the lake.

3. The Afternoon.

At about a quarter past two, in other words late, because it was almost impossible to find a parking space in the Old Town, we arrived at "the house," which differed from other houses in this narrow street solely by the fact that in front of it stood Knobel, my warder, in mufti. We were the first. Addressing himself exclusively to my public prosecutor, Knobel said: "I've got the keys." In a dark, rather musty passage stood bicyles, a rather antiquated pram and garbage pails

Knobel was not carrying the keys in his coat pocket, but took them out of a rather rusty letter-box bearing the name A. Stiller. There was no indication of profession. From a backyard came a noise like a tinsmith's workshop, or perhaps a plumber's; I saw moss-grown cobblestones and the long, already bare branches of a plane tree on which the sun probably shone only at midday in the summer, and also a waterless little fountain of sandstone, likewise overgrown with moss; there was a certain idyllic quality about it all. I also saw bundles of iron pipes, short and long; one of these bundles of pipes still bore the little red tag that had been attached when it was brought here by lorry. Then Rolf, my friend, who seemed to be paying his first visit to this house, remarked:

"I think we'll go straight up—"

Since I made no attempt to lead the way, Knobel pointed to the one and only staircase of old and tread-worn walnut, an aristocratic staircase, broad and not at all steep, flanked by banisters with worm-eaten volutes. On the fourth floor, where it smelt of sauerkraut, these stairs came to an end. Knobel informed the Herr Staatsanwalt that this was not the top; opened a partition and invited us to mount a narrow and suddenly very steep staircase of deal. They kept me in the middle all the time, either by chance or design. The taciturn gravity of the whole proceedings, especially on the part of Knobel, who had cut me dead since the morning, was funny; but even my friend and prosecutor was mute in a way that suggested we were approaching the scene of a tragedy with an unknown number of corpses.

"Yes—," he said, when we reached the top, once more half to me and half to Knobel, "I hope the others will soon be here . . ."

There were three doors here, the first was fitted with a padlock, the second bore a humorous sign indicating a lavatory, the third led into the missing man's studio. Knobel unlocked the door; as an official on duty he went in first, while the public prosecutor said to me, "After you." To avoid giving the impression that I felt in any way at home here, I took advantage of his politeness, and I also noticed that at this moment Rolf, my friend, was feeling far more uncomfortable than I, more edgy than I had ever known him. No sooner were we inside the studio than he asked me:

"Where's the wardrobe?"

Knobel pointed to a nail on the blue door.

"Yes," said the public prosecutor, immediately rubbing his hands together, "—open a window, Knobel, the air in here is ghastly."

I felt sorry for my friend; as I knew, this studio had once assumed a certain importance in his own life, a disproportionate importance, as he now very well knew; but that is the infamy of these outside hearings —they are intended to overwhelm the prisoner with long-buried memories by suddenly placing him in a familiar environment. Fortunately I didn't have time to utter any well-meant remark, for at that very moment the bell rang, and we were both glad of it. Knobel looked for the press-button that opened the door downstairs and found it. I still didn't know who was actually attending this idiotic investigation, presumably my counsel, possibly also Julika, I thought, and I didn't even take my coat off: I had no intention of making myself at home here. The good Knobel obviously hadn't pressed hard enough, for at that moment the bell rang again. The public prosecutor exclaimed:

"Why don't you press it?"

"I am pressing," said Knobel, "I am pressing."

Meanwhile I took a look round, my hands in my trouser pockets under my open coat and my hat on my head—after all it wasn't a dwelling in which anyone dwelt. There was a lot of art standing about. Apart from the thick dust on every sill, every spatula, every easel, every stand, every piece of furniture—so

that for this reason alone one felt unwilling to touch
anything—it was just such a studio as I had imagined
from Frau Sibylle's descriptions, rather topsy-turvy,
like a workshop that was lived in, half proletarian, half
romantic; a stovepipe running right across the room
demonstrated with an inescapable gesture that con-
vention had no place here, and yet it was precisely
the stovepipe you find in every Paris studio, the conventional symbol of a certain bohemianism. I should
worry! For the rest, it was a large, and to that extent
agreeable room, a kind of garret with rough deal
planks that creaked softly when we walked on them,
and plenty of light on a sunny autumn day like today.
Below a sloping roof, exactly as Frau Sibylle had remembered it, stood an old gas cooker, its enamel
scarred with rust, a terrazzo sink and a crooked cupboard containing crockery, on the top shelf of which
—obviously intended as a joke—was displayed stolen
crockery bearing various inscriptions: Hôtel des
Alpes, Bodega Granada, Kronenhalle Zürich, and so
on. The rubber tube on the tap, once no doubt red,
now a gray and mildewed rubber mummy, was still
attached with string; it was dripping and I wondered
whether it had been dripping like that for six years, a
passing idea that somehow irritated me, reminding me
of the dripping in the Carlsbad caves. On a nail hung a
dishcloth spotted with blackish mould like a leper, and
naturally enough there was no lack of spider's webs,
for example on the telephone, which stood next to the
couch and presumably no longer rang, having fallen
silent under the burden of unpaid bills. The couch
was broad, big enough for two, also covered in dust,
so that nobody sat on it, which gave this piece of furniture an obtrusive importance, as though it were
standing in a museum with a notice saying Do Not
Touch, like King Philip's bed in the Escorial.

My public prosecutor, I noticed, also kept his hands
in his pockets to avoid touching anything. He was

looking at the two bookcases. To call what the missing man left behind a library would be an exaggeration. Alongside a small volume of Plato and one or two things by Hegel stood names which today have been forgotten even by secondhand booksellers; Brecht rubbed shoulders with Gorki, Nietzsche and a great many paperbacks, some of which contained opera texts; Count Keyserling was also there, but with the black imprint of a public library; then there were all sorts of art books, especially modern ones, and an anthology of Swiss poetry; *Mein Kampf* was flanked by André Gide and supported on the other side by a White Paper on the Spanish Civil War; there were various volumes in the Insel series, though not a single complete set of anything, isolated volumes like *Westöstlicher Diwan* and *Faust* and *Gespräche mit Eckermann, Don Quijote de la Mancha, Der Zauberberg,* the only work by Thomas Mann, the *Iliad,* Dante's *Commedia,* Erich Kästner, *Mozarts Reise nach Prag,* also Mörike's poems, *Till Eulenspiegel,* then again Marcel Proust, but not the whole of *La Recherche, Huttens Letzte Tage,* of Gottfried Keller's works only the Diaries and Letters, a book by C. G. Jung, *The Black Spider,* something by Arp and suddenly Strindberg's *Dream Play,* some early Hesse, too, Chekhov, Pirandello, all in German translation, Lawrence's Mexican story, *The Woman Who Rode Away;* a good deal by a Swiss called Albin Zollinger, of Dostoyevsky only *The House of the Dead,* Garcia Lorca's first poems in Spanish, *Petite Prose* by Claudel and *Das Kapital,* the latter supported by Hölderlin; a few thrillers, Lichtenberg, Tagore, Ringelnatz, Schopenhauer, again with the black imprint of a public library, Hemingway (on bullfighting) next door to Georg Trakl; piles of periodicals ready to fall apart, a Spanish-German dictionary with a very tattered cover, the *Communist Manifesto,* a book on Gandhi and so on. Anyhow, it would be a difficult job to make a spiritual warrant of arrest out of this lot, especially as no one knew which of these books the missing man had read, which of those he had read he had understood or simply not understood or misunderstood in a way that was valuable to him, and my prosecutor and friend had the look of a man who cannot quite find what he wants. For a moment, when in spite of the dust he pulled out a single India-paper volume with a crimson leather back, I thought: Perhaps he is looking for books out of his own library. But he put the leatherbound volume back on the shelf and instead turned the pages of *Anna Karenina* . . .

Apart from the bookcases, the main article of furniture in the studio was a broad and long table of ordinary planks, like a bench, on trestles with the name of a plaster-caster stenciled on them and also smeared with plaster. Some good fairy seemed to have tidied the place up, all the ashtrays had been emptied and so had the garbage pail in the kitchen recess under the sloping roof. On the wall. as Frau Sibylle had described them, I found two gaily colored but faded *banderillas* from Spain, an African mask of very dubious authenticity, all sorts of photographs so faded as to be unrecognizable, the fine fragment of a Celtic axe and a poster by Toulouse-Lautrec, also completely faded. At one point the public prosecutor said:

"Why are they taking such a long time?"

"Don't know," said Knobel. "I pressed the button."

I didn't meddle in their on-the-spot investigation, which didn't seem to be going too well; I was here in the role of prisoner, so I just looked out of the window during their worried confabulation.

"Do you think they have lost their way?"

"How could they?" said Knobel. "The lady knows her way around here, she was the one who showed me everything."

Now I knew whom I had to expect. I lit a cigarette and couldn't believe that Julika, if she loved me, would lend herself to this farce. I was waiting eagerly to see what would happen, but I felt confident and certain of victory; in the last resort everything depended upon Julika, upon Julika alone . . .

As regards my own part in this performance, I couldn't imagine any place where I should feel more of a stranger than here. A few works in clay, which the vanished Stiller had left behind, were wrapped in brown sacking to prevent the clay from drying; but since this sacking had not been wetted for years, it was probable that the clay had completely dried out and was only held together by the sacking. I didn't touch it, naturally. All that was needed to complete this on-the-spot hearing was to unroll these strips of sacking, and everything would crumble into dust like a mummy. My friend and prosecutor could not escape the same impression and was likewise reminded of mummies, such as you see in ethnological museums where, with good reason, they are put behind glass. In particular, he scrutinized the plaster head of the company director whom he had met in the flesh that morning, but he refrained from any expression of opinion. One or two of the things had actually been cast in bronze which in my opinion was more than they were worth; bronze, a metal of some durability after all, took away the spurious charm that came from their unfinished look and created a feeling of expectancy which more or less counterbalanced their weaknesses; what remained in bronze was not enough to constitute a grown man's testimony. No wonder Stiller (who must have seen this for himself at some point) made off! A single glance round his dusty studio and one couldn't help thinking: How much labor, oh, how much dogged perseverance, how much sweat and grind, and yet one doesn't even feel an urge to raise one's hat to the result. It was rather sad, no more—and I was glad the bell rang again.

The public prosecutor grew somewhat irascible and

told Knobel to go downstairs and let in the lady and the gentleman, who, there seemed every reason to suppose, were unable to open the front door—and be quick about it. My warder, understandably offended, since he had pressed the button as hard as he could, went to the door and found himself face to face with the old hawker who had been serving the other floors and was now standing outside our studio, an open suitcase on his trembling arm. This, of course, was something we had none of us reckoned with, but nor had the hawker reckoned with us. "No!" said Knobel angrily, in the tone in which he himself had just been addressed, "nothing." Naturally, the hawker had no idea that we were not the occupants of this garret, that there had been no life here for the last six years; he insisted on his right at least to show his wares, most useful wares, as Knobel did not venture to deny. Since we were three gentlemen he particularly recommended razor blades, shaving soap, styptics and so forth. Knobel tried to cut him short, so that Herr Staatsanwalt should not get angry again; on the other hand the hawker couldn't understand how the three of us could live here without a single toothbrush, without fly paper, without toilet paper and without shoe polish, without anything, but particularly without razor blades. Knobel couldn't get rid of the little old man. As though he actually had come to doubt our masculinity, the hawker pushed everything he had so far shown us back into his case and tried saucepan brushes, sewing things, elastic garters, best-quality pine-needle oil and finally even hair-slides, an article that is forever getting lost and is always wanted again. Knobel kept saying, "That's enough, that's enough!" but without the slightest success. Finally my public prosecutor intervened and with a superior air bought something or other, possibly razor blades, and once more we were alone, but still without the other participants in this on-the-spot investigation, who evidently

(it was striking 2:45) hadn't even rung the front door
bell yet.

"I've got to be in court by 3:30," said Rolf, adding
rather inconsequently: "This is a fine studio—?"

I nodded vigorously. "And very good light."

Then Knobel, in order not to be as superfluous as
he had been just before with the hawker, made himself important or useful with his knowledge of the lay
of the land by saying, not to me, but to the public
prosecutor:

"This leads out on to the parapet."

And since we had no urge to go out on to the parapet:

"There's still some mail here, Herr Staatsanwalt,
the mail since last Saturday—"

"Mail?"

"Printed matter," said Knobel and read out: "Old
age and dependents insurance, but Herr Dr. Bohnenblust already has the whole pile of unpaid contribu-
tions. And this letter is for Herr Stiller personally—"

Since I had no intention of reading their vanished
Stiller's letters, my friend and prosecutor took the liberty of slitting open the envelope. To judge by his expression it was of no importance. Only considerations
of tidiness prevented him from throwing it in the
wastepaper basket.

"An anonymous patriot abuses you," he said laconically. "People take it very much amiss that you don't
grasp the opportunity of being Swiss as a boon—and
therefore unconditionally."

Later, since the people we were waiting for still
didn't ring the bell, we stepped out on to the parapet
after all; like everything else here, it tallied exactly
with the Frau Staatsanwalt's recollections. Fragments
of tiles smashed by a hailstorm lay around, proving
that they were in nobody's way. The weeds on the
roughcast roof were probably higher than ever; a few
stalks of autumnal yellow swayed in the wind. My

friend and prosecutor seemed also to be finding everything much as he had expected; he looked at the rotten frame of an armchair with no fabric covering that
still lay in the corner, and we stood without a word,
Rolf and I, while someone beat a mattress on the parapet opposite. I was well aware how Rolf, my new
friend, must be noticing all these irrelevant details. He
had no eye for the splendid view over gables and sky-
lights and chimneys and party walls, a view that even
contained a wedge of the lake that glittered under
the hazy autumn light when a steamboat set its lazy
waves in motion—a really delightful view, it seemed
to me. He was smoking rather nervously. Why did
we have to come to this place where there were so
many things to cause him pain, irrelevant details that
were not meant like that at all and nevertheless assumed for him, Sibylle's husband, a distressing significance, whether it was this mattress that was just being beaten in front of our eyes, or the elastic garters
the hawker had offered him, the best quality pine-
needle oil for the bath, or the hair-slides that are for
ever getting lost and are always wanted again; why, I
mean, did we have to look at this place which his wife
and he had inwardly overcome long ago? I could see
from his lips that it was costing him more than he had
anticipated, and to no purpose. I don't know what he
was thinking about during those two or three minutes
during which he smoked his cigarette down to the tip;
but it was futile, no doubt about it, there are tests
which are completely off the mark, like this one. The
rotten frame of an armchair, on which his wife may
never have sat, because the fabric was already missing
seven years ago, was all at once sufficient to cast fresh
doubt on their love after years of certainty, to appear
to show in one minute that they had made no progress
in six or seven years, and to conjure up mental images
of agonizing precision, images of the past, which in
any case, whether accurate or inaccurate, could only

leave a bad taste in the mouth. Or did my friend expect of himself that he should be able to bear these torments, which only the inert physical surroundings re-awakened in him, without distress? It was futile. What had all this stuff here, even if it were not rotten, to do with his living Sibylle, with his relationship to her? There is a disgust that can never come to an end, a disgust that is the inevitable punishment for harboring mental images that have nothing to do with us, or so I believe. Why did he inflict this on himself? It is possible to overcome jealousy, to overcome it from within and in relation to one's partner, to overcome it as a whole, as he had succeeded in doing; but it is nonsense to imagine that one must also be able to swallow the individual fragments without turning a hair. His smile was rather strained. Didn't he know, my friend and prosecutor, who had accompanied so many people to the scene of the crime, didn't he know that there is often something diabolical about inert objects? Naturally, I didn't know what to say to him on this parapet. It was such an unnecessary humiliation, and for the first time I realized what false reactions can be evoked by an on-the-spot investigation, when a person is confronted with inert objects, as if there existed a truth outside time . . . As he said nothing, I asked rather abruptly:

"How old is your wife now, by the way?"

"Sibylle—?"

"Hannes must be nearly ready to go to grammar school," I went on chattily, "and now this little one, that must be wonderful for your wife, and a girl too—!"

"Yes," he said, "it's wonderful."

"For you, too—"

"Yes," he said, "it is."

The good Knobel, who, as a petty official, was not yet used to being so inactive while on duty, left us no peace and warned us about the rusty balustrade it would be better not to touch. So we didn't touch it. Pigeons were cooing on the roof. We could also see the blue ridge of hills where we had been at midday.

"It was glorious up there," I said, "in that open-air restaurant—"

"Wasn't it?"

"Of course I don't mean an angel with wings," I said, recalling the question he had asked up there. "Not an artist's angel like you see in sculptures and the theater. It may be that the people who first invented this image of the angel had experienced something like I experienced, that is to say something incommunicable. All I really know is that I experienced something—"

To my distress (it made me feel as though I'd been gagged) the bells of the nearby cathedral began to ring just at that moment. I couldn't see what it was for—a wedding perhaps or a final departure; anyhow, there was a ghastly booming. A swarm of pigeons whirred off over our heads. At this close range we didn't hear any notes at all, only a metallic tremor in the air, the noise of clappers that seemed as though it would burst our ear drums. We left the parapet, and when we stepped back into the studio to escape from some of the din they were already there—Julika and my defense counsel, who was just helping her off with her new Paris coat. Although we shut the window, conversation was out of the question. Julika was more attractive than ever. We greeted each other with a kiss. The fact that Julika was wearing her glorious hair rather more blonde again, more unobtrusive, as was appropriate for Zurich, did not escape me; it made me more convinced than ever that she had finally said goodbye to Paris and Monsieur Dmitritch. I was rather strangely affected, I must admit, by the little dog that Julika had brought here just because she did not intend to return to Paris; it was another fox terrier. I stood there stroking it, since the frightful din of the bells made speech impossible. Everyone lit a cigarette. Julika fetched ashtrays with the air of a hostess and invited us with a gesture to sit down. But it was far too dusty.

I waited with eager anticipation to see what would happen when the bells stopped ringing and we could speak again. It seemed to me that the comedy of the situation would resolve all our problems at one stroke, if only it dawned on us. My counsel, who was fumbling through his brief-case as usual, was naturally the main source of comedy, precisely because he could see nothing comic in the situation. The bells went on and on ringing. Knobel did his best to pretend he wasn't there, and Rolf, my public prosecutor, spent as long as he could taking his overcoat off the nail. It was not his fault that the others (probably on Foxli's account) had come so late. At last, when we were beginning to get used to this pantomime, the Cathedral fell silent . . .

"Well—?" inquired Julika.

Julika seemed to have expected to find my confession already made, and when the public prosecutor informed her to the contrary and moreover had unfortunately to take his leave, Julika sat down on the dusty couch as though staggered by a telegram containing bad news. My counsel didn't know whom to stare at, the public prosecutor or me. The disappointed Julika had probably already started crying; but we didn't notice it yet. My counsel tried unsuccessfully to stop the public prosecutor leaving. As he shook hands with me I had the feeling my new friend was deserting me; but I soon realized that precisely because he was my friend the last thing he wanted was to be present at this monstrous performance, which he had not been able to refuse my official defense counsel. When I noticed that the beautiful Julika was crying, I asked:

"Do you love me?"

My counsel tried to say something—

"I'm asking the lady," I interrupted, sitting down beside Julika on the dusty couch. "Do you love me, Julika, or don't you?"

She sobbed more and more bitterly.

"Look," I said as tenderly as I could in the presence of an official defense counsel and a warder, "everything depends on that now. Everything depends on you, Julika, and no one else!"

"Why?" she sobbed. "Why on me?"

Still with the warm tranquility of confidence I endeavored to explain to Julika why, as long as she really loved me she needed no confession from me that I was her lost husband. It seemed to me so simple, so self-evident. Nonetheless, I went on talking for quite a while, far too long, and as time went on I grew confused, as always happens. Never in my life have I been able to cope with this situation: as soon as I feel that I am alone with a simple and self-evident truth I lose sight of its self-evidence, blurring it with hasty similes that are supposed to help the other person to understand me, but in reality only confuse what was originally a clear realization, and finally defending what I have ruined with arguments that are sheer nonsense. I could see exactly what I was doing. But as the lovely Julika said nothing at all, not even nonsense that would at least have re-established an equilibrium of mutual helplessness, I couldn't stop. Why didn't she help me? I held her tear-stained hand as though we were alone, and could think of nothing else than to repeat my question as to whether she loved me and wait—

"How much longer are you going to torment this unfortunate woman?" said my counsel, no doubt with the best intentions. "That Frau Julika loves you, God knows, is obvious enough—"

He also spoke for much too long.

"—and altogether," he finally concluded, "have you no feeling for this woman? It's monstrous the way you treat this frail woman. Instead of making up your mind to confess at last! Now this woman has come all the way from Paris for your sake, has given up her dancing school for your sake, and you treat her—One may really wonder how a person like Frau Julika can have deserved to be married to you!"

At this I looked at him.

"Yes indeed!" he added forcefully.

Thereupon, not at once, but after some hesitation, after waiting in the hope that Julika might correct him after all, I rose, suddenly felt my legs very heavy, dusted my overcoat to leave time for some happier turn of events, and finally walked over to the door, which (I shall never forget the feeling in my hand) was locked. Locked. It was no illusion and the door wasn't jammed; it was simply locked.

"Knobel," I said and heard myself utter a laugh that even I didn't like,"—give me the key."

Knobel, his ears scarlet, said nothing.

"What do you want from me?" I asked.

Meanwhile Julika, the traitress, had placed herself between me and the door, the knob of which was still in my hand—at least this gave me a chance to ask without being overheard: "Why do you betray me?" Her innocent face with the exceptionally beautiful eyes and the arches of her plucked eyebrows, which give her such a charming expression of permanent childlike surprise, did not show the slightest hint that she understood why I was acting as I did; her incomprehension struck me dumb. Likewise under her breath she said: "Don't act like that!" And it was quite true that, carried away by some burst of primitive emotion, I had all too often done the wrong thing; the possibility existed that I was wronging everyone, but especially Julika, who a moment ago had been my only, but confident, hope. Why was I acting like this, really? So now I stood arm in arm with Julika, whom I perhaps just didn't understand,

in front of my counsel, who also thought Julika a
wonderful woman, and in front of Knobel, my
warder, who had the key in his trouser pocket, and
furthermore surrounded by these sackcloth mummies,
which Julika began to introduce to me as my life's
work. For a little while, as though my consciousness was temporarily paralyzed, I let her go on, let
Julika lead me around, almost touched by the fact
that this stuff meant so much to her, permitted myself
little jokes—for instance about the company director's
head in plaster . . .

I don't know what paralyzed me in this way, nor
how long it lasted. Suddenly awake again, and apparently having lost all recollection of the locked door
and the impertinent remarks of my counsel, as
though waking from a silly dream that was already
forgotten and conscious that it had only been a dream,
I found myself right back at the question I had
asked already once, directly before this dream about
the locked door: Did Julika love me or not? That, I
realized, was the point at which we had lost the
thread, and I interrupted her touching commentary
on the sackcloth mummies by reiterating this question. I could understand, to some extent, that it was
difficult for a shy and reserved person like Julika to
answer it in the presence of an official defense counsel
and a warder; I was very conscious of the enormity
of my question in these surroundings. Perhaps for
that very reason I couldn't tolerate my counsel opening his mouth to help the mute Julika, as he imagined.

"Devil take you," I shouted in his face. "What's
this got to do with you? I don't deny I'm having an
affair with this lady—"

Julika, offended:

"Anatol—?!"

I yelled:

"What's Anatol got to do with it? What's Anatol got
to do with it? Don't imagine that's going to make me

take over this load of rubbish from your lost husband
—There!" I cried, laughing with an anger that had
never really left me and ripping off a sackcloth wrapping. As I expected—nothing but dust, which no defense counsel could hold together, a heap of crumbling clay, and the next likewise, mummies, nothing but
mummies, then a scaffold of rusty iron and twisted
wire—that was all there was left of their vanished
Stiller, dust to dust, as clergymen say, a few grayish-
brown lumps on the floor, but above all a cloud of
brown dust when I shook the sacking. Unfortunately
the bell rang. Unfortunately; for dumbfounded themselves by the art that was coming to light, they
wouldn't have stopped me from making a clean sweep
of the lot. But the ringing irritated me.

"Whom else are you bringing here," I asked my
counsel, "to drive me crazy?"

At this instant I had a very definite suspicion, and I
saw how Knobel, at a sign from my embarrassed
counsel, finally took the key out of his trouser
pocket to open the door and go downstairs. Then ·I
forgot my very correct suspicion under a torrent of
words from my counsel, who once more (how many
times already?) admonished and adjured me: I
should come to my senses, my last chance of making
a confession, otherwise there'd be a court verdict,
distressing for Frau Julika, just a single sensible
word and I'd be free, things weren't so black as they
looked to me, a fine studio with good light, friends
were planning a welcome home, so chin up and out
with the confession, Stiller a highly esteemed artist,
not a great artist, who is great? but esteemed and the
Arts Council ready to meet the legal costs, everyone so nice to me, my ridiculous obstinacy hurt no
one but myself, just a bit of commonsense called for,
Julika a fine and worthy person, marriage never child's
play, but Julika forbearance and kindness personified,
so chin up and make a fresh start, flight never a real

solution, liberty only in attachment, marriage a moral obligation, not a pleasure, a little maturity called for, a little good will and everything would be all right, Julika's hard years in Paris and her magnanimous renunciation of her successful dancing school, Julika's sacrifice, nothing but a woman's sacrifice, I ought to show some gratitude, so once again chin up, shake hands and hallelujah!

During this speech we stood arm in arm again, either because Julika was afraid I might take advantage of the now unlocked door, or because she clung to me out of genuine affection; I could feel the warmth of her body.

My counsel was still speaking: So chin up, there's no place like home, an occasional trip abroad of course, so that we learn to appreciate our homeland afresh, but man needs roots and so no doubt does the artist in me, roots, that's the important thing, roots and again roots, millions homeless, so I should be thankful, mustn't always look on the black side, a little love for mankind, the Swiss are only human too, nobody can change his skin, a more positive attitude called for on my part, more composure, no smashing things up like just now, all due deference to self-criticism, but one shouldn't make a filthy mess of dust and fragments, all due deference to temperament, but moderation in all things, things weren't as bad as I thought, and Zurich was just about the finest city in the world, but as he'd said, a more positive attitude was essential, enough nihilism in the world today, every individual must do his bit to improve the world, if everyone wholeheartedly desired the good, things would be all right, like Frau Julika for example, Frau Julika was a model in every way, all respect for Frau Julika, nothing could divert her from womanly fidelity to me, a rare woman, but a typical woman, a wonderful woman, men often stubborn and egoistic, women so different, motherly, difficult in her way, certainly, but only because I didn't understand her, her wealth of emotion, Julika's inner life so much richer than most other women's, heart in the right place, a little more feeling on my part, the eternal feminine draws us upward, enough intellectualism in the world today, mustn't always think and doubt, but hope, chin up and hope, no marriage without hope, without hope no peace between individuals and peoples, anyone can see that, without hope no true art as in the Middle Ages, in short, without hope no hope, so hand on heart and no silly fuss, Stiller, too, good at heart, my counsel convinced of his good heart, everything else dust in the balance, the name for example, but we must have order, everyone has to bear a name, my counsel no bureaucrat, naturally, my counsel positively shattered by his glimpse into this marriage of two estimable people, my counsel married himself, been through all the difficulties, got over them all, but sacrifice needed, sacrifice and again sacrifice, the recompense a soul at peace, the soul the most important thing of all, enough materialism in the world nowadays, a little trust in the Almighty indispensable, destruction of true values by the speed of modern traffic, also by the cinema and sport, for instance by the building of stadia that make masses out of us, but above all by Communism, but my counsel broadminded and no grudge against Stiller for his youthful exploits in Spain, forget it, my counsel was also at one time a member of a party that ceased to exist, forget it, to err is human and Franco important for Europe, Stiller couldn't know what was going to happen, no, nor could my counsel, the eternal laws therefore all the more important, the Ten Commandments still the best, thou shalt not make unto thee any images, as Frau Julika says over and over again, quite right, quite right, but also thou shalt not lust and certainly not kill, anyhow not in peacetime, as a machine-gunner it's a bit different, naturally, antimilitarism out of date long ago, but that's not what we are talking about, no, thou shalt not kill, my friend, not even in thought, we don't do that here, the family the germ-cell of the nation, Frau Julika not too old for children, it was always her secret wish, only working people reproduce themselves *en masse*, a serious failure on the part of the intellectuals over this point, it's not a question of income but of the inner will, besides, a decent artist can earn so much in Switzerland that a moderate level of procreation may be considered perfectly feasible, splendid grants in the last resort, provided the artist is of good character, this proviso quite right, heaven knows, no children of drunkards and people suspected of leftist tendencies, liberty is something to be valued, in short, Switzerland is still an ideal country and not to be compared with unhappy France that does nothing but strike, so once again, chin up, hand on heart and forget the past, everything will be all right, my friend, everything will be all right, it must be, even a lawyer has to keep starting all over again, human destiny, but anything's possible with a little trust in the Almighty, mustn't be fanatic about that either, of course, but everything with good Swiss commonsense, a social conscience goes without saying and then another point: Stiller mustn't forget his stepfather in the old age home, or as Goethe so magnificently puts it: The gifts of your fathers you must earn to possess—speaking spiritually, speaking humanly, it isn't nice to forget your stepfather in an old age home, one doesn't do that, a spot of piety, Stiller not alone in the world, damn it all, but a member of the community, a stake in the community, a sense of duty called for, but everything with a little love, not always thinking of yourself, Herr Stiller, take an example from Frau Julika, once again all respect for this fine and valiant woman who took it upon herself to marry such a difficult man, so once again: Shake hands, there's no more point in denying

it, proof overwhelming, nothing left but a voluntary
confession, Herr Stiller, so courage and a bit of commonsense, a little trust in the Almighty and Frau
Julika, in marriage, in Switzerland, in the good in myself, a bit of—

Thus my Doktor Bohnenblust.

I give Julika great credit for the fact that as they
brought in the little old man from the old age home
she at least blushed, like a wife when the disguised
mental nurses come into the house with a straitjacket.
The first moment, I took him for the hawker who'd
been up before, and I was astounded when my counsel quickly offered him a chair with a politeness that
was due to embarrassment; he probably hadn't imagined the situation would be so painful. He only
wanted to knock a little sense into me by means of a
confrontation, as is often done with obstinate prisoners; none of the other confrontations had affected
me. So what else could my counsel do? Knobel sat
the little old man down in the dusty rocking chair,
where he positively wilted with respect for the court
and the authorities and the Herr Doktor and the
dancer from Paris. I wept when I recognized him, and
I noticed that he could not see my tears. He was
pretty doddering. I turned away, too fainthearted for
this sight, which at bottom didn't surprise me; when
he came to my mind that night in the Bowery I pic-
tured him much like this. Now I could only hear them
behind my back, his malicious, highpitched old man's
voice: Soso, you're back are you? Soso! He giggled
and my counsel had to point out to him which of the
men present might possibly be his son. He giggled: A
nice son, yes, yes, doesn't bother his head about me,
soso. My counsel asked him whether he would recognize me. Soso, he giggled, goes off without a word, a
nice son, and when he comes back to the country
years later he doesn't think of asking whether I'm still

alive, a nice son! . . . Of course I did quite the wrong thing.

"Stop that drivel!" I said as insolently as I could. "I don't know you."

Soso, he giggled, soso.

"That's enough," I shouted, and I felt I was cutting an utterly ridiculous figure and the situation was so unbearable—out of pure helplessness I picked up some plaster object, at first only as a threat, but then I saw the lovely Julika's cool, calm face and her scarcely smiling certainty that I, her Stiller, would never dare to throw anything at her, and true enough, I didn't dare. I flung the plaster object at random, aware of the ridiculous figure I was cutting, as I have said, and furious at my own absurd behavior (the others were behaving with impeccable dignity) I took the nearest thing, a head, and hurled it on the floor, where it merely rolled along without breaking in pieces; I felt a nightmare impotence, an unparalleled impotence, however hard I threw the things—and no one hindered me, even my counsel and Knobel just watched in amazement, but entirely convinced that I was the missing Stiller and therefore had the right to smash everything in this studio to pieces, only the little dog barked, and I felt paralyzed by their misunderstanding, so that in some cases I could barely lift the things off their stands—so I kept to the smaller figures, flinging them at the wall, where some of them did shatter to bits after all, which delighted me, but I could already see the humiliating possibility that my rage would not be sufficient to smash everything, but only the smaller objects, while the larger works, because I couldn't lift them off their stands, would survive my fury. I felt I couldn't bear such a humiliation, which was all they were waiting for, and it was really fear of this humiliation that compelled me to go on wreaking havoc. It was some

job! And nobody uttered a word, so convinced were
they that at any moment I should give it up, only the
little dog went on barking, and I was in despair at my
own vanity which forbade me to stop this idiocy,
this smashing of plaster objects that no one mourned,
there seemed no end to it, until, armed now with an
iron clamp, I had smashed all the plaster stuff in
pieces or at least mutilated it beyond repair; now
there remained the bronzes, of which there were not
many, but some all the same; the first was so heavy
that throwing was out of the question, but now I
simply had to complete the job and finish off the
bronzes as well, the bronzes especially; exerting all
my strength I could just manage to lift it and drop it
on the floor; I was the only one who laughed to see
how little effect it had on the bronze to thud once or
twice or ten times on the floor—then out of the window with it!

Now, of course, they jumped up, alarmed by the
thought that there might be someone in the courtyard down below; the crash as it hit the corrugated
iron roof was balm to my soul, oh yes, now my delight in this holocaust returned, so did my physical
strength, Knobel seized me by the arm, but he was
afraid I might simply drop a bronze on his foot and
kept his distance, so that in spite of all appeals I
reached the window with my next bronze, crash, the
corrugated iron reverberated and a storm of voices
rose from the courtyard, an alarm of curses, there
was a cracking as though of shots, and dripping with
sweat I looked round to see what was left and tore
open cupboards; small objects flew out through the
window in an arch, someone was ringing the bell
like mad, although now only sketchbooks, spatulas,
tins and suchlike were raining down; of the people in
the studio I saw nothing, I was merely aware of their
presence, and as long as I could still find something—
the African mask, the *banderillas*, the Celtic axe-

head—anything with which to enliven the corrugated
iron roof, I felt at ease—at ease is not the right expression, I was free from the fear of doing the wrong
thing, and once more myself. But the moment which
seemed to me, although I was now satisfied with myself, the most miserable moment in my life—the moment when I could find nothing more on any sill or
easel with which to make the corrugated roof rattle
and scrape and echo, the moment when I could not
imagine what was going to happen next, a moment
that was quiet and rather empty and transient like
every moment and for that very reason so wretched
—came at last . . .

I was sweating. Knobel had gone out to pacify the
people in the tinsmith's or plumber's workshop and
tell them that the hail of bronze was now at an end. I
tried to smile, and then, as I couldn't manage it, at
least to laugh, and found myself alone with my laughter and too exhausted to laugh on my own. Now I
saw Julika again, lovely Julika. She was the first to
speak:

"What now?"

Julika was sitting holding on her lap the little fox
terrier, which had been so terribly upset by my behavior, but was now safe in Julika's arms. During
the whole of my rampage, I don't think she even
stood up. She didn't shake her head, but merely
looked at me as she would look at a man who had
spilt wine or trodden on a lady's evening gown: it was
pardonable but embarrassing. But pardonable. And I
couldn't believe my eyes: her face with the great big
beautiful eyes was so unchanged that I now asked
myself what I had actually expected. She smoothed
her red hair—unnecessarily, for Julika hadn't budged;
I was the only one who had so heated myself with all
my rampaging that I was now sweating from every
pore, my shirt drenched, my hair in disorder, my tie
crumpled, and for that very reason Julika smoothed

her hair again, a gesture of embarrassment, understandable embarrassment. Was she waiting for me to apologize?

A loud buzz of conversation could be heard from the stairs; it seemed no one had been hit, otherwise there would have been silence. But there was a great deal of hostility and indignation, understandably, I could see that. Julika took out a cigarette, whereupon I offered her a light. Yes, she was right: What now? For a few seconds, as I looked at my Julika with the lighter still in my hand, I thought I should burst into scalding tears and the next moment fall on my knees with both hands over my face, until Julika freed my sobbing, ugly, ludicrous face. I should have liked to, but I didn't; it was as though the tears flowed inwards, and I stood there as unchanged as she. Her arrogance (her forbearance) was so stubborn and unshakable; she was smiling like a victress who couldn't help the fact that I always came off worst, or like a mother, more like a mother, who loved her incorrigible son in spite of everything, and her superiority seemed to me so immense, her innocuousness so incomprehensible, her imperturbability so murderous, her lack of response so idiotic, that I went on staring at Julika dumbfounded. And how beautiful she was, I shall never forget it—her red hair, her alabaster complexion, her girlish lips, her blue or possibly colorless eyes, oh, so big and so beautiful, as I have said, and so limpid and without a background, her aristocratic nose with the rather large nostrils, and her charming ear, and this noble and erect and slender throat with the really very gentle voice emerging from it. I shall never forget it! And the gracefulness of her wrist as she sat there smoking—for a moment I felt as though I was going to take Julika by the windpipe and throttle her. But I didn't do that either, naturally . . . Then Knobel came back and informed my counsel of the approximate extent of the damage.

"God be praised," said my counsel, "at least no one's been hurt, at least that—!"

They had to explain to my stepfather what had happened; the noise hadn't escaped him and he wanted to know what it was all about, for after all he had been sent for personally, personally, as he emphasized several times.

P.S. Now, as I can see in full awareness of my impotence, is the moment to tell everything, to tell the truth. But what does this everything of mine amount to? As soon as I try to explain it, there is nothing left. Should I not otherwise have explained it long ago, this everything of mine, this experience of mine—?

What I can say is this:

About two years ago, I tried to take my life. The decision was an old one. I was convinced, as probably most suicides are, that once it was done everything would be over, lights out, end of the performance. About this I had no doubt, and therefore no fear. Failure was due to purely technical causes. The little firearm I found in the shingle hut—an old-fashioned thing that functioned after being thoroughly cleaned —had a much lower pressure-point than I was used to from my rifle, or perhaps none at all. The weapon probably went off prematurely, so that the projectile (there was one single bullet belonging to this ancient weapon in the drawer with it) only grazed the skull without penetrating, on the right above the ear. Later, they showed me the X-ray. I remember that my head was held by two hands as though by two clamps, above me was the face of Florence, the only person who had heard the shot, and then everything went blank—except for a round opening in the distance (as boys we used to crawl through a sewer, the distant hole filled with daylight seemed far too small for us ever to get out—it was just like that) and the condition was unbearable, yet not painful. More like a craving for pain. The feeling of being called and possessing no voice myself. Later, when I was already in the City Hospital, I am supposed to have said something like this and to have begged for sleep. Looking· back on it I think the terrible pain consisted in suddenly being unable to do anything more, unable to move either backwards or forwards, not being able to fall, no longer having any above or below and yet being still there, motionless without end, without death. Just as one knows in dreams that it is a dream, so I knew that this was not death, even if I now died. Put prosaically, I felt tremendously perplexed, rather as though I had jumped over a high wall in order to dash myself in pieces, but the ground didn't come, it never came, there was nothing but falling, a falling that was actually no falling, a state of total powerlessness accompanied by total wakefulness, only time had disappeared, as I said, time as the medium within which we normally act; everything stayed as it was, nothing passed away, everything remained like that once and for all. As I was told later, I was given injections at short intervals. It was probably these palliatives, restoratives, narcotics—no doubt necessary for my sensitive and injured body—which repeatedly brought me close to the terror that took on vivid form while I was in a coma and afterwards reverberated in my memory. That's what I think, at least; I've never talked about it to anyone. Can one talk about a thing like that? All I can say here is that it is this terror I call "my angel" . . .

(Interrupted by the information that today's final hearing with judgment, originally fixed for 4 P.M., has been put forward to 10:30 A.M.)

As I said, I have never talked about this business to anyone—quite rightly: you can't make the incomprehensible comprehensible without losing it completely, and I notice now the way I involuntarily keep trying, as I set down this declaration, to sort things out and give everything a "meaning." Yet I have nothing to give. I have merely received the "meaning." And I have to preserve it . . .

Of the dreams that came to me in a never-ending stream during that period I remember little, since I could not tell them to anyone. (Once Florence, the mulatto girl, paid me a visit in the City Hospital; I understood her very well, although I couldn't utter more than a word or two.) One of the dreams went like this:

Just as I am strangling Little Gray I realize that it is not the cat, but Julika, who is laughing in a way I have never known her to laugh, Julika is altogether quite different, gay, I strangle the cat with all my strength, Julika mocks me in front of an audience that is invisible to me, the cat doesn't defend itself, but afterwards jumps up on the window sill and licks itself, Julika was never my wife, it was all just my imagination . . .

Another dream:

Mother is lying in my bed, ghastly although smiling, a wax doll, hair like brush bristles, I am filled with horror, I try to switch on the electric light but can't, I try to ring Julika but can't, everything has been cut off, darkness through the whole house and yet I can see my wax mother perfectly clearly, utterly horrified I fall to my knees with a cry in order to wake up, suddenly I am holding in my hands an Easter egg as big as a head . . .

Other dreams I can remember even less clearly. They all seemed to be about the same thing, and they continued while I was in a coma, for instance . . .

(Interrupted by Dr. Bohnenblust, my defense counsel, who gave me the same information orally. I am to hold myself in readiness.)

All I can really say is that I had a premonition. It is
not shame that prevents me from laying my cards on
the table, but sheer inability. I never felt ashamed of
my action. I threw away a life that had never been a
life. Even if the way I did so was ridiculous. I was left
with the memory of an immense freedom: everything
depended on me. I could decide whether I wanted
to live again, but this time so that a real death took
place. Everything depended upon me alone, as I have
already said. I have never been closer to the essence of
grace. And I realized that, certain of grace, I had decided in favor of life, by the fact that I began to feel
a terrible pain. I had the distinct sensation that I was
now being born for the first time, and with a certainty that need not fear even ridicule. I felt ready to
be nobody but the person as whom I had just been
born and to seek no other life than this, which I could
not cast from me. That was about two years ago and
I was already thirty-eight. The day I was finally discharged from the City Hospital . . .

(Interrupted again!)

The judgment of the court is expected: I am (for
them) identical with the Anatol Ludwig Stiller, citizen of Zurich, sculptor, last address 11 Steingartengasse, Zurich, married to Frau Julika Stiller-Tschudy,
at present domiciled in Paris, who disappeared six
years, nine months and twenty-one days ago, and is
now condemned to various fines in respect of the box
on the ears inflicted on a Swiss customs officer, in
respect of all sorts of acts of culpable negligence including failing to apply for permission to leave the
country (as a result of which a hundred and seven
different reminders have now been addressed to Stiller
by various government departments); further, discharge of debts in respect of government tax, military
tax, old age and dependents insurance; further, dam-

ages in respect of a Swiss army rifle; plus one third of
the legal costs: total 9,361.05 francs, payable within
thirty days of the signature of the present judgment.
Moreover: After conclusion of these proceedings remand in custody is to continue until possible connections with the Smyrnov affair have been cleared up
in the course of subsequent proceedings, if no appeal
is lodged against the present judgment.

I waived the right to a final speech.

I waived the right to appeal.

Frau Julika Stiller-Tschudy, as from today's date
my legal wife, is now busy trying to console Herr Dr.
Bohnenblust, the counsel for the defense provided by
the court. This man has done really everything he possibly could and deserves my heartfelt gratitude today.
I had intended to give expression to a kind of gratitude, but then forgot all about it. Herr Direktor
Schmitz, the millionaire, was also in court; he has
lodged an action for slander as from today's date. As
regards the Smyrnov affair I shall very soon disappoint
the federal police, who have now taken me over: as-
suming that the good Theo Hofer, my former comrade in Spain, a Czech, who later lived in the
Bronx, New York, as a hairdresser and took me in
when I first arrived in America, is still alive, it should
be possible to produce my alibi for the relevant date,
18.1.1946, within a few days.

I have just heard Julika coming along the corridor—
My angel keep me on the alert.

PART · II

Postscript
by the Public Prosecutor

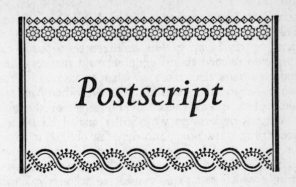

Postscript

WE were sorry that Stiller, after writing the foregoing "Notes in Prison"—reproduced here unabridged and of course unaltered, with the permission of those of the people involved who are still alive—did not follow them up with "Notes in Freedom." Our attempts to persuade him did not shake his resolve for a moment. Stiller felt no urge to continue his notes. Subsequently, we realized ourselves that it was a mistake to try and persuade him. His sudden loss of voice, if one wants to call it that, was in fact an essential, perhaps even the decisive step towards his inner liberation—a liberation which we could observe not only in our friend himself, but even more clearly in those nearest to him and in an almost imperceptibly slow but nevertheless real change in our relationship with him. It became possible to be his friend: Stiller had become free of the morbid impulse to convince.

The Smyrnov affair requires no further mention here. Stiller's alibi for the crucial date was irrefutable: long before 18.1.1946 he was in New York, where he stayed for the first few weeks with his Czech friend. Stiller could not prove this until he had given up denying his identity. His indifference towards this suspicion seemed to me genuine from the very first, more genuine than most of what he said and wrote while remanded in custody. On the other hand the authorities, lacking personal knowledge of the man, could not understand why Stiller denied his obvious identity so obstinately, and they felt obliged to examine any possible links with previously unsolved crimes, as indeed was their duty. Among the unsolved crimes which had to be considered were two Zurich murders; about these Stiller knew nothing. In every instance an unambiguously negative verdict was quickly reached, and his release took place the same month.

Stiller lived first in a small *pension* on Lake Geneva, accompanied by his wife, who was resolved to live with him again. Both of them probably found it difficult to imagine how their life together would work out. For my part I was more than curious. He preferred not to move into our small, primitive but heatable country cottage on the Forch, "because it's too damned close to Zurich." Fortunately his home town had decided, after tough opposition inside the council, to give him two thousand francs as an encouragement, a sum which, at that time, was sufficient to keep a married couple going for two or three months. So they lived on this and the hope of further miracles beside Lake Geneva. We found it hard to imagine Stiller at Territet, a district which, to the best of our recollection, consisted of hotels, tennis courts, funicular railways and chalets with turrets and garden dwarfs. But friends had been able to make arrangements on a friendly basis for him there.

When we heard absolutely nothing from them over Christmas we began to feel worried. Then Stiller's first letter arrived at last, still addressed to "My dear friend and prosecutor" and asking for the loan of an electric cooker. It was winter, and apart from a hot breakfast included in their arrangements, they were living on cold snacks in their hotel bedroom. In this short letter Stiller thanked me "for everything" with an alarming servility. We felt anxious about the two of them, a possibly attractive but isolated hotel bedroom in a holiday resort out of season appeared to us the most unpromising setting for this couple's renewed encounter with each other.

Eventually, one week-end towards the end of February, my wife and I drove out to Territet and found them both, tanned by the sun, in a really pleasant little room with a small balcony that afforded a little extra space; their piled-up trunks made the room even smaller. Seen from their window, Lake Geneva looked all the larger by contrast. Stiller behaved gaily, a little too gaily; he took his wife by the arm and introduced "a couple of Swiss inland emigrants." Any mention of their future was avoided. Downstairs in the dining-room we none of us succeeded in passing beyond a rather laborious conversation. Although the room was practically empty and the whole place had a family atmosphere, Stiller and his wife sat there as awkwardly as though they had never dined off a white tablecloth before. Apart from ourselves there was hardly anyone in the dining-room—an aged Englishman who was partially paralyzed, so that a nurse had to cut up his meat for him, and a French marquis reading a book over his soup, outsiders, solitaries, except for a young German couple whose wedding rings, as I noticed immediately, were not of the same gold, two happy but strikingly shy people. A young waiter, a German Swiss, made them blush scarlet with his French. Anyhow, we could see no reason why Stiller and his wife should be so ill at ease.

Unfortunately it rained the whole week-end. Walking was out of the question, and Stiller and his wife fought shy of the empty lounge. So we spent almost the whole time sitting in their small bedroom among the trunks. I cannot remember any particular conversation, but their appearance has stuck in my mind. His wife, elegant even in shabby clothes, kept walking up and down, said practically nothing, listened to other people and smoked incessantly. They looked to us like Russians in Paris, or, as my wife said, like German Jews in New York—people to whom nothing belonged. Frau Julika and my wife were meeting for the first time; apart from conventional politenesses they hardly exchanged a word. Stiller made several attempts to save the situation with his humor. All in all it was depressing, an endless afternoon with rain on the window, tea and a great deal of smoke, really a disappointment—probably for all parties. Their money was running out, it was easy to guess that. It seemed virtually impossible to find work at all in keeping with their abilities, for which there was not much demand. To return to the Paris dancing school, which incidentally did not belong to Frau Julika, but to Monsieur Dmitritch, was presumably out of the question. Stiller laughed about this utterly hopeless outlook. Frau Julika stood waiting for the water in the electric cooker, her slender hands in the pockets of her tailor-made costume, smoking, while Stiller squatted on a trunk, his hands clasped round his up-drawn knees. One had the feeling that they must live very much the same when they were alone together, perfectly friendly and therefore rather taciturn, two people in chains who had the good sense to put up with one another. Stiller asked for books.

For a long time we heard nothing of them. I couldn't think of anything to write myself, after our visit even less than before. I felt I ought to write, but I just didn't know what to say. I sent a large parcel of books, including Kierkegaard, but received no reply. For months the Stillers seemed not to exist.

We felt that in any case they had probably changed their address. We give little thought to people whose life we cannot visualize, even if we imagine they may need us. I neglected them completely; my wife, for her part, had different reasons for feeling she couldn't write, worthier reasons.

After about half a year, in the late summer, came the elated letter in which Stiller announced: "As a reward from God for all the months I spent in the remand prison, we have just found, rented and moved into the house of our dreams, *une ferme vaudoise!*" We breathed a sigh of relief. It really seemed to be a godsend. A fabulously low rent suggested an equally fabulous state of dilapidation, but our friend did not tire of singing the praises of his *ferme vaudoise* in lengthy descriptions. Anyhow, he seemed to be thoroughly happy. We had to imagine a capacious house, originally a Vaudois farm-house, perhaps even a winegrower's house, Stiller wasn't sure about that; attached to it were a vineyard, a wine-press of venerable age, an airy barn that made an ample studio, and an avenue of plane-trees that gave the whole estate a manorial touch. In other letters they were not planes, but elms. In subsequent letters the barn vanished altogether. Instead other joys made their appearance: Stiller suddenly wrote about the old well in the courtyard whose wrought ironwork he drew for us, about the beehive or the rose garden. He described all this with affectionate good-humor as rather overgrown, rather rusty, rather dried up, and everything was smothered in dark ivy. At times our imagination was severely strained, especially as we knew the district round Glion. We could only suppose that our happy friend was exaggerating a bit. Sketches by his hand showed a steep tiled roof with ends as well as sides inclined, as is usual in the Vaud, a broad terrace with fruit trees all round and in the background the mountains of Savoy; the avenue with the eighty elms was missing. My wife took the liberty of inquiring about this. A special sketch—as a sketch so charming that we hung it up in a passepartout—showed the interior with a great farmhouse chimney and Frau Julika kneeling in front of it making up the fire; on the edge of the sheet was a cordial invitation to a *raclette*.

"When are you coming?" every letter soon began. At the end of the letter he wrote: "I must impress on you once again that you can't come here with the car. Nobody will be able to tell you the way. Just garage your car at Montreux. I'll come and fetch you; otherwise you will never find my *ferme vaudoise!*"

Winter came and we did not see Stiller. He hadn't the money to come to Zurich, and no desire, even if we had invited him. Spring also went by without a meeting. Today this surprises me. Stiller wrote to us quite often; Frau Julika appeared in his letters fairly frequently. We knew that she had worked for a time as shop assistant in a grocery. But on the important point, their married life together, his letters gave not the slightest hint. Instead he devoted two or three pages to descriptions of sunsets. Fundamentally he said nothing at all; to me it was always as though his letters had reached me in a bottle carried by the waves from some distant outpost, and I had no right to break his silence as in a legal interrogation, either by a direct or leading question or by putting a provocative misconstruction on what he had said. He did his best to write in a humorous vein.

"I suppose you don't believe that I have found the house of my dreams," he wrote again. "Why don't you come? I admit we see Chillon Castle and the Dents du Midi, and that when the west wind is blowing you can hear the State Railway, loudspeakers from an international regatta and the jingle-jangle of dance orchestras playing for the visitors to our spa, and I don't deny that you can see from here a few Montreux hotels, the whole lot in fact, but we are simply above them, inwardly above them as well, you know. You'll see! The cellar—I haven't told you about this before—is full of empty barrels, if you shout into them your flesh creeps at the sound of your own voice, and if you keep quite still you can hear the mice in the beams, perhaps rats too, anyhow it's a sign that the beams are genuine, and that's the point, you see, everything here is genuine, even the swallows under my roof that I have spent a whole week patching up to the perpetual horror of Julika, who was afraid I might fall off. And yet I am now caution personified, I cling to life as never before, you see I always have the feeling death is on my heels—that's quite natural, you know, a sign of life. Seriously, I have rarely felt like this: I almost always look forward to the next morning and only hope the following day will be like the one that has just gone by, for the present suffices me to an extent that is often astounding. And then I'm going to fit up a workshop, I can't spend all my time reading your Kierkegaard and similar heavy stuff, I've got to tie up vines, pull up weeds and then buy glass-paper, artificial fertilizer, snail powder—as you can see, it is a case of *retour à la nature*. By the way, will you tell your wife they're not planes, but elms, unfortunately diseased like almost all elms nowadays, nobody can explain why; elms don't like our times and when they have to be felled it cuts us to the quick, even if they belong to our neighbors. Will you see them before they go? I'm already waiting for you in spirit on the platform at Montreux; then I shall lead you up a rather steep and stony *vieux sentier* flanked by vine-clad walls that is as hot as an oven in summer, but more airy in autumn, overgrown with moss for decades and only used today by woodcutters and *le ménage* Stiller (pronounced Stillair). But why should I describe this countryside to you? You can read about it in your, and now also my, beloved Ramuz. When are you coming at last? I beg you, come before the old walls tumble down, the moss covers my feet and ivy grows out of our eyes."

When we received letters like this we always recalled with a smile Stiller's former jeers at country life as "sentimental escapism"; now he seemed to be feeling better in his *ferme vaudoise* than ever before. We were particularly relieved to hear that Frau Stiller had found a satisfactory part-time job; she was teaching eurhythmics in a Montreux girls' school. And Stiller himself had started working. On my wife's birthday she received a whole consignment of pottery —bowls and jugs and plates, most useful things. Stiller had never breathed a word about this. Now he wrote in connection with his present:

"Here in Glion, you must know, in case you ever come, I've been a potter from birth. I'm making a lot of money now. And once I've got my own kiln things will really start humming. And when I'm tired of making money I shall go up to Caux, which is quite near here, ten minutes on the little railway. But I haven't reached that point yet; I'm not doing my own firing yet. For preference I sell my wares to Americans with good taste. I've got a notice on my garden gate saying "Swiss Pottery," in English. Americans who know something about pottery are frequently astonished to find almost the same decorative patterns in Switzerland that they have seen with their own eyes among the Indians around Los Alamos, New Mexico, and especially in the Indian Museum at Santa Fé."

Stiller never lost his delight in mischievous pranks. He needed a certain measure of disguise in order to feel at ease with people. After my wife had visited Stiller in Glion on her way to the South of France with the children, I asked her about his *ferme vaudoise*; she merely laughed loudly. I must see it for myself! In reality things were probably not so fabulous as in his letters. Frau Stiller had once more to go "into the mountains." It was during this period of solitude that he kept ringing me up in the evening. His calls were often a nuisance, coming just when we had company. As a rule Stiller had been drinking; he began talking about Kierkegaard and pretended to be in urgent need of elucidation from me. He made these calls from a tavern—his own telephone had been cut off because he hadn't paid the bill. I was never an expert on Kierkegaard; I sent him the book following a conversation about melancholy as a symptom of the aesthetic attitude to life. When he rang me I hadn't got the book handy, and nor had Stiller. Above all, it was obvious that he had scarcely read Kierkegaard yet, so there must have been something else on his mind. He used to hang on for a quarter of an hour or more, half an hour sometimes, probably just to listen to a voice. In the background I could hear sounds from the tavern, the clink of glasses being rinsed, the clank of a pin-table. I could scarcely make out what he was saying. He must often have thought me a miserly skinflint and cursed me in his heart. I knew his economic position and tried to bring these expensive conversations to an end. I probably wasn't sufficiently capable of putting myself in his place. His jokes did not deceive me as to the degree of his loneliness, his longing for a friend. It was precisely because I was so clearly aware of this that I felt so helpless. All too often I simply couldn't provide what he expected, for I hadn't got it, and consequently he was doing me an injustice with his sudden question: "Are you mean?" Then he would continue: "Say something for heaven's sake, I don't care what, but say something!" And he regularly concluded with the words: "If you ever come to Glion, though I don't believe now that you ever will—!" and fell silent, without replacing his receiver. Then I would say goodbye several times but continue to hear the clink of glasses being rinsed and a French waitress calling out the orders. Stiller waited for me to ring off without saying goodbye himself. We feared these nightly calls. Sometimes we just didn't pick up the receiver; then he would go on ringing until two in the morning.

It was over eighteen months since we had last met, when finally I alighted at Montreux one sunny October day. I didn't recognize him at once on the platform; my own discarded suit gave him a positively bourgeois appearance, and strange to say Stiller did not take a single step towards me. Our greeting was a trifle strained. With his steep and stony *vieux sentier* in mind I had only brought an attaché case; Stiller wanted to carry it, but I wouldn't let him. To look at, Stiller was miraculously unchanged, his thin hair slightly grayer and slightly more thin, his bald patch more extensive. My old suit was too short for him, especially at the sleeves, which gave him a boyish look. Stiller immediately asked after my wife and then inquired very heartily about the children, whom he had seen. After a few paces, conversation was no longer the least bit difficult. The fact that I had allowed eighteen months to pass without seeing him was due partly to pressure of work, but partly to other reasons. I realized that now. I had felt slightly afraid of this reunion: our friendship sprang from the time when he was remanded in custody, and it might now have proved, against our wishes, out of date, a recollection instead of a present reality.

Before leaving Montreux Stiller bought wine, St. Saphorin, "to support local industry." He forced two bottles into his coat pockets and held the third against his neck like a hand grenade. Then we set off. In fact, and almost to my surprise, there was a *vieux sentier* to Glion. Stony and steep, as described, it led upwards between vine-clad walls. As we advanced we began to feel our age; rather out of breath we stood still and looked at Chillon Castle, below us Territet with its hotels, tennis courts, funicular railways and chalets, but beyond it the great blue Lake Geneva. It was almost like being by the Mediterranean. Once you can forget the shoddy-looking chalets, this landscape has a liberating breadth that is unusual in our country. Whereabouts on this vandalized hillside a *ferme vaudoise* could possibly be concealed was a puzzle to me. And we must be almost at Glion. Our conversation dealt with wine-growing, then with the concept of culture, of leisure as a prerequisite for culture and with the nobility of enjoyment, with the fundamental difference between potatos and vines, the spiritual serenity of all districts devoted to viticulture, the connection between luxury and human dignity and so forth—I did not fail to see the little sign on the iron garden gate bearing the inscription "Swiss Pottery" in English. Stiller pushed the rusty little gate open with his foot, and without interrupting the conversation led me along a moss-grown path, past all sorts of garden dwarfs, to his dream-house.

One glance at the universal dilapidation showed why the rent was so low. Vases of cast iron liberally decorated with arabesques, some of them damaged, a sandstone Aphrodite or Artemis with a broken arm, a little jungle that was doubtless supposed to be the rose garden, lots of steps everywhere, crooked, flanked on both sides by banisters, some of them crumbling away, revealing that they were all only cement, a moss-grown fountain, an old kennel, weed-grown terraces—this must have been the garden, populated by a considerable number of jolly garden dwarfs of brightly painted pottery, some broken, some undamaged. I still thought this was no more than the path leading to his own estate. Stiller talked and talked, unperturbed by the nauseating surroundings, with which he was familiar. The house itself, a chalet, was fortunately smothered by ivy, only the upper part emerged in all its fake antiquity—a brickbuilt turret with cute little loopholes. In addition there was a wooden façade covered in scroll-work that looked as though it had been made with a fretsaw, and elsewhere blocks of tufa. Everything was united under a roof with enormous eaves. And the whole place was not large, but tiny, like a toy; I couldn't believe my eyes. It was a Swiss chalet distantly related to a Scottish castle.

Stiller now pulled the two bottles out of his jacket pockets, hauled a key from his trousers and announced that Frau Julika would be back from her girls' school in about an hour.

So there we were. As on so many chalets of this kind, there was a fake marble tablet bearing in gilt letters, some of which had already turned black, the inscription MON REPOS. The interior held no more surprises. A wooden bear stood ready to receive umbrellas and above it was a badly tarnished mirror. It was a sunny afternoon and on the ceilings of all the rooms the light reflected off Lake Geneva flickered over gray stucco or bare lath and plaster. A greenish light, like that of an aquarium, filtered in through a veranda with *art nouveau* leaded windows. You could hear the State Railway about as loudly as it must sound in a line-keeper's cottage, and the greased cable of a funicular railway hummed close by.

Stiller was busy, so I was able or compelled to look around to pass the time; he was standing our white wine under a jet of cold water. Later, we sat out of doors on a mossy balustrade surrounded by the ever jolly garden dwarfs, and at last I had to say it: "So this is your *ferme vaudoise?!*" Stiller seemed unwilling to discuss any discrepancy between his description and the reality, he merely said: "It's a terrible pity you never saw my eighty elms, they were supposed to be diseased." And with that the joke was over. I asked, "How are you?" and received the impression that Stiller had made up his mind not to complain. "How's your wife?" he asked back. In subsequent conversations, too, he avoided uttering her name; I don't know why. Apart from this he did not inquire after anyone, and conversation was really a great effort.

"Why don't you put these garden dwarfs in the tool-shed?" I asked, for the sake of something to say. Stiller shrugged his shoulders: "I haven't got time, I don't know, they don't bother me." But in spite of everything I felt he was glad of the visit. "When Julika comes," he said, "we'll drink our wine." Meanwhile we smoked . . .

I remember that insignificant quarter of an hour very well. What does man do with the days of his life? I was scarcely aware of the question, it just irritated me. How could Stiller bear to face this question unprotected by affairs or social or professional importance, without any defenses? He sat on the weather-worn balustrade, one knee drawn up and his hands clasped round it; when I looked at him I could not imagine how he could bear this existence, how any man can bear his existence once he has learnt from his experiences and is consequently free from vain expectations . . .

His pottery was situated in an underground chamber with a good light cut into the side of the hill lower down—once a wash-house with a drying room and a storehouse for garden furniture, formerly whitewashed, but now papered with gray mold although the sun shone in from midday till dusk. I was relieved: here I found it easier to imagine my friend's days. "One has to do something," he commented as we looked at his finished wares, the "Swiss pottery" with which he earned his meager livelihood. "Julika still likes these shallow bowls best," he said. Another time: "Everything has to be learnt, you know, and I shall never become a proper potter now." Stiller took particular pleasure in displaying a potter's wheel he had made himself. As a layman, I considered him a master of his craft when he talked about the pottery of various peoples and periods, about the mystery of certain glazes. In what way had he changed? It seemed to me that his mind was directed more towards things themselves than it had been. Once he had spoken only of himself when he talked about marriage in general, about negroes, volcanoes and heaven knows what else: now he talked about "his" pots, "his" wheel, "his" glaze, even "his" skill, without speaking of himself at all.

"Herr Staatsanwalt!" Frau Julika greeted me. And Stiller gave her a kiss on the cheek; his hands were rather dirty from the potter's wheel. I found Frau Julika noticeably older, an unusually beautiful woman still, her striking girlish hair with its almost natural sheen stranger than ever. "He never misses a good excuse to drink wine!" she remarked when Stiller went to fetch his bottles, having first put the two wobbly armchairs out in the garden for us. "It's nice here," said Frau Julika, "isn't it?" In spite of the growing sympathy I felt for this unusual woman, I never quite knew what to talk to her about. It would be wrong to take her cool manner, which was probably only a mask to cover her shyness, personally. In all likelihood she had no inkling how little she communicated herself, and couldn't understand it when people failed to notice her goodwill, her delight at seeing someone or in a little present. She looked at the little handprinted cloth. "You can't get anything like that round here," was all she said. I think she had a profound aversion to expressing herself in words, but on the other hand the way Frau Julika immediately put the little cloth aside, although she probably liked it, made me feel thoroughly embarrassed too, as though I had been expecting a speech of thanks. Now I inquired about her job at the girls' school down in the valley, but learnt practically nothing and had to think what else might interest her. She had cushioned her head on her coppery hair, understandably tired after her day's work.

"Our Stiller has become a real potter!" I began, and she nodded. Earlier on, in the underground chamber, I had been struck by Stiller's remark: Julika still likes these shallow bowls best. This suggested a limited appreciation on his wife's part, a lack of interest or even scepticism regarding his endeavors, yes, the good Stiller seemed to miss something, something like encouragement, criticism within the framework of enthusiasm; down in the underground chamber one got the impression that Frau Julika really regarded his whole activity as a potter as humbug. Now she said to me: "Don't you think it's amazing what he's done in these two years?" I did think so. "You should tell him that," I remarked. "He'd like to hear it."—"Don't I tell him?"—"You know what we men are like," I said evasively. "We like to make an impression on the woman we love, and if we can't manage that we try the public." I meant it more as a joke. "I don't know," said Frau Julika, rubbing her eyes with both hands, "what he expects of me. Haven't I told him? Can I help it if he doesn't listen?" I had no intention of interposing myself in the role of guardian, so I broke off the conversation.

"You're very formal with one another," burst in Stiller, making our embarrassment complete. "Well, *prosit!*" he said to bridge the gap, and Stiller and I went to work on the cool little glasses. "Aren't you drinking?" he inquired when Julika did not pick up the glass he had filled for her, because she didn't feel like it. He repeated, "Well, *prosit!*" For a moment I really wondered whether Julika might not be expecting a child; her refusal to drink wine was as mute as it was definite, as though she wasn't allowed to, and I thought it a pity she didn't at least take a sip. In some way she shut herself out from the start. There is nothing trickier, I find again and again, than a three-cornered gathering. I made a great effort not to be drawn into an alliance with Stiller. It was easy with him, he has a feminine gift of adaptability, and for her part Frau Julika did nothing to prevent herself from being shut out. She lay back among her long hair without a word; her face, which I saw in profile, entranced and disturbed me in equal measure, it seemed to wear an expression of mute terror that had become permanent. Stiller paid no heed to this, but let himself go in witty persiflage, frequently directing his remarks to Frau Julika with an undertone of tender entreaty, half consideration and half coercion. Several times I thought: He makes it too easy for himself, he pays with charm, of which he has plenty, that doesn't cost him anything. It also seemed to me that Stiller was perpetually trying to make amends for something; on such occasions he became polite to the point of timidity.

"Take it away," said Frau Julika. "I don't need a cushion, really I don't." Stiller felt rejected, to judge by his brief glance at Julika, unjustly rejected. If I had been asked to act as arbiter, I should have had to take Frau Julika's part as regards the superfluousness of the proferred cushion. "Where are you going to set up your kiln?" I asked, to change the subject; but Stiller didn't hear. "Why don't you want this cushion?" he insisted, until poor Frau Julika finally took it for the sake of peace, without thanking him, and instead of putting it behind her head pushed it under her knees, where it was less in the way. Two well-meaning people! I thought and praised the delicious wine.

For no particular reason I recalled the little story someone had told me recently. "You once discovered Mexico," I said, "this will interest you. Some chap was breeding pigs there, I don't know where exactly, anyhow it didn't pay, he sweated his guts out, but to no avail, and he had invested all his means and half his

life in it, and all his ambition; to cut a long story
short, the business simply didn't pay, and then on top
of everything else there came a devastating drought.
That happens, doesn't it? The river dried up, I don't
know which one; and then apparently things got so
bad that the crocodiles migrated overland to the nearest water. One fine day a convoy of these crocodiles
started heading straight across his pig farm. What was
he to do? The unfortunate fellow could have climbed
up on to a roof, for example, and shot the crocodiles dead. But he didn't. He let them eat all his pigs,
which had never paid anyway, made a stronger fence
round the whole place, acquired a crocodile farm, went
into the handbag business and made a fortune." Stiller laugher loudly. "It's supposed to be true," I added.
"Isn't that wonderful?" exclaimed Stiller, turning to
Frau Julika. Her laugh was completely forced, and as
a matter of fact, when I look back, I can't remember
this woman ever laughing in any other way. Her
laughter always stayed on her face; it was as though
she had no inward laughter, as though she had lost it.
It was quite useless trying to cheer Frau Julika up;
afterwards one felt utterly silly.

Now I was annoyed at myself. What was the point
of all this talk? It was a late afternoon in autumn with
a gentle sun, the hour Stiller had described in his letter:
"—and then, my dear sir, when we sit outside and the
autumn sun is enough to make you happy, when there
are grapes again, when a metallic haze hangs over
the lake, but the mountaintops are clear and bright
with golden woods against a Mediterranean sky and
the light lies across the lake in a pathway of pure
quicksilver, later of gleaming brass, then of copper—"
The quicksilver phase was already over, the lake was
at the brass stage.

Every now and then I had to look round again; the
ever jolly garden dwarfs, the chalet with its turret,
the weeds, the gray Aphrodite, the empty, moss-

grown fountain with its basin choked by dead leaves
and its rusty water-pipe, the veranda with its *art
nouveau* leaded windows, the ivy, the funicular railway blood-red in the setting sun, all this remained
pretty incredible. They themselves, Stiller and Frau
Julika, wore this environment like an alien suit of
clothes with the unexpressed awareness that ultimately
every suit of clothes is alien and provisional. I admired
them. What really belonged to them was the sun with
its vast radiance on the surface of Lake Geneva, the
pottery down below in the underground chamber, all
kinds of difficulties such as are usual among human
beings, and no doubt also their helpless guest. As
soon as one left Frau Julika in peace everything went
smoothly. Now, however, Stiller wanted to know
whether I believed in the educational value of eurhythmics. Frau Julika pleaded its cause without any
real conviction, Stiller was of the opinion that Julika
should devote herself to purely artistic work again and
start a ballet school of her own at Lausanne. The discussion never got as far as a consideration of the practical obstacles; Frau Julika was positively vehement,
Stiller sorrowful because she would accept nothing
from him, neither a cushion nor his belated belief in
her artistic gifts. He rose disconsolately to fetch the
other bottle . . .

"Rolf," she said the moment we were alone, "you
must talk him out of that idea! I beg you, talk him
out of it! He's driving me crazy with this scheme!" My
attempt to examine the idea from a practical standpoint, to consider what Stiller hoped Frau Julika might
gain from it, and to ask what future Frau Julika herself desired, fell on totally deaf ears; since it was impossible to talk to me either, she had thrown herself
back in the chair again and was shaking her head as
she lay. "What does he want of me?" she said at last, in
a tired voice, as I remained silent. Her eyes were
glistening; with her slender, pale hands she was

grasping the arms of the chair as one does at the dentist's to stop oneself trembling. Her whole behavior, I must admit, struck me as overwrought and I felt I was being called upon to take sides in a long-standing argument, something I had no wish to do, particularly as I lacked all expert knowledge in the matter. "Stiller has made a pretty fool of me with his *ferme vaudoise*," I said. She didn't react at all. "But this position!" I chatted on, "what I like most about Lake Geneva—" She heard neither my small talk nor my effort to pass beyond it to a genuine conversation: "Talk him out of it!" she begged again, just as excited as before. "How do you imagine I could do it?" she protested with a violence that was also directed against me and which she toned down by adding in a gentler voice: "It's impossible, believe me. Impossible." And soon afterwards: "Of course, he can't know."—"What can't he know?"—"Don't ask," she begged, pulling herself together and taking another cigarette. I clicked my lighter. "I shouldn't smoke all the time," she remarked as though frightened or something, as though I were forcing her, in any case without thanking me for the light, which she did not use. "He can't know," she said to herself, "I've been to see the doctor—" I'm sure Frau Julika did not intend to talk to anyone about it and was sorry she had started; naturally I waited to hear more, though in silence. "The whole of my left lung," she said. "I don't want him to know yet. It's got to be done. As soon as possible." Her sudden calm, a kind of composure that made me think the unhappy woman had no idea what it was all about, although she herself subsequently employed the medical expression, which she head learned not from her doctor, but from her own commonsense; her lack of complaint amazed me, so that I stared at the ground, as though searching for something in the gravel, and dared not look her in the face for fear of showing by my expression what I could not help thinking. "Yes," she said drily, "that's the way it is." I assumed the same dry tone. "When is the operation to be?" I asked. "I don't know yet. As soon as I am no longer afraid."

A moment later Stiller arrived with the other bottle. He was just going up to Glion, he said, to fetch some grapes . . .

"Talk him out of it!" repeated Frau Julika, as though the ballet school idea was still the topic of conversation. She was lying back with her head cushioned in her girlish hair again. I don't think I've seen a lonelier person than this woman. Between her suffering and the world there seemed to be an impenetrable wall, not merely detachment but rather a kind of certainty she would not be heard, an old and hopeless, absolutely indelible conviction derived from experience, unreproachful but incurable, that her partner could hear only himself. I wanted to ask whether she had never been loved in her life. Of course I didn't ask. And did she herself love? I involuntarily tried to picture her as a child. Was it due to the fact that she was an orphan? Expecting every minute that Frau Julika would begin to pour her heart out, I too remained silent, listening to her regular, muffled breathing. What had happened to this woman? I found it impossible to believe that any human being could have been like this from the outset, so completely unable to express herself even at a moment of agonizing misery. Who had made her like this? Stiller had been gone a quarter of an hour already, in another quarter of an hour he would be back. "Now you too," she began at last, "are waiting for me to say something. I've nothing to say. How can I change? I am as I am. Why does Stiller always want to change me?"—"Does he want to?"—"I know," she said, "he probably means well, and he is convinced he loves me."—"What about you?" I asked, "do you love him too?"—"I understand him less and less," she replied after painful thought. "Do you know what he's always wanting me to do, Rolf?" . . .

After this, to take my mind off what she had said, but of course without being able to forget her horrifying revelation, I tried to put into words my current ideas about Stiller, about his human disposition, his actual make up and his potentialities, his development during the last few years as I had sensed it; I tried to express myself in a way that neither blamed nor defended and scarcely excused, and for a long time I was under the impression that Frau Julika was listening to me. Certainly, I found it easier to "understand" Stiller than Frau Julika, and after her last question I felt that in any case this was my task for the moment. As I spoke I drew with a twig in the gravel. When I glanced up to try at least to read from her expression her opinion about an idea, a question, which I as a man could not decide, I saw an utterly distorted face. I shall never forget this face that was no longer a face. Her mouth was open as in antique masks. She was trying in vain to bite her lips. Her mouth remained open as though paralyzed, trembling. I saw her sobs, but it was as though I were deaf. Her eyes were open, but unseeing, blurred by silent tears, her two little fists in her lap, her body shaking—there she sat, unrecognizable, beyond the reach of any cry, with no personal characteristic left, no voice, nothing but a despairing body, flesh screaming soundlessly in the terror of death. I can't remember what I did . . .

Later, when I held her two little fists that were still trembling convulsively, while her face had grown calm with exhaustion, she said: "You mustn't tell him." I nodded in order to give her some sort of feeling of support. "Promise me!" she begged.

Soon afterwards Stiller arrived with his grapes, Frau Julika rose quickly to her feet with head averted; from the distance she said something about sweets and was gone. Stiller absolutely insisted on my trying the grapes, which were for dessert. Whether he really saw no signs of what I had been through, or only acted as though he didn't, I could not decide. Stiller said how glad he was I had come and promised himself a merry evening. I steered the conversation on to the subject of the wine when Stiller asked casually what I thought of Julika. "I mean, as regards her health," he said. "Isn't she looking splendid?" We stood drinking, our left hands in our trouser pockets. When Julika finally came back with the sweets, she was wearing a woollen jacket and looking splendid. She had powdered her face; but that wasn't the only reason. She herself seemed to know nothing. I had the irritating feeling that it wasn't the same person at all; as though I had merely dreamed of this woman. It really was growing cool, and we went indoors. I couldn't imagine how we were going to get through the evening; but to Stiller everything was just as usual, and so it was to Frau Julika.

At that time I had not yet read the foregoing notes, though I knew that Stiller had written something like a diary in custody. It is not my purpose in this postscript to rectify Stiller's statements. The mischievous element in Stiller's notes, his subjectivity which occasionally did not shrink from falsification, seem to me obvious enough; as the report of a subjective experience they may be honest. The picture which these notes give of Frau Julika amazes me; it appears to me to reveal more about the person who drew the picture than about the person who is so grossly misrepresented by it. Whether there is not something inhuman in the very attempt to portray a living human being is a major question, and one that applies substantially to Stiller. Most of us do not keep notebooks, but perhaps we do the same thing in a less manifest way, and the result is in every case bitter.

My visit to Glion naturally exercised my mind for a

long time. Soon after my return I received a letter from Frau Julika in which, without giving any reason, she once more adjured me to say nothing. Whatever might be my own opinion, I had no right to break from without this silence between a couple, unasked, merely because I happened to have come into possession of the facts by chance and probably against the will of the person concerned. Did the unhappy Julika fear that Stiller would lose his head and bring about an impossible situation? I don't know. Or had she reason to hope that perhaps the operation would not be necessary after all?

The other thing that occupied my mind was, of course, Stiller himself. Something had happened to Stiller, it seemed to me. The tiresome question of whom we took him for had lapsed, so had his fear of being confused with someone else. In his company I felt as though I had been liberated from some hitherto barely conscious constraint; I myself became freer. As long as a person does not accept himself, he will always have this fear of being misunderstood and misconstrued by his environment; he attaches much too much importance to how we see him, and precisely because of his own obtuse fear of being pushed by us into the wrong rôle, he inevitably makes us obtuse as well. He wants us to set him free; but he doesn't set us free. He doesn't permit us to confuse him with somebody else. Who is misrepresenting whom? On this point much could be said. The self-knowledge that gradually or abruptly alienates a person from his previous life is merely the first step, indispensable but by no means sufficient in itself. How many people we know who come to a halt after this first step, who are satisfied with the melancholy that comes of mere self-knowledge and who make this melancholy look like maturity! Stiller, I believe, had already passed beyond this stage when he first disappeared. He was in the process of taking the second and much more difficult

step, of emerging from resigned regret that one is not
what one would so much have liked to be and of becoming what one is. Nothing is harder than to accept
oneself. Actually only the naive succeed in doing it,
and I have so far met few people in my world who
could be described as naive in this positive sense. In
my view Stiller, when we met him in custody, had already achieved this painful self-acceptance to a pronounced degree. Why did he nonetheless defend
himself in such a childish way against his whole environment, against his former companions? I had the
good fortune never to have been directly acquainted
with that earlier Stiller. This made a sensible relationship much easier: we were meeting for the first time.
In spite of all his self-acceptance, in spite of all his
will to self-acceptance, there was one thing our friend
had failed to achieve, he had not been able to forego
recognition by those around him. He felt himself a
different man—quite rightly, he was a different man
from that Stiller as whom people immediately recognized him—and he wanted to convince everyone of
this: that was the childish thing. But how can we
forego being recognized, at least by those nearest to
us, in the reality that we ourselves do not know, but
at best can only live? This renunciation of recognition will never become possible without a certitude
that our life is directed by a suprahuman authority,
without at least the passionate hope that such an
authority exists. Stiller reached this certitude very
late. Had he reached it? After my visit in autumn I
gained the impression that he had, although Stiller
never mentioned the subject—perhaps precisely because he never mentioned it. Stiller himself—and this,
no doubt, was an essential reason for his silence—had
absolutely no desire to announce his metamorphosis.
His new work did not serve the purpose of expression
either; he made plates and cups and bowls, useful
things which in my opinion showed a great deal of

good taste, but this work was no longer a form of self-portrayal. He was free from the fear of not being recognized, and in consequence one felt freer in one's attitude to him, as though released from a spell. Now I could understand why, in spite of all my friendly feelings towards him, I had always felt rather afraid of meeting Stiller. The word "silence" may be misleading. Naturally, Stiller was by no means untalkative. But like everyone who has arrived at himself, he looked at people and things outside himself, and what surrounded him was beginning to be world, something other than projections of his self, which he no longer had to seek or conceal in the world. He himself was beginning to be in the world. That was my impression after my first visit to Glion, and incidentally it was confirmed by his letters, insofar as they did not concern Frau Julika.

Things were, understandably, most difficult in relation to Frau Julika, his wife from before; with her he had the greatest temptation to relapse into old fears and destructive perplexities, to be at a less advanced level of development that he really was in relation to other people. A shared past is no small matter; the habituation that springs up whenever our energy is naturally at a low ebb, the habits that present themselves at every stop, can be diabolical. They are like water-weeds to a swimmer—who doesn't know that? On the other hand, I believe, our friend was now aware of the impossibility of flight: it was no use starting a new life by simply leaving the old one behind. Was not Stiller's main concern to really do away with the past in his relationship with this woman, the sterile force that had knit the two of them together, not to flee it but to melt it down in the new living present? Otherwise this new present would never become quite real. That's what it was all about—to realize potentialities or suffer failure, to breathe or suffocate, in this sense to live or die; more accurately, to live or waste away. Naturally, the relationship with a woman, in the sense of marriage, need not always become this ultimate touchstone; in this case it had become so. There are all kinds of touchstones: Stiller had found his. Our hope, as I have already mentioned, was based on our own happy experience that Stiller, at least in his dealings with his friends, had attained a living, fearless, not merely willed but real and natural openness, that the further he penetrated into himself the more he was able to pay heed to people and things outside himself. These he loved or hated. Caux, for example, he hated wholeheartedly and intolerantly, and boundlessly. Stiller remained a man of temperament, a turbulent spirit; there was no gentle universal love in our friend, but more love than ever before in his life, I believe, and it was to be hoped that this love would also reach Frau Julika, who had such need of it.

The winter passed without another meeting. Naturally I waited from letter to letter to hear that the operation was imminent or perhaps even happily over. I interpreted every remark I could not understand (P.S. "How does one behave under a curse?") as meaning that our friend was now also informed. But the very next letter proved me wrong, since he barely replied to my inquiry after Julika's state of health, or said it was excellent. Meanwhile it was already February. The dreaded operation seemed to have been unnecessary after all, and in my relief I was merely surprised that Frau Julika, knowing my concern, had never written about it. But that was her way. At one point the seven notebooks he had filled in custody arrived. "Here are my papers" was the only comment Stiller made in his letter. Why he had sent these notebooks, which I never expected to receive, was not clear to me. Did he want them out of the house so as not to be haunted by their ghost? After reading bits of them, I hoped more than ever that Stiller would at last be able to advance to a condition of living reality also in his relationship to Frau Julika, who appeared to me in these papers as having been shockingly misrepresented; at the same time the fear crept over me that time would be too short.

The operation took place in March. We were unaware of the fact, my wife and I, when we went to Glion for Easter. Our visit of two or three days, to be combined with a short trip through France, had been arranged long ago. To our surprise, the doors of MON REPOS were locked and bolted. For a while, as I walked round the chalet and shouted from every side, I had the feeling that Stiller and his wife were no longer there, no longer in Glion, no longer on the earth, that they had vanished, leaving behind them this nauseating example of architectural bad taste that had never belonged to them. The glass door of the underground chamber was not locked, but there was no one in the pottery. Nevertheless there were signs of recent work here: a once blue, now washed-out apron lay on the table as though flung down in haste, a lump of damp clay stood on the wheel. We decided to wait. It was a rainy day, mist hung over Lake Geneva; we sat in our raincoats on the wet balustrade, doing our best to convince one another that there was nothing to worry about. The wet and hence especially shiny garden dwarfs, the house with its ivy and the brick turret, the rusty iron fence, the fake marble tablet bearing the inscription, of which the letters had mostly fallen out, the wet and consequently blackish moss and the cracked fountain—everything was still there and totally unchanged, but in the absence of sunshine extremely lugubrious. We tried to cheer ourselves up by cracking jokes, but with no success. The red funicular railway was empty. After an hour dusk began to fall; the State Railway ran along the floor of the valley with its lights on, the hotels of Montreux were ablaze with light, around us was nothing but gray, and no light went on in our friend's house. Drops of water were dripping from the trees. "Let's go to a hotel," I suggested, "and ring up later." My wife was undecided. "Now that we've waited so long . . ." she suggested. So we smoked one more cigarette. The lights of Montreux, although they did not stand up to the comparison, reminded us of the shimmering Babylon we had once seen at our feet, years ago, from the Rainbow Bar . . .

Stiller arrived without coat or hat and apologized for not having pinned a note on the door—he had actually forgotten all about us. He had just come from the Val Mont Nursing Home: Frau Julika had been operated on that morning. He addressed his not very clear explanations primarily to my wife, who sat on the balustrade as though paralyzed, her hands in the pockets of her raincoat. It was now raining as well. Stiller, full of timid trust in the doctor's statement, reported that the operation had been successful, very successful indeed, as successful as it possibly could be. I wasn't sure whether he understood what the operation meant, whether he was merely minimizing it to us so as not to have to bear our horror too. Frau Julika hadn't recognized him and wasn't able to speak. A great deal now hung on this night, he explained, clinging to the doctor's permission for another visit to his wife next morning at nine o'clock as though it were an objective consolation.

"What are we standing here in the rain for?" he exclaimed. "Let's go indoors, I'm glad you've come." Indoors, in the light, he was deathly pale, busied himself with our cases, and insisted on cooking up a proper supper. My wife was no doubt right not to attempt to dissuade him, but actually to encourage him by saying she just felt like something hot to eat. "Yes, that'll be nice, won't it?" he said. She also did very little to help him; action was now the only thing that could possibly help our friend to relax. "You know," he declared to me, "this operation is very common." To hear him, one would have thought that people with two whole lungs were quite an exception. He cooked and prepared and laid the table in the kitchen, without taking off his jacket; if he had been wearing an overcoat, he wouldn't have taken that off either. It was as though he had only dropped in for a moment; and yet it was another fourteen hours before his morning visit to the nearby nursing home. "You know," he said to me, "it happened quite suddenly; it had to be done, the quicker the better."

He cooked us a magnificent rice dish; of course we only ate to keep each other's courage up. We all smoked one or more cigarettes with the meal. My wife did the washing up, while Stiller dried; then she went to bed early. She had driven our car, and Stiller believed her when she said she was tired. Alone with me, from about nine o'clock on, he seemed to have no desire to speak of the crucial matter or of Frau Julika at all. We discovered that we had both once played chess and wanted to find out whether we could still manage it. I couldn't remember where the castles and bishops went. He showed me. Even Stiller had forgotten which way round the board was supposed to go, whether there should be a white or a black square on the right-hand side. But we played. It was a kind of vigil. We played until four in the morning, when the darkness outside the window slowly turned to gray. A fine Easter day seemed to be breaking; the sky was starry. Stiller took it as a sign.

Frau Julika survived the night, all things considered she got through it excellently in fact, and our friend came back from the nursing home like a man reprieved; we breathed a sigh of relief. On top of that it was a sunny morning and Easter; Stiller suggested we should go for a walk with him. "She recognized me!" he said. I have never seen our friend so happy.

We strolled along the riverside promenade to Chillon, my wife in between us. Stiller was very talkative in an absent-minded way, all sorts of things occurred to him in confusion—his brother's last visit, jokes, then he talked enthusiastically about new friends at Lausanne, about a bookseller and his girl-friend, the world was full of nice people. At intervals he fell very silent, and also deaf. On the sun-warmed stones of the railway embankment we watched the wriggling love-play of two lizards. I asked our friend what he had against Chillon Castle, which he had always referred to scornfully in his letters, not against the hackneyed little pictures on chocolates and musical boxes, but against the reality before our eyes. He had nothing against it, and we found Chillon Castle with its walls lit by the morning sunshine very beautiful. Stiller didn't even notice that I had been teasing him a little about his former disparagement of everything to do with this country. (As regards this disparagement, which vexed me when I first read his notebooks—probably unjustly, since he never expressed himself in these terms to me—it is clear that once our friend accepted himself he had no further reason for playing the foreigner; he accepted the fact of being Swiss.) It was a hazy blue March day, the nearby Valais mountains appeared quite thin and light and silvery gray. "How are your children?" he inquired. Rather ostentatiously, he always addressed me, never my wife, although she was walking between us. We lunched at the Hôtel du Port, Villeneuve—fish washed down with wine from the nearby slopes. As was natural, at the back of his mind he was thinking almost incessantly of Frau Julika. I believe that from the hotel you can see the Val Mont Nursing Home. Between the soup and the main course, he rang up. "She's sleeping," he reported. Only Stiller remained completely clear in the head after the exquisite, but not exactly light white wine. Stiller had been drinking pretty regularly during the last few years.

The only sign here that it was Easter, once the morning bells of the churches had fallen silent, was an excessive quantity of traffic on the main road. We wandered into the Rhone delta, rather dazzled by the sun and muzzy from the wine. Fishing nets were hanging up to dry. Fishing skiffs lay bottom up on the riverbank waiting for a fresh coat of paint; others were floating in a canal surrounded by swans. "On a working day you're quite alone here," said Stiller, but even today there weren't many people about. Our path led through sparse woodland beside the reed-beds. There were clumps of alders, birches, beeches and here and there an oak; all the trees were still bare and so we could see a great deal of airy blue all the time. The ground was covered with the gray autumn leaves of the previous year, not yet hidden by any green growth, and in places the earth was almost black, a bog. I recollect this walk as one of the most enjoyable I ever went for. On the right, away over the dun-colored reeds, we could see Lake Geneva; on the left the other blue of the equally broad, flat valley of the Rhone enclosed by precipitous mountains. Unusually large flocks of birds were gathering on a distant high-tension cable; we could not make out the species, but in any case they were gathering for their great flight northwards. Two lads in blue track trousers and stripped to the waist were burning reeds on a pile that gave off bright, transparent flames. The smoke recalled autumn, yet it was March and the birds were twittering. I regretted now that my head was heavy with wine, for a long time I walked along as though under a veil, and Stiller kept asking questions. He inquired about my work and my views on education. We found an utterly deserted spot on the riverbank, though it was really quite noisy: a hum of distant trains came to us over the water, we kept hearing the signals from a railway station, and all the time gurgling, rustling, whispering sounds came from among the reeds, birds cried and beat the smooth water with their wings as they took off. The sun made us very warm, the soil on the other hand, proved damp and cold. Stiller tore up the dry reeds in bundles to make a comfortable place for my wife to sit. He did not stop even when I offered him one of his favorite cigars, and finally it became a veritable nest; my wife gave his work the praise it deserved, lowered herself on to the dry reeds and shut her eyes against the sun. Stiller stroked her brow with his hand. At moments like this, which were rare, I became very conscious of the past; then the present shared by the three of us astounded me, seeming impossible, or at least unexpected. So we smoked our cigars.

Unfortunately the obtrusive hotel up at Caux was again visible from here, and Stiller couldn't help launching out on the subject once more. His standpoint: "They work miracles up there, no doubt about it, they produce Christianity not with the poor, but with the rich, where it apparently pays better, and they really manage to fix it so that one of those bandits, after he's collected sufficient swag, repents and spends two, three, four or nine million for the peace of his soul, or at least so that a better ideology can quickly be opposed to Communism; he only keeps one single million for himself so that he shan't be a burden to the community in his old age. I can't stand that sort of Christianity. Seven millions are better than nothing, they say, and it's all given back in such a voluntary and human way, you know, so that the workers of the world, if they have any tact at all, can never take action against a bandit, for the possibility that one of these capitalist bandits may suddenly repent and improve the world from the center outwards has been proved once and for all in that hotel up there—so please, if you want a better world, no revolutions please!"

My wife had meanwhile fallen asleep, and to avoid waking her by our voices Stiller and I walked down to the riverbank, where we discussed flints and other geological matters about which we knew practically nothing. Then we tried playing ducks and drakes, as we used to when we were boys, making flat stones bounce over the surface to the water. We took off our Sunday jackets and had a little competition. For a time everything seemed forgotten, we could see the Val Mont Nursing Home, but we knew that poor Frau Julika was, so to speak, doing fine. We were really fascinated by our game.

After a time our lady urged that we should continue our walk. The later afternoon, although still just as cloudless, seemed to be part of quite a different day from the morning. I felt as though the morning lay years back in the past. On the way home Stiller talked about almost nothing but Frau Julika. I have never heard her express any regret at not having children; Stiller was convinced that she did regret it and made this regret his own, or the other way round. He spoke without reproach, without self-reproach. No doubt things couldn't have been different, he commented, but his voice was heavy with regret. Finally, as we stood beside the funicular railway, he concluded with the remark: "It's a pity you never had a chance of really getting to know Julika!" When I answered that there was still plenty of time, Stiller seemed shocked by what he himself had said.

Stiller came back very quickly from his visit that Easter Sunday evening. She was doing fine! he reported. The doctor had asked him not to go in and see her. "I can come back tomorrow," said Stiller and immediately dispersed our secret alarm: "She's doing fine, but she still needs complete rest." We all understood, and Stiller was very optimistic; there was nothing to prevent him from preparing the *raclette* he had so often promised, from organizing a sociable and jolly evening, making up an open fire, cooling off white wine and cutting three pointed sticks with which to toast the cheese over the fire. Of course it was no farmhouse chimneypiece like that shown in his sketch, but rather an over-decorated fake marble fireplace in an equally spurious *art nouveau* style. By German-Swiss standards, at least, our *raclette* was highly successful; we were hungry after our walk. Stiller drank a great deal. Whenever the party seemed on the verge of breaking up, he uncorked another bottle, and we carried on like this to the accompaniment of desultory conversation till eleven o'clock. He wasn't drunk. He drank hurriedly in little sips from the slender Vaudois white-wine glasses and remained more wide-awake than we. But we could see he wasn't listening to anything we said. His eyes seemed close to tears. Even when I tried to talk about Frau Julika, he didn't listen. It was all a great strain. Perhaps if he had been alone with either of us, my wife or me, he would have felt like talking. But there we sat, the three of us, and all we could produce was a rather cheap attempt at gaiety, to which Stiller contributed more than we did. After half an hour of relative conviviality, we said good night and went up to our room in the turret. Stiller remained standing in the hall down below—just as after his nightly telephone calls, without any salutation at the end, not even in response to our repeated "good nights"; I thought it shocking bad manners, a sentimental kind of coercion, the way he stood there without a word until I broke off, either by replacing the receiver or by shutting the door . . . Despite our fatigue, my wife and I could not sleep.

Around one o'clock I got up again. The light was out in the hall, but not in the living-room, and I went downstairs just as I was, in pajamas and barefoot, hence almost soundlessly. Our friend was sitting in front of the cold fireplace and seemed to have fallen asleep. I went over, intending to cover him up with something. But his eyes were open. "Why aren't you asleep?" he said, and his voice was thick. Stiller was now very drunk. "There's no point in drinking any more . . ." I said. He filled his glass again as though in defiance and looked me up and down. I said all sorts of sensible things. Stiller drained his glass, and as he rose to his feet he staggered visibly. "Childish," he said, "I've drunk too much, I know it's in bad taste, disgusting, childish . . ." He shook his head and glanced round as though he had lost something, supporting himself on the back of a chair. "Is she going to die?" he asked, without looking at me. I tried to calm him, but he didn't hear a word I said: he had picked up the fire tongs and didn't know what to do with them. His eyes were swimming in tears, which didn't impress me, in view of his drunkenness. "Come," I said, "let's go to bed." He looked at me. "Yesterday afternoon," he began, "when I thought she was dying—yesterday afternoon . . ." I waited in vain; he didn't finish the sentence. Stiller had not reckoned with having someone to talk to, now he was prevented by the knowledge that his speech was thick. "Too late," he said laconically. "What's too late?" I inquired. I was beginning to shiver. "Everything," he replied at last. "Two years, my dear fellow, two years! I've tried, God knows, I've tried—" He belched wine. "Pardon," he said and fell silent. Perhaps he was less drunk than I had first thought. He had started to say something, I reminded him: "You've tried—?" Now he had to sit down again. "It doesn't matter," he said.

I had never seen Stiller in this state and I felt sorry for him in his physical and mental discomfort that was at the same time ridiculous. I didn't know what to do. I felt that my commonsense approach was very shallow. "Is she going to die?" he asked as though for the first time, his head in his hands; he seemed to be giddy. "You talked to the doctor yourself," I replied. "What did the doctor tell you? Exactly?" Even when he was sitting down he swayed, without noticing it, nor did he notice that he kept taking hold of the matches by the wrong end; finally he gave it up and sat with an unlit, bent and crushed cigarette in his mouth. "It's never too late," I said, found this a sadly commonplace remark and then couldn't remember what I had really wanted to say. "Never too late!" he said with a dull laugh. "Just make a fresh start. And suppose it just can't be done—because it's too late?" All of a sudden Stiller seemed to be much more wide awake. "Rolf," he said quite clearly, quite firmly, in spite of his thick voice, "—I can kill a person, but I can't bring her back to life again . . ." And he evidently imagined that explained everything. He reached for the bottle again, but fortunately it was empty and only a few drops trickled out. "What," I inquired, "what can't be done?" He merely shook his head. "Do you love her, then?" I asked. "Do you want to—" He shook his head, without having heard me. "She can't take anything more from me," he said, "can't take anything more from me. She says so herself. 'Leave me alone,' she says, and there you stand. Honest as she is. I don't know what's wrong, Rolf. I never ask. I've ruined that woman . . ." His fingers were twisting the disintegrating cigarette and trembling, but at least he had started talking. "I'm driving her mad. I know. I'm always expecting something. A miracle! And then I start trembling the moment I see her. My mistake, maybe. Probably. She hasn't changed much. No desire to change. 'Leave me alone,' she says, and there you stand. I can't make her out. That's all there is to it. I can't make contact with her. Then I hate her. I perish if I can't love, and she—" He tore his cigarette in shreds. "How do you know, Stiller, that she too doesn't—" He shook his head. "Stiller," I said, "you're self-righteous."—"Isn't she?"

—"Her self-righteousness is her own affair," I commented. He said nothing. "What do you mean by love?" I asked, but meanwhile Stiller had found another bottle, which nearly filled his glass after all. "Stop that drinking!" I told him. He drank. "That's absurd," he said, "you're shivering, Rolf, you've got no slippers on . . . What do I mean by love?" he mused and tried to drain the empty glass again: "I can't love on my own, Rolf, I'm not a saint . . ."

It was really too cold now; I had looked around in vain for a rug or something of the sort, now I crouched down, snatched a newspaper from the low table and bundled it into the fireplace. There were still a few pine logs in the hearth and even a large beech stump. For a while I was occupied . . .

"What am I to do?" I suddenly heard Stiller at my back. "What am I to do? What?" He had risen from the chair again and I just caught sight of him drumming with his fists against his forehead. He was chalky white and still unsteady on his legs; but the alcohol seemed to be leaving his brain. His speech was no longer thick. "Why could I never make contact with that woman? Never. Not for one day, Rolf, not for one hour in all this time. Never! Why was that?" he asked. "Tell me."—"What did you expect?"—"Expect?" he asked back. "Yes," I repeated, "what did you expect, Stiller, two years ago, I mean, when you came here. To live with one another. I'm asking you because I don't know. It seems to me you expected a transformation—on her part."—"On my part, too."—"Don't be offended," I said, lighting the fire, "but that makes me think of novels. Transformation? A person realizes he has wronged somebody, and himself as well, and one day he is prepared to make amends for everything—provided the other person is transformed . . . Isn't such an expectation a bit cheap, my dear fellow?"—"Like everything about me," I heard him say. I disregarded this and asked: "What did you really expect?" Stiller seemed to be thinking it over, I had to busy myself with the fire. "Everything—except what was humanly possible," I finally answered myself. "Even in your letters it sometimes seems to me as though you are not talking about love at all, but about tenderness, about well, yes, about Eros in some form or other. Men of our age need that, Stiller, and I think it's wonderful if one has it . . . Only," I added, "that's not the point here."

The fire was now crackling cheerfully, and Stiller was leaving all the talking to me, more than I fancied. But now I had started. "Things don't go right, you said, and that really surprises you? After so many years' experience? And then, you say, you've tried? There are times when one might imagine you think yourself a magician who can change this Frau Julika into her opposite. And all the time, it seems to me, that's the only thing you worry about—It's hard to put into words. Julika has become your whole life, Stiller, that's a fact. Why did you return from Mexico? Simply because you had come to realize that. What a couple you are . . . Bring her to life! That's your old nonsense, Stiller, if you don't mind my saying so—your murderous conceit. You your own savior!" Stiller said nothing. "Over one point," I went on after a pause, "perhaps I understand you only too well. One gives in, one comes back in order to give in, but one never gives in for good and all. For then, who knows, it would be only spineless resignation, no more, a decision to make the best of things prompted by some sort of narrow-minded conventionality . . . You tremble, you said. Tremble! You tremble because again and again the same surrender is expected of you—Stiller?" I called him, "what are you thinking about?"

Stiller was standing; I was sitting on the stool, my bare feet stretched out to the warming fire; he said nothing. "You don't imagine," I said, "that with a different, perhaps more open woman—Sibylle, for example—one can get over everything one has in oneself? Or do you imagine that?" As I turned round I only saw his face from below; he was staring over my head into the fire. "You let me go on telling you a whole lot of stuff you already know," I finished off.

Stiller wasn't asleep, he was standing with his hands in his trouser pockets, and his eyes were open, awake, but empty, expressionless. "Stiller," I said, "you love her!" He seemed to hear nothing at all. "Tell me," I said to him, "if you want to be alone." In the warmth streaming out from the glowing embers I suddenly felt my fatigue again and had to suppress a yawn. "What's the time?" asked Stiller. It was getting on for two o'clock. "—She waited, you see, and I didn't wait. For her! From our first walk onwards. For her—for some sign for some utterance, for help, for joy, for anything, for a single sign in all these years! I humiliated her, you see, and she didn't humiliate me! . . . Isn't that so?" he asked. "Who says so?" I countered. Now he gazed at me with piercing eyes. "Rolf," he declared, "she wants to die!" He only nodded: "That's the way it is." He was deaf to everything I produced for the next five to ten minutes by way of contradiction; he only spoke to murmur "Pardon" when he belched wine!—"You'll keep on until one day it will really be too late, Stiller," I said. "Are you going to continue bickering even when she's in the nursing home?"—"I know I'm being ridiculous," he said. "You've gone a long way, Stiller, you mustn't make yourself ridiculous. What you said just now, you don't believe yourself. Whoever dies to please or spite someone else? You overestimate your importance. I mean your importance to her. She doesn't need you as you would like to be needed . . . Stiller," I called, as he began to sink into himself once more, feigning drunkenness, "why are you suddenly afraid she is going to die?"—"I overestimate my importance?"—"Yes," I replied. "This woman never made you her purpose in life. Only you made something of the sort of her, I think, from the beginning. As I've told you already, you set yourself up as her savior, you wanted to be the one who gave her life and joy. You! That's the way you loved her, I'm sure, until you bled yourself to death. You wanted her to be your creation. And now you're afraid she might die on you. She didn't become what you expected. An unfinished life's work! . . ."

Stiller walked over to the window and opened it. "Are you feeling sick?" I asked. "Why don't you sit down?" He turned his back to me and wiped his brow with a handkerchief. "Just go on talking," he begged. "I'll get you some water," I said, putting down the fire tongs ready to stand up. "Did she write you many letters?" "Only one," I replied. "Why?" He wiped his forehead again. "Doesn't matter," he said, dismissing the subject. "I don't imagine, Stiller, that I understand your wife, that I understand her better than you do. We're almost complete strangers, your wife and I, we've scarcely talked to one another. Her letter was very short, anyhow." He nodded sadly: "You understand her. Yes, yes. It's lucky for her." And then: "I feel lousy, you must forgive me." Nevertheless, Stiller didn't go out and relieve himself, as I had expected. He was like wax, and every time I saw his eyes I knew that there was actually only one question for him: Is she going to die? He made an effort to think about something else. And to that extent, he was glad someone was talking. "Weren't you going to say something?" he asked. But I could no longer remember at what point our conversation had been interrupted.

Now I remarked casually: "By the way . . . I've read your papers."—"Burn them!"—"What do you hope to gain by burning them?" I replied. "That's what you wrote them for . . . You've striven for this woman, as the saying goes. I understand her perhaps over one single point. Who would ever think of asking his savior how he was himself? In all those years, you see, she got used to the idea that you didn't want to be a poor, weak man, but her savior." Stiller smiled. "Why don't you say it straight out?" I didn't know what he meant, his vague smile baffled me. When I looked at him he was shaking in every limb; he had the shivers. "It's nothing," he said, "just this idiotic drinking!" At this I steered him over to the only chair with a high back against which he could rest his head, and shut the window. "Wouldn't it be better," I asked, "if I were to take you up to bed?" He shook his head. I placed the beech stump in the glowing embers. "What can I do?" he asked from under the hands that supported his face. "I can't be born again, Rolf. I don't want to either . . . What have I done wrong? Tell me. I don't know. What have I done? Tell me, I'm an idiot. Tell me!"—"I've read your papers," I repeated. "In them you know quite a lot." He took his hands away from his face. "If knowing would do it!" he said and sat for a long time unspeaking, his hands dangling, his elbows resting on his knees. "Do you remember last autumn" he asked, "the evening the three of us spent together? It was nothing special. But everything went smoothly. So I thought. For me it was a feast . . . The whole of this winter we never managed another evening like that, she and I. We just sit, she there, I here. It's enough to kill me, but she's quite satisfied!"—"How do you know she's satisfied, Stiller?"—"Why doesn't she cry out?" he demanded. "I'm proud am I? Isn't she? She waited. Do you hear? She waited for my understanding. For how many years? Two years, fourteen years. What does it matter. That's why she's worn out, do you see. I've made a wreck of her. And she hasn't done the same to me!" —"Who says that?"—"She," he answered with a scornful laugh, resting his head on the wooden chair-back. "I have humiliated her—hasn't she humiliated me?"—"Stiller," I commented, "it's no good feeling sorry for yourself now. What did you expect after all that had happened? That she would go down on her knees? To you of all people?" He kept silent, his head resting on the back of the chair, his eyes staring at the ceiling. "I can quite believe, Stiller, that there are times when you feel ready for anything, for all kinds of things. Then you rise in revolt again—in self-pity, in hate, in hopelessness. Because you expect mercy from her—from a human being. Isn't that so?" I asked. "Your occasional kneeling is out of place."—"I hate her," he said to himself, "sometimes I hate her." And then: "What good is it to me, what she says to other people? I'm the one who is waiting for her. I! Not a wise friend or a venerable aunt, but I, Rolf, I'm the one who needs a sign!" He was enjoying his anger, it seemed to me. "Why didn't you separate?" I asked. "You know, that's what most people do when things don't work out. Why did you come back like that? I suppose it was because you love her. And because we can't just switch over to another life when things go wrong. After all, it's our life that has gone wrong. Our one and only life. And then—" Stiller made as if to interrupt me; but when I stopped, he said nothing either. "I don't know," I said, "what you mean by guilt. At least you've reached the point of no longer seeking it in other people. But perhaps, I don't know, you think it could have been avoided. Guilt is the sum total of one's own faults that could have been avoided, is that how you mean it? Anyhow, I think guilt is something different. Guilt is ourselves—" Stiller broke in: "Why did I come back? You've never seen anything like it. Sheer lunacy, nothing else, utter pig-headedness! Can't you understand? When you've stood half a lifetime knocking at a door, great God, unsuccessfully as I stood before this woman, absolutely without success, great God—then see if you can pass on! See if you can forget a door like that, after wasting ten years knocking at it! Give it up and move on! . . . Where does love come into it? I couldn't forget her. That's all. As one can't forget a defeat. Why did I go back? Out of drunkenness, my dear chap, out of spite. You with your noble views! Go into a casino and just watch the way they go on playing when they lose, the way they keep on sitting there. It's just the same. Because there comes a point when it simply isn't worth while giving up. Out of spite, out of jealousy. You can lose a woman when you've won her. Let someone else come along! But when you've never won her yourself, never made contact with her, never fulfilled her? Forget a door like that, let others go in, pass on! You're quite right: Why didn't we separate? Because I'm a coward."

Stiller tried to laugh. "You're saying just the same in different words," I commented, "only I don't consider it cowardly."—"A sacrifice, you think? A reciprocal sacrifice, in which both perish!"—"Of course, there are cases where people can separate," I said, "where they ought to separate, and if they don't it's cowardice, inertia. How many there are who I wish would separate, the quicker the better; there are certainly episodes, inside or outside marriage, and when they're over you can finish with them. Not every couple become one another's cross! But when it is like that, when we have made it like that, when it isn't an episode, but the central theme of our lives—" Stiller protested: "Cross!"—"Call it what you like."—"Why don't you say it frankly" he asked. "You don't say it openly in your letters either."—"What?"—"What you mean: His will be done! God has given and blessed are they who accept, and dead they who cannot hear, like myself, who cannot love in the name of God, the accursed like myself, who hate because they want to love by their own efforts, for God alone is the love and the power and the glory—that's what you mean, isn't it?" He didn't look at me, but sat with his head resting against the wooden chair-back and the same

vague smile on his face once more. "And lost are the
proud," he went on, "those with the murderous pride
who seek to bring back to life what they have slain,
those with the miserly regret, who calculate and la-
ment at a time like this when things take a different
course or don't move at all, the deaf and the blind,
who hope for mercy at a time like this, the small-
minded like myself, those with a childish spite against
suffering, yes, let them get drunk, the arrogant who
sin against hope, the stubborn, the unbelieving, the
greedy, who want to be happy, yes let them get drunk
and chatter, those who refuse to be broken in their
pride, the unbelieving, those who put their earthly
hope in Julika! But blessed are the others, blessed are
those who can love in His name, for in God alone . . .
Is that it?" he asked. "Is that what you've been trying
to say all the time?"—"I'm your friend," I answered,
"I'm trying to tell you what I think about Julika and
you, about your loneliness with each other. That's
all."—"Well, what do you think then?" he asked, his
head against the wooden chair-back. "I've told you."
Stiller seemed unable to remember. "You love her," I
repeated. "That's what you think," he retorted. "But
you expect from your love something like a miracle,
my dear chap, and that is probably what you feel
hasn't worked out."—"I love her?"—"Yes," I asserted,
"whether it suits you or not. You would rather have
loved someone else. I know. And she knows too! Perhaps Anya, or whatever her name was, your Polish
girl in Spain, or Sibylle upstairs . . . Only it's not
Julika's fault that she isn't the girl you might have
made happy."—"No," he said. "Julika can't help that
either."—"You love without being able to make the
creature you love happy. That is your suffering. A
real suffering—apart from all our vanity, for one
would like to play God Almighty a bit, to take the
world out of one's pocket, to conjure life on to the
table, hey presto! And then, certainly, we should like

to be happy ourselves when we love . . . That doesn't always happen!" I said, and as he did not smile, I added: "That's roughly what I think, and if you ask me what you should do—" His thoughts were elsewhere. "Since autumn!" he said, and his lips were trembling. "She has known since autumn. I found out today from the doctor. Since autumn! And there was I whistling away in my underground chamber with no idea at all, no idea at all . . . What I should do," he exclaimed, vigorously on the defensive against me. "I can't walk on the water!"—"Who's asking you to?" —"Yesterday afternoon, when I thought she was dying . . . Rolf," he said, "I wept! And then I asked myself whether—if that might save her—I should be willing to go through it all over again with her, all over again. And I shook my head, I wept, for fourteen years she's been dying day by day, sitting at the table with me . . ." I felt sorry for Stiller. "You know she went to the nursing home alone?" he asked. "Without me."—"Why without you?"—"Her things were all packed. There was another hour to wait. We didn't know what to talk about. Flowers don't help, I know. But I just had to get some. There was nothing she would have liked in Territet. So I went on to Montreux. In forty minutes I was back at the house, in just forty minutes—well, she went to the nursing home alone." He forced himself to smile. "Perhaps you think nothing of it," he added, "you with your commonsense?"—"What do you think of it?"—"Without me!" he answered. "Without me! That gave her more kick than flowers, you see. To leave this house perhaps for the last time, alone, unescorted, oh yes, that lasts longer than all the flowers in the world!" I didn't accept his explanation. "Rolf," he retorted, "that woman is spiteful. Perhaps I made her spiteful. One day you can't believe in love any more . . . I was too late!"

Stiller had risen to his feet. He looked as though he

would fall down any minute, I didn't know what kept
him upright at all. "Have a white brandy," he said,
"and then we'll go to bed." But he couldn't find the
glasses, which I could see on a tray lower down, and
seemed to forget what he had meant to do. He just
stood there, the brandy bottle in his hand, lost in silent thoughts. "There is no one who is more of a
stranger to me than that woman," he said. "I don't
want to bore you, Rolf, but I must just say this: I
shall be grateful, I shan't wait for a miracle. I shan't
wait for some other Julika, I shall be grateful for
every day if she comes back to this house again—
now, yes, now, when I can't sleep, can't stay awake
for fear it's all too late, now—Rolf!" he said, but he
was so weak that he had to sit down on the nearby
window sill in order to continue; he spoke like a
frightened child after a nightmare: "What will happen
when she is sitting there again? She there and I here?
Suppose everything is just the same as it was? Exactly
the same? She there and I here—" He sat, still holding
the brandy bottle in his hand, and looked at the room,
at the two empty armchairs. "What then?" he asked
himself, and a few moments later he addressed the
same question to me: "What then, my dear chap, what
then? Am I to dissolve in smoke, so as not to be a
nuisance to her? Or what? Shall I fast until she gives
a sign, and show her that one can die of hunger waiting? Or what?"—"Stiller," I replied, "things won't be
as they were before. Things won't be the same for
you, even if Julika never changes. Yesterday afternoon
you thought she was dying—" As soon as he realized
what I was leading up to, he broke in. "I know what
you mean," he said. He showed me he was feeling
sick, to stop me from talking, so I said no more. "How
many revelations I've already had, how many decisions I have reached!" he said. "But what will happen when she is sitting here again? I'm gradually getting to know myself. I'm weak"—"Once you know

you're weak," I commented, "that is already a big step forward. Perhaps you have only just found out. Since yesterday afternoon, when you thought she was dying. Often you hate her, you say? Because she, too, is weak and poor? She can't give you what you need. Quite true. And her love is so necessary to you. More so than any other. There are things which are very necessary, Stiller, and yet we can't manage them. Why should Julika be able to manage it? Do you idolize her—still—or do you love her?" Stiller let me talk. "Yes, yes," he said, "but speaking practically, when she's there and I'm here, what am I to do? Quite practically?" He looked at me. "You see, Rolf, even you can't answer that!" he said, and it seemed to satisfy him. "You've gone a long way," I said, "I sometimes have the impression that one more step is all you need."—"And we'll be sitting here in the middle of a wedding, you mean?"—"And you will no longer expect Julika to be able to absolve you from your life or the other way round. You know what that means in practical terms."—"No."—"There'll be no change," I said, "you will live together, you with your work in the underground chamber down there, she with her one lung, God willing. The only difference will be that you won't go on tormenting yourselves day after day with this crazy notion that we can change people, somebody else or ourselves, with this presumptuous despair . . . Quite practically—you will learn to pray for one another." Stiller had risen to his feet. "Yes," I concluded, "that's really all I can say to you on the subject." Stiller put the brandy bottle down on the little table, and we looked at each other; the vague smile he had worn before did not reappear. "One has to know how to pray!" was all he said, and there followed a lengthy silence . . .

Later, much later, I often wondered how I ought to have behaved that night, unexpectedly confronted with a task that went beyond the powers of a friendship. When Stiller left the room to relieve himself at last, I stood there helpless. I felt my lack of any official status, for whatever I might have said remained merely my personal opinion. At best I could do no more than offer friendly resistance whenever my friend, who was being tested, tried to evade the test . . .

I poured myself out a glass of white brandy, and when Stiller returned about ten minutes later—unfortunately not without bumping into a piece of furniture in the dark hall and causing a clatter—he found me with the empty glass in my hand. "How do you feel?" I asked. Stiller only nodded. He had emptied his stomach, and obviously also washed his face, which was green with inflamed eyes. "What's the right time?" he inquired afresh, sitting down on the clothes press and supporting himself on his outspread arms. "You're right," he said, "this idiotic drinking—!" Stiller seemed to want to forget our unfinished conversation. It seemed that in order to go upstairs to bed all we needed was an appropriate phrase, an optimistic cliché—Tomorrow is another day, or something like that. The clock struck half past two. Of course we both thought of time in the nursing home. There time was important, not here. I involuntarily visualized the sick-room, the night nurse sitting by the white bed taking her pulse—let's hope she doesn't have to ring the doctor—and for the first time I felt afraid. I saw the telephone on the clothes press, which might ring at any moment, and felt that the worst was possible. I remembered the doctor's refusal to let Stiller pay Julika an evening visit. "What are you thinking about?" asked Stiller, and I had to say something. "All you have to do now is to be sensible, Stiller, not to see ghosts. You love her. You have begun to love her, and Julika isn't dead, everything is still possible . . ." I felt slightly ashamed, but this was just the sort of hackneyed phrase that seemed to pacify Stiller. "Have you got another cigarette?" he asked to avoid going to bed and being alone. I was in pajamas: I had no cigarettes. "I'm sure your wife won't have been able to sleep," remarked Stiller, "I loved your wife—I still love her," he added to get everything straight, "but you know that." His silences grew longer and longer. "Leave them," he muttered, as I pushed the empty bottles a little to one side, so that Stiller shouldn't fall over them and make a fresh clatter. "Or do you think I've never loved at all?" he asked uncertainly. "Never loved at all?" His face appeared to be visibly disintegrating with fatigue. "If only I weren't so damned wide awake!" he expostulated and looked as though he were on the point of vomiting. "You must rest," I said. "You'll see her at nine tomorrow morning—" His cigarettes, the blue Gauloises, were lying on the carpet by the chair. "Thanks," said Stiller when I offered him his own packet, and put a Gauloise in his mouth; but he took it out again, in spite of the lighted match I held out to him. "I shall see her at nine tomorrow! . . ." Then he smoked as though the smoke were a food.

"You don't think," he asked, "that Julika is going to die?" At this I said something imprudent: "As long as your telephone doesn't ring, Stiller, there's no reason to fear anything of the sort." Once it was said it was said, and I could not take back the senseless remark that had given his fear a physical object to which it could attach itself. Stiller looked at the black telephone. So I went on speaking. "You must be prepared for that," I said. "One day Julika, too, will die. Sooner or later. Like the rest of us. You must be prepared for that now." Stiller smoked and said nothing. I had no idea what he was thinking. At last he threw his cigarette into the fireplace, or at least close to it, ready to bring the conversation to a final close. I was freezing: the fire was going out and there was no more wood. "It was probably a good thing," I said, descending to clichés again, "for us to have had this talk—" Stiller nodded without conviction and continued to sit on the clothes press, supported on his outspread arms; he seemed to be waiting for strength. "The truth is, I'm at exactly the point where I ought to have begun two years ago," he remarked, "not a step further. Only another two years have been lost— I don't want to bore you, Rolf, but . . ." He saw that I was shivering. "Rolf," he said, "everything would have been all right. Without a miracle, believe me, we should have got on all right, the two of us, just as we are—not then, but now; I mean two years ago. Now for the first time, here and now . . ." Stiller didn't want to cry, he fought against it and stood up. "This morning in the nursing home," he said, "—no, that was yesterday—" Tears streamed all over his face, which was in no way that of a man in tears; he tried to say something. "Everything would have been all right —," he repeated, but got no further. "Then it will be all right!" I said. "It will be all right!"

What happened next was strange; for a time we both acted as though Stiller were not crying at all. He stood somewhere in the room, his hands in his trouser pockets, unable to speak. I saw his back, not his face, knew that Stiller was crying and because he was crying could hear nothing, and talked about his "notebooks," simply to avoid being a mute spectator. "—anyhow, you know the essential point," I said among other things, "you know that nothing is settled by putting a bullet in your temple, for example. How one learns that is something that cannot be described. But you know it, unimaginable as it is. Perhaps you have a queer idea of what it means to believe; perhaps you think one is certain when one believes, so to speak wise and saved and so on. You feel yourself to be anything but certain, so you simply don't believe you're a believer. Isn't that so? You can't picture God, so you tell yourself you have never experienced Him

. . ." Stiller seemed glad I was talking. "As far as I know your life," I said, "you have again and again thrown everything away because you were uncertain. You are not truth. You are a man and you have often been willing to give up an untruth, to be uncertain. What else does that mean, Stiller, but that you believe in a truth? And in a truth that we cannot change and cannot even kill—a truth that is life."

The grandfather clock out in the hall began to clank as it always did before striking the hour; it was three o'clock. "I got an odd impression from your notebooks," I went on, for the sake of something else to say. "You kept trying to accept yourself without accepting anything like God. And now this proves an impossibility. He is the power which can help you really to accept yourself. You've learnt all that. And yet you say you can't pray; you write it too. You cling to your powerlessness, which you take for your personality, and yet you know your powerlessness so well —and all this as though out of spite because you are not power. Isn't that so?" Of course Stiller didn't answer. "You feel it must compel you, otherwise it's not genuine. You don't want to kid yourself. You're annoyed because you have to beg for belief; then you're afraid God might simply be your own invention . . ."

I went on talking for a long time before finally coming to a stop. As I have said, I did not expect Stiller to listen: I only talked to avoid being a mute spectator of his weeping. His thoughts were elsewhere. "Her face," said Stiller, "that isn't her face at all, it never was—!" He was unable to express himself any further. Stiller was now crying as I have rarely seen a man cry. And all the time he stood there with his hands in his trouser pockets. I didn't leave the room; my presence no longer carried any weight . . . During those minutes I made a great effort to recall her face, but only saw it as it was last autumn, when it was no longer a face at all; I saw her sobbing with her mouth wide

open and rigid, her equally rigid fists in her lap, the
dumb trembling of a blind body filled with the fear of
death; but I didn't want to be reminded of that now. I
resolved to go to the nursing home myself the following morning, to see Frau Julika, if only for a moment.

"Say something," begged Stiller when finally, exhausted by his crying, he became aware of my presence again. "I've said all I can say to you: Julika hasn't
died," I repeated, "and you love her." At this Stiller
looked at me as though I had uttered a revelation. His
legs were still unsteady, his eyes watery, but his head
was sober, I believe. He made some complimentary
remark about our friendship, about my kindness in
staying up with him again almost a whole night, and
rubbed his waxen forehead. "If you've got a head-
ache," I said, "I have some Saridone tablets upstairs."
His thoughts were already elsewhere again. "You're
right," he repeated several times, "I shall see her at
nine o'clock tomorrow—" At last we stood in the
doorway, I myself utterly exhausted, and Stiller put
out the chandelier with its watery light. "Pray for me
that she shall not die!" I heard him say, and suddenly
we were in darkness: Stiller had forgotten to switch
the hall light on first. "I love her—" I heard him say.
At last Stiller found the hall switch, and we shook
hands and said good night. Stiller went out into the
garden. "I must have some air," he said, "I've certainly
had too much to drink." He was very calm.

The following morning, Easter Monday, my wife
and I came downstairs at about nine o'clock. Our
breakfast was standing ready on the table by the open
window—coffee under the cozy and places laid with
everything complete for two people. Neither salt cellar nor ashtray were missing. The soft-boiled eggs,
one of them with "3 mins." written on it to show it
was especially lightly boiled for Sibylle, as well as the
toast under the table napkin, were still warm: our
friend must have heard us washing and couldn't have

been long out of the house. My wife had heard the crash during the night, but knew only that we had stayed up late talking. Naturally we assumed Stiller was already at the nursing home. Our long conversation during the night seemed almost like a dream, lacking any true connection with daylight reality, as we sat down at the table with the sun glinting on the knives and spoons and the exquisite view out over the forget-me-not-blue Lake Geneva to the snow-covered Savoy Alps. On the assumption that another satisfied client would come out of the nursing home, we decided to drive on in the course of the day via Chèbres, Yverdon, Murten or Neuenburg and spend a day's holiday on our own on St. Peter's Island in Lake Biel. The weather was absolutely glorious. A magnolia was already in full blossom in a neighboring garden, forsythia was hanging over the fences in sheafs of brilliant yellow, the blood-red funicular railway came down empty between green slopes covered in cowslips and went up full of trippers. It was a world painted in colors of positively childish brilliance, such as are only appropriate to an Easter day; the birds were twittering so loud they were really noisy, and a white pleasure steamer was chugging across the lake to Chillon Castle, somewhere in the distance a brass band was playing Sunday music, the State Railway rumbled by.

Stiller came in while we were still comfortably breakfasting. Our immediate but rather anxious question, how's it going? naturally referred to Frau Julika; our friend had not come from the nursing home, however, but from his underground chamber. Stiller hadn't slept a wink; he had probably spent the rest of the night in the garden and the early morning in his pottery. Of course he looked pale and exhausted. Why he hadn't gone to the nursing home at nine o'clock I don't know; he was still unshaven too. Was he afraid? With apparent optimism, as though Frau Julika were on the point of being discharged from the nursing home, he talked about something else. He hadn't even telephoned. He asked me to call at the nursing home and tell his wife he would come around eleven o'clock. Not one of his excuses would hold water. He had to shave! Then again we heard that some V.I.P. who was passing that way had asked to see his pottery and was arriving at about ten—which was true, but not an adequate excuse. Perhaps Stiller felt ashamed to stand beside the sick-bed stinking of liquor. He kept his distance from my wife too, in a way that couldn't be overlooked. "I stink," he said. A real or fancied odor of wine was no reason for not at least ringing the nursing home, but Stiller didn't want to. I couldn't force him.

In the end my wife and I drove to the nearby Val Mont Nursing Home, where my wife waited in the car; it was bound to be only a short visit, if a visit from someone not a relative was allowed at all. I felt a real desire at least to see Frau Julika before we drove on. The moment I announced myself I knew what had happened. I had to wait another anxious quarter of an hour in a sunny corridor with flower vases standing in front of the doors and silent nurses hurrying this way and that, before the young doctor informed me of her decease. At my urgent request he promised that Herr Stiller should not be notified over the telephone. Death had supervened half an hour earlier, and it had obviously come as a surprise to the doctor. My other wish, to see Frau Stiller, was at first refused. But in the end my face (I was probably crying) was sufficient to make the doctor change his mind—or was it my identity papers? Anyhow, the matron was told to take me to the dead woman.

"Her hair is red, very red in fact, in keeping with the new fashion, not like rose-hip jam, however, but more like dry minium powder. Very curious. And with it a very fine complexion—alabaster with freckles. Also very curious, but beautiful. And her eyes? I should say they are glittering, somehow watery, even when she is not crying, bluish-green like the edges of colorless window-glass. Unfortunately her eyebrows have been plucked to a thin line, which gives her face a graceful hardness, but also a slightly masklike appearance, as though perpetually miming surprise. Her nose looks very aristocratic, especially from the side; there is a great deal of involuntary expression in the nostrils. Her lips are rather thin for my taste, not without sensuality, but they must first be aroused. Her loose hair is gloriously silky and as light as gossamer. Her front teeth are splendid, not without fillings, but otherwise gleaming like mother of pearl. I looked at her as though she were an object; as though she were just any unknown woman . . ." That was exactly how she lay on the deathbed, and I suddenly had the monstrous feeling that from the very beginning Stiller had only seen her as a dead woman; for the first time, too, I felt the deep unqualified consciousness of his sin, a consciousness no human word would obliterate.

The only thing left was to bring the heavy tidings to my friend. A few words were enough; Stiller already knew. Although almost an hour had passed since I left the nursing home, they had not telephoned; but he knew the moment he saw me, and I believe Stiller uttered my news himself; I won't say "calmly," for it was the terrifying calm of someone whose mind is wandering. I waited a long time to drive Stiller to the nursing home. He went up to his room, to fetch his coat, so he said. We heard nothing, no footsteps, no sobs, only the noise of the birds outside, and after a time my wife was manifestly afraid our friend might have done something to himself. I didn't believe this for an instant, but as he still didn't come I went upstairs and knocked at his door. There was no answer, so I went in. Stiller was standing in the middle of the room, his hands in his trouser pockets as so often. "I'm coming," he said. I drove him to the nursing home and waited outside in the car. The picture of the dead woman was so much stronger than anything I could see with open eyes—the picture of a being who was dead and had never been recognized by anyone while she was alive, least of all by the one who had striven for her with his human love. After a quarter of an hour Stiller came back and sat down beside me in the car. "She is beautiful," he said. I had my leave extended and remained in Glion for a few days, after my wife had left, to relieve him of all sorts of things that have to be done after a death. Moreover, I had the feeling that Stiller needed me, although there were no further conversations between us. The medical report did not interest him and there was little else to say; the decision had been reached. The evening after the little funeral in an alien cemetery, when I had to leave him, Stiller was working in his underground chamber, or at least trying to. He accompanied me to the little iron gate with the funny notice-board, his thoughts elsewhere, so that I had to shake hands with him two or three times. We saw one another now and then; he made no more late-night telephone calls and his letters were uncommunicative. Stiller remained in Glion and lived alone.

MAX FRISCH was born in Zurich, Switzerland, the son of an architect. In 1933 he was forced by economic circumstances to abandon the study of German literature at Zurich University, and turned to journalism as a livelihood, traveling throughout Europe, writing news, reports and articles on sport.

Able at last to renew his education, he became a trained architect and in 1943 won a public competition for the construction of a building in Zurich, thus enabling him to open his own architect's office.

It was before this, however, during war service with the frontier guard, that he broke his own secret pledge "to write no more." The first outcome was his work, *Leaves from a Knapsack*. In 1943, his novel, *The Difficult One*, appeared.

Encouraged to try the theatre by the dramatist, Kurt Hirschfeld, Frisch wrote his first play, *Santa Cruz*. His requiem for the death of World War II, *Now They Sing Again*, quickly made his name known throughout Germany.

In 1952, he spent a year in the United States and Mexico on a grant from the Rockefeller Foundation. In the meantime, his work had been gaining its present place in the front rank of those writing in German, through his half-dozen frequently performed and much discussed plays, and above all by his novel, *I'm Not Stiller*, which has been translated into all the major European languages.

Max Frisch is married and lives at Mannedorf in Switzerland.

THIS BOOK was set on the Linotype in Janson, an excellent example of the influential and sturdy Dutch types that prevailed in England prior to the development by William Caslon of his own designs, which he evolved from these Dutch faces. Of Janson himself little is known except that he was a practicing type-founder in Leipzig during the years 1660 to 1687. Composed, printed and bound by H. WOLFF BOOK MANUFACTURING, New York. Cover design by GIOVANNI GUARCELLO.

VINTAGE FICTION, POETRY, AND PLAYS

V-814   **ABE, KOBO** / The Woman in the Dunes
V-2014   **AUDEN, W. H.** / Collected Longer Poems
V-2015   **AUDEN, W. H.** / Collected Shorter Poems 1927-1957
V-102   **AUDEN, W. H.** / Selected Poetry of W. H. Auden
V-601   **AUDEN, W. H. AND PAUL B. TAYLOR (trans.)** / The Elder Edda
V-20   **BABIN, MARIA-THERESA AND STAN STEINER (eds.)** / Borinquen: An Anthology of Puerto-Rican Literature
V-271   **BEDIER, JOSEPH** / Tristan and Iseult
V-523   **BELLAMY, JOE DAVID (ed.)** / Superfiction or The American Story Transformed: An Anthology
V-72   **BERNIKOW, LOUISE (ed.)** / The World Split Open: Four Centuries of Women Poets in England and America 1552-1950
V-321   **BOLT, ROBERT** / A Man for All Seasons
V-21   **BOWEN, ELIZABETH** / The Death of the Heart
V-294   **BRADBURY, RAY** / The Vintage Bradbury
V-670   **BRECHT, BERTOLT (ed. by Ralph Manheim and John Willett)** / Collected Plays, Vol. 1
V-759   **BRECHT, BERTOLT (ed. by Ralph Manheim and John Willett)** / Collected Plays, Vol. 5
V-216   **BRECHT, BERTOLT (ed. by Ralph Manheim and John Willett)** / Collected Plays, Vol. 7
V-819   **BRECHT, BERTOLT (ed. by Ralph Manheim and John Willett)** / Collected Plays, Vol. 9
V-841   **BYNNER, WITTER AND KIANG KANG-HU (eds.)** / The Jade Mountain: A Chinese Anthology
V-207   **CAMUS, ALBERT** / Caligula & Three Other Plays
V-281   **CAMUS, ALBERT** / Exile and the Kingdom
V-223   **CAMUS, ALBERT** / The Fall
V-865   **CAMUS, ALBERT** / A Happy Death: A Novel
V-626   **CAMUS, ALBERT** / Lyrical and Critical Essays
V-75   **CAMUS, ALBERT** / The Myth of Sisyphus and Other Essays
V-258   **CAMUS, ALBERT** / The Plague
V-245   **CAMUS, ALBERT** / The Possessed
V-30   **CAMUS, ALBERT** / The Rebel
V-2   **CAMUS, ALBERT** / The Stranger
V-28   **CATHER, WILLA** / Five Stories
V-705   **CATHER, WILLA** / A Lost Lady
V-200   **CATHER, WILLA** / My Mortal Enemy
V-179   **CATHER, WILLA** / Obscure Destinies
V-252   **CATHER, WILLA** / One of Ours
V-913   **CATHER, WILLA** / The Professor's House
V-434   **CATHER, WILLA** / Sapphira and the Slave Girl
V-680   **CATHER, WILLA** / Shadows on the Rock
V-684   **CATHER, WILLA** / Youth and the Bright Medusa
V-140   **CERF, BENNETT (ed.)** / Famous Ghost Stories
V-203   **CERF, BENNETT (ed.)** / Four Contemporary American Plays
V-127   **CERF, BENNETT (ed.)** / Great Modern Short Stories
V-326   **CERF, CHRISTOPHER (ed.)** / The Vintage Anthology of Science Fantasy

V-293   **CHAUCER, GEOFFREY** / The Canterbury Tales (a prose version in Modern English)

V-142   **CHAUCER, GEOFFREY** / Troilus and Cressida

V-723   **CHERNYSHEVSKY, N. G.** / What Is to Be Done?

V-173   **CONFUCIUS (trans. by Arthur Waley)** / Analects

V-155   **CONRAD, JOSEPH** / Three Great Tales: The Nigger of the Narcissus, Heart of Darkness, Youth

V-10   **CRANE, STEPHEN** / Stories and Tales

V-126   **DANTE, ALIGHIERI** / The Divine Comedy

V-177   **DINESEN, ISAK** / Anecdotes of Destiny

V-431   **DINESEN, ISAK** / Ehrengard

V-752   **DINESEN, ISAK** / Last Tales

V-740   **DINESEN, ISAK** / Out of Africa

V-807   **DINESEN, ISAK** / Seven Gothic Tales

V-62   **DINESEN, ISAK** / Shadows on the Grass

V-205   **DINESEN, ISAK** / Winter's Tales

V-721   **DOSTOYEVSKY, FYODOR** / Crime and Punishment

V-722   **DOSTOYEVSKY, FYODOR** / The Brothers Karamazov

V-780   **FAULKNER, WILLIAM** / Absalom, Absalom!

V-254   **FAULKNER, WILLIAM** / As I Lay Dying

V-884   **FAULKNER, WILLIAM** / Go Down, Moses

V-139   **FAULKNER, WILLIAM** / The Hamlet

V-792   **FAULKNER, WILLIAM** / Intruder in the Dust

V-189   **FAULKNER, WILLIAM** / Light in August

V-282   **FAULKNER, WILLIAM** / The Mansion

V-339   **FAULKNER, WILLIAM** / The Reivers

V-412   **FAULKNER, WILLIAM** / Requiem For A Nun

V-381   **FAULKNER, WILLIAM** / Sanctuary

V-5   **FAULKNER, WILLIAM** / The Sound and the Fury

V-184   **FAULKNER, WILLIAM** / The Town

V-351   **FAULKNER, WILLIAM** / The Unvanquished

V-262   **FAULKNER, WILLIAM** / The Wild Palms

V-149   **FAULKNER, WILLIAM** / Three Famous Short Novels: Spotted Horses, Old Man, The Bear

V-45   **FORD, FORD MADOX** / The Good Soldier

V-7   **FORSTER, E. M.** Howards End

V-40   **FORSTER, E. M.** / The Longest Journey

V-187   **FORSTER, E. M.** / A Room With a View

V-61   **FORSTER, E. M.** / Where Angels Fear to Tread

V-219   **FRISCH, MAX** / I'm Not Stiller

V-842   **GIDE, ANDRE** / The Counterfeiters

V-8   **GIDE, ANDRE** / The Immoralist

V-96   **GIDE, ANDRE** / Lafcadio's Adventures

V-27   **GIDE, ANDRE** / Strait Is the Gate

V-66   **GIDE, ANDRE** / Two Legends: Oedipus and Theseus

V-958   **von GOETHE, JOHANN WOLFGANG (ELIZABETH MAYER, LOUISE BOGAN & W. H. AUDEN, trans.)** / The Sorrows of Young Werther and Novella

V-300   **GRASS, GUNTER** / The Tin Drum

V-425   **GRAVES, ROBERT** / Claudius the God

V-182   **GRAVES, ROBERT** / I, Claudius

V-717   **GUERNEY, B. G. (ed.)** / An Anthology of Russian Literature in the Soviet Period: From Gorki to Pasternak

V-829 **HAMMETT, DASHIELL** / The Big Knockover
V-2013 **HAMMETT, DASHIELL** / The Continental Op
V-827 **HAMMETT, DASHIELL** / The Dain Curse
V-773 **HAMMETT, DASHIELL** / The Glass Key
V-772 **HAMMETT, DASHIELL** / The Maltese Falcon
V-828 **HAMMETT, DASHIELL** / The Red Harvest
V-774 **HAMMETT, DASHIELL** / The Thin Man
V-781 **HAMSUN, KNUT** / Growth of the Soil
V-896 **HATCH, JAMES AND VICTORIA SULLIVAN (eds.)** / Plays by and About Women
V-15 **HAWTHORNE, NATHANIEL** / Short Stories
V-610 **HSU, KAI-YU** / The Chinese Literary Scene: A Writer's Visit to the People's Republic
V-910 **HUGHES, LANGSTON** / Selected Poems of Langston Hughes
V-304 **HUGHES, LANGSTON** / The Ways of White Folks
V-158 **ISHERWOOD, CHRISTOPHER AND W. H. AUDEN** / Two Plays: The Dog Beneath the Skin and The Ascent of F6
V-295 **JEFFERS, ROBINSON** / Selected Poems
V-380 **JOYCE, JAMES** / Ulysses
V-991 **KAFKA, FRANZ** / The Castle
V-484 **KAFKA, FRANZ** / The Trial
V-841 **KANG-HU, KIANG AND WITTER BYNNER** / The Jade Mountain: A Chinese Anthology
V-508 **KOCH, KENNETH** / The Art of Love
V-915 **KOCH, KENNETH** / A Change of Hearts
V-467 **KOCH, KENNETH** / The Red Robbins
V-82 **KOCH, KENNETH** / Wishes, Lies and Dreams
V-134 **LAGERKVIST, PAR** / Barabbas
V-240 **LAGERKVIST, PAR** / The Sibyl
V-776 **LAING, R. D.** / Knots
V-23 **LAWRENCE, D. H.** / The Plumed Serpent
V-71 **LAWRENCE, D. H.** / St. Mawr & The Man Who Died
V-329 **LINDBERGH, ANNE MORROW** / Gift from the Sea
V-822 **LINDBERGH, ANNE MORROW** / The Unicorn and Other Poems
V-479 **MALRAUX, ANDRE** / Man's Fate
V-180 **MANN, THOMAS** / Buddenbrooks
V-3 **MANN, THOMAS** / Death in Venice and Seven Other Stories
V-297 **MANN, THOMAS** / Doctor Faustus
V-497 **MANN, THOMAS** / The Magic Mountain
V-86 **MANN, THOMAS** / The Transposed Heads
V-36 **MANSFIELD, KATHERINE** / Stories
V-137 **MAUGHAM, W. SOMERSET** / Of Human Bondage
V-720 **MIRSKY, D. S.** / A History of Russian Literature: From Its Beginnings to 1900
V-883 **MISHIMA, YUKIO** / Five Modern Nō Plays
V-151 **MOFFAT, MARY JANE AND CHARLOTTE PAINTER** / Revelations: Diaries of Women
V-851 **MORGAN, ROBIN** / Monster
V-926 **MUSTARD, HELEN (trans.)** / Heinrich Heine: Selected Works
V-901 **NEMIROFF, ROBERT (ed.)** / Les Blancs: The Collected Last Plays of Lorraine Hansberry
V-925 **NGUYEN, DU** / The Tale of Kieu

V-125   **OATES, WHITNEY J. AND EUGENE O'NEILL, Jr. (eds.) /** Seven Famous Greek Plays

V-973   **O'HARA, FRANK /** Selected Poems of Frank O'Hara

V-855   **O'NEILL, EUGENE /** Anna Christie, The Emperor Jones, The Hairy Ape

V-18   **O'NEILL, EUGENE /** The Iceman Cometh

V-236   **O'NEILL, EUGENE /** A Moon For the Misbegotten

V-856   **O'NEILL, EUGENE /** Seven Plays of the Sea

V-276   **O'NEILL, EUGENE /** Six Short Plays

V-165   **O'NEILL, EUGENE /** Three Plays: Desire Under the Elms, Strange Interlude, Mourning Becomes Electra

V-125   **O'NEILL, EUGENE, JR. AND WHITNEY J. OATES (eds.) /** Seven Famous Greek Plays

V-151   **PAINTER, CHARLOTTE AND MARY JANE MOFFAT /** Revelations: Diaries of Women

V-907   **PERELMAN, S. J. /** Crazy Like a Fox

V-466   **PLATH, SYLVIA /** The Colossus and Other Poems

V-232   **PRITCHETT, V. S. /** Midnight Oil

V-598   **PROUST, MARCEL /** The Captive

V-597   **PROUST, MARCEL /** Cities of the Plain

V-596   **PROUST, MARCEL /** The Guermantes Way

V-600   **PROUST, MARCEL /** The Past Recaptured

V-594   **PROUST, MARCEL /** Swann's Way

V-599   **PROUST, MARCEL /** The Sweet Cheat Gone

V-595   **PROUST, MARCEL /** Within A Budding Grove

V-714   **PUSHKIN, ALEXANDER /** The Captain's Daughter and Other Stories

V-976   **QUASHA, GEORGE AND JEROME ROTHENBERG (eds.) /** America a Prophecy: A Reading of American Poetry from Pre-Columbian Times to the Present

V-80   **REDDY, T. J. /** Less Than a Score, But A Point: Poems by T. J. Reddy

V-504   **RENAULT, MARY /** The Bull From the Sea

V-653   **RENAULT, MARY /** The Last of the Wine

V-24   **RHYS, JEAN /** After Leaving Mr. Mackenzie

V-42   **RHYS, JEAN /** Good Morning Midnight

V-319   **RHYS, JEAN /** Quartet

V-2016   **ROSEN, KENNETH (ed.) /** The Man to Send Rain Clouds: Contemporary Stories by American Indians

V-976   **ROTHENBERG, JEROME AND GEORGE QUASHA (eds.) /** America a Prophecy: A New Reading of American Poetry From Pre-Columbian Times to the Present

V-41   **SARGENT, PAMELA (ed.) /** Women of Wonder: Science Fiction Stories by Women About Women

V-838   **SARTRE, JEAN-PAUL /** The Age of Reason

V-238   **SARTRE, JEAN-PAUL /** The Condemned of Altona

V-65   **SARTRE, JEAN-PAUL /** The Devil & The Good Lord & Two Other Plays

V-16   **SARTRE, JEAN-PAUL /** No Exit and Three Other Plays

V-839   **SARTRE, JEAN-PAUL /** The Reprieve

V-74   **SARTRE, JEAN-PAUL /** The Trojan Women: Euripides

V-840   **SARTRE, JEAN-PAUL /** Troubled Sleep

V-607 **SCORTIA, THOMAS N. AND GEORGE ZEBROWSKI (eds.)** / Human-Machines: An Anthology of Stories About Cyborgs
V-330 **SHOLOKHOV, MIKHAIL** / And Quiet Flows the Don
V-331 **SHOLOKHOV, MIKHAIL** / The Don Flows Home to the Sea
V-447 **SILVERBERG, ROBERT** / Born With the Dead: Three Novellas About the Spirit of Man
V-945 **SNOW, LOIS WHEELER** / China On Stage
V-133 **STEIN, GERTRUDE** / Autobiography of Alice B. Toklas
V-826 **STEIN, GERTRUDE** / Everybody's Autobiography
V-941 **STEIN, GERTRUDE** / The Geographical History of America
V-797 **STEIN, GERTRUDE** / Ida
V-695 **STEIN, GERTRUDE** / Last Operas and Plays
V-477 **STEIN, GERTRUDE** / Lectures in America
V-153 **STEIN, GERTRUDE** / Three Lives
V-710 **STEIN, GERTRUDE & CARL VAN VECHTEN (ed.)** / Selected Writings of Gertrude Stein
V-20 **STEINER, STAN AND MARIA-THERESA BABIN (eds.)** / Borinquen: An Anthology of Puerto-Rican Literature
V-770 **STEINER, STAN AND LUIS VALDEZ (eds.)** / Aztlan: An Anthology of Mexican-American Literature
V-769 **STEINER, STAN AND SHIRLEY HILL WITT (eds.)** / The Way: An Anthology of American Indian Literature
V-768 **STEVENS, HOLLY (ed.)** / The Palm at the End of the Mind: Selected Poems & A Play by Wallace Stevens
V-278 **STEVENS, WALLACE** / The Necessary Angel
V-896 **SULLIVAN, VICTORIA AND JAMES HATCH (eds.)** / Plays By and About Women
V-63 **SVEVO, ITALO** / Confessions of Zeno
V-178 **SYNGE, J. M.** / Complete Plays
V-601 **TAYLOR, PAUL B. AND W. H. AUDEN (trans.)** / The Elder Edda
V-443 **TROUPE, QUINCY AND RAINER SCHULTE (eds.)** / Giant Talk: An Anthology of Third World Writings
V-770 **VALDEZ, LUIS AND STAN STEINER (eds.)** / Aztlan: An Anthology of Mexican-American Literature
V-710 **VAN VECHTEN, CARL (ed.) AND GERTRUDE STEIN** / Selected Writings of Gertrude Stein
V-870 **WIESEL, ELIE** / Souls on Fire
V-769 **WITT, SHIRLEY HILL AND STAN STEINER (eds.)** / The Way: An Anthology of American Indian Literature
V-2028 **WODEHOUSE, P. G.** / The Code of the Woosters
V-2026 **WODEHOUSE, P. G.** / Leave It to Psmith
V-2027 **WODEHOUSE, P. G.** / Mulliner Nights
V-607 **ZEBROWSKI, GEORGE AND THOMAS N. SCORTIA (eds.)** / Human-Machines: An Anthology of Stories About Cyborgs